ALSO BY DIANE M[...]

Isabella's Heart
BOOK 2 IN THE JEWELED DAGGER SERIES
"Fans of historical romance are sure to love this adventurous tale of intrigue, family bonds, and a love that will not be denied."
—BLUEINK REVIEWS

"Wigginton tells an absorbing tale, peppered with witty, flirtatious dialogue." "A captivating, adventurous tale."
—KIRKUS REVIEWS

"Isabella's Heart is a fun and imaginative tale of romance with strong themes of family and loyalty." "Wigginton has created a unique series, following the mother-daughter link of strong, thrill-seeking woman."
—FOREWORD REVIEWS

Angelina's Secret
BOOK I IN THE JEWELED DAGGER SERIES
"A sweeping and engaging historical romance, Angelina's Secret has emotion, action, suspense and above all, an epic and timeless love. Filled with heroic, dashing pirates and brave, beautiful ladies, this is a fantastic read."
—BLUEINK REVIEWS (STARRED REVIEW)

"Diane Merrill Wigginton's period tale, Angelina's Secret, has romance and action in spades."
—FOREWORD REVIEWS

"Save for a rainy day and escape into this suspenseful, bodice-ripping romp."
—KIRKUS REVIEWS

JEWELED DAGGER PUBLISHING COMPANY
www.jeweleddaggerpublishing.com

© Copyright 2017 by Diane Merrill Wigginton

All rights reserved. Except as permitted under the U.S. Copyright Act of 1976, no part of this publication may be reproduced, distributed, or transmitted in any form or by any means, or stored in a database or retrieval system, electronically or otherwise, or by use of a technology or retrieval system now known or to be invented, without the prior written permission of the author and publisher.

Designed by Fine Design

First edition August 1, 2017

ISBN 978-1-946146-08-3—Olivia's Promise eBook
ISBN 978-1-946146-07-6— Olivia's Promise Paperback
IBSN 978-1-946146-06-9— Olivia's Promise Hardback

*This story is about friendships and unwavering family bonds. So, I wish to dedicate this book to my beautiful girlfriends, sister-in-laws, daughter-in-laws and dear women who support and inspire me every day. I am grateful for your sweet encouragement that propels me forward, through thick and thin, no matter how many miles separate us. I send out to you my unwavering love and devotion—
Gigi, Teresa, Karol, Linda, Sheri, Annie, Debbie, Phyllis Nicole, Lauren B, Sarah B, Lauren W, Suzanne
& my mother, Margaret.*

OLIVIA'S PROMISE

Diane Merrill Wigginton

JEWELED DAGGER
PUBLISHING

Prologue

IRELAND 1807

I BEGAN KEEPING THIS JOURNAL A few years back, just as my mother had done and her mother before her. My reasons for keeping a journal were simple, I needed a way to analyze and untangle the web of emotions that I experienced during a particularly difficult time in my life. And it was my way of leaving my mark. In truth, a testament to my posterity, so they would know who I was and understand why I did the things that I did. A way of holding up a mirror before my face so that I could take a good hard look at myself.

I grew up knowing that I was different from other children and why I was born this way, but it didn't make the shunning by the other girls my age any easier. Crueler still were the parents of my peers.

Of course, people gossiped and whispered behind my back about things of which they had no real knowledge. This fact made me even more grateful for those brave souls who chose to disregard the harsh criticisms of others and reach out a hand of friendship. I called them my true believers.

One family in particular— the Collins sisters: Lilly, Rose and Iris. Their mother dearly loved them and named them after her favorite flowers. Mrs. Collins died giving birth to her fourth child, a little boy, who was buried alongside her.

Mrs. Collins' spirit came to me after her death with the wee baby boy still cradled in her arms. She needed me to pass along a message of comfort to her daughters. Mrs. Collins explained that she could not find peace during her journey to the afterlife, knowing that her girls were so bereaved and devastated by her passing.

It then became my duty to find a way of relaying this message to Lilly, Rose and Iris, without looking like a complete idiot. And for a young girl of twelve, that was no small feat.

The day I went to express my condolences, and pass along Mrs. Collins' message, truly was a bleak day. The girls sensed my hesitation, Lilly more so than the other two.

She was two years older than me and we had been friends for a year and a half when this tragedy befell the family. Lilly sweetly put her arms around me to comfort me, even though she was the one grieving. I was so touched by her compassion that I told her the truth about my deepest darkest secret that day, and we have been the best of friends ever since.

Beautiful Lilly, with her alabaster skin and reddish-brown hair that shone so brilliantly in the sun, was the prettiest of the three girls, with her dark eyes that danced with merriment when she teased her younger siblings. I loved her joy and the pure essence of her soul, which was always so good and kind. The very thought of her even now makes me smile.

My family has its secrets, like most families do, yet my family is very different from any other. Certain members of my family possess unique mystical talents that the average, closed-minded person could not comprehend.

Great-grandmother Clarisse Stewart could tell when something bad was about happen. She had this instinctive nature that allowed her to know what to do or how to help. That's not to say that she didn't have her fair share of heartache, but, to her credit, she managed to keep tragedy at bay by directing more than a few family members down the right path.

Grandmother Angelina Deveraux could also sense things that were about to happen or had happened, blessed with the ability of premonition. And she could see into a person's heart and tell the true nature of them.

Coco and I looked up to our grandmother and from our perspective, she was a living angel, telling us hair-raising tales of adventures from her and Grandfather Jude's younger years. Sometimes she would leave things out, but even at my young age, I knew enough to know that certain things were sacred, to be shared between husband and wife.

My mother is Isabella Deveraux, the daughter of Angelina and Jude Deveraux. Isabella has a twin brother, Charlie, and the two of them share a special bond. Connected at the hip from the time they drew their first breath, mother and Charlie have a unique ability to link their minds, knowing when something is wrong with the other, no matter how many miles separate them.

Mother was like a homing pigeon when Charlie went missing on the eve of their nineteenth birthday. Charlie and two of his school mates had managed to get themselves kidnapped by a group of Irish thugs. They belonged to a secret society known as The Hearts of Oak gang, but that is an entirely different story.

I was blessed from a very young age with the ability to see spirits. To me they were like friends who stopped by at any hour of the day or night. I was never afraid of them because they were always kind. Some of the younger spirits stayed to play for a while before continuing their journey. I received requests from a few, asking me to pass along a message to a loved one before they could peacefully cross over to the afterlife.

The first time I met my sister, Coco, she was a spirit. I was three and a half and just discovering my unique abilities.

Coco was such a pretty little thing, with her strawberry curls and almond-shaped eyes. I often marvel at her perfectly-shaped lips and delicate little eyebrows. I remember her standing in the corner of my room, watching me for an entire day. She didn't try to come near or say a word to me, but stood as still as she could, in the shadows.

Finally, I said something to her and then motioned for her to come closer. At first she looked shocked, then surprised when she realized that I could see her. Coco and I began talking and we never stopped. If one of us lied, the other would swear to it, even if it landed us both into trouble, and Coco and I were always in trouble.

I was born on the seventh day of November, in the year of our Lord, seventeen hundred and eighty-two. My parents christened me Lady Olivia Sophia Allen Townsend.

When my sister was born on the same date, exactly four years later, she was christened Lady Catherine Elizabeth Townsend. My parents' hopes of blessing their second daughter with a regal name befitting her station were dashed when they were forced to concede defeat. Coco's name had been decided long before she ever drew a breath.

Coco and I had strawberry blond hair with rich brown under-tones. Our eyes, blue like father's, were fringed with long dark lashes. Where I was daring, Coco was the voice of caution. This kept me in check, most of the time.

We grew up with all the finer things in life afforded the daughters of a Viscount: privilege, grace, lovely clothes and, above all else, an education.

With the passing of Grandfather John, my father's father, on February twentieth, seventeen hundred and ninety-two, my father became the forth Earl of Buckinghamshire, The Right Honorable Lord Lieutenant of Ireland.

I will be the first to admit that before father's advancement in station that we were deemed a handful, but certainly afterwards, the two of us became holy terrors. We caused no less than three nannies and one tutor in a short span of time, eighteen months no less, to retire early from their chosen vocations. To be fair, two of the nannies were older than dirt and the other one was far too young and inexperienced for the position she had retained.

I also admit that I felt somewhat guilty at the time for chasing Miss Abigail Jones away in such a terrible way, but she had it coming.

The day I noticed her eyes wondering toward my father was the day of her undoing. I knew she had to go, and so an idea formed in my young mind.

Coco convinced Miss Jones that we had a message for her from the great beyond. I then proceeded to spin a tale so frightening and horrible that she ran screaming from our home in fear for her life, vowing never to return. And true to her word, she never did. It wasn't until three months later a relative of hers visited our home to retrieve her belongings.

The reason for Miss Jones's hasty retreat was simple. I convinced her that she was being punished by the spirits of our ancestors for her unclean thoughts towards our father. I tipped the scales even farther by telling her that they wouldn't stop until they scared her to death.

She believed our wild story because it came on the heels of three very long, tortuous nights of mysterious hauntings. My sister and I snuck into her room through the secret panel from the nursery to the nanny's quarters. Then we hid behind the changing screen until we heard her steady, even breathing, telling us she was asleep. Maneuvering through the room, hiding ourselves behind the ample curtains and furniture, we opened windows, banged shutters and knocked over chairs.

Her blood-curdling screams were heard throughout the servant's quarters. When everyone came running, Coco and I slipped back through the panel during all the confusion and tucked ourselves into bed, with no one the wiser.

For months after Miss Jones' sudden departure from our home, Coco and I heard whispers in the hallway about her mysterious afflictions. Staff said she shut herself away in her aunt's home, refusing to step foot outside. If truth be told, who could blame her?

Thank goodness we grew up and learned to behave like proper young ladies, instead of the rabble rousers and heathens we were back then.

Coco also inherited the family gift, but her gift was truly unique. All she needed to do was touch a person's bare skin and mental flashes came to her. Sometimes she could simply touch an object someone possessed and impressions would flood her mind. That is why she rarely took her gloves off in public.

Most of the time I could tell if Coco was experiencing a vision because she would become very still for a moment, as if she was thinking about something a little longer than normal, then pick up with the conversation as if nothing had happened. But there was always a telltale look in her eyes that I recognized.

A few times, getting a strange look in her eyes, Coco immediately turned loose of an object as if she couldn't get it out of her hands fast enough. Sometimes she confided in me about what she had seen, but other times she brushed it off, explaining that the situation was far too tragic to discuss, causing me to drop the subject forever.

Some adults found our abilities unnerving, even peculiar by nature, and called us any number of unflattering names. Our parents, being forward thinkers by nature, understood and empathized with our plight. They never made us feel embarrassed or ashamed, and mother did her best to reassure us that the prejudice and judgement would pass, but they didn't.

Yet, even after these many talks, I found myself hiding my gifts from the world. I'm ashamed to say that I chose to keep the lost spirits at arm's length, pretended not to see them when they came to me or passed me on the street. The lost and empty looks in their eyes broke my heart and I was haunted by them for days. The experiences taught me that people could be narrow minded and short sighted as I continued to rebel against my gifts.

I had recently turned twenty a few months prior to my world suddenly turning upside down. I was about to discover that fate, like life, is very unpredictable.

So now, I begin my story and pray you don't judge me too harshly, because I did not find this a time to retell the truth to suite my own needs, but instead, a time for cold hard facts. I begin my story from the moment it all went tragically wrong.

I

JANUARY 9, 1804
DUBLIN CASTLE, DUBLIN, IRELAND
12 O'CLOCK MIDNIGHT

"OLIVIA, WAKE UP." THE HOARSE whisper sounded harsh next to my ear.

Slowly I opened my sleep-filled eyes and recognized my best friend, whom I hadn't seen in months, "Lilly. What is it? What's the matter?" I asked, with a degree of shock at seeing her dress disheveled and torn, standing in my bed chambers. Slowly sitting up in bed, I rubbed the sleep from my eyes.

"I need your help," she said, pulling her shawl tightly around her slender shoulders and sounding desperate as she walked to the end of my bed.

Reaching over to the night stand, I struck the flint and lit the candle, while absently answering her, "Anything, Lilly. Name it," I replied, turning back around to get a better look at her.

As my eyes adjusted and fell on Lilly, my heart sank to my stomach, because I just realized that she was no longer among the living. She was now just one of the many spirits paying me a midnight visit before crossing over to the other side.

Quickly bringing my hand to my mouth to keep from crying out, tears filled my eyes and all I could do was stare at her ethereal form. The feeling of loss was so raw it hurt. I swallowed a gasp, at least I thought I had.

Lilly's eyes flew to my face. "What's wrong? Why are you staring at me like that, Olivia?"

"What happened to you, Lilly?" I cried, feeling despair overwhelm me. "I have been inquiring after you for months now, but all your sisters would say is that you were away visiting a relative in England."

"I can't remember off the top of my head where I've been exactly, but I don't believe I went to England," Lilly replied, with a stricken look.

"Then tell me where you did go."

"That's just it, I can't remember. The only thing I do recall is feeling happy and excited that I was going someplace. Ever since Mama died, I've wanted to be happy again, Olivia," Lilly whined. "Truly happy!" she added, with emphasis, poking out her bottom lip slightly. "I grew tired of the mask I wore every day to appear happy to everyone." Lilly clutched her fist to her belly, then, wringing her hands in her gown, she began looking around with confusion, unable to remember how she had come to be there.

"We will figure this out. I just need you to stay calm. I have something to tell you and I'm not entirely certain how you are going to take it," I prefaced my next statement, while climbing out of bed and walking over to her.

"Don't be silly, Olivia, you can tell me anything."

"Forgive me for being blunt, Lilly, but I don't know any other way to say this," I stated, through sniffles while trying to soften the blow. "You're dead, Lilly."

"That is ridiculous, Olivia Townsend. You don't know what you are talking about," Lilly retorted, looking down at her bare feet and torn dress, before running over to the full-length mirror. I followed behind her with my candle in hand.

"I'm so sorry, Lilly."

"No, no, no, no, no, no..." she kept repeating, bringing her hands to her face in disbelief, when she couldn't see herself in the mirror. Her celestial form began to fade before my eyes.

"Lilly. Lilly, come back here. I insist you come back here this minute!" I stomped my bare foot on the hardwood floor. "Oh please, Lilly, I promise everything will be alright." I cried, holding the candle a little higher. "Please come back, Lilly," I sobbed.

The door to my room slowly opened and I turned suddenly in surprise.

"Olivia?" Coco's voice was tentative as she looked back over her shoulder before stepping into my room and shutting the door. "Who were you talking to? I heard you calling out to Lilly and thought maybe you were having a bad dream."

"It wasn't a bad dream, Coco. It's was a nightmare," I sobbed into my hands, slumping into the nearest chair, wondering what I was going to do next.

"I don't understand, Olivia. Tell me about your nightmare," she sweetly coaxed, setting her candle down on the dresser and kneeling beside me.

"Oh, Coco," I gasped, placing the candle next to me on the little table and covering my mouth with the back of my hand.

"What is it, Olivia? What's happened?"

"Why have I been cursed with this ability?" I snapped, suddenly angry that I had been given the ability to see spirits. I'd always considered it a gift and a blessing to help people to cross over to the other side when I was younger, but lately it had become a curse.

"What are you talking about, Olivia?" Coco questioned, "I don't understand. You're not making any sense." "Oh, never mind," she uttered, reaching out to take my hand and easily slipping away to the place she goes when she sought answers. Coco closed her eyes and fell silent.

Quickly turning loose of my hand, Coco jumped to her feet and gasped. Her beautiful eyes registered her shock and horror at what she had just witnessed. "This can't be, Olivia! *I* don't believe it."

"*You* don't believe it," I sniffed, "I don't believe it!"

"How did this happen to her?"

"I never got that far in our conversation. When I told Lily she was dead, she disappeared on me, and I don't know where she went," I cried again as tears trailed down my cheeks.

"But she is coming back?"

"Where else would she go?" I bluntly stated.

"Olivia?" Lilly whispered, causing me to nearly jump out of my skin as I turned my head toward her voice and re-affirmed body.

"Is she back, Olivia? Olivia, answer me!" Coco demanded, growing impatient with my silence. Coco took a hold of my hand so that she could see what I was seeing.

"Lilly, I was so worried about you. Where did you go?" I asked, sniffing loudly and drying my tears with the back of my hand.

"I was scared and when I couldn't remember what happened to me… well, I just felt myself begin to fade away, and I didn't know how to stop it." Lilly's voice cracked with emotion.

"Well, did you remember anything more?" I questioned with a loud sniff. "I want to help you, but I need to know where to start. Did you leave your home with someone? Did you take a carriage or a ship? Do you remember if you stayed in Ireland or sailed to another country? Was it a man or a woman that you went to meet, and did you know them well? What is the very last thing you do remember?" I asked in quick succession without taking a breath in between questions.

"Stop it, Olivia. Just stop! You must give me a minute to catch my breath. I did just find out that I am dead. Give a girl a chance to blink, would you?" Lilly responded, shaking her head and turning her back to me as she looked off someplace far away, falling silent for a few minutes.

Reaching back into, her memories, Lilly quickly turned back around, excitedly by her new revelation. "I remember, there was a man and we were in love. Oh, Olivia, I was in love! He was terribly handsome too, now *that*, I do recall."

"Can you describe him to me?"

"He is very tall and has the most beauty hair. Oh, and a beard. He has a beard and the sweetest brown eyes. I felt like I was melting inside every time he looked at me," Lilly swooned.

"Yes, yes, that's all very nice, Lilly, but you still haven't told me anything about the man or what he does for a living. Telling me that he is handsome and beautiful brown eyes gets us nowhere," I stated with irritation. "You have to give me more to go on than that he makes your insides melt," I was pointing out when I got an idea.

I separated Coco's hands and gave her a gentle shake.

"Why did you do that?" she complained.

"Because, Coco, I need you to do something for me. Run and get your sketch pad, and be quick about it," I added, watching my sister snatch up her candle and move quickly toward the door. "I need you to sketch the man as Lilly describes him to us. Then we will at least have a picture of him," I said, sitting down in the chair next to me with a plop, before murmuring under my breath, "I hope!"

Coco quickly returned with sketch pad in hand, drawing the man as Lilly gave us every detail of him.

Holding Lilly's gaze, I said very solemnly, "Lilly, I am going to make you a promise. I swear that I will find out what happened to you, and with my last breath, I will make the person responsible for hurting you pay dearly."

An hour later we had an accurate drawing of our mystery man, a few more details from Lilly of what she could recall of this man, including where he was from and what he did for a living. Then I formed a plan of attack, one that I was not sharing with anyone else.

I was certain Coco would try and stop me, or at the least talk some sense into me if she knew what I was planning. I was even more certain our mother would know instantly what I had in mind if I put words to it and return home on the next tide. So, I kept all thoughts of my crazy plan to myself.

Thank goodness my parents were out of the country and not due back for another five to seven days. I seriously doubted that they would go along with my crazy scheme.

2

SATURDAY, JANUARY 10, 1804

Let the Hunt for Answers Begin

P ACKING MY TRUNK FOR MY journey, I went over in my mind everything I needed. Two forged letters, a ship, lovely dresses and enough scrip to pull the whole thing off. Check, check, check and check!

The first letter had a dual purpose, first to introduce me to the American Cotton Growers' Cooperative, selling cotton at the market and the second purpose to give me authorization to negotiate on behalf of my family for raw cotton. I would be acting under the assumed guise of doing business for *Stewart Textiles of London*, the family business Mother and Uncle Charlie took over from their parents who were semi-retired, taking a lesser position from the day-to-day running of the company. Mother was grooming Coco and me to take it over one day, but I think, if she knew what I was up to now, she would launch herself into the air and explode like the annual, royal fireworks display.

Well, as I like to say, better to beg forgiveness after the fact, then to ask permission before hand, I thought to myself.

The other letter would be presented to Captain Bellamy of the *Trinity*, a two hundred and fifty-ton vessel with three masts of square rigging. The *Trinity* was the fastest ship in our fleet, but certainly not the largest.

I forged the two letters with father's signatures and knew that I was sealing my fate when I placed the family seal upon the letters. I knew I was risking everything, including my parents confidence, but I had to find out what happened to Lilly.

I was nearly ready to go and all my plans appeared to be falling into place, yet something kept nagging at me.

I had sent William, the house boy, off earlier that morning to deliver my letter to Captain Bellamy, informing him of our impending departure. I also informed Margot, my very loyal lady's maid, that she would be accompanying me on my journey to America. The one person I had not informed was Coco. I was unsure how she would take the news that I had left for New York without her, but I hoped that she would not be too angry.

I slipped the bundle of scrip into the pink satin reticule that matched my Grecian, high-waisted gown of thin gossamer material. I chose my heaviest wool cape to fend off the cold of the ocean breeze, and slipped on a pair of white gloves with purpose. Placing my jeweled dagger that I inherited from mother, who inherited it from her mother, into my pocket, I was ready to depart. Opening the bedroom door, I motioned for the footman to take my heavy trunk to the carriage.

I fully expected Coco to appear at my door the moment I opened it, and at the same time was relieved when I didn't have to face her to explain why I was making the trip to America alone. I even told myself that she was exhausted from our late-night escapades and had slept in. It was better this way.

I gave two hand-written notes to Flora, the upstairs maid, and requested that she give the first one to Coco when she awoke and the other to my parents when they returned home. Then, taking one last look around, deciding I had everything, I calmly walked down the stairs to the waiting carriage.

You can imagine my surprise when I opened the carriage door to find Coco seated next to Margot. "What are you doing here?" I harshly whispered, looking behind me, to see where the driver was.

"Shush! Get in here," Coco demanded sternly. I stepped through the door and sat across from her, with a feigned smile upon my face, as the driver appeared at the door.

"Please be a dear and close the door, Mr. Watts. We are in a terrible rush and need to leave immediately," Coco interjected, with a sweet smile. "We wouldn't want to keep Captain Bellamy waiting. You know how he gets if he misses an outgoing tide."

I was momentarily struck speechless while I tried to figure out how Coco had outsmarted me. Forcing my gaping mouth closed, I waited for the carriage door to be closed. Then, turning on Coco after the door slammed shut and the carriage began to move, I immediately starting in on her. "What are you doing here and how could you possibly know what I was going to do?" I grumbled under my breath while roughly removing my gloves, setting them in my lap.

"You didn't think I would let you go off on this crazy goose chase without me, did you?" Coco sweetly replied, before gesturing towards Margot with her head. "Could we not do this in front of the help?"

"Oh," I scoffed loudly. "It's just Margot. I can trust her with my deepest, darkest secrets. She would never betray me. She is as loyal as the day is long," I reassured her.

"I'm glad to hear it. That makes one person in this carriage I know I can trust," Coco retorted with more than a little sarcasm dripping from her lips.

"What's that supposed to mean?" I asked, folding my arms across my chest and scrutinizing her.

Mirroring my movement, Coco narrowed her eyes, "You know what I mean. Don't play dumb with me. You were going to leave me behind."

"Oh, never mind that. How did you know what I was planning?" I demanded, before remembering that she had touched my arm before retiring to her own chambers earlier that morning. "Never mind, I remember now. Mother is going to kill me!"

"Better to beg forgiveness than ask permission." Coco mimicked my motto.

"Oh, you're impossible," I grumbled, before turning to stare out the window.

Coco's good mood was annoying as she sat across from me, a triumphant look upon her face. All the way to the wharf, it caused my own foul mood to sour even more.

Our carriage stopped, and I spotted Captain Bellamy waiting at the top of the gang plank for us and knew he would have questions.

"Margot, I want you to march up that gang plank with authority and demand to see the first mate. You will demand to be shown to the master's quarters, then immediately begin unpacking. I will follow shortly," I ordered, as I chewed on my nail contemplating what I would do next. Grabbing ahold of Coco's arm before she stepped out of the carriage behind Margot, I uttered, "I need you to let me do all the talking! Understand?"

"Aye, aye, Capitan," Coco said, saluting me before disembarking the carriage and waiting for me to join her. We marched up the gangplank with an air of authority. Never letting my eyes stray from Captain Bellamy's gaze from the moment I stepped from the carriage, I quickly spoke before he could. "Good morning, Captain Bellamy. Looks to be a fine day for a sea voyage. Wouldn't you agree?"

"Begging your pardon, Miss, but I take my orders from Lord Townsend or the Missess," Captain Bellamy said, gruffly.

"Well, today, Captain Bellamy, you will be taking your orders from me. My father sent word late last night that he would be delayed by two weeks due to unforeseen circumstances. He also expressed his concern to me about missing out on the best selection of cotton at the market this season. He feels that I am ready to take a more active role in the family business and requested that I take his place. You did receive the letter his lordship sent to you? He specifically stated that he would be forwarding a letter to you." I added with a lift of my chin, hoping that he wouldn't question me further.

"Well... I'm not sure," Bellamy hesitated, looking uncertain.

"You did receive the letter, did you not?"

"Yes, but —"

"Wonderful! Then the matter is settled. We set sail on the next tide, which by my calculations should be in the next twenty minutes," I stated flatly, while checking the pocket of my coat for the twentieth time, to make sure that I hadn't forgotten my dagger. "Well, we wish to get settled in. Come along, Coco."

"Of course, Olivia, I am right behind you." Coco replied, never making eye contact with the captain.

I heard Captain Bellamy mumbling something to himself, which I pretended not to hear.

"That was close, Olivia," Coco muttered quietly once we were out of earshot of the captain.

"Not even a little," I assured her, exhaling the breath I'd been holding.

I continued to the sleeping chamber that we would call home for the next three to five weeks, depending on weather and tides. Margot busily arranging trunks to fit in the confines of our small little space as Lilly Collins sat upon my bunk, watching her.

"I hope you don't expect to share a bunk with me," I stated flatly, looking directly at Lilly.

"Oh no, Miss, that would be highly improper," Margot replied.

"Not you, Margot, our spirited guest over there," I said, gesturing toward the bunk, "where Miss Lilly Collins is making herself at home on my bunk," I said without humor.

"She's here?" Margot gasped.

"Where else would she be?" I replied, crossing the room with purpose.

"I don't take up much room." Lilly retorted.

"That's not really the point, now is it?" I shooed her with my hands. "It's the principle," I added, taking a possessive stance, sprawling across my bunk.

"Lilly can bunk with me," Coco generously offered. "I'm sure that I won't even know she is there. But don't get mad if I roll over on you in the middle of the night." She smiled, looking at the same spot I had been.

"Tell Coco thank you for the generous offer, but I will find my own accommodations," Lilly retorted coolly, disappearing in a huff.

"Lilly thanks you for your kind offer, Coco, but she has made other arrangements."

Margot shivered, crossing herself to ward off any evil spirits. One would think that after six years in my employ she would be a little less skittish over the mention of a spirit or two.

3

WEDNESDAY, FEBRUARY 4TH, 1804

Spirits That Walk Among Us

THREE WEEKS AND FOUR DAYS after leaving Dublin, with favorable winds and even more favorable tides, we reached the port of New York. Our ship skimmed across the water at times, as if helped along by unseen hands.

I was half way down the gang plank before the *Trinity* crew had finished tying her off. I used the excuse that I needed to obtain lodgings for us, before Margot and Coco could disembark.

Truth of the matter was I couldn't wait to add distance between me and my three cabin mates. I was never happier in all my life to vacate our cramped quarters. Turns out that the journey was three weeks too long for my taste. Between Coco wanting to know everything I was seeing or doing, and a talkative spirit yammering on and on in my ear all day, I thought I would lose my mind.

As it began to drizzle, I pulled the hood of my cloak over my head to ward off the cold. A breeze caused an involuntary shiver to course through me. Another stiff breeze off the water blew up the skirt of my dress, and I pulled the collar of my coat closed with frigid fingers. It was less than ideal weather, but I didn't care because the air in the cabin was stifling, and I was determined to place distance between me and the *Trinity*.

I had been to New York City two years earlier, on a buying exposition with mother and Uncle Charlie, but things had changed slightly and my eyes continued to search for familiar land marks.

Walking quickly over the slick, cobble stone streets, dodging puddles, I made my way to the main street that ran in front of the wharf.

A man was stepping down from his hired carriage when I called out to the driver. "Excuse me, sir, are you free?"

"Yes, Miss. Do you need a lift?" he replied.

"I am looking for lodgings and would like a lift to the Carmichael Hotel, if you please."

"Certainly, Miss, it would be my pleasure," he graciously replied, waving his hand, indicating that I should climb in.

Stepping into the dry carriage, the door closed behind me as I sat down. "Where are you off to in such a hurry, Olivia Townsend?" Lilly inquired.

Nearly jumping out of my skin, I grabbed my chest. "Holly Mother of…" I cried. "You scared five years from my life, Lilly Collins," I continued in a loud whisper, not wanting to attract unwanted attention from the driver.

"So answer the question," Lilly pouted, sitting across from me.

"I simply wish to secure our lodgings so we may get off that ship," I answered, taking a deep breath to comport myself.

"Liar!" she said in an accusatory tone. "I saw the way you leaped from the gang plank. I believe you would have flown from that ship if you knew how to sprout wings."

Feigning offence, before thinking better of it, I decided to come clean. "Truth be told, I'm not accustomed to being cooped up in a tiny cabin with three other people — sorry, two people and a ghost," I corrected, "who, I might add, is constantly droning on about something in my ear! I was feeling a little closed in," I grudgingly admitted. "So, yes, I would have flown like a bird, if I could have, from that ship. I hope you can understand that I just needed a minute."

"Did you say something to me, Miss?" the driver called down to me through the small door, he'd slid open.

Trying to appear normal, I smiled pleasantly back at him. "No, I was just singing to myself. I do that sometimes after a long ocean crossing. Sorry for disturbing you. I will try to keep it down."

"No worries, I hum to myself as well. It makes the time pass quicker," he said, giving me a shy smile, before closing the slot.

"You need to stay with Coco and Margot on the ship. I must take care of our lodgings and, if you keep talking to me, I may slip up and start talking back to you. Then people most likely will start talking about me behind their hand, crossing the street to avoid me because they think I'm crazy," I concluded, with a lopsided smile.

"But Olivia," Lilly whined, "I remembered something and I could be of help to you."

"You and all the other wounded and confused spirits, aimlessly wondering the streets of New York?" I retorted, peering out of the carriage window at three lost souls, who didn't yet realize that they were dead. My heart went out to them, but not enough to do anything about it directly. "Maybe you could be helpful and let them know that they need to walk into the light. But whatever you do, don't bring them to me, I have my hands full." I was feeling weary from the voyage.

"Sure, Olivia, I can do that, if you think it will help," Lilly said, excited that she could do something useful. She looked out the window at the souls I pointed out to her. Then bringing her attention back to me, she continued, "Did you hear what I said? I remembered something else."

"Yes, I heard you. Well, out with it." I impatiently prodded, absently gazing out the window.

"I remember Rosewood, and being unmistakably drawn to a man with the most beautiful eyes," Lilly announced triumphantly.

Tearing my eyes away from the street, I queried, "What is this Rosewood? Is it a person's name?"

"I'm not really sure, but the word keeps coming to my mind," she replied.

Taking an exasperated breath and blowing it out, I smiled. "Thank you, Lilly. Not sure how that helps us yet, but I will keep that in mind. Now, can you help them, or not?" I whispered, hoping to occupy her for a while. "Don't forget to direct them toward the light, but whatever you do, don't go yourself. I will never untangle this situation without you."

With a look of confusion, Lilly continued. "Did you hear me? I said that I was drawn to this man."

"I heard you. I just chose to ignore that part. Who is drawn to another person?" I scoffed, looking impatiently at her.

Uncertainty flashed across her features. "Well, I was, I think."

"Well?" I questioned, gesturing towards the wondering souls behind us as the carriage came to a stop, waiting for the cross traffic to pass before making a left turn.

"You can count on me," Lilly said with a forced smile, before disappearing.

I looked down the street as the carriage turned the corner and saw her conversing with them. I hadn't realized how tense I was. The muscles in my neck and shoulders were so tight they ached. Leaning back against the seat I took another deep breath, and felt myself begin to relax.

The voyage had been strenuous, and to keep my body and mind occupied I had volunteered to help in any way I could. I had even scrubbed decks, peeled potatoes and helped serve the meals. I was rolling my head from side to side, remembering the faces of the grateful crew when the carriage pulled up to the Carmichael Hotel. The driver opened the slot once again as I pulled out a couple of coins from my reticule and handed them to him. "Thank you very much for delivering me safely to my destination. Would you be able to wait for me? If they have a room available, I will only be a moment. Then I will need to go back to the ship, to retrieve my sister and maid."

"It would be my pleasure, Miss," he said, giving me a large smile. He stepped down to open the door for me.

"You are terribly kind and I thank you, good sir."

"Think nothing of it, Miss."

I walked through the enormous hotel doors held open by the doorman dressed in a black coat and tales. His crisp white shirt and gold cravat accentuated the two rows of shiny, brass buttons down the front of his perfectly tailored coat and pants, which had a strip of gold brocade running down the side of the pants. His black top hat sat smartly upon his head. The hotel was just as I had remembered it, very grand.

Walking up to the front desk, I smiled politely to the clerk. "I would like to procure a suite, if I may. Preferably with two rooms and maid's quarters for the remainder of the week."

The man behind the counter gave me the once over and then looked down his nose at me. "I am afraid we do not have any rooms left, Miss," he announced, in a snobbish tone.

"I don't understand?" I complained, "my family has always been accommodated when we are in town. How can this be?" shrugging my shoulders, baffled by his shabby treatment and snobbish attitude.

"And who might your family be, Miss?" he inquired with an uppity sniff.

"Townsend. My mother is Lady Isabella Townsend and my father is the second Earl of Buckinghamshire." I replied, turning to leave, my disappointment apparent by my dejected tone.

"I am terribly sorry, my lady, it seems I have misspoken. I hope that you can forgive my terrible mistake. We seem to have a suite available." He blathered on, snapping his fingers several times to get the bellboy's attention. "I am sorry again for the mix up. I'm sure this room will be suitable for your needs."

"Truly? Oh, I am so grateful. How can I thank you enough, Mr. —" I said, leaving the question open ended.

"Mr. Jones. Ah, William Jones, at your service. And if there is anything more I may do for you, please don't hesitate to ask. Just sign here, Lady Townsend?" Mr. Jones continued in a loud voice.

"Please, Mr. Jones, there is no need to make such a fuss," I added, looking to around to see if anyone had noticed. "You may call me Miss.

Townsend, if you please. No need to be so formal." I continued. "I will need a man to take the trunks up to the room when my sister arrives. Do you think it possible to have someone run a note to my sister for me? She is on the *Trinity*, docked at the wharf," I sweetly asked, knowing that Mr. Jones would bend over backward at this point to make up for his lapse in protocol.

"Excuse me, Mr. Jones, would you mind handing me the key for room 325! And please hurry, I am in a bit of a rush," a man said, stepping up to the counter while standing too close to me for propriety's sake.

"Of course, Mr. Beaumont, right away, sir," Jones answered, snapping to attention. "Please forgive me, Lady Townsend, I will only be a moment," he added, before stepping away to fetch the key for the gentleman.

"Of course, Mr. Jones, think nothing of it," I grudgingly replied, thinking all the while how rude this man was for blatantly interrupting us. Who did he think he was!

Trying to mind my own business, I continued to stare straight ahead. A strange, nagging feeling clawed at me and something told me to turn around. I wrestled with myself for a split second longer before turning to look at the gentleman, but was not prepared for what I saw.

Upon turning, I realized that he had been staring intently at me, so I smiled cordially, giving him a quick assessment, before turning back around. He was a very handsome man, with striking eyes and a beautiful beard. Realization hit me and I had to catch myself before my jaw came unhinged. Smiling shyly at the man, I turned again to look at him. I could feel my heart banging against my ribs and worried that he would hear it. I felt light-headed, unable to think or breathe as blood rushed to my head all at once. Then I sneezed two times in quick succession, and diverted my face, covering my mouth with my gloved hand.

The hotel clerk, Mr. Jones, had called Mr. Beaumont, leaned in even closer and said, "God bless you," as he offered me a clean, white handkerchief before I turned back around to thank him.

Looking at the outstretched offering as if it were a snake, I considered refusing, but changed my mind. "Thank you." I begrudgingly said, taking the handkerchief and wiping my nose. "I will see that you get it back."

"There really is no need. I have more handkerchiefs than any sane man should," he replied with a cordial smile.

Mr. Jones returned, placing the key into Beaumont's out-stretched hand. As he walked away my eyes landed on his profile and then the back of his head. "Who is that man, Mr. Jones? He looks familiar to me." I said, lying through my teeth while digging my finger nails into the solid wooden counter of the front desk.

"That would be one of the Beaumont boys. I can't be sure, but I do believe that was Mr. Brody Beaumont. He has a twin brother by the name of Quinton. It really is remarkable how much they look alike. I have a hard time telling them apart, unless I see them together. One is often mistaken for the other, if truth be told. However, there are a few subtle differences between them," he added, leaning over the counter, close to me. Mr. Quinton has brown eyes and Mr. Brody has hazel eyes, like his dear departed mother. God rest her soul. Annabelle Beaumont was a pillar of society. It was really a tragedy how she died," Mr. Jones said with a polite smile, as if he had just said too much. "The family is in the cotton business. They hail from West Virginia. I've been told the Rosewood plantation is one of the most beautiful plantations around. But then it would only be hear-say, since I have never actually seen the place."

My mind began to spin the moment, Mr. Jones, mentioned the word *Rosewood* Plantation.

"You are just a wealth of information Mr. Jones." I said, flattering his ego. "I thought maybe I knew him, but I am certain now that I was mistaken." I coyly smiled at him while my heart raced in my chest.

Mr. Jones had just given me all the information I needed. In the back of my mind I was thinking that Mr. Beaumont looked exactly like the picture Coco had drawn of Lilly's gentleman, but which one was he? If he had a twin, how would I tell them apart?

I made a mental note of his room number when Mr. Jones passed him his key and the name of his plantation. I would be sure to stop by his booth, the day after tomorrow, when Kingsley Hall opened for business. Then I would look them both in the eye, so I could see for myself just how much they looked alike and would gauge for myself if either one of them was the cause of Lilly's death.

I managed to sweet talk Mr. Jones into giving me a suite on the same floor as Mr. Beaumont. Then I paid the carriage driver double his normal fee to return to the wharf and retrieve my sister, Coco and Margot from the ship.

With room key in hand, the bellboy and I made our way upstairs to find my room on the third floor. I peered down the hallway towards room 325, just before closing my own door. My gut told me that I was another step closer to unraveling the mystery of Lilly's death. I felt certain that one of those Beaumont boys had to be the key.

While sitting alone in the room waiting for Coco and Margot to arrive, I judiciously worked out a plan in my head. It felt like an eternity before they appeared. I bided my time, waiting for the two young porters to carry in our trunks and deposit them in the other room.

"Margot, would you mind giving my sister and me a little privacy? I want to discuss something with her."

"Don't mind me. I'll just be in the next room unpacking," Margot hesitated. "And don't forget what time it is. I don't know about you, but I could use a decent meal. I'm not sure I could have forced one more bowl of pea soup, corned pork or dandy funk down my throat. I was seriously considering throwing myself overboard for the fishes to eat," she proclaimed, while walking into the next room.

"I hear you, Margot, and I would have been right behind you," Coco laughed.

Waiting for Margot to shut the door, before leading Coco by the arm, I steered her to a chair and gave a small shove. "I believe the man we are searching for is in room 325. Do the names Brody or Quinton

Beaumont sound at all familiar to you, Lilly?" I asked, looking over my shoulder directly at Lilly who was now sitting motionless on the couch behind me, trying not to be noticed. "Did you think I wouldn't see you sitting there if you didn't move or say a word?" I accused.

Lilly looked embarrassed at first and then she shrugged her shoulders and gave me a devil-may-care look. "Maybe. Besides, being dead has to have some advantages."

"If you want to be sneaky, next time stay out of sight," I said, with a little sarcasm.

"I'll keep that in mind!" she retorted, before saying the names a couple of times. Suddenly sitting up straighter, Lilly's face lit up with excitement. "Something is familiar, I have to see them!" Lilly cried, disappearing through the wall.

"You found the man in my drawing already? That is impossible." Coco stated.

"Yes, I did, and Lilly has gone to see for herself. She needed to see him with her own eyes, before she can say with certainly, but —"

"How can this be? We haven't even been here a full day. Do you really think it is him?" Coco cried, coming out of her chair and walking over to peer out of the window. "That's plain crazy, Olivia."

"That is what some call fate or maybe destiny, I don't know which," I stated, matter of fact. "We knew his family was in the cotton business before we left Dublin because Lilly was able to remember that much. And I was counting on him being here for the opening of the cotton market. What I wasn't counting on is two of them to contend with. This will complicate things." I muttered out loud as I began to pace back and forth.

"Two of them!" Coco gasped.

"Yes," I answered, absently, "two of them."

"What a coincidence that we should all end up in the same hotel, on the same floor, all by happenstance," she added with suspicion.

"Oh that." I sheepishly shrugged. "It was no coincidence really. This is the finest hotel in the city. It makes sense that a well-to-do cotton man would be staying here." I pointed out. "As for him coming along at the precise moment I just happened to be standing at the counter, procuring our room, now *that*, I will admit, was strange to me, as well. Something else struck me as odd. While I was arranging for a room, Mr. Brody Beaumont came up next to me and asked the desk clerk for his room key. At least I think that was his name. Mr. Jones wasn't sure as to which Beaumont it was," I said, waving her skepticism aside. "Anyway, something kept nagging at me when he was standing so close to me, then I nearly swallowed my tongue, when I did look up. But then it happened and I felt…" I said, hesitating.

"Felt what, Olivia? What did you feel?" Coco whispered.

"I felt something strange, like I knew him. It was truly quite eerie. After he walked away, I asked the desk clerk to tell me his name, pretending that I know him, of course." I said, launching in to my story, when Lilly reappeared with a stricken look on her face.

"Well?" I prodded. "Is either one of them, the man?"

"I think so. They both look so familiar. Yet I am not certain why," Lilly replied with tears in her eyes.

"Why are you crying, Lilly?"

"Lilly is crying? Why is Lilly crying, Olivia? Oh, never mind." Coco made a sound of disgust, pulling her gloves off so she could touch my arm.

"I'm crying because I miss being alive and I can't remember why I am dead." Lilly sobbed.

"Oh Lilly, I am so sorry," I said with tears forming in my own eyes. "I promise that I will get to the bottom of this. I will leave no stone unturned. I would climb to the highest mountain for you, Lilly. I will find out what happened to you. I swear it," I boldly proclaimed, patting the couch cushion next to me. "You are my best friend, Lilly. Tell me how to make this better."

"I wish my mother was here with me," she cried, looking forlornly at me with her big blue eyes.

"I know Lilly, and you will be reunited with her soon. I just need your help to understand everything that happened. I can't do this without you," I insisted softly as tears softly rolled down my cheeks.

"Tomorrow is another day," Lilly replied, pulling herself out of her gloomy mood, suddenly forcing a half smile to her lips as she dried her tears. "I am really tired now, Olivia. If you will excuse me, I need to go someplace and be alone."

"Oh Lilly, please, don't go again," I cried, as she turned her back to me and walked away.

I watched as Lilly disappeared, into a mist of light. "I wish my mother was here too." I lamented, slumping into the couch. "Somehow I think she would handle this whole thing better than me," I murmured under my breath, allowing the tears to fall freely.

Letting go of my arm, Coco slipped her gloves back on, "Olivia, don't talk like that. You're Lilly's best friend and only chance of finding out what happened. You will figure this out," Coco assured me, attempting to comfort me. "And I will help too."

"I love you, Coco. You always know what to say," I added, wiping at the tears with my hand.

"Margot poked her head out of the room and looked around. "Is the coast clear of spirits?" she wearily asked, crossing herself. "I could really use something to eat."

Coco and I looked at one another and began to laugh. "Yes, Margot, the coast is clear. Let's order room service and put our feet up. I believe I could eat an entire cow myself," I joked with a sad chuckle.

"Just as long as they aren't serving dried salted meats and pea soup," Margot announced.

"I'm in," Coco added.

4

FRIDAY, FEBRUARY 6TH, 1804
9 O'CLOCK IN THE MORNING

Kingsley Hall

THE DAY WAS BLEAK AND the downpour began early that morning, around two o'clock, and I prayed that this was not a sign of things to come.

The flimsy materials of my fashionable, Grecian-style gown was no match for the cold, New York weather. I donned my heavy wool cape, pulling it close about myself, in an attempt to keep the cold at bay.

Coco wore a similar gown, but was smart enough to have brought a heavy woolen coat that covered her ankles, keeping her warm and dry.

A wooden plank lay leveraged from the hotel steps to the carriage step-up, allowing us to keep our delicate slippers dry. Coco and I stepped daintily across the plank, while holding the hand of the brave driver as we climbed into the waiting carriage. Lilly simply appeared in a seat, and I had to stop Coco from sitting on her by directing her to sit in another spot. The twenty-minute ride to Kingsley Hall, where all the cotton sellers and buyers gathered two times a year, was uneventful.

"This is it," I announced, as we pulled up to the hall. "I need you to try to stay dispassionate, Coco. Think of it as a game of poker with Father. You don't want to give anything away, so you need to control your emotions. Follow my lead and whatever you do, don't take off your gloves," I counseled, taking her hands in mine. "Are you sure you're up for this particular brand of poker game?"

"I will be fine, Olivia. I'm not a child. I am seventeen, after all." Coco grumbled, drawing her hands back.

"I know. It's just that I worry about you."

"Well, don't," she said, with a perfunctory tone, pushing away from me as the door opened.

I turned to look at Lilly, but she had already disappeared, following behind Coco as she walked through the double doors held open for her by two well-dressed men in uniform.

I gave a shy smile to the coachman, feeling slightly embarrassed for making him stand so long in the rain. I took his offered hand and stepped out of the rig, pulling my hood over my head. Stopping at the large wooden doors of Kingsley Hall, I took a deep breath to calm my rattled nerves and prepare myself for whatever came next.

Coco and Lilly were wandering around looking at the samples of raw cotton each seller had displayed before them. The hall was very large and well-lit for such a dreary day, but I was interested in finding the Beaumont table.

My eyes wandered around the large hall, but I didn't see Mr. Beaumont anywhere, and wondered if perhaps he wasn't there. Out of the corner of my eye I noticed a door that led to another room. Things had changed from the last time I was here. There were more buyers, and more sellers, hence, the need for more room. Stepping through the large door, my eyes immediately began to search and I noticed a tall man with dark, chestnut-colored hair, with his back to me. His table was in the middle of the room and he was talking to a merchant, standing between two tables.

Removing my gloves, I tucked them into the pocket of my wet cape and handed it to a woman who hung it up. Making my way towards the center of the room, I pulled at the fibers of cotton testing the fiber length and density to determine the quality. Placing the cotton back down, I turned my attention to the next table and did the same. This second sample was less dense, and the fibers were shorter than the first cotton sample, but still of fine quality, and the color was unusual. I was still trying to decide whether or not to bid on this lot, when I turned to my left and picked up a third sample from the next table.

"Can I help you, Miss?" a man asked, coming out from behind his stand to greet me.

"No, I don't believe you can," I replied, turning my back to him and walking back to the previous two tables.

"There's no need to get so uppity, little lady," the man angrily added, following closely behind me.

"It's my accent," I stated blandly. "It makes everything I say sound uppity, good man," I retorted, without stopping or turning around. Grabbing me by the shoulder, the man spun me around to face him. "Unhand me this instant you —" I demanded, with a cold, calculating tone, automatically dipping my hand into my gowns hidden pocket to feel for the handle of my blade.

"Now there is no cause for this fuss," came a voice behind me. Another figure stepped between us both to prevent any further discourse. "Tom, I'm certain the young lady meant no disrespect. Now, did you?" he cajoled, in a rich melodic tone that reverberated and oozed masculinity.

I turned and was staring up into hazel green eyes, fringed with thick, dark lashes. The air between us crackled with electricity. "Of course not," I quietly replied, staring up into the strikingly handsome face of the man I had met only once before.

"Allow me to make introductions," he soothed pleasantly with his southern drawl. "This is Thomas Bartholomew, from Virginia. His family has been in the cotton business for three generations now," he added, with a congenial smile. "And this good looking gentleman to your left is my neighbor and good friend, Jackson Montgomery. Now *his* family has been in the cotton business *five* generations?"

"Six, if you count me," Jackson chimed in, giving me a very broad smile that showed off a row of beautifully white teeth.

"Nobody truly counts you, Jackson," Brody quipped.

"Hey now, you cut me to the quick," Jackson cried, feigning hurt.

"That would first require you to possess feelings, my dear friend," the man continued teasing, turning back to me. "Allow me to introduce another gentleman, who just happens to be manning our family booth behind you — my brother, Quinton Beaumont, and my name is Brody. Brody Beaumont, and before you question your own eyesight, let me assure you that you are not mistaken, we are identical twins," Brody teased, smiling broadly showing off his own white teeth. "So I do believe that just leaves you," he asked cordially. "Who might you be, little lady, with the beautiful accent?"

"I am, Olivia Townsend, representing Stewart Textiles, of London," I boldly proclaimed, thrusting my hand out to shake Brody's hand. "It is a pleasure to make your acquaintance," I stammered, boldly gazing into smoldering green eyes.

I felt a jolt travel up my arm when Brody took my hand in his, and I could tell by the look in his eyes that he felt it too. His handshake was unapologetically firm and his palms were calloused and warm as he held my hand longer than necessary, or even proper.

I felt a blush creeping up my cheeks before clearing my throat and removing my hand from his grasp. Turning to the two other men in turn, I shook their hands before turning back to Brody. "Perhaps we could do a bit of business, Mr. Beaumont," I added with a business-like tone, noticing him scrutinizing me.

"It would be my pleasure, Miss Townsend. It is *Miss* Townsend?" Brody prodded.

"Yes, of course, why do you ask?"

"Oh, no reason," he grinned. "Please, call me, Brody. Now, if you would be so kind as to follow me," he gestured, directed my gaze to the back of the hall were tables and chairs had been arranged.

Putting my hand out to take Quinton's, I hoped I didn't sound overly eager. "It is a pleasure to meet you, Mr. Beaumont." I said, being direct.

But something in his gaze made me feel uneasy, and I quickly retrieved my hand. "Gentlemen," I added with a nod.

"I know your family. The Stewart name, that is. My father has done business with a Charles Deveraux and I remember him being accompanied by a woman." Quinton looked down as he thought a moment. "I believe her name was Mrs. Townsend. You wouldn't be any relation, would you?"

"Why yes, I would, as a matter of fact."

"How is Mr. Deveraux doing?"

"Uncle Charlie was well last time I spoke him, and Mrs. Townsend would be my mother. She is well. Thank you for asking," I answered, turning to leave.

"Isn't your family some kind of royalty back in England?" Quinton asked.

Blushing slightly, I turned and saw Coco making her way to me, affording me the perfect opportunity to throw the attention back on someone else. Smiling widely, I stretched out my hand to pull her into the group. "Gentlemen, allow me to introduce to you my sister, Lady Catherine Townsend."

Giving me that sour look she always gives whenever I use her full name, Coco rolled her eyes at me. "Coco, this is Mr. Quinton Beaumont and his twin brother, Brody, and their very good friend, Mr. Jackson Montgomery." Smiling pleasantly at her, I winked and slowly backed up. "Gentlemen, it has been a pleasure to meet you, but I need to conduct a little business. I will leave you in the capable hands of my sister now."

"Please, call me Coco," she smoothly transitioned, shaking hands with the three men. "No one calls me Catherine, except my grandmother," she added, trying not to stare at the two men in front of her who looked identical to her sketch.

"Close your mouth, Coco, they are twins. Isn't that astounding?" I whispered in her ear.

"Astounding," Coco quietly echoed.

"Now, Mr. Beaumont," I said, "shall we adjourn to conduct our business?"

"That sounds delightful. Please, follow me," Brody gestured, waving his hand to the back of the room. I turned to follow, but not before I noticed a look pass between Brody and Quinton.

I had been to market with Uncle Charlie a few times when I was quite young and learned that a bale was a compressed bundle of cotton, weighing anywhere from four hundred to five hundred pounds. Merchants bid on the number of bales and haggled over the amount that they were willing to pay, per pound.

Winding his way past booths and several tables, Brody maneuvered his way to a particular table. Pulling out a chair for me to sit in, he called to the steward and requested tea and pastries be brought over. Then he sat down across from me and pulled out a small book and a pencil from his pocket. "Perhaps you will find me too forward, but I had hoped to run into you again."

I blushed, reminded of the first time we met at the Carmichael, but couldn't think of anything witty in reply when the steward approached. Setting the tray on the table he poured the tea. "Cream and sugar?" he inquired.

"Two lumps, no cream. I prefer mine on the sweeter side," I said, feeling like the cat playing with a mouse. Just a little closer and I would have him. "I understand that you live on a plantation. Is it a large plantation?" I innocently asked.

"We own five hundred acres of the richest West Virginia soil you could ever hope to see," he informed me, picking out a pastry from the tray. "Why, my daddy likes to say that God made the land himself just for growing cotton," Brody quipped in a tone that smacked of bragging.

"You don't say?" I replied, purposely trying to sound skeptical, as I leaned forward in my chair. "Well, I don't think I've ever seen a real live working plantation before," I casually mentioned, eyeing the pastry tray and selecting a scone with raisins. "We don't have plantations in Dublin. Not like you have here in the Colony."

"Well, is that so?" Brody smiled even broader. "I think we are going to have to change that."

"What do you mean, Mr. Beaumont?" I questioned, playing naive to the hilt.

"Why, our plantation home is so large that you and your sister could have an entire suite to yourselves and we wouldn't run into each other for two whole days, if you're of a mind to avoid me," Brody teased.

"Somehow I think you might be, as you southerners like to say, pulling my leg." I teased him with a glint of mischief in my eyes.

"Well, maybe just a little, but the place is huge. You and your sister truly should come out, if you have time. My brother and I would love to discuss textiles with you. But more importantly our father loves anyone with a foreign accent."

"If we are going to be perfectly honest with one another, I am rather enjoying your accent." I replied, leaning back in my chair with my tea cup in hand.

"This is what they call a southern drawl, Miss Townsend, not an accent," Brody corrected with a seductive smile. "Now, let us get down to business, shall we? How many bales were you considering?"

"I wish to purchase fifteen bales, at ten cents a pound," I coolly offered, taking a sip of tea.

"Twenty cents a pound," he countered, with a straight face.

"Your product Mr. Beaumont is of high quality, I will give you that, but it isn't made of gold, sir. I will give you twelve cents a pound and not a penny more," I scolded, giving him my best poker face, knowing that he could easily get fifteen cents or more a pound. I sipped my tea, peering at him over the rim.

Brody narrowed his eyes slightly and studied my face for a few silent moments. "Fourteen and a half, is a fair price."

"I will take seventeen bales at twelve cents a pound or I take my business elsewhere," I countered, placing my cup down with purpose.

Brody studied my face again to determine how serious I was. I refused to blink first, choosing instead to stand up and stick out my hand. "It was a pleasure to meet you, Mr. Beaumont. I'm terribly sorry that we couldn't come to an understanding."

Taking my hand in his, Brody rolled my fingers through his hand, staring silently up at me again. Hesitation flickered in his eyes before answering. "You have yourself a deal, but on one condition. You agree to come back to my family's plantation with me."

Tiny nervous butterfly wings fluttered about in my stomach. How could this be? These feelings were ridiculous. Brody Beaumont was truly a formidable foe, and I was suddenly scared and thrilled, all at the same time. Part of me wanted to run as far from those soul-searching eyes as I could get, and the other part of me wanted to see where this all would lead. I was definitely playing a dangerous game, and it involved fire. I stood there a few seconds longer, weighing my options and marveling at his cool calculating demeanor. It was as if he thrived on risky it all. I watched the steady pulse as it beat in his throat and noticed his beautiful eyes had been gazing at me, and waiting. I don't remember seeing him breathe. Or was that me?

Feelings of trepidation and apprehension fluttered through my veins. This is what I wanted from the moment I set my eyes upon Brody Beaumont. I felt myself hesitate, nervously licking my dry lips. I hoped I was doing the right thing. Then Lilly appeared behind Brody, her eyes looked so haunting. I couldn't read her thoughts, but I could read her face. She was unsure about something. What was she unsure of?

"Thank you, Mr. Beaumont. Your kind invitation is most generous, if not completely unorthodox," I coolly stated, exhaling the breath I'd been holding. Placing a pleasant smile on my lips, I continued. "Coco and I would be honored to accompany you back to your family plantation for a few days. But don't you have to stay until the end of the venue?"

"Our foreman, Mr. Madison will be taking over for us later this afternoon. Quinton and I are needed at home. We will be leaving tomorrow," Brody answered, giving me a sly smile.

"We will certainly need a little time to pack. Shall we say, tomorrow, around ten o'clock?"

"Splendid," he replied, clapping his hands together as his rich seductive voice sliced through me like a knife. "I will make all of the arrangements and send a carriage around to your hotel by ten then."

"How far is it by carriage?" I asked.

"We won't be traveling all that way by carriage, Lady Townsend. Our ship, the *Channing*, is moored at the wharf and we will sail it down the coast, then travel the rest of the way by carriage."

"In that case, Mr. Beaumont, we are staying at the —" I began when Brody cut me off.

"I know where you are staying. Room 320, if I am not mistake," he said smoothly, "and please, I insist you call me Brody."

My eyes couldn't help sliding back up to Lilly's, still standing behind Brody. Her sorrow was palpable as it reflected in her eyes. I felt as if I had somehow betrayed her, as if she could read my thoughts and know what I was feeling. I kept telling myself that I was simply playing a part when I agreed to accompany Brody Beaumont to his plantation. But my sudden racing pulse and pounding heart told me otherwise. I was drawn to him by some magnetic pull, and I could not resist the force that was Brody Beaumont.

Magnetic pull aside, nothing was going to keep me from fulfilling my promise to Lilly. I would find out what happened to her, and that person, whether it be Brody Beaumont or someone else, would pay dearly for taking her life.

5

SATURDAY, FEBRUARY 7, 1804

Rosewood Plantation

THE MORNING WAS GLOOMY AND cold with a light snow falling. I wanted to return to our ship, the *Trinity*, and go straight back home, but I had a promise to keep.

At nine twenty, Margot pulled on the call rope, signaling the hotel staff that we needed our trunks taken down stairs. Coco and I were finishing our breakfast of tea, biscuits and plum preserves when there came a knock on the door. "I'm sure that must be the young men come to fetch the trunks." Margot called out, over her shoulder as she went to answer the door.

"I'm worried about Lilly," I commented, before taking another sip of tea. "She never came back with us last night, and I haven't seen a glimmer of her since."

"She will show herself sooner or later. Maybe she is still observing the Beaumont's and trying to remember," Coco added, with a well-natured smile. "I certainly couldn't help but notice Mr. Beaumont making eyes at you yesterday. Maybe he felt encouraged, just a bit," she added, giving me a measured look over the rim of her tea cup.

Setting my cup down, I eyed the young men as they walked past us, with heads bowed, to retrieve the trunks from the next room. "I certainly can't be held responsible for another person's behavior," I whispered loudly, irritated at my sister for saying such a thing. And yet, if I was being completely honest with myself, I would admit that I was more irritated at myself for the duplicitous, underhanded part I played, just to get what I wanted. A bloody invitation to the Beaumont plantation.

Glancing at Coco over my own cup of tea, my inner emotions and frustration got the better of me. I'd been conflicted for weeks over Lilly's death and couldn't get myself or my conflicting emotions under control. I finally decided to concede this one point to Coco. "Well, maybe you're right, and let's just say that I can see your point. After all, I'm playing a part in this little game of cat and mouse," I stated, glancing at her from the corner of my eye. She arched an eyebrow at me, like Father did when he doubted a person's sincerity. "Stop looking at me like that, Coco," I retorted sharply, wiping my mouth with the napkin. "What would you have me do, come out directly and ask the Beaumont twins if either one of them is responsible for Lilly's death?"

"Excuse me, my lady, I was informed that the carriages have arrived early. This was also delivered for you, Olivia," Margot said, handing me a note with masculine handwriting on it.

The two men tried not to gawk at us as they passed through the room again with our trunks in tow. I could only assume they had heard some portion, here and there of our conversation, and were trying to figure out if they should contact the authorities.

"Well?" Coco questioned, coming to stand next to me.

"Well, what?"

"The note, what does it say?" she queried.

I blankly stared at the sealed note in my hand for a few seconds, before breaking the seal and reading the words. "It is from Mr. Brody Beaumont. He apologizes for the inconvenience of calling on us before the appointed time, but the tide is set to go out earlier than anticipated today and there appears to be a storm blowing in. He hopes that we will forgive the rush," I concluded and chanced another glance at Coco, who was now standing next to me, with a strange smile on her lips. "Well, you've told me that I could negotiate with the Devil himself and come out ahead. Shall we find out if you are correct?" I added with a strained smile. "Did you happen to leave out the heavy coat that I purchased yesterday, Margot? It looks like it is going to be a very cold day indeed."

"Yes. I will just go and fetch it for you, my lady," she replied, playing the proper lady's maid.

A few minutes later Coco and I stood together in the lobby, when I remembered that I had written a letter to our parents. "I have to take care of something before we leave. You go ahead to the carriage and I will be right behind you."

"Don't be long," Coco called to my retreating back.

Stepping up to the front desk, I waited until I caught Mr. Jones's eye. He put down the papers he was looking through and leaned in towards me. Leaning over the desk slightly, I looked around to make sure that no unintended ears were listening to what I had to say. "Mr. Jones, I was wondering if you could do me two favors," I shyly asked, looking around once again.

"Of course, Lady Townsend, I would be happy to," he replied, looking over the rim of his perfectly spotless, shiny spectacles.

"I need you to have someone run this letter to Captain Bellamy of the *Trinity*," I said, presenting him with a letter that I pulled from my coat pocket. The letter stated that I wished Captain Bellamy to wait for the purchase cotton to be delivered, then to sail the ship down the coast to the Virginia Port and wait for me. He was to send word of his arrival to the Rosewood Plantation, owned by the Beaumont's, and then wait further instructions. Then opening my delicate white reticule, I produced another envelope. "I also need you to give this letter to my mother and father when they arrive here looking for me."

"I did not realize that Lord and Lady Townsend would be staying with us," he exclaimed. Genuine surprise registered on Mr. Jones's normally placid features.

I smiled awkwardly and said, "I cannot guarantee they will be staying, once they receive my letter," I quickly corrected, after reflecting on how my original words may have sounded. "That is not to say that I did not enjoy my stay with you, Mr. Jones. My sister and I wish to express our deepest appreciation for your wonderful assistance and fine service while we stayed with you." I smiled awkwardly again, not knowing what else to say. "Well, good day to you, Mr. Jones," I concluded by offering my hand to him.

"And good day to you, Lady Townsend," Mr. Jones replied with a polite smile, taking the two letters from me as I slipped him a few coins.

I'd written to Mother and Father, explaining everything in detail, letting them know where Coco and I would be. I hoped to diffuse some of their anger I was certain had been building, as they made the long journey here, only to find out that Coco and I had left.

Stepping from the Carmichael Hotel, I pulled the collar of my coat up even higher. The frigid breeze chilled me to the bone. Snow was still falling gently, touching the ground where a light dusting had deposited itself earlier.

I eyed the two carriages to my left, and smiled. Brody Beaumont had thought of everything. One carriage for our many trunks and the other for our comfort.

"Right this way, Lady Townsend, Mr. Beaumont has arranged everything to ensure that you and your sister are accommodated. I have placed blankets in the carriage to keep you warm, but please don't hesitate to let me know if you need anything else." The driver nervously babbled, while leading me to the carriage door. "Mr. Beaumont has insisted that I make any stops along the way to pick up any essentials before delivering you to the ship. Would you like me to make any stops before we reach the wharf?" he asked while opening the carriage door and assisting me inside.

Smiling sweetly, I replied, "No thank you, sir. I do believe my sister and I are adequately supplied," I answered, sitting down next to Coco and snuggled myself under the blanket she offered. "Thank you for your kindness."

As soon as the door closed, Lilly appeared on the seat across from us and next to Margot, with a forlorn expression marring her pretty features.

"Where have you been, Miss Lilly?" I asked, my concern quickly turning to consternation. "I was so worried. Don't you ever do that to me again!"

"Lilly is here?" Coco and Margot cried, simultaneously, both for different reasons. Coco was excited, while Margot was surprised Lilly was still around.

"Shush you two, I want to hear her explain herself," I insisted.

"His eyes," was all she said, before staring longingly out the window.

"What about his eyes?" I asked.

"What is she saying, Olivia? Oh, never mind," Coco said impatiently, removing her gloves, while Margot crossed herself and stared out the opposite window.

"There is something different about his eyes. Brody's eyes are hazel, but sometimes brown," Lilly pondered, looking off into the distance again. "I only remember his eyes being brown. The other one, Quinton has brown eyes, but no beard. I definitely remember there being a beard," she murmured to herself. "Why can't I remember, Olivia? Why am I always so cold? I can't seem to get warm," Lilly complained, pulling her shawl tighter around her shoulders.

"Sometimes when the soul is separated from the body too quickly or in a particularly traumatic way, it causes confusion. It becomes disorientation," I said gently. "I'm sure your memory will come back to you, Lilly. Just be patient. I'm sure you won't have to endure the feeling of being cold much longer." At least I hoped she wouldn't. I was lost in thought, remembering the time a few years back I had witnessed one soul that didn't want to leave this earth. He'd chosen to stick around his family, causing trouble for his wife and two sons. What some might call a good, old-fashioned haunting. The entire thing was very destructive to all parties involved, and it got very messy before I could convince him to leave.

"I was jealous of you yesterday, Olivia. The way, Brody kept looked at you. It made me angry," Lilly pouted.

"You were jealous of me? Why?" I retorted, "I've never heard of anything so ridiculous in all my life, Lilly Collins."

"You have a future to look forward to, Olivia Townsend. I'm stuck here, in between heaven and hell," Lilly lamented, with a catch in her voice. "No one can hear me, or touch me. It isn't fair. All I've ever wanted is to feel the love of someone's arms around me." She shivered. "This damnable, bone chilling cold is enough to drive a soul crazy," Lilly complained, looking at me with unshed tears glistening in her eyes.

"Lilly, I truly am sorry for what has happened to you," I assured her, holding back tears of my own. I felt such empathy for her plight. "I also realize that I cannot change what has already occurred. But I bloody well can find out what happened and why it happened," I added with conviction, "I swear, I will make someone pay dearly. No matter who it is."

"Me too, Lilly," Coco chimed in as several tears ran down her cheeks.

I was so focused on Lilly that I failed to realize we had arrived at our destination, until the door opened suddenly. "I thought you would never get here," Brody cheerfully blurted out, sticking his head inside. "Well, come along, ladies, daylight is upon us and the tide is going out."

Coco turned her head and wiped her tears, pulling on her gloves again before taking hold of Brody's hand and climbing from the carriage first. Margot followed behind her and I took a last look at Lilly, before turning away. Taking ahold of Brody's hand I gazed into his eyes, while my words to Lilly still rang in my ears. Apprehension twisted my stomach as I suddenly questioned my decision to leave with Brody and his twin brother. Had I lost my mind?

"It certainly is a cold morning for a leisurely jaunt down the coast today. Are you sure we shouldn't wait until tomorrow?" I asked, stepping out of the carriage.

"Captain says there's a storm coming and we need to leave while we can," Brody said, patting my hand confidently as he tucked it into the crook of his arm. Giving a reassuring squeeze, he led me up the gangplank and on to the *Channing*. "It won't be a long trip and we have transportation waiting when we reach Virginia. We will most likely arrive at the plantation close to midnight, if all goes well."

"Here's to all going well." I awkwardly smiled, crossing the fingers of my other hand.

"Here's to smooth sailing," Brody echoed with a smile, squeezing my hand again.

6

SUNDAY, FEBRUARY 8, 1804
12:30 IN THE MORNING

An Evil That Lurks Within...

EVERYTHING DID GO WELL ON our journey down the coast, if you don't count the rough waters, and stiff winds. I became concerned when Margot and Coco both turned ashen, and it was at that moment I decided to go up on deck to breathe the fresh brisk air.

Upon arriving at the port of Virginia, two Rosewood carriages were waiting for us. They were custom-designed, painted a glossy black which shone brightly against the gloomy gray of low hanging clouds. No doubt, countless hours had been spent polishing them to their brilliant gloss, so you could see your reflection in the inky black paint. The plantations gold leaf insignia was prominently displayed on the door. Two stems intertwined, one with a delicate rose in full bloom and the other with a cotton ball. Truth be told, the impressive design left me speechless.

The conversation was pleasant and lively as we traveled from Virginia to the Rosewood Plantation in West Virginia and somewhere between ten o'clock and midnight, Coco and I fell asleep. That was until the driver slid the small compartment open, to announced that we had arrived. Lilly had popped in and out of our carriage during the ride and now had a strange look on her face, just before disappearing. I was unable to ask her what was wrong because of the occupants currently sitting near me.

The mansion was lit up and several blurry-eyed footmen and maids waited for us at the bottom of the steps, along with the proprietor of Rosewood.

The mansion was very grand, with eight, large, two-story gallery posts. The entire house was painted white with large, black shutters and two glossy, black-paneled doors. Four steps led up to the massive wrapped-around porch that ran the entire length of the front and both sides of the house.

Brody and Quinton stepped down from the carriage, greeting their father with a large hug, and several hearty slaps to the back, before turning toward the carriage.

Coco looked at me in the dark interior of the carriage as if trying to decide what to do next. "Well, Olivia, this is it, the moment of truth," she said, with a mysterious smile. "Take a deep breath and follow me." Reaching out to take ahold of Quinton's outstretched hand, she stepped effortlessly down from the carriage.

"Father, allow me to introduce Lady Catherine Townsend, of the Stewart Textiles of London," Quinton announced, causing me to cringe inwardly, because I knew Coco was bristling at the proper use of her name. "Catherine, this is my father, Harrison Beaumont."

"It is a pleasure to meet you, Mr. Beaumont, and please call me Coco."

"Well I'll be hung. If that isn't the damnedest thing I've ever heard?" Harrison loudly proclaimed, with a hearty laugh. Then peering into the carriage, Harrison squinted, trying to see into the darkened interior. "I thought your telegram said there were two of them."

Brody walked to the carriage door, reaching his hand in to take ahold of my hand. "Allow me to introduce to you Lady Olivia Townsend, of Dublin, Father," he announced proudly, as if this were a formal gathering and I was the Queen of England.

Ducking my head, I stepped down less gracefully than my sister, but short of falling upon my face. I forced a smile to my lips, looking up into Harrison Beaumont's eyes. To look at him, one could tell that he was a man of authority, very disciplined and structured, commanding of respect. For a man of his age, he was in good shape. His hair meticulously combed, face recently shaved and a fresh set of clothes and crisp white shirt completed the picture.

Stepping closer, I extended my hand to Harrison, "My sister and I would like to thank you for graciously offering to take us in for a few days, Mr. Beaumont."

"Nonsense, it is my pleasure and we are honored that you would stay with us," he said, sweeping his hand towards the door. "Let me be the first to welcome you both into our humble home." Harrison's voice boomed loudly in the darkness. "And may I also say that you are in for a real treat. We are preparing for our annual Winter Ball. I do hope you can stay for it."

I stood staring at this bigger-than-life man who exuded enthusiasm and strength, and I marveled at his apparent physical strength. But all of this paled in comparison with the extraordinary woman standing quietly by his side.

She was the most exquisite creature I had ever seen, holding herself so regally she could have been royalty. Her piercing hazel green eyes burrowed through me as the line was clearly being drawn in the proverbial sand. The look she gave me said that she had marked her territory a long time ago, and I that I was treading upon it. But one reaction was unmistakable. The moment she realized I could see her. The shadow of disbelief then shock flashed across her delicate features, distorting her features before they quickly became replaced with an angry scowl. I was considering the unscrupulous, malignant eyes of this cold-hearted spirit, whom I assumed to be Brody and Quinton's dearly departed mother, the saintly pillar of society that Mr. Jones had spoken of.

"Why, Mr. Beaumont, my sister and I would love to stay long enough to enjoy such festivities. Perhaps we can discuss the particulars of your celebration in the morning. It truly has been a long day," I begged, drawing my eyes back to engage Harrison.

"But of course, my dear. How rude of me," Harrison gushed. "Mrs. Bell will show you the way. Your luggage has already been delivered upstairs to your rooms."

"You are too kind, sir," I concluded, giving him a proper curtsy as Coco silently followed behind me.

Tiny goosebumps ran up and down my arms when I walked through the massive wooden doors of the Beaumont mansion, led by Mrs. Bell, a petite woman in her early forties. Coco and I held hands as we followed her to our rooms, and to be perfectly honest, I was afraid to let go of her. As we were led through the west wing, I was surprised by the number of lit candles that lined the hallways and the fires still burning in the hearths at such a late hour. Yet, despite all of this light glowing throughout the Beaumont home, it felt neither warm nor cozy. There was a palpable chill over the house that I felt every time I breathed in.

I also felt the venomous eyes of the dead upon me, long after she dematerialized into the night, moments after realizing I could see her.

Our suite of rooms was adorned in a rose décor. Tiny roses speckled the off-white paper back ground with green vines climbing upwards. It made the room feel slightly warmer than the rest of the house, despite the apparent spiteful spirit residing there.

The canopy and top quilt were made of a warm, rich burgundy brocade, designed to keep the occupant warm and cozy on cold wintery nights, like the one we were experiencing.

I marveled at how quickly Margot could turn a simple room into an oasis. She had followed the trunks upstairs while Coco and I made introductions, and laid out our night clothes and laid back the quilts on our beds. I watched as she released the heavy drapes from their gold tassels, and they fell across the cold, dark windows.

"Is everyone alright?" I asked, wondering if either one of them had felt as I did.

Margot replied in the negative while, Coco shivered. "I felt something," she replied.

I felt it best to say nothing at the time regarding the angry spirit of Annabelle Beaumont, in hopes that ignorance might truly prove to be bliss.

Retiring to our own rooms, Coco and I changed and climbed into bed. Then one by one, I watched as the candles were extinguished in our rooms, with exception to the one on my bedside table. There was a degree of comfort afforded me with that one single candle still glowing brightly, next to me.

7

Shanty Row, and Forgotten Ghosts

FEELING AS IF I HAD barely closed my eyes, I was jolted awake by a heavy clunking noise as books fell from a desk, hitting the floor. There was little doubt in my mind how such a thing may have happened, never-the-less I was left with a racing heart. Sitting straight up in bed, a scream stuck midway in my throat.

Crawling out of my warm bed and walking across the cold wood floor, I pulled back the curtains and saw dawn barely cresting the top of a hill. The surrounding terrain, a mixture of small hills and meadows were covered in a variety trees. Pines, cedars, aspens and cottonwoods dotted the landscape and the glorious scent of pines wafted through the window as I cracked the window open. The clean, crisp morning breeze was like a balm to my frazzled nerves. The storm we'd experienced the day before had blown away, leaving behind a glorious day and feelings of hopeful expectation. And even though my eyes felt rough and scratchy like sandpaper, I looked forward to what the day might reveal.

I poured water into a basin, then scooped the ice cold water on my face. With towel still in hand, I rang for the upstairs maid, Grace, who arrived with a small pot of strong tea, milk and biscuits, still warm from the oven. Grace informed me that breakfast would be served precisely at eight thirty, in the sun room. Considering that it was only six o'clock, I was grateful that she had thought to provide fresh biscuits and jam.

After eating and drinking my fill of tea and biscuits, I looked in on Coco and found her still sleeping soundly. Not wishing to disturb Margot after the late hour she had retired the night before, I quietly dressed in a green wool gown, then I dug a pair of boots out of the trunk and slipped them on.

Stepping into the hallway just as the clock chimed six-thirty, I stood for a moment, listening for any movement. A hall boy bustled past, barely noticing me, with his arms loaded down with wood, a broom, dustpan and metal pail which hung from his left arm.

I went off in the direction the young man had come from and found the back stairs. Descending the staircase, I slipped past the servants' quarters and out the back door through the kitchen entrance. Pulling the collar of my coat up around my neck, the air was colder than I'd expected as it hit me. Quickly buttoned the top button, then pulling on a pair of gloves from my pocket, I was concerned about Lilly and decided to seek her out.

Making my way through the garden, I followed a path that led me to a large barn. Lilly loved animals and especially horses, so I figured the barn would be a logical place to start. The heavy wood door had been pushed partially open, so I stepped inside. I was surprised at how warm the large building was as I looked around. Cows were in stalls to the left, fresh hay in their troughs, while chickens gathered in the center of the room, scratching and pecking at the grain on the ground.

I didn't see or hear anyone, so I felt it safe to softly call to Lilly, without being thought of as mad. "Lilly. Lilly, are you in here?" Spying another row of stalls to my right, I started in that direction, still calling out to her when I nearly jumped out of my skin. A feral cat hissed with its claws out, taking a swipe at me, before racing past me. Undaunted, I continued my search for Lilly. Poking my head into each stall, I looked around and called out, but there was no sign of her. Stopping to scratch a particularly friendly horse behind the ear, I was about to leave when I heard a quiet whisper.

"Are you alone?" Spinning around, I found Lilly, timidly looking at me.

"Yes. Everyone else is still sleeping," I replied.

"No. I mean that evil woman who stands guard at the door," Lilly replied, wearily looking around her. "She scares me!"

"Me too!" I whispered. "Do you know who she is?"

"I don't remember seeing her before."

"I assume she is Annabelle Beaumont, the woman Mr. Jones from the Carmichael Hotel told me about. The dearly-departed mother and wife of the Beaumont men. And I say assume because she won't acknowledge me. Honestly, she is just as bad as the feral cat that just greeted me. They both make my skin crawl."

"Did you say something, Miss?" A polite voice asked, standing a mere four feet away.

Awkwardly I turned and smiled. "I was just talking to the horse. Sorry I disturbed you," I answered. "Let's get out of here," I whispered as I turned back around and headed for the opened door at the far end of the barn.

Stepping outside, I shivered when the cold air hit me again. Wrapping my arms around myself, I ran my hands up and down my arms to generate some warmth. "Burr, it certainly is a cold morning," I commented, trying to break the ice.

"I wouldn't know, since I only feel cold these days," Lilly tersely replied.

Following the path from the back of the barn, I saw wooden structures through the trees. Lilly and I silently walked along, down the path for a few minutes, both of us lost in our own thoughts.

"I was worried about you when you didn't follow me into the house last night. But after coming face to face with that accursed spirit guarding the entrance, I understand," I finally said, glancing over at her. "Did you remember anything more about this place?"

"Well, I remember this place. I've ridden on that horse you were scratching. His name is Old Pete. I remember this path, the main house, Quinton, and his brother Brody. I even remember their father, Harrison, the irascible old sod," Lilly answered, as if just saying Harrison's name left a bad taste in her mouth.

"Now what would make you say such a thing, Lilly Ann Collins? Since when have you ever bantered about such slanderous words?" I scolded.

"Have you ever noticed that when you meet someone, your life is forever changed?" she lamented. "Sometimes it is for the better and sometimes for the worse, but none the less, it is changed forever," Lilly continued, waxing nostalgic.

I hesitated a moment before replying to Lilly's thought-provoking question while we came around a bend in the path. "I never really thought too deeply on the matter, Lilly, but you're right. Everyone you meet changes your life, in some way or another."

Before us stood rows of houses that were really broken down shacks at this point. I imagined them to have been built many years before for migrant workers or hired help. Each building was one long bunk house with two separate doors along the front. A porch ran the entire length of each building, with several chairs lined up, as if the occupants would return soon. A dilapidated fence surrounding the small community was falling apart. A few posts, which looked as if someone had attempted to repair them here and there, were now overgrown with foliage. Vines, like gnarled fingers, wrapped around the wood buildings, and climbed up along the roof lines, as if the vegetation was attempting to reclaim the old wood as part of the forest again.

Continuing down the path, seven more buildings still stood. Some looked to be in decent shape, while others were uninhabitable. One row house leaned at an angle as if it would collapse at any time.

We stopped at the last row of buildings before I realized my mistake. Several people sat around talking as we approached. At first glance, I thought nothing of the field hands sitting on the porch, until I looked closer. The men wore very worn pants and shirts, thread-barren in spots. The women wore gowns that were old and out of date, also thread-barren in spots. They all began to stare at us when they noticed us looking in their direction. Three men, two women and a young male child, maybe ten years old, and all of African descent. All conversation ended abruptly as they stared at us.

"Don't look at them, Lilly," I blurted out, looking away as fast as I could. "Do you think they saw us?" I asked, looking at the ground and trying to act as if I hadn't seen them.

"Oh, they saw us all right."

"Olivia!" Brody called out, barrowing down the path on his powerful black stallion. I turned in his direction and came face to face with two of the men from the porch. They were now standing directly in front of me, blocking my path.

"Can you sees us or not?" the older man asked.

"She can sees you, Joseph. I knew it! Didn't I tells you she was a lookin at us."

"Yes, but I can't talk to you just now," I quietly replied, looking down at the ground, as if I had just noticed something terribly interesting. "Lilly, please, do something," I pleaded, under my breath.

"What are you doing over here?" Brody asked, coming to a sliding halt next to me. "If I knew you were such an early riser, I would have invited you to come riding with me."

The disappointed looked I received from the two men as I looked up from the ground made me ill as I felt my heart shrink two sizes. I placed a smile on my lips and looked past them as if they weren't even there.

"Why don't you boys come along with me and leave the nice lady alone," Lilly said, gathering them up, like a mother hen, as she led them away from me.

"What kind of nonsense is she about?" Joseph complained, giving me one last nasty glare.

Looking up at Brody, who was still seated on his horse, I brought my hand up to block the sun. "New surroundings, different noises, you know how it is. I couldn't sleep, so I decided to take a walk before breakfast," I answered, placing my hands in the small of my back and leaning back, stretching, somewhat dramatically.

"Do you like to ride?"

"I tend to avoid it, whenever possible," I answered, placing my hand to my forehead again as I looked up at this tall, handsome figure of a man and tried to act normal. I could still feel disbelieving eyes staring at the back of my head. I gave a little shiver and as hard as I tried, I couldn't stop my eyes from straying back to that porch.

With a skeptical look, Brody climbed down from his horse and took me by the hand. Then leading me around to the other side with a laugh that said you must be jesting, he placed my hand on the neck of his horse. Trailing my fingers through the silky, thick mane with his assistance, he continued. "Nonsense, you just haven't had the proper riding partner. This is Zeus. He stands seventeen hands high and is what they call a Friesian," Brody proudly proclaimed. "I traveled all the way to England, just for the pleasure of paying top dollar for him," he added with a half-smile on his handsome, full lips. Then he chuckled as if he had just told a great joke. "I knew the moment I laid eyes on him that Zeus was meant to be mine. He and I have been together for three years now, and to tell you the truth, I can't remember what I did without him."

Zeus nervously pawed at the ground with his powerful front legs, as his coal black eyes stared in the direction of the porch. Soon he began to prance around, restlessly and snort.

"Maybe we should lead Zeus back down the path. He seems spooked by something," I suggested, knowing full well what was spooking him.

"It's these buildings. He always gets like this whenever we ride through here," Brody said solemnly, looking towards the rundown wooden structures. "Ghosts from the past, I suppose," he added while staring at the porch, as if he could see people standing there.

I nervously laughed, knowing he didn't realize how true that statement was. Steering his attention away from the porch and back to his spooked horse, I pulled on his sleeve. "I still think that it would be prudent to walk Zeus out of here."

"Now that's just crazy talk. You will be perfectly safe with me," Brody boastfully stated, slowly dragging his eyes from the porch. With a confident smile, Brody boldly looked at me now. Placing the leather reins in my hands with purpose, Brody grasped either side of my waist and lifted me onto his horse.

Sitting sideways, with one leg over the saddle horn, while Brody hoisted himself up behind me, I was afraid to move. But at the same time, I didn't miss the fact that his well worn pants were faded in all the right places, as if he wore them often, while riding or performing manual labor. His boots, while broken in, shone black with a fresh coat of polish and his white shirt, minus a formal cravat, was paired with a dark gray waist coat which accentuated the green of his eyes.

My heart began to beat wildly against my ribs as he came in close behind me, hooked one arm around my waist and slid me back against his chest and hips. "How is that? Are you still afraid that you might slip off?" Brody asked with confidence.

"No, Mr. Beaumont, I am no longer afraid of falling from this great beast of a horse. I am, however, concerned that your father or someone else may see us and call for a priest to marry us post haste."

Throwing his head back and laughing, Brody tightened his grip around my waist even more, crushing my lungs as he kicked Zeus in the side. Turning around on the path, we headed for the stables. "Oh, my dear woman, you are, if nothing else, entertaining. I am truly grateful that you agreed to come."

With a terse smile, I took one last look at Lilly and the others still on the porch, giving the slightest nod of my head. Lilly knew what to do, and I knew that I could find her again if I needed to.

Brody called out as we rode into stable area. "Jamie, take care of Zeus for me. I must show Lady Townsend something," he bellowed, pulling me unceremoniously from the back of Zeus like a rag doll. "And don't forget to give him extra grain. It's going to be cold tonight."

"Yes, sir," Jamie replied, spiriting Zeus away, the moment Brody had spoken.

"Where are you taking me, Brody Beaumont?" I tersely asked, attempting to pull my hand from his grasp. Tightening his grip, Brody smile mischievously and continued to pull me behind him.

"I told you. I need to show you something," he said with an air of mystery mixed with excitement. "And you will just have to be patient, we're almost there." Pulling me towards the house, he stepped onto the porch and wound around to the left side of the house.

A dog house, mimicking the main house in structure, sat off the ground on stilts about two feet high. A gently sloping ramp was attached, with two large paws and a dog's snout rested upon it.

"Here girl, I have a treat," Brody called out and drew closer.

At first, only a gray nose popped out and sniffed the air, then a head peaked around the corner followed by the rest of the dog. A beautiful, gray, hunting dog walked down the ramp wagging a stub of a tail, rubbed up against Brody and obediently sat down next to him. Her short, shiny, slick coat was beautiful. Brody placed his hand next to her muzzle and gave her a piece of meat from his pocket.

"Oh Brody, she is a beauty. I have never seen anything like her. Are her eyes gray or blue? I can't tell," I asked, squatting down to look closer.

"They are a little of both," he said. "She's a German Weimaraner and built for hunting. I took her off the hands of a merchant ship captain last year. Unfortunately, she tangled with one of Jackson's hunting dogs and now the pups are worthless."

"How can you say such a thing, Brody Beaumont?" I scolded. "All life is precious."

"They are mutts, Olivia."

"What kind of dog does Jackson have? And was it really such a hideous match?" I asked, scratching the dog behind her ears.

"You need to be careful, Olivia. She isn't always so friendly to strangers."

"Don't be ridiculous, she isn't going to bite me. I think she recognizes a dog lover when she sees one," I replied.

"To answer your question about the dogs, separately they are both a beautiful breed, but together the Chesapeake Bay retriever mixed with a Weimaraner, well, let's just say that I haven't decided yet," Brody answered, retrieving two of the puppies from the dog house to show me. "The Retriever is a stockier breed, where the Weimaraner has a finer bone structure and body." He handed me one of the pups. "As you can see they are merely round little balls of fur now."

The puppy had a dark brown coat with a slight gray tinge to it, so I couldn't tell whether she would be chocolate brown or gray, like the mother. Either way, the puppies would end up with short slick hair.

"Oh Brody, they are precious. How can you call them mutts, as if they are an abomination? I think they will surprise you and be stunning" I defended, holding the puppy up to inspect her. "Just look at her! She is beautiful and her eyes are amazing. Those are the eyes of a very smart dog," I assured. "Why, I will bet you that these puppies will be something truly wonderful. You'll see. They might surprise you and turn out to be excellent hunting dogs to boot."

"Do you always see the good in every situation?"

I laughed when the pup licked my nose. "I dare say, I might just take this one home with me. Ever since Winnie died a few years ago, I haven't had the heart to replace her. But perhaps it is time." I laughed again, nuzzling my nose to the puppy's. "She really is sweet, Brody, just look at her, I can tell she is going to be very smart."

A blood curdling scream came from somewhere inside the house and time stood still for a moment, before instincts kicked in. "Coco," I yelled, shoving the puppy into Brody's hands and pivoting on my heels. I picked up the hem of my skirt and bolted for the house, heart pounding wildly in my chest. Time felt like it had slowed down as I moved towards the door throwing it open and screamed for my sister. "Coco, where are you?" I bellowed, racing through the foyer towards the back hallway, stopping momentarily to get my bearings. I looked left, and then franticly looked right, noticing a gathering of servants in the middle of the long hallway. Racing down the hall with Brody close behind me, I pushed my way through the crowd. "Move out of my way," I demanded, pushing people to one side. "Coco! Coco!" I frantically called, before seeing her sitting on the floor, propped up against the bookshelf. "Coco, are you alright?" I dropped to my knees next to her. "What happened?" I cried, looking to Harrison and then Quinton, who knelt next to her.

"All I've been able to ascertain is that she slipped trying to retrieve a book from the shelf up there," Harrison indicated with his finger while looking up through the rungs of the library ladder.

Taking Coco's hand in mine, I touched her cheek, brushing back the stray hairs that had fallen across her eyes. An angry red mark already forming on her forehead and cheek. "What happened to you?" I demanded, as fear caused me to sound harsher than I meant to.

"I'm fine, really. I was looking for a book and the next thing I knew something hit me in the face, and then I fell into the bookcase, hitting my face," Coco softly said, placing her hand over the mark on her forehead, then pulling it away to check for blood. "Please, tell them to stop gawking at me," Coco said, with a flip of her head towards the door. "I am terribly embarrassed."

I looked up at Harrison, Brody, then Quinton, and noticed a strange look pass between the three of them. A group of staff members had collected behind them.

Harrison reacted first. "Go back to work. There is nothing to see here. You heard her. She merely slipped and bumped her head. Go on, be gone, the entire lot of you," he barked irritably. Servants hesitated, still standing in the doorway whispering. Quinton moved towards the door, causing servants one by one grudgingly to disperse.

"Jane, make sure the tea is hot and ready for breakfast, and see that Miss Coco gets a cold towel for her head. Get the water from the well. It will be colder," Quinton called down the hallway.

"Right away, sir," Jane answered, hurrying off to do as she was told.

"Let's get you off this floor, little lady," Harrison said, trying to sound cheerful and upbeat.

They were covering something up. It didn't matter how the three of them tried to play it off, I sensed tension between them. It hung in the air like the terrible smell that lingered in this room. Then I saw her, merely a shadow really, lingering in the far corner. Our eyes met for a full minute, neither one of us looking away. It was in that moment I knew Coco hadn't simply slipped and fallen. She had been pushed and somehow I believe the Beaumont men knew it too.

"Olivia, did you hear what I said?" Brody asked, stepping between me and his mother. He touched my arm to draw my eyes up to his. "Is everything alright?"

"Yes. Why wouldn't it be?" I deflected. A part of me wanted him to know that I was on to him, and that I knew he wasn't being completely honest with me.

A strange look crossed Brody's face before he masked it. "Quinton and my father took Coco to the sunroom for breakfast. I thought you might want to join us," he said, confused by my reaction.

"I would be delighted to join everyone for breakfast. There seems to be far too many ghosts residing in this room," I snapped, looking him dead in the eye. Gauging his reaction, I knew I hit a nerve when his pupils grew larger. It was a slight twitch before he blinked, laughing awkwardly as he took ahold of my hand and led me down the hall to the sunroom.

The remainder of the day was uneventful. I knew Annabelle lurked in the shadows, refusing to show herself again that day, but I felt her, and it made my skin crawl. I'd never had this kind of reaction to a person's spirit before.

I tried convincing Coco fresh air would make her feel better, but she wanted to go upstairs and lay down. I finally lured her outside with the promise of new puppies to play with. She was so excited that she forgot all about the morning's incident and spent the rest of the day playing with the puppies.

And I breathed more easily for the first time that day.

8

MONDAY, FEBRUARY 9ᵀᴴ, 1804
10 O'CLOCK IN THE MORNING

A New Day Dawns and All is Well

COCO SLUMBERED THAT NIGHT IN my bed. This arrangement was more for my benefit and peace of mind than it was for hers. Somewhere around midnight I drifted off to sleep, but it was fitful rather than a restful one.

I awoke with a start to find Coco gone. Panicked, I leapt from the bed, ran to her room and found it empty.

"Margot, where are you, woman?" I shouted, the sound of my own voice reverberated off the walls. The rooms were empty.

Quickly dressing in a Grecian-inspired, muslin white gown with tiny pink rosebuds embroidered around the neckline and hem, I picked up a soft pink shawl to keep my arms warm and left the room. Half way down the stairs, I could hear loud laughter coming from the sunroom. One voice in particular was very familiar — my father's. His booming laughter quickened my steps and, as I rounded the corner, I hesitated a moment. I was not sure of the reception I would receive. Composing myself before stepping through the doorway, I decided the doting daughter would be my best move in this situation.

I rushed through the door and immediately came face to face with Father. Throwing myself into his arms, I greeted him as if I hadn't seen him in months, which I hadn't. "Oh father, you finally arrived. I have missed you so," I cried, planting kisses on both his cheeks. Then turning to my mother, I made a dramatic show of throwing my arms around her as well. "And Mother, it has been an eternity. How was your trip? Uneventful I hope," I rambled, embracing her and kissing both of her cheeks. "Coco was just saying last night, how she hoped you would receive our message in time to attend the Beaumont's annual party, and here you are!"

"Yes, here we are," Mother repeated, in a tone that let me know she wasn't for one minute buying what I was selling.

"How fortuitous," I stated gleefully, feeling like a trapped animal.

"Yes, how fortuitous, indeed," Father mimicked, with a death stare that made my insides turn liquid. A nervous laugh bubbled up from somewhere inside escaping my lips, while I turned three shades of red.

"I can only assume that everyone has introduced themselves."

"Yes, and I have already made arrangements for your parents to stay in the same wing of the house as you and your sister," Harrison said, gesturing towards the table. "Perhaps we can all sit down and enjoy a lovely breakfast together."

"Yes, thank you, Mr. Beaumont, that would be most hospitable of you, considering my daughters have already intruded upon your generosity," Mother stated, taking ahold of my arm, escorting me to the table, while Father flanked me on the other side, like a pair of armed guards escorting a prisoner.

My eyes wandered over to Coco in hopes that she would help me in some way. But she suddenly found something interesting to stare at in her lap. *Coward!*

"We haven't decided to stay," Father informed me, then cleared his throat. "I've sent Captain Bellamy home to unload his cargo. So it seems that you and your sister will be traveling back with us."

"If you will allow me to say, sir, Olivia is a tough negotiator. I believe I may have lost money on our deal," Brody interjected, seeing the stricken look in my eyes.

"You don't say!" Father turned to give Brody the full measure of his scrutiny.

"Why, yes. She wouldn't budge from the amount she was willing to pay. I tried everything, but Olivia didn't blink. She was very convincing when she stood up and thanked me for my time," Brody laughed and shook his head. "I believe she would have actually walked away. In the end, I was the one who blinked."

"You don't say," Mother mused, looking at me with fresh eyes.

"Your daughter truly is a shrewd negotiator, Lady Townsend," Brody replied, never averting his eyes, even when I blushed and looked away. I smiled to myself, taking the seat next to Coco, who finally decided to look up at me. The little turn coat!

"You didn't give the farm away, did you, boy?" Harrison choked on his coffee, sputtering and coughing into his white linen napkin.

"No Father, I did not give the farm away. I simply did as I was taught. I made up the difference on the next deal I made," Brody assured him, before giving me a wry smile and a wink.

This caused Coco to giggle into her napkin, then cover it up with a cough, while reaching for her cup of tea. "Something in my throat…"

"I would expect nothing less of Olivia," Father stated with pride. "I taught her to play poker when she was only six. Take my word on this one, she is very good at a bluff."

Brody gave a hearty laugh. "Believe me, I know."

"Excuse me, sir, you have a guest," the butler announced from the doorway, "Prince William Alexander of the Netherlands."

Making a grand entrance the moment his name was announced, Prince William, sauntered in with opened arms. "My dear friends, I am so happy to see you again. I hope that you don't think me rude, but I didn't wish to miss this year," he exclaimed, giving Quinton two solid slaps to the back in greeting, before taking Brody by the arm and pulling him close, repeating his greeting. Prince William stood five feet eleven inches tall, with a wiry physique and dark brown hair, cut short, just above his ears with thick side burns and piercing brown eyes that didn't miss a thing.

"You know that you are always welcome in our home, William. We are so delighted that you have honored us," Harrison responded, standing up to greet his honored guest. "And I personally would never consider your presence an inconvenience."

"I was sad to miss your celebration last year, but it couldn't be helped. As I'm sure you've heard, my father has taken ill and is preparing to step down. I had some business in the States, so I took the opportunity to stop in for a visit."

"I believe I heard something about your father when we were in Europe a few months back," Quinton said, leading the prince to an empty seat. "How is your lovely wife, Wilhelmina?"

"She is doing well, but couldn't make the trip. We are expecting again and her physician advised against her accompanying me," Prince William announced proudly. "Ships make her terribly sick under normal circumstances, as you may recall." Quinton, Brody and Harrison simultaneously congratulated him on the good news.

"Where are my manners?" Brody said, turning back to the table. "Please allow me to make the introductions. This is Lady Olivia Townsend and her sister, Lady Catherine Townsend of Buckinghamshire. Although Lady Catherine prefers to be addressed as Coco," Brody said as a side note to the prince. Then with a sweep of his hand, "let us not forget the young lady's parents, Lord Aiden Townsend, the Earl of Buckinghamshire, The Right Honorable Lord Lieutenant of Ireland and his lovely wife, Countess of Buckinghamshire, Lady Isabella Townsend."

With a sly look, Prince William leaned over and whispered in Brody's ear. "The older sister, she is important to you?"

"We are simply business acquaintances," Brody assured him, then cleared his throat.

"Although I hear your words of denial, I see your face and it tells me otherwise. I know of what I speak," Prince William said from behind his hand. Turning back towards me with a self-assured grin, he continued. "Forgive me if I have embarrassed you, my dear. It is my pleasure to make the acquaintance of you and your family, but I am afraid I must beg your forgiveness. There is a little matter to attend, and I must steal my old friends away. I have a gift for them and did not think it would be appropriate to bring inside," William said with a slyly smile and a wink.

"You know, William, we do not expect anything from you when you come for a visit, old friend," Quinton said, with a large smile. "That being said, it would be very rude of us to refuse a gift from a prince. Especially when he carried it all the way here for us, Brody."

Brody and Quinton looked at each other over the prince's head, then, with juvenile enthusiasm, they both took the prince by the arm escorting him from the room.

"What's the rush boys?" William teased, while looking between them. "One might think that you were excited to find out what I have brought you. Are you not concerned that your breakfast will grow cold?"

"No," they said simultaneously, picking William off the ground to hurry him along. We all stood and followed the three men down the hall and out the front door. We congregated in the courtyard, near a large black carriage. Quinton and Brody put the prince on the ground, then William let loose with an ear splitting whistle and two men stepped out from behind the carriage, leading a pair of matching horses. We all gasped in unison as Prince William clapped his hands again and the two men brought the horses closer. The horses were long and lanky in stature, with delicate features, and brilliant, iridescent blond coat, with a sheen that reflected golden, in the mid-day sunlight.

"I present to you a perfectly matched pair of Akhal-Teke mating horses from Turkmenistan," William proudly proclaimed.

"This is unbelievable. I am simply overwhelmed, my friend," Brody whispered in awe. Walking toward the horses, he slowly reached his hand out to touch them. Quinton looked as if he was in a state of shock, as words momentarily escaped him.

"William, old friend, you spoil these boys," Harrison exclaimed. "We couldn't possibly accept such a prized possession."

"Nonsense," William protested, "I insist." Coco and I stepped forward to get a better look. I wanted to touch their coat. It looked like spun gold.

The female horse had almond-shaped eyes with long straight ears that stood straight up. She was smaller than the male horse and stood about fifteen hands high. The large male horse stood between sixteen and a half to seventeen hands tall. Their manes and tails were not as full as an average quarter horse but, none-the-less, they were the most magnificent creature I had ever seen. The male stared intently at me, making me feel uneasy as his eyes followed my every move.

"This horse is tamed, correct?" I asked.

"But of course," William laughed.

"They are magnificent. I've never seen anything like them. Thank you, my friend," Quinton said, turning to Prince William. "My brother and I are indebted to you for your most generous gift."

"This is a most unexpected, surprise, William. I too wish to thank you for your generous gift," Brody added, still stroking the stallion's coat.

"They are simply gifts boys, think nothing more of it. I have several pair of my own. They truly are magnificent creatures. I will caution you to watch out for that stallion," Prince William indicated with a toss of his head. "He can be a handful."

While stroking the coat of the female horse, I was admiring her beauty, when a foul odor permeated the air near me. I didn't think anything about it until I saw something strange from the corner of my eye. Something dark, and sinister hovered around the stallion. The stallion pawed restlessly at the ground, darting his eyes toward the shadowy figure. Suddenly he jerked on his lead, causing the man holding him to frantically look around and call out.

"See what I mean? This one has a mind of his own." Prince William said, throwing up his hands as he stepped closer to the stallion. "Shh…shh…shh," he said, trying to sooth the beast.

I spotted Annabelle sitting on the beast's back, screeching with laughter when the stallion abruptly reared up, pawing the air with his powerful hooves as I turned to prevent from being trampled. Hitting the ground hard, I rolled, narrowing dodging the horse's pounding hooves.

I'd heard that your life passes before your eyes moments before you die, but it wasn't my life I saw the instant the air was knocked from my lungs, unable to breathe, writhing in pain, while I rolled around on the ground. It was the cold, calculating, evil of someone so devoid of humanity that she attempted to kill me, just because she could.

9

MONDAY, FEBRUARY 9, 1804

Something Foul This Way Cometh

EVERYONE WAS IN A STATE of shock following my near fatal trampling. Brody and Coco reached my side first and the horrified, tear-streaked face of my sister told me she thought I was dead. Brody did not hesitate to immediately pick me up and hurry toward the front door, while my parents followed close behind, trying to get a look at me to see if I had been disfigured or mortally injured.

I heard Harrison giving orders to someone to fetch the physician. Then I was deposited into my bed and told that under no circumstance was I to move from that spot until after the doctor attended me.

I did not share with anyone that day what I had witnessed, for fear that I would be immediately whisked away to our ship and taken back home. I knew for sure that someone in this household held the key to what had happened to Lilly. Besides, I had never considered myself a quitter, not even if my life was in danger from a spiteful spirit.

I had never been afraid of dying before. Death was not some unknown entity to me. I knew there was an afterlife, like some people knew that the sky was blue or the grass was green and so, therefore, I did not fear what came afterwards because I knew. But admittedly, I felt a moment of apprehension and unbridled terror when I saw the stallion charging directly at me with Annabelle at the reins.

People came in and out of my room like it was a fancy hotel with a revolving door, once the doctor left, pronouncing me unharmed.

I'd twisted my wrist and banged my knee when I fell, but nothing was permanently damaged.

Mother and Father stood at the foot of my bed discussing how they would whisk me away the instant I woke. So I pretended to be asleep, because I knew that once I made a miraculous recovery, they would forget all about leaving.

They finally left me in peace and I slept deeply that night until I awoke early, sitting in the darkness, watching the sun cresting over the hill top. I was pondering my next move, mesmerized by the changing hues, when the hall boy entered my room.

With bucket and broom in hand, I watched as he cringed, then froze in place when his bucket loudly rattled and clanked against the dust pan. He appeared to be about fourteen years old, and I figured if anyone knew what went on in this place, it would be him.

I came alive, knowing what I needed to do.

"Boy, what is your name?" I called out, startling him.

Dropping his dust pan and broom, I saw him physically cringe. "I'm terribly sorry, Miss, I did not mean to disturb you. I only came in to check the fire and noticed yours was out. I can come back later." He apologized, gathering his things quickly. He reminded me of a frightened mouse that scurries away when you cast a light into the room.

"Wait, I didn't mean for you to leave. I only wanted to talk with you," I said anxiously. Agilely leaping from bed, I cut him off before he reached the door.

"You wish to speak with me?" he questioned.

"Yes, with you," I assured him, gesturing for him to continue his work. "Please, don't stop. It is rather chilly in here. How long have you lived in this house?" I asked quietly, knowing the walls had ears that never rested.

"All my life, Miss," he answered without looking at me.

"What is your name?"

"My name, Miss?"

"Yes. What do people call you?"

"Sam. My name is Sam, Miss. But people call me Dusty, because I'm always covered in ashes," he replied, looking down at the ground as he stood up. Nervously he shuffled his feet and I could tell he was anxious to leave, but I wasn't done questioning him.

"Which do you prefer to be called, Sam or Dusty?" I asked, gently tipping his chin up, forcing him to make eye contact with me.

"I've gotten used to being referred to as Dusty, Miss, but me mum calls me Sam," he said, bravely glance at me, before looking away.

"Then I shall call you Sam," I announced, bringing a slight smile to his lips. "Sam, please don't run off. It is early and truly I would enjoy having someone to talk with. Please," I begged. "Would you like to sit?" I gestured for him to take a seat.

Sam shook his head. "No, Miss. I will just get ashes everywhere," he said quietly, picking up the wood and piling it in one arm. "I don't wish to bother you further, Miss," he cautiously added, eyeing the door, before his eyes wandered back to the unlit hearth.

"You would be doing me a favor. It is rather chilly in here," I added, attempting to put Sam at ease.

"I'm not very good at talking, miss. People don't notice me enough to speak to," Sam said with a scoff, leaning over to stack logs next to the hearth.

"Then this will be a rare treat for both of us. How old are you, Sam?" I asked, smiling when he turned his head slightly to look at me.

"Almost fifteen," he replied, look at me out of the corner of his eye while scooping the ashes from the night before into his metal pail.

I could see a few embers still glowing red hot as he dumped them into the metal container.

"So, you have seen some strange things occur in this household. Maybe, even unexplainable things?" I pressed.

"Why, did something happen?" his tone of concern as he turned to look at me.

"I'm fine, Sam, but I need you to tell me the truth. Have you seen strange things that couldn't be explained?" I quietly demanded, quickly glancing around the room. "How long has your dead mistress been haunting this home?"

Suddenly the light went out in Sam's eyes and his face lost all its color. I watched as his entire countenance changed. "We don't speak of her. Ever!" Sam shook with conviction as he spoke a little harsher than he intended. "I beg your forgiveness, Miss."

"Think nothing of it, Sam. Even I can see that you are scared," I whispered, touching his shoulders. "Please tell me how long the mistress has been gone?"

"I'm not scared," Sam said, glaring defiantly at me.

"It's alright if you are, Sam. Sometimes I get scared too. Being scared isn't necessarily a bad thing. It takes someone with common sense to know when it is warranted," I admitted.

"I've seen some things, Miss. Some bloody awful things that I never wish to see again," he stated so quietly that I was forced to turn my ear towards him to hear. "Most nights I find a corner so far away from the main house, behind a chair or curtain and hope that she can't find me."

"Who, Sam? So who doesn't find you?" I asked.

"Her, Miss. The mistress." He whispered next to my ear. "She still walks the halls at night, I've seen her. Sometimes she knocks vases off a table when I pass by, so I get in trouble. One time, a sword fell off the mantle, just as I finished cleaning the main hearth downstairs. It landed next to my leg and stuck into the floorboard. When I stood up, I noticed that my pant leg was cut. I was scared then," Sam admitted.

"I would have been frightened too, Sam," I conceded. "Then what happened?"

"I ran out of the house and didn't come back for three days. I told me mum what happened and she told me not to ever mention the incident or mistress's name again," Sam added with finality, pulling away from me.

"Sam, it isn't people speaking of the mistress or thinking of her that keeps her here," I said.

"It isn't?" Sam asked, not sure if he believed me or not.

"No, Sam, it isn't. There is something else going on here, that is keeping her spirit bound to this house. I don't know what that is yet, but I intend to find out."

"What are you saying, Miss?" Sam questioned, turning to look at me.

Unable to stop myself, I smiled. "Just between you and me, Sam, I can see spirits. I've had the gift since I was very young, and I have seen Mistress Beaumont. She is a foul sort of spirit, the like of which I have never come across before, and she needs to leave this place, before someone truly gets hurt," I stated flatly.

Sam cringed and turned back to the fire that he had just started.

"Maybe you doubt me because you don't know me yet, Sam. But you will. For now, I just need you to keep this between the two of us," I said with a wink. "It will be our little secret."

"Describe her to me if you've truly seen her," Sam insisted, not bothering to turn and look at me now while he put the lid back on his pail of ashes.

"Annabelle has on a white taffeta gown with tiny black rosebuds around the collar. She has striking hazel green eyes, and dark chestnut hair," I replied, looking up to the ceiling, trying to recall as many details as possible. "Oh, yes, she has this disconcerting way of looking at you, that says you could never make her happy, regardless of how hard you tied."

"How could you possibly know what she was wearing the day she was laid to rest?" Sam asked in awe.

I took this as a positive sign and pressed my point. "I told you, Sam, I've seen her."

"Mrs. Beaumont died the night Mr. Brody and Mr. Quinton's celebrated their birthdays, eight years ago. Mr. Beaumont has never cancelled his son's annual celebration, even though every year there is an incident," Sam said reverently, crossing himself. "One of these times, something truly bad is going to happen. My mum said so. She told me Mrs. Beaumont's spirit is unhappy."

"Well, I can tell you with complete confidence, that your mum is spot on. The only question is why is she so unhappy?" I mused.

Sam's chore complete, he turned and took a step towards me, just as a clump of soot landed in the middle of the freshly lit fire. We both jumped back, startled by the noise, when a fireball shot out, catching his pants on fire. Sam screamed and I ran to get the pitcher of water from the night stand. He was running in a circle, panicked. He continued to thrash at me when I knocked him to the ground. "Sam, stop it!" I yelled, dousing his pants and extinguishing the flames.

His leg was red and blistered and the hairs were either singed or gone. There were no words to express my complete and utter shock.

"I have to leave," Sam said, jumping up and running from the room without his tools.

"Wait Sam," I yelled, grabbing for his arm. Sam was too quick for me as he scurried from the room before I could blink. When I reached the door, I looked up and down the hallway, there was no sign of him.

Coco stood in the doorway tying the sash to her robe. "Good heavens, Olivia, what is all the screaming about?" Coco asked breathlessly.

"We are in real trouble here, Coco." I whispered, not sure I hadn't merely dreamed that a fireball shot out of the fireplace.

"What are you talking about?"

Soundlessly I walked back into the room and stood over the spot, where I had doused Sam's pants with water. "She lit him on fire and I put him out. Right there, with my pitcher of water," I said, pointing at the spot on the floor. "I know I did."

"Who was lit on fire, Olivia?"

"Sam, the hall boy. We were talking and he was preparing my fire. Then Annabelle lit his pants on fire."

Margo walked to the doorway carrying a tray of tea. "I was told that you were up, so I brought — what is it, ladies?" she questioned, bewildered by our blank stares.

"Shut the door!" I ordered. Taking three steps back, Margot gently kicked the door shut with her foot. Then setting the tray down, she came over to where we stood.

"What is it? What's wrong?"

"If I hadn't seen it with my own eyes I would never have believed it," I began. "What we say in this room, does not leave this room. Swear it. You too, Margot. Swear!" Both nodded their head.

"Young Sam was preparing the fire and discussing strange occurrences in the house hold when something exploded down the chimney catching Sam's pants on fire. He was nearly burned alive in front of me. Annabelle Beaumont did this."

"Who is Annabelle Beaumont, and why haven't I met her?" Coco asked before Margot could get the question out. I began to shake uncontrollably as tears formed in the back of my eyes.

"And yesterday when that stallion nearly trampled me, Annabelle was on the back of that stallion. I think she meant to kill me," I said, swallowing the lump in my throat.

Touching my arm, Coco gasped as vision of both events flashed through her mind. She released my arm suddenly. "Olivia, we cannot stay here," she cried.

Taking her shoulders in my hands, I said with a deadly calm, "Coco, you have to leave."

"I will be only too happy to leave this place. I felt something was off when I walked through the door," she stated through clenched teeth. "Why didn't you say something?" she narrowed her eyes at me. "You saw her that night."

"Saw who?" Margot asked suspiciously. "What are you both talking about?"

"The woman whose portrait hangs over the fireplace downstairs," I said, exasperated because Margo didn't understand what I was trying to say. "Mrs. Annabelle Beaumont died eight years ago after the annual celebration. That is all I know so far. Please try to keep up, Margot."

"We have to leave, today," Coco stated emphatically.

"You have to leave. I'm staying."

"You can't be serious. I am not leaving here without you," Coco insisted, stomping her foot for emphasis.

"I'm mean it, Coco, you have to go before something bad happens to you. Tell her, Margot!"

"And I said I'm not leaving without you. If you stay, I stay," she argued, petulantly lifting her chin.

"You are the most stubborn —" I began, then sniffed the air. A foul odor permeated my room, and I quickly turned to find Annabelle standing a mere three feet away. My sudden silence alerted both women that something was terribly wrong.

"Is it her, Olivia?" Coco asked, her voice shaking.

I braced myself in front of them like a human shield, as if by shear will alone I could protect them from the evil that was Annabelle Beaumont. Slowly nodding my head, Coco took ahold of my hand. Somehow I was comforted by her presence and the fact that I wasn't alone.

"What is it that you want, Annabelle?" I asserted, with a voice that was neither confident or potent. The noise of my heartbeat pounded between my ears, like waves hitting the shore. "Why do you stay earthbound, tormenting people?"

Annabelle simply smiled, narrowing her eyes as she advanced on me causing me to step back pushing Coco and Margot as I went. The sound of Annabelle as she threw her head back and laughed was more demonic than joyful, before she leveled her eyes at me. Hovering inches from my face, she smirked and vaporized into thin air, without answering the question.

I felt Coco's hand trembling before turning loose and she dropped into a nearby chair, as I dropped to my knees on the floor. I was left feeling weak and breathless, as if someone had punched me in the gut. My breaths came out in harsh gasps for air as I omitted a guttural noise that was somewhere between a growl and a scream of frustration.

"Not a word of this incident is to ever pass from your lips, Catherine Elizabeth. Not one word," I said more harshly than I intended. "And that goes double for you, Margot."

"But Olivia…"

"I mean it. Not one word. Swear it!" I growled threateningly as I cut her off. "Swear this instant, Catherine Elizabeth!" I repeated when she didn't instantly recite the oath.

Letting out the breath she'd been holding, Coco conceded. "Yes, yes, I swear. Not one word of what has transpired here, in this room this morning will ever pass from my lips, to another living soul, as long as I have breath in my body. I swear until the day I die." Coco chafed, rolling her eyes as she repeated our childhood oath.

"Margot!" I bellowed, staring her down.

"You know my loyalty lies with you, Olivia," Margot prefaced, "but your parents should know about this."

"Margot, I'm afraid you are going to have to declare an oath of silence, on penalty of death."

Margot looked at me and Coco, who pursed her lips and nodded her head, affirming the seriousness of the situation. "Fine!" she finally proclaimed, exasperated by our antics. "But you are both crazy," Margot announced, leaving the room. "Hope you don't mind pouring your own bloody tea. It's probably cold to boot."

I glanced over at Coco, and knew she was still somewhat annoyed at me. Coco and I kept one another's secrets, and would rather cut off a body part than break that oath. Truth is, I wasn't entirely certain she wasn't angrier over the fact that I use her full name. "Tea?"

"I'd love some."

After tea, I desperately needed to escape the confined of Rosewood itself and its demonic spirit. "I think I will go for a brisk walk. Want to come?" I asked, opening the lid of my traveling trunk to retrieve a pair of men's breeches, white shirt and a pair of well-worn boots.

"You're not going outside dressed like that, are you?" Coco's incredulous tone scolded.

"I most certainly am," I said adamantly. "I'm not doing anything mother hasn't done before."

"The circumstances were different, and you know it. We are staying with respectable people," Coco retorted, her voice ringing with distain. "Just wait until Margot finds out."

"If you help me, she won't find out. Please, Coco, I must get out of here and it is far too cold to wear a flimsy dress," I pleaded. "Besides, I would snag the hem on a branch or something and ruin it beyond repair," I added reasonably.

"Fine. But if you get caught, I want no part of it, or the repercussion," Coco warned, picking up the shirt to help me dress.

"Deal!" I gladly conceded, slipping the breeches on, tying the draw string.

10

TUESDAY, FEBRUARY 10

Nearly Trampled Again

A FEW MINUTES LATER, I SLIPPED down the back staircase, through the kitchen, and out the servant's entrance. I headed straight for the trail running parallel with the forest and away from the house. My unruly red hair tucked discretely beneath a wool cap, I buttoned up the brown wool coat covering my neck. Frost crystals formed in front of my face with each breath and the ground crunched beneath my feet. A thin layer of ice coated the blades of grass and fallen leaves. Shoving my hands deep into my pockets to keep them warm, I scolded myself for not remembering to grab a pair of gloves before leaving. It was colder than I anticipated, yet no amount of money could persuade me to turn around and go back to retrieve them. I wanted to put as much distance between me and that house.

I briskly walked for twenty minutes before the ground began to vibrate beneath my feet and I heard thundering horse hooves pounding the ground behind me. Quickly turning to see three riders coming straight at me, left precious little time to think.

"Get out of the way, boy," Jackson yelled, just before forcing me to dive off the road and into the ditch, as they barreled past me.

"And to think I've been worried about demonic spirits, when I really should have been worried about getting trampled by a horse." Retrieving my cap from the ditch I currently found myself in, I assessed the damages and began to curse in Gaelic when I realized that I had ripped my favorite coat and skinned my knee, again!

Covered in twigs, leaves and dirt, I crawled from the ditch, and turned in the direction of the retreating riders, as one of them pulled up short and turned around.

Using the cap to brush the leaves and grass from my clothes, I looked up to see Brody riding towards me. "Do the three of you make it a habit of running helpless individuals off the road and into ditches very often?" I glared up at him.

Brody jumped down from his horse just as Jackson and Quinton came to a skidding halt next to us. "Well, we don't really make it a habit, but I will admit that it has happened once or twice." He chuckled.

"And exactly what do you find so humorous about this situation, Mr. Beaumont?" I grumbled, narrowing my eyes at him. Standing up straight, I was all of five feet, seven inches tall. Placing my hands on my hips, I glared at the three offending men.

Brody and Quinton both stood an impressive six feet, three inches tall while Jackson Montgomery was about two inches shorter. The fact that they found humor in my pain irked me, and I nearly kicked them all in the shin, but thought better of it. "Well?" I demanded, with a stomp of my booted foot.

"We really didn't mean to run you off the road, Olivia. Say, why are you dressed like that?" Brody asked with another chuckle, removing a handkerchief from his pocket and wetting the corner with his tongue. Dodging his attempts at cleaning the smudge of dirt from my face with his spittle and handkerchief, I resorted to swatting his hand away, when he wouldn't give up.

"Have you ever taken a walk on a brisk morning, without your britches on?" I asked, with a self-righteous indignant tone, I snatching the cloth from his hand to wipe my own face.

"Well, no," Brody replied. "Why would I?" He continued, reaching over and removing a smudge I'd missed, with his thumb, earning him another nasty glare.

"That's crazy. We'd freeze our… uh… " Jackson stammered, unsure that he should finish that sentence.

"Exactly! You'd freeze your Netherlands off." I boldly stated. "That is exactly my point, gentlemen. Thin, flimsy material is no barrier against your cold, West Virginia winters. I would freeze parts of me that I guarantee wouldn't thaw out until next spring."

"I like her, Brody. She's spunky and speaks her mind. Most refreshing in a woman, if you ask me," Quinton laughed heartily, giving me a firm slap on the back, earning him a sour look. "And she appears to be very sturdy. Not like all those prissy little things that you normally attract. Why, most of them look like they would break at the merest of touches. I swear, Brody, she's virtually indestructible. Nearly trampled by two horses and look, she's still standing," Quinton said, poking his brother in the stomach with his elbow.

"My, how you flatter me so, Quinton Beaumont," I said sarcastically, before punching him in the arm. "Aye, I do speak my mind, you feckless savage. But that does not give you leave to man-handle me like your prized mare," I admonished, distain dripping from my lips. Quinton and Jackson both laughed off my insult, shoving the other as they turned their backs to me, dismissively.

"I'll show you indestructible," I grumbled, adding a few Gaelic insults under my breath, as I prepared to attack Quinton from behind. Brody acted quickly, stepping between us, diverting a disaster he saw coming. With a jovial smile, he took me by the arm, leading me over to Zeus.

Jackson and Quinton were none the wiser as they gathered up their mounts.

"She's fine. Now let's get back to the real matter at hand. The winner of our race has yet to be determined. Since none of us completed the race to the finish line, we have to start over again," Jackson said, as if nothing had happened, while climbing back on to his horse.

"Oh you are so going to lose, Montgomery," Quinton heckled over his shoulder, while placing his foot in the stirrup and hoisting himself up, completely forgetting about the insult I had paid him. "Are you coming, Brody?" he asked, craning his neck to see Brody, as his horse pranced about, ready to race.

"No. You go ahead. I will see that Olivia doesn't get trampled by anymore horses today," Brody answered, with a smile. "You two go ahead. I'll catch up to you later."

"You know what that means?" Quinton grinned back at Jackson.

"Brody forfeits!" Jackson crowed like a rooster.

The two men began to chant, "Brody forfeits, Brody forfeits," as they as pranced their mounts around us.

"Go on, get out of here," Brody laughed, slapping Jackson's horse on the rump, sending him off like a shot, closely followed by Quinton's horse, not wanting to be left behind.

"You really don't need to worry about me. I am perfectly capable of finding my own way back to the house," I said tersely, turning my back on Brody as I began to walk away.

"It's quite a walk back to the house and you're limping."

"I'm fine. It's merely a scratch, nothing more." I dismissed his concern, as I sharply sucked in air. "I will be fine," I called over my shoulder. Taking the reins in his hand, Brody ran to catch up to me.

"I really am sorry that we almost ran you over, Olivia."

"That's twice that I was nearly run over by one of your horses." I scoffed, holding two fingers up, as I walked away.

Brody reached out a hand, to bring me to a halt. "I'm sorry that two of my horses have tried to run you down, twice," Brody said softly, pulling me closer, making it impossible for me to continue to ignore him. "You must give me the opportunity to make it up to you," he pleaded, tipping my chin up and gazing into my eyes with a hopeful smile.

After a brief pause, I cleared my throat and conceded. "Fine. What did you have in mind?" I asked sullenly, knowing in my heart that I couldn't stay mad at him.

"Here, hold these," Brody insisted, jamming the reins into my hands just before unceremoniously throwing me on to his stallion, Zeus, before I could say a word of protest. "Isn't this nice?" he said, after climbing up behind me.

"I prefer walking, Mr. Beaumont!" I retorted, shifting my weight. "I'm sure you can understand, nearly being trampled and all."

"I insist you drop the 'Mister' nonsense and call me Brody. I was hoping to run into you this morning, just not in the way I did. I want to show you something, but you truly have to sit still," Brody cautioned, pulling me even tighter against him with one arm. "I would hate for Zeus to get spooked and take off running."

I was not fond of horses to begin with. They always made me nervous, and the thought of this one running wildly down the road with me precariously perched atop of him did not thrill me, so I took his warning to heart and sat very still. Pulling on the reins, Brody directed Zeus down a trail to the left of the main road and we were now headed east, directly into the sun.

"Where are we going?" I asked again, this time with a resigned tone.

"I want to show you something, but you really must be patient," Brody insisted. "Besides, this will give us time to become better acquainted. You can tell me something about you, and then I can tell you something about me."

"How very modern of you," I quipped, crossing my arms. "You go first."

"I would be happy to," Brody said, well naturedly. "My mother died on my birthday, eight years ago Saturday."

I felt as if someone had just punched me in the gut, for the second time that morning. I was completely unprepared for Brody's honest, heartfelt confession.

Uncrossing my arms, I shifted in the saddle so that I could see his face. "I'm terribly sorry that your mother died on your birthday, Brody. That must have been very hard on you and your brother," I said sympathetically. "How did she die?"

"The maid found her that evening, floating in her bath tub. She must have slipped and hit her head on the side of the tub."

"That's awful," I added, gently touching his face. "Tell me about her."

"My mother was very beautiful. My father tells me I have her eyes." Brody looked away as he directed Zeus down another path to our right. "But as beautiful as she was, my mother was very vain and self-centered. I don't think I ever remember a time when she did something for Quinton or me that wasn't self-serving." He said this so matter-of-factly, it sent chills up my arms. "Now your turn, tell me something personal about yourself that you don't talk about to just anyone."

Narrowing my eyes, I had a sneaking feeling that there was something on his mind, "Perhaps you can tell me what it is in particular, you wish to know about me."

"Very well, tell me about your gift," he asked so bluntly that I felt my insides begin to vibrate, like a string on a violin when someone plucks it. My mouth went dry and I hoped that I had heard wrong.

"What did you just say?" I questioned softly.

"Your gift, I wish to know about your gift," Brody repeated.

"I don't know what you are talking about." I heard myself saying, as my voice faltered.

"Of course you do. When Quinton and I were in Dublin a few months back, Lilly told us this incredible story about a young woman and her amazing gift. Your amazing gift. I just need to know if it is true. Can you really see ghosts?"

Chewing at my lower lip, I silently studied his face, unsure of what to say. If I told him the truth, would he think me an unholy, abomination of nature? An oddity to be placed on display in some traveling side show? Or did Brody Beaumont have an ulterior motive that he had been hiding all along?

"I can see you thinking to yourself, do I tell him the truth, or do I deny the entire matter?" Brody said off handed, bringing Zeus to a full stop. "I knew who you were the first time I saw you standing at the counter of the Carmichael Hotel, in New York. To be honest, I was caught off guard and a little unsure of how to approach you. Why do you think I made up that ridiculous ploy, about retrieving my room key when I had it in my pocket the entire time?"

"But how could you have known me, when we have never met?" I questioned.

"Lilly showed me a framed sketching of the two of you, sitting in her garden. It was your eyes. I would have known you anywhere. The artist truly captured your essence." Brody concluded.

"The drawing Coco did of Lilly and me sitting under the Weeping Willow?"

"Yes, that's the one."

"I saw the desk clerk retrieve your key with my own eyes," I gasped accusingly.

"That was Quinton's key. And boy was he mad when he came back and discovered that I had taken his key."

I felt fear well up inside of me as I gazed into his hazel green eyes. Experience had taught me not to trust outsiders. "So you admit that you knew my best friend Lilly?" I exhaled.

"What an odd question to ask," Brody said, giving me a strange look. "Of course I know Lilly. She is a lovely girl," he stated, curiously tilting his head to study me. "You know that Quinton is in love with her. But I'm assuming she told you all of this when she went back home." Tears formed at the back of my eyes, but Brody continued to explain. "Quinton and Lilly were planning to be wed. That is until she up and left in the middle of the night, leaving nothing but a note behind."

"Lilly left a note?" I questioned, feeling a knot forming in the pit of my stomach. "What did this not say?"

"It said that she was home sick and that she was going back home. Maybe you couldn't tell by the cavalier front Quinton presents to the world, but he was devastated and heartbroken over the matter."

Brody looked visibly shocked as I gasped, stifling a cry with the back of my hand. His words confused me. Then something moved in the tree line. Merely a shadow at first, when I turned my head to look, and saw Lilly standing there, watching us, a sad look on her face. My eyes locked with hers for a moment and I thought it strange the way she cautiously looking around, as if she was afraid to approach. Then just a quickly, she disappeared back into the forest.

"What is it?" Brody asked, looking back over his shoulder to see what I was staring at. "Did you see something?"

A full minute passed as I decided how to proceed. Did I tell him the truth, and chance his ridicule, or did I carry on as if he was the one who was crazy? Taking a deep breath, I decided to be honest. "Lilly is dead," I quietly stated, still watching his expression carefully. I could tell that the news had come as a shock to him. I looked away. "She came to me just over a month ago, in the middle of the night." Bringing my eyes back up to look at him, I braced myself for the reaction my next words would bring. "And yes, it is true that I am able to see the dead," I said without blinking. I had a slight catch in my voice as I continued. "But I refer to people who have passed away as spirits not ghosts. When the soul separates from the physical body, you are left with a person's spirit, their essence."

"I don't understand, what happened to her?" Brody stammered. "Forgive me if I am a little confused."

"Well, that makes two of us," I conceded, still trying to determine whether or not I trusted him. And if he didn't have anything to do with Lilly's death, who did?

"Stop looking at me like that, Olivia. I swear, I didn't know about Lilly's death. Can't you just ask her what happened? I'm sure she will tell you that I didn't do it. Honest!" Brody cried, trying to absorb the shocking news.

"That's just it, Lilly can't remember what happened to her. I've seen this happen one time before. That person's death was very traumatic and sudden," I said, taking a deep breath to calm my jangled nerves. "Mark my words, I intend to find out what happened to her, regardless of who is involved," I boldly stated.

Hazel green eyes locked with mine. "What is that supposed to mean? Brody asked. "You can't still believe that I had anything to do with her death," his eyes pleaded for me to believe him. "I liked Lilly. I had no reason to hurt her."

"The only way I can rule you out completely is for you to speak with Coco."

"And why is that?" he asked cautiously.

"Nice to know that Lilly didn't give away all of the family's secrets," I said derisively, turning around and presenting my back to him. That way, I could ignore the stab of guilt I felt when I looked into his pleading eyes.

"Olivia, what does that mean?" Brody questioned, bringing me back around, forcing me to meet his gaze. Defiantly tipping my chin up and away from his grasp, I squared my shoulders and turned back around.

"It means I still have a few tricks up my sleeve," I stiffened my back and sniffed. "I think I would like to go back to the house now. I am feeling chilled and need to change my clothes."

11

The Truth Will Come Out, One Way or Another

CHANGING INTO MORE SUITABLE CLOTHES, I went to search for Coco to fill her in on all that had happened. Brody gave consent to have Coco look into his very soul, if it ruled him out as a suspect.

My nerves were raw and my stomach was in a massive knot. Every time he touched my arm I felt a jolt go through me. It was disconcerting but what was worse, the way his eyes followed my every move distracted me. I will admit I found the attentions flattering because no one had ever looked at me like that before. But, at the same time, I was unnerved by the uncertainty of my situation. I needed to stay focused and solve this mystery so that I could return home, quickly. My life was settled at home. Everything made sense and there was a predictability to my days. In this strange place, nothing made sense and I constantly felt off kilter and out of sorts.

I needed to believe Brody when he said he was innocent. In fact, if I was perfectly honest with myself, I would have to say that I believed him to be a good, honest man, with true and virtuous intentions. But what if I was being short sighted, blinded by his handsome face and hazel eyes that made me believe as gospel everything that came out of his mouth. No, I would rely on Coco's judgement, since mine was a bit off regarding this particular Beaumont.

I sat on the settee pondering matters when I heard a knock at the door. Margot arranged the tray of tea and finger cakes on the table in front of me, then went to answer the door.

Brody stood at the door with an unusually somber Quinton. The two men entered and I could tell Quinton had been crying as he averting his eyes downward, to hide the fact. I noticed his nose was red and swollen while his lashes appeared to still be moist from tears.

"Thank you, Margot, but I think I can serve the afternoon tea today. I won't need you for about an hour or so," I called, dismissing her.

Margot stopped in mid-step and gave me a look. "Very good, Miss, I will just tend to a few things before dinner. Ring downstairs if you need me," she said, keeping her voice even and professional in tone, before leaving the room with a basket of clothes.

I indicated with a wave of my hand for them to take a seat across from me, without looking up. "Do you take sugar or cream in your tea, gentlemen?" I politely asked, chancing a glance through my lashes.

I marveled at the beauty of the porcelain set, as I poured out tea into the matching cups sitting on sturdy little saucers, with their pink rose bud design.

Clearing his throat first before answering, "I like two sugars, no cream," Brody said, with a new formality he had not expressed towards me before. "And Quinton will take cream, one sugar, if you please."

Coco was standing at the window gazing out at the landscape and people working in the courtyard below when she turned to join us. I didn't need to ask her how she took her tea. It had been the same way ever since she was very young, cream first, then tea followed by one sugar.

"I wish to clear up something before we begin this little journey of ours. I will touch you both, one at a time, of course," Coco said, looking Brody directly in the eye. "Please do not attempt to touch me. I truly hate people touching me when I am unprepared. It's a terrible shock to my system," she added, with a wry smile, taking the cup of tea from my hand, instinctively knowing that I had just fixed it for her.

I leaned over to hand Quinton his cup of tea, then Brody as his fingers brushed my hand, and our eyes locked. Coco cleared her throat.

Quinton sat motionless in his seat, staring into his cup of tea silent and brooding. "Is something wrong with your tea, Quinton?" Coco inquired of him when she noticed his strange daze.

"Uh, no, it's, it's just fine. Thank you for your concern," he replied, without making eye contact or looking up from his cup.

"I've tried to prepare Quinton for what is to come. But since I am, myself, somewhat at a loss… well…" Brody awkwardly stammered, shrugging his shoulders and leaving his sentence unfinished.

"That is because it is difficult to describe what Coco does. I believe you will understand when she begins. Who would like to go first?" I asked cheerfully, as if we were preparing to play a parlor game. I took a sip of tea before putting my cup down. "Perhaps you would be more comfortable over here on the settee. I will switch places with you so that you and Coco may sit together, Brody," I suggested, before standing to exchanging places.

Awkwardly, Brody and I tried to move past each other, without touching, both moving in the same direction, at the same time, then correcting ourselves. Placing his hands on my shoulders to keep me in place, Brody stepped around me with a chuckle. "Shall we dance, Miss. Townsend?" he teased.

"Maybe later, Mr. Beaumont," I answered. "My dance card is rather full at the moment."

"Isn't that always the way," he lamented, gazing down at me. "The pretty ones are always taken," he concluded with a humorless smile before sitting down on the settee.

Coco again cleared her throat, bringing Brody's eyes back around to hers. "I will remove my gloves and take your hands in mine. I need you to sit quietly for a moment, until I begin to speak," Coco instructed as if she were speaking to a child.

"But what if I need to ask a question?" Brody interjected.

"When I am through speaking you will have time to ask your questions, Mr. Beaumont," Coco said, sounding patient even as she sucked in air, and rolled her eyes as she gave me a look.

"Then, I am ready to proceed, if you are," Brody announced, giving Quinton a quick glance to make sure that he was still with us. Quinton continued to sit staring into his cup of tea, bringing it to his lips slowly. His hand trembled slightly, and I thought how odd his behavior was, until I noticed a single tear fall from his chin and land in his tea.

I brought my eyes back around to find Brody studying me as our gazes locked again, for a minute. I was trying to read him, like I had done others, hundreds of times before. Yet I felt something was blocking me from doing so. I gave Coco the signal to begin with a slight tip of my chin, prying my eyes away from his.

Coco took a deep breath, bracing herself for the images and shock to her person when she touched someone. Taking Brody's large hands in hers, Coco closed her eyes and breathed in and out slowly. She remained like this for a full five minutes, before turning loose of Brody's work callused hands.

"Well, tell me something," Brody insisted, leaning back against the cushions and placing his hands in his lap.

"Where do I start?" Coco said, with a deep breath. "You remember your mother well, but not necessarily in a fond way. She was a very selfish, self-centered individual, with a wandering eye. You and Quinton are very close and always have been since childhood. In fact, you have always shared everything. Does he know about you and Lilly and the terribly guilt you have?"

Jumping to his feet, Brody's face turned three shades of red. "What kind of witchcraft is this?" he cried defensively.

"No witchcraft, Mr. Beaumont. I know a lot of things about you. For instance, I know that you stole the house keeper's locket when you were five years old. You thought the picture of her daughter was beautiful.

I know that you never returned that locket, and it still sits at the bottom of your old brown, leather trunk," Coco stated defiantly.

Brody shifted uncomfortably, looking between me and my sister, "I... l... How did you...?" He stammered, looking like a cornered animal, not sure which way to turn.

Coco didn't give Brody the opportunity to finish his statement. "There are no tricks or magic involved. Would you like me to go on?" She innocently asked in a tone that left no doubt that she would happily spill all of his deepest, darkest secrets.

"I believe you. Now, please stop," Brody begged. "I swear, I had completely forgotten about the locket. I will return it today and make restitution for my actions as a delinquent five-year-old."

"He may have been guilty of some bad choices in the past, but he had nothing to do with Lilly's death," Coco assured me as she turned to stare at Quinton, who had just let out a low growl as he glared at Brody. With a deadly calm, Quinton set his cup and saucer on the tray.

"What happened between you and Lilly, Brody?" he asked through clenched teeth, suddenly standing up with a menacing stance.

Brody stiffened and looked at me, then back at his brother. "I swear, it was completely innocent, Quinton. Lilly was confused. I think she thought I was you."

"What did you do, Brody?" Quinton growled again, flexing the muscles of his jaw.

"To be fair, Brody wasn't completely at fault. Lilly knew what she was doing," Coco chimed in, as if that would make everything alright.

"I think you are missing the point here, Quinton," I said, stepping between them, like a human shield. "Brody had nothing to do with Lilly's death."

"I'm going to ask you one more time, Brody," Quinton's tone threatening, when he took a step forward as if he meant to go through me to get to Brody. "What happened between you and Lilly?"

"Lilly kissed me, alright? She kissed me and when I pushed her away, she played it off, as if she thought I was you," Brody blurted out, raking his fingers through his hair, loudly exhaling the breath he had been holding. "The thing was, I always felt she knew exactly what she was doing, I just didn't know why she did it."

Quinton took a step back. A terrible sound of anguish gurgled up from somewhere deep down in his gut and I saw him visibly retreat to a secret place inside of himself. I felt bad for him, but at the same time I still had no idea whether he had anything to do with Lilly's death.

Gently touching his arm to draw him back to reality, I softly called, "Quinton, I need you to hear me, and the only way I know that you are listening to me, is if you look at me."

Shock and grief showed in his eyes, but slowly Quinton rubbed his free hand over his face and brought his gaze down from the ceiling, to look at me. "I know that you are in a lot of pain. Believe me, Quinton, I was just as shocked and devastated by Lilly's death as you are. She was my best friend and I loved her as I love my own sister," I added gently, before the words caught in my throat. I reached up and touched his face to keep him focused on me. "I dare say that I have no misconceptions about Lilly and her childish games, but you need to hear what your brother is saying to you. You have known him all your life. If he is telling you that he had nothing to do with what transpired between himself and Lilly, don't you think that you should give him the benefit of the doubt?" I pleaded. "I know that if it were my sister, standing before me, swearing to something like this, I would."

I watched Quinton's eyes, which had been clouded over with so much grief and anger only seconds before, begin to grow clearer. I held my breath as his dark brown eyes stared back at me while he pondered my words. Finally, Quinton gave an affirming nod.

Stepping into him, I gave Quinton a hug, suddenly overwhelmed by my own raw emotions of pain and anger. We shared a bond, in that instant. "I beg your forgiveness, Quinton," I whispered, wiping tears from my face with my hand. I was embarrassed by my own demonstrative show of emotions. "I can't imagine what came over me," I added, backing up and taking a seat next to Coco, without looking up.

"Now, shall we continue?" Coco asked. "I believe it is your turn, Quinton. When you are ready, of course."

"If you will excuse me. I'm not feeling well at the moment and need some air," Quinton stated abruptly, before rushing from the room, not bothering to close the door behind him.

Brody looked between us apologetically, "It was a terrible shock to Quinton when I told him Lilly was dead. He really did love her, you know." Pulling his fingers through his hair, I could tell he was trying to decide what to do next.

"Go after him, Brody. He may be very upset right now, but he will forgive you, once he has a chance to think everything through." That was all he needed to hear. Turning on his heels, Brody rushed from the room, closing the door behind him, with a loud clank.

"Well, one man cleared and only fifty or a hundred more people to eliminate from our pool of suspects," Coco quipped sardonically.

"What are you talking about? We merely need to rule out Quinton and his father."

"When I described Annabelle Beaumont as a selfish, self-centered individual, I was being kind, for her son's sake. The woman was a holy terror," Coco blurted out, making a high pitched whistle through her teeth. "I'm not ruling anybody out just yet, except for Brody, that is. Which means everyone from the head housekeeper to the butler could have done it, as far as I am concerned."

"Oh Coco, you're just being dramatic. We don't even know if Annabelle slipped and hit her head or if someone actually killed her. Besides, nobody can be that bad, right? I'm going to focus my energies on what happened to Lilly. Let them figure out the thing with their mother on their own," I scoffed.

"What I mean by holy terror is she could have had a broom and rode around on it every full moon. You don't know what I know, Olivia," Coco fired back. "Brody was a wealth of information, and now I understand."

"You understand *what* exactly?" I questioned.

"Why this place is haunted and why their mother has stayed. She was an evil person when she was alive, it makes perfect sense that she wouldn't want to move on."

"What do you mean, Coco?" I questioned, then narrowed my eyes at her.

"The woman was vain and jealous and heartless. I have this strange, nagging feeling that it is all somehow connected."

"That makes me want to stop and ask myself what made her that way? Was she always a heartless pariah or did something happen to her to make her that way?" I asked, walking over to the window in time to look down and see Quinton taking off like a madman, on their new stallion. Moments later, Brody shot out of the barn on the back of Zeus. "Oh, that can't be good," I commented. Coco had come up behind me to see what I was looking at.

"What's not good?"

Pointing my finger at the two retreating figures on horseback I replied, "Quinton and Brody, riding down the road again like crazy people."

"They will be fine. A little hung over in the morning, but they will work it out," Coco added with a knowing smile and a wink.

"Are you sure?" I asked, prying my eyes away from the fading figures, to look at her.

"Yes, I'm sure." She laughed. "Don't be surprised if Brody comes back with a sore jaw. Quinton leads with his left. Brody never sees it coming. Afterwards, all is forgiven and their world is set to right again. Don't worry. I know what I'm talking about," she assured me with a confident smile as she gave the servant's bell a pull. "I need some hot tea and biscuits with jam. Do you want anything?"

"No, but thank you for asking," I answered over my shoulder as I walked to the door. I was still digesting Coco's words and the ease with which she regurgitated so much information about someone's life. It never ceased to amaze me. "I think I need some air as well. I won't be long."

"Now?" Coco asked, sounding terribly incredulous. I paused with my hand on the doorknob.

Looking over my shoulder, I answered, "Yes, now! I need to speak with Lilly, right now. I saw her earlier today, but she disappeared so quickly, like she was frightened of something. I'm worried."

"Well, I can't guarantee that there will be any biscuits and jam left when you return. The air here makes me want to eat all the time," Coco admitted with a sigh, as she plopped down on the cushions.

"Just be careful that you don't eat too much and sink us all as we return home," I teased, ducking as a pillow sailed across the room directly at my head.

12

Searching for Answers in All the Wrong Places…

I BORROWED A HEAVY WOOL COAT from the hook nearest the back door. I figured it belonged to one of the housekeepers and would not be missed until that night when the person needed to go home. By then I would have returned it and no one would be the wiser.

Heading toward the barn, I cut around to the right and walked quickly towards the rear of the building, quietly calling Lilly's name in hopes that she would materialize. When she didn't appear, I walked down the path to the rundown row of share cropper's buildings. I was sure that she had gone there to see if she could find more lost souls to help.

Walking down the dirt path to the last row of buildings, the seven lost souls were no longer around, and I felt relieved. Pulling out a chair to sit and rest my weary mind and feet for a moment I called Lilly's name again. "Lilly, where are you. I need to talk to you," I called, but still no answer came. Tipping my head back against the high backed chair I closed my eyes.

"Well, aren't you a pretty young thing," the sound of an unfamiliar male voice came from the doorway. "It looks as if we has ourselves some company, Boyd," he said, sauntering onto the porch. "Boyd, get over here and have yourself a look-see."

"Who the bloody hell are you?" I questioned, as I felt my insides sour. Jumping from the chair I'd been relaxing in, I slowly backed away.

"My names Emmitt and my friend here's Boyd," he answered with a large grin on his beard-stubbled face.

"I'm sorry. I did not realize that anyone was living here," I stammered, knowing darn well that no one was supposed to be here until cotton picking time.

"Oh, we don't live here. We just needed a place to hold up for a while," Emmitt admitted, while the man he called Boyd poked his head out the door, before stepping out onto the porch to join us.

Boyd was tall and lanky, I would guess well over six feet, with greasy black hair that blended into a scraggly beard, that never grew in completely. I couldn't tell his true height, because he slouched over at the shoulders when he walked, like a Neanderthal. His hair was shoulder length and hung in filthy ringlets that kept falling into his eyes, causing him to constantly toss his head to the side in order to see. When he smiled, one tooth in the front of his mouth was completely blackened and two others were partially rotted away. Boyd made this strange noise that was somewhere between a laugh and a scoff, that reminded me of a baying donkey.

I sensed Emmitt and Boyd were toying with me, and I felt trapped, like a hapless animal that would be extinguished once they were done having their fun.

"I would offer something to eat, my lovely, but Boyd here's too lazy to trap anything for us," Emmitt confessed with a patronizing undertone, stepping closer to me as he spoke.

"That's quite alright, I've already eaten. Well, I will be on my way. I am terribly sorry for disturbing you both," I apologized, feeling my way along the railing as I backed away from them. Instinctively I knew that I was in serious trouble. Feeling the steps to my left, I smiled awkwardly and quickly turned to leave as Emmitt jumped over the railing and landed on the ground in front of me. I screamed and jumped back up the steps, two at a time.

"You really are quite agile," I blurted out, while trying to keep distance between Emmitt and myself, when Boyd stepped in front of me, halting my retreat. "I really must be going now, people will be looking for me," I insisted, jamming my hand in my coat pocket. Only this wasn't my coat, and my jeweled dagger wasn't there. I had neglected to bring the weapon with me. Panic ran through me, turning my blood to ice. I couldn't breathe. What was I to do now? I had nothing but my wits to protect me. I was doomed!

"Olivia, help is coming. Just hold on. Your father and the others are on their way," Lilly whispered in my ear.

"Now you show up!" I murmured louder then I intended to.

"Looks like we's going to have us some fun, Emmitt," Boyd bayed like a donkey, grabbing my arms from behind.

"Lilly, where have you been, I've been looking everywhere for you?" I cried, turning my head in her direction, causing Boyd and Emmitt to panic, looking around to see who I was talking to. "You boys can't see my friend, Lilly because she is a ghost," I said with distain. The two men looked at one another as if I had lost my mind.

"We gots us a crazy one here, Boyd," Emmitt cried, narrowing his eyes at me, before looking over his shoulder again to see what I was staring at.

"You just keep telling yourself I'm crazy, Emmitt," I yelled, unable to hide my confident tone. "But if I were you, I'd be high stepping it out of here."

"Oh, and why's that?" Emmitt asked, leaning in close to my face. The stench of his fetid breath caused me to turn my head.

"Because my father is coming for me and he is no one to be trifled with," I snarled, braving his stench as I turned to face him.

"I don't see nobody coming. She's lying, Emmitt," Boyd said with a sniff, tightening his grip on my arms. "Emmitt, do you think she's worth anything? Maybe we could get some money, if'n we sells her."

"Nothing has worth to a dead man," I stated flatly. "And that is exactly what you both will be when my father gets his hands on you."

"Shut your mouth," Boyd yelled, giving me a shake.

"The girl's got a sense of humor," Emmitt said, sounding less confident as he looked over his shoulder again. "Let's get her out of sight, before someone comes along and sees us," he said, gesturing with his head.

"Olivia Townsend, you better punch him in the nose. Your father taught you better." Lilly screamed in my face, trying to rile me up, putting up her fists as if she would take the man on herself if I didn't, Lilly danced about, shifting from side to side.

"Now, Lilly, you just look ridiculous. You don't do it like that," I said calmly, before bringing both feet up and kicking Emmitt in the stomach. Boyd stumbled backwards, trying to keep his balance while Emmitt tumbled down the steps, landing in a heap at the bottom. I stomped on Boyd's toe when I came down, he turned loose of my arms and fell backwards against the wall. Seizing the moment, I ran down the steps as fast as I could. The only sound I could hear was the sound of my heart beating in my ears.

I screamed in surprise as Emmitt grabbed my foot, toppling me over and I hit the ground with a loud thud. Emmitt was on top of me before I could blink. Frantically flailing my arms and legs at him to free myself, I quickly ran out of air. "Woo wee, she's a fighter, Boyd," Emmitt crowed excitedly, with a nefarious glint in his eyes, slapping me across the face.

Looking up, I saw Lilly standing over Emmitt's shoulder. "Your father is nearly here, Olivia, just hold on," she said, anxiously wringing her hands together and looking down the road.

"Get off me, you filthy disgusting pig," I rasped, gasping for air with a full grown man sitting on top of me.

"I reckon a tongue is good for something girly, it just aint talking," Emmitt glared down at me, before pulling me to my feet by my hair.

I screamed out of frustration, praying my father truly was near. "If you wanted me to get up, all you had to do was ask nicely," I ground out through clenched teeth.

"This is me asking nicely," Emmitt chuckled, yanking my hair again as he dragged me up the steps. "Get up, you idiot," he grumbled, kicking Boyd in the side as he passed, never breaking stride as he continued to drag me toward the door.

Emmitt stopped in his tracks at the sound of approaching riders. "Take her inside and keeps quiet. I'll get rid of them. Then we can have us some fun," he said, passing me off to Boyd who pushed me through the doorway and attempting to clamp a filthy hand over my mouth.

Moving my head from side to side, I managed to avoid Boyd's dirt-caked hand across my mouth. He kicked the door shut with his booted foot at the same time I kicked him in the knee and elbowed him in the stomach. Boyd propelled me forward and I landed on the wooden floor with a thud.

A familiar foul odor, or should I say stench, began to permeate the air in the tiny cabin. I looked around to see Annabelle Beaumont lurking in the far corner of the room. Stepping from the darkened shadows with a smile on her face, she reminded me of a very content cat with a cornered mouse.

"You need to listen to me, Boyd. You are about to make a serious mistake," I cautioned, putting up my hand to ward him off.

"How's that?" Boyd asked, narrowing his eyes, taking a step closer, as I took a step back. Just then we heard Emmitt raise his voice conspicuously as he backed up to the door of the shack.

"Because any minute now, my father will be coming through that door, looking for someone's hide to nail to the wall. Do you really want it to be yours?" I asked with confidence. We heard a muffled yelp, then a loud thud, as something hit the door hard.

"That was the sound of your friend, Emmitt, hitting the door, most likely, with a very large knife protruding from his body," I said with a nasty smile. "It really depends on who threw the knife." I continued to back up while desperately searching for something to defend myself with. "Now if it was Mother who threw the knife, Emmitt got it in the head. She's very accurate and precise," I taunted. "On the other hand, if Father killed Emmitt, that knife could be anywhere. Father doesn't particularly care where he hits his victims, as long as they die," I concluded morbidly.

Annabelle drew closer, coming up behind Boyd, who was now looking nervously at the door, trying to decide if he believed me or not. Meanwhile I inched my way along the floor toward a broom handle that would make an excellent weapon. Just five more inches and I would have it in my hand.

"Emmitt, you alright?" Boyd called nervously to his friend. "What happened to Emmitt?"

"I told you. It all depends on who threw the knife," I answered, lunging for the broom handle.

"Hey, what's you doing?" Boyd yelled, leaping for the broom at the same time. I reached the handle first, kicked Boyd in the stomach and knocked him to the floor. He rolled around on the ground clutching his belly, gasping for air. Not waiting for him to recover, I wacked him on the head with the wooden stick three times and ran for the door. Annabelle stood in front of the door, as if she could stop me from opening it. "What is your problem?" I screamed.

"I want you to leave my home," Annabelle growled, her eyes looking like narrow slits.

"So you can speak."

"Of course I can speak, you imbecile," she growled. "Now, get out. Leave my home, before I cause something truly terrible to happen to you and your family. I have tolerated your presence long enough!"

"Not until I get what I came for," I spat out between clenched teeth.

"It's your funeral," she quipped, disappearing through the wall as the door banged open. Father came through the door first, followed closely by my mother who carefully stepping over the dead body of Emmitt, who had a large knife protruding gruesomely from his neck.

"Let me guess, Mother beat you to the throw," I questioned, lifting an eyebrow while looking down at the lifeless body of my tormenter.

"Only because she kicked my horse and made him skitter to the side," Father retorted defensively.

"Oh, Olivia, what were you thinking? I was so worried!" Mother cried, roughly pulling me into her arms. "Can't you manage to stay out of trouble for one day? Don't you ever scare me like that again!" she mumbled into my hair.

Looking past Mother, I gave Father a questioning look. Wrapping his arms tightly around us both he squeezed. Hearing the bombastic voice of Harrison Beaumont, I pushed against my parent's embrace, to see what was going on.

"What in tar nation is all of this?" Harrison asked, stepping over Emmitt's lifeless form in the doorway, being careful not to get blood on his fancy shoes. Disbelief marred his features as he walked over and kicked Boyd with his foot. Boyd laid on the dusty wooden planks, out cold with a nasty looking bump on his head where I had conked him with the broom handle.

"I was taking a walk and ran across these two miscreants. Somebody should have warned me that this kind of rabble frequented the property," I haughtily announced, hoping that Harrison would be so put out by my harsh words that he wouldn't ask any more questions.

Annabelle reappeared over Harrison's shoulders and it looked as if she was whispering in his ear. Harrison swatted at his left ear several times, as if he was bothered by a pesky fly. "Yes yes, well, there's no accounting for what the wind blows in," Harrison absently answered, still looking bothered by something. Turning on his heels, he pressed a white handkerchief to his nose.

"Dandy," Father said in disgust under his breath, the moment Harrison turned the corner. "No accounting for what passes for a man these days."

"Murmuring is very unbecoming, Father," I teased, taking his arm and walking from the room, with Mother on the other side of me, as Harrison's men came in to clean up the mess.

13

WEDNESDAY, FEBRUARY 11, 1804

An Unexpected Turn of Events...

DRESSING IN A SIMPLE BROWN gown, I tucked my jeweled dagger into my pocket before going down to breakfast, making certain that I would not be without it again.

Quinton and Brody did not appear for breakfast the next morning and Coco gave me her all-knowing look. With the Beaumont boys otherwise occupied, Coco and I decided to entertain ourselves. We enjoyed a brisk walk around the grounds with Harrison Beaumont, Prince William and two body guards assigned to us. After the incident the day before, Harrison made it clear that Coco and I were not allowed to wander off on our own.

The staff busily prepared for Saturday's festivities as everyone nervously buzzed about polishing and shining everything from the chandeliers to the hardwood floors.

I was on my way up the stairs to search for Sam, the hall boy, when Quinton and Brody decided to grace us with an appearance at twelve thirty in the afternoon. Quinton looked no worse for wear, with a devilish grin on his lips as he sauntered past me, freshly shaven and dressed in a casual pair of brown trousers and white linen shirt. He saluted and grinned before passing me on the steps. Brody, on the other hand, walked down the steps as if his head were about to fall off his shoulders. His glorious full beard was now shorter especially on one side. His hand kept coming up to his right jaw as if it pained him to open and close it properly.

"Well, don't you look bloody awful," I teased, standing two steps below him.

"Thanks," he rasped, squinting his eyes against the sudden bright light that flooded the downstairs rooms. "Aren't you a ray of sunshine early in the morning?"

"I'm afraid you slept through the morning and it is now afternoon. What happened to your beard?" Taking a seat on the step, so he wouldn't tumble forward, Brody waved his hand at me, and patted the step next to him.

"You look a little woozy, why don't you take a seat, before you fall down the steps?" he said, covering his mouth as a small burp escaped. "I'm afraid my twin, the devil, incarnated!" Brody yelled at the back of his twin, wincing in pain. Quinton turned with a smirk, blowing Brody a kiss in the air before disappearing around the corner.

"Carnivorous, three-headed dog!" he shouted, despite the obvious pain it caused. "Ooh, ah, well," Brody added, bringing his hand up and resting it against his cheek, trying to ease the pain that shot through his jaw. "See what I mean? He has an evil streak running clean through him."

"Let me guess, Quinton led with his left and you never saw it coming," I said blandly, prying his hand away from his jaw, so I could get a better look.

"How could you possibly know that?" Brody asked, turning to look at me, as if I had just sprung three heads.

"Stop being a baby and let me look at you," I insisted, pulling his hand back. I gently felt along his jaw line and cheeks checking for abnormalities or lumps, Brody winced again, and then closed his eyes as if my touch brought some relief to his throbbing pain. "Coco told me. I was worried that one of you would be seriously hurt after the way you two tore out of here yesterday. I was going to come after you before she stopped me. She insisted the two of you needed to work it out."

Bringing his left hand up to his temple, Brody began to massage that spot. "It would have been nice to know all of this before Quinton sucker-punched me. I think I even blacked out for a minute," he added with a questioning look.

"Well, you look no worse for wear to me. And you worked out your differences, right?" I asked, studying his expression. "You did work out your differences, didn't you?"

"Yes, but that's not the point."

"Then exactly what is the point, Mr. Beaumont?" I asked in a tone that was slightly harsher than I meant it to be. At the same time I pulled my hand away and placed it in my lap. "You kissed your brother's intended and then kept your mouth shut about it for months. How did you expect Quinton to react?" I asded plainly, offering him no sympathy.

"Why are you getting so mad? You act as if you were the one betrayed." Then Brody's eyes opened wider, as if he suddenly understood. "Are you jealous? You are, aren't you? he scoffed. "You're jealous!"

"Don't be ridiculous, Brody Beaumont," I asserted defensively, standing up to leave.

Before I could step past him, Brody grabbed my hand and stood up as well. "Wait!" he blurted, sounding like an order instead of a request. "Are you upset with me?"

"I have no reason to be angry with you. We hardly know each other," I stated flatly.

"Because I didn't kiss, Lilly. She kissed me," Brody assured, looking down at me.

"I don't care who you kissed or intend to kiss in the future, Brody Beaumont," I added, lifting my chin just a touch higher as my eyes defiantly glared back at him.

"Your mouth says one thing, but your eyes say another," Brody countered with a slow, seductive grin.

"Aghh... men," I cried with disgust, shaking him off as I turned to leave. "You are ridiculous, Brody Beaumont, to be sure."

Suddenly Brody pulled hard on my arm, forcing me to turn back around. His strong hands took a hold of my shoulders as I suddenly realized what he intended. His mouth clamp down hard upon mine as I struggled and pushed at his chest. His arms wrapped around my waist, ignoring my feeble attempts to free myself until I shifted, entwining my fingers through his hair. Pulling him closer, momentary thoughts of impropriety quickly dissipated as the kiss deepened into a passionate embrace. His hand cupped my chin as his velvety tongue desperately searched for answers that my words alone couldn't express. My arms and hands, that only moments before pushed against his hard, solid chest, now pulled him even closer as a sigh escaped my lips.

Slowly, Brody pulled back as my lashes gradually fluttered open, and I gazed questioningly up into his hazel eyes that appeared suddenly more golden brown than green. "Why did you do that?" I whispered, still trying to catch my breath.

"I have wanted to do that from the moment we first met. I also wanted to make a point," Brody countered.

"And what point would that be?" I asked tersely.

Looking down at me, with a very serious look he asked. "Did I kiss you or did you just kiss me? Who kissed who?" his lips turned up into a glib smirk. "Tell me if you can."

"You mean whom," I corrected with a superior tone, bristling then shoving at his chest with the heal of my hands. "Cretin," I mumbled under my breath, along with a few choice Gallic words.

"What? What!?" he asked, refusing to let me out of the embrace as confusion replaced his smugness.

I felt the strains of embarrassment streak across my face as I noticed the servants averted their eyes, pretending they hadn't seen anything. "There are easier, if not better ways to make one's point," I said under my breath, with such distain that Brody threw his head back and laughed before he could stop himself. I tried to push my way past him again, only to feel his hand grab a hold of my arm to stop me.

My furrowed brow should have been a warning enough, but Brody chose to ignore it. Never looking away from Brody's gaze,

I lifted my dainty boot and stomped on the top of his bare foot. The response was immediate as he tripped on the step behind him, rescuing his wounded foot. Then to add insult to injury, Brody grabbed his head when he landed hard on the step behind him. "Oh, oh… ouch! Why would you do that?" he cried, leveling his eyes at me. "That really hurt."

"Good," I peevishly snipped over my shoulder as I continued up the steps, a string of Irish expletives tripping off my tongue.

"I'll come find you later. After I get a tonic for my pounding head, and you are in a better mood," Brody softly called, slowly getting to his feet.

"Don't bother, I'm sure I will be otherwise engaged, and still angry," I bantered, not bothering to turn around and address him directly. I was rewarded with another short burst of laughter from Brody. Stopping mid-step, I silently smiled to myself as I waited for the eventual groan of pain I knew would come, before Brody realized his triumph was short lived.

I began to climb the steps when an ear-splitting scream echoed through the hallways, interrupting my quiet celebration. I pinpointed the scream to be coming from upstairs and, gathering my hem up, bolted up the rest of the steps. I heard heavy clomping of Brody's feet as he came up the stairs behind me.

Momentarily frozen at the top of the stairs to get my bearings when another ear splintering scream echoed through the hallway bouncing off the walls, I began to run again, when Brody bumped into me as he passed me.

Quickly catching up to him, he took hold of my arm, bringing me to an abrupt halt. "Where do you think you are going?"

"Someone is in trouble. I'm going to help," I said frantically, trying to loosen his grip from my arm.

"Oh, no you are not! You are staying here! I mean it, Olivia. Stay here!" he ordered, before heading down the hallway.

Momentarily stunned by his tone, I took a breath and then started after him. "The hell you say," I called out, winning a nasty glare over his shoulder as I hurried after him.

At the end of the hall was a narrow doorway that led up to the attic, where extra furniture, old clothes and discarded party decorations were stored. Brody pulled several people out of the way, so he could continue up the narrow flight of stairs to the attic. The screaming had been replaced by loud sobs. One of the downstairs maids quickly ran past me, covering her mouth, a look of horror in her eyes.

I stopped a second to watch her push her way past the gawkers at the bottom of the stairs. I took another deep breath and told myself that I would not be deterred. Running up the last few steps, I was stopped dead in my tracks as I was taken aback by the terrifying sight of the still swinging body of Sam, the hall boy.

I must have audibly gasped, because Brody turned and looked at me before trying to block my view, taking me by the arm as he walked back to the top of the steps. "Someone get me a blanket and a sharp knife." He yelled down the steps, at the servants still standing at the foot of the steps, too frightened to see for themselves what had happened. "You don't want to see this," Brody insisted, turning to me and trying to force me down the steps, before running back to the body.

"That's Sam," I blurted out, still in shock. "I was just looking for him."

Brody grabbed the legs and lifted him up slightly. "Maybe he is still alive. Tell them to hurry up with that knife. We need to cut him down," he yelled frantically.

"Do you hear that?" I said, standing perfectly still to listen.

"Hear what?" Brody's tone sounded annoyed.

"I hear someone crying, over there in that corner." I cautiously pointed with my shaking hand to the darkened corner just beyond him. "Why can't you hear it?" I asked, looking toward the corner of the dimly lit room. "Sam, is that you?" I called softly.

"Who the devil is Sam? Olivia, help me hold up Dusty. Maybe he's still alive." Brody called to me. "I can assure you, he isn't making any noise," Brody said, struggling with the body.

"Brody, the young man whose feet you are currently holding is named Sam. Everyone in this household has nicknamed him Dusty, because he is always covered in ashes," I corrected, picking up a lantern from the table and holding it above my head. "Sam, is that you?" I called out again, seeing a shadow move, then curl up in to a tight ball in the corner.

"Who in the world are you talking to, Olivia?" Brody demanded. "I need you to tell them to hurry up with that blade. I don't know how much longer I can hold him up."

Taking my jeweled dagger from my pocket, I stepped closer to Brody. "It's too late for that, Sam is dead. You better stop his mother at the bottom of the steps so she doesn't see him like this." I said, cutting the rope and watching as Sam's lifeless body crumpled into Brody's arms. Then placing a gentle hand on his arm, I looked into his eyes. "Keep everyone downstairs for a few moments, while I see if I can help him."

"Handle what, Olivia? I don't understand." Confusion and grief shadowed Brody's eyes.

"I know," I added sympathetically, taking my dagger and placing it back into my pocket. "But this is what I do and I will explain it to you in detail later. For now, just keep everyone away, until I come back downstairs, and close the door on your way out. Oh, please warn the mother ahead of time, so that she can brace herself. Screaming and wailing is very disconcerting to the dead."

Walking towards the quiet sobs in the corner, I stepped around a trunk and two chairs to get to Sam. I watched as Brody quietly walked to the stairs, giving me a measured look before descending. I could hear him gathering people as he went, "There's nothing to be done for him now. I need everyone to go back down stairs, please," he said, shooing them out the door and then quietly closing it.

I stood there looking down at Sam who was hugging his knees to his chest and rocking back and forth, quietly sobbing.

"Sam, I would like to help you, if you will let me," I said. Remember me? I'm Olivia, you came to my room yesterday. Can you tell me what happened to you? Did you mean to kill yourself?" I gently prodded, crouching down and sitting across from him on the floor. "Sam, talk to me. I truly wish to help."

The sobbing stopped before Sam raised his head up slowly to look at me. "Yes, I remember you, but I don't remember what happened. I don't even remember coming up here."

"Do you remember tying the rope that you hung yourself with?"

"No," came his reply, before dropping his head forward and resting it on his arms as he began to rock back and forth.

"Sam, it's alright to be scared. Being scared just means you are about to do something very brave. Now, look at me! There has to be more to your story than that," I said, indicating the middle of the room, where moments before his lifeless body swung from the rafters. "One doesn't just end up hanging himself by accident. Were you upset about something?" I prodded, then watched as he shook his head, no. "Then what do you remember, Sam?"

"I don't remember anything," Sam sobbed pitifully.

"Sam, you must snap out of this. I can't help you if you won't stop feeling sorry for yourself and think. We don't have much time. Sam! Sam, listen to me! Was something bothering you? Were you scared, or anxious? Honestly Sam, you must remember something, anything," I said impatiently, firing off questions in quick succession as I got to my feet to pace the floor in front of him.

"I remember being scared yesterday, really scared and I've been afraid ever since we talked." Sam sniffed, brushing at the residual tears with the back of his hand. "I remember hiding behind the curtains of the window seat last night, the ones that faces to the west. I love watching the sunsets, and I especially enjoyed last night's. Then I decided to curl up and go to sleep on the window seat." Bewilderment shone is his eyes, as his gaze became confused. "I swear to you that is the last thing I remember."

"Have you seen a bright light yet or maybe someone who has died from your family?" I asked, keeping my voice calm and soothing.

"No! Nothing but complete darkness. I'm scared Olivia. What… what do I do now?" Sam stammered, a tear dropping from his large brown eyes. "My mum is going to be so disappointed. The priests won't bury me next to me Dad now, because I killed myself." Sam cried, tears rolling flow down his face in earnest.

"Sam, you are a good person. You're not going to hell," I assured, kneeling next to him. "Now, please, stop crying," I begged, wishing I could brush the tears from his cheeks. "The first thing you need to do is stop being scared. Can you do that for me, Sam?"

Sniffing, Sam swiped at his nose and wiped his tears with rough, work worn fingers. "I think I can," he answered, lifting his chin just a touch. "Being dead isn't what I thought it would be."

"That is the problem, isn't it. Our imaginings quickly disappear when faced with the reality of it all," I added wistfully, looking down at him. "Now, it's time to face what is before us. What do you say, are you up to the task? No more fear, and certainly, no more useless tears," I warned. Sniffing loudly, Sam braced himself to stand, pushing against the wall for support.

"Will you tell me Mum that I was brave?"

"The bravest," I said, with a forced smile. "Now, no more bad thoughts. That's an order," I insisted, trying to look stern, but missing the mark as I couldn't help smiling again. "Only happy ones will do. That's the ticket."

Sam forced a brave smile to his lips, just before we both heard the hauntingly, primal cries of his mother, coming from the bottom of the stairs. I watched as Sam's entire countenance fell, marring his young face with uncertainty and fear.

"Sam, look at me." I snapped my fingers in front of him to bring his attentions back to me. "It's never the condition of our reality or situation that is difficult for us to face." I stated with authority, as Sam brought his gaze back around to meet mine. "It's our actions, and the affect it has on those we are forced to leave behind. They are the ones who suffer, Sam. There simply is no way around it. I will do my best to comfort your mother, but you must do your part as well," I said as compassionately as I could. "Now, I need you to look for a bright light and go into it." I insisted, snapping my fingers in front of him again, as his gaze drifted toward the screaming and wailing noises his mother was making at the bottom of the steps. "Do you hear me, Sam?"

"Yes…ah… yes, of course." Sam stammered, uncertainty creeping into his eyes.

"Sam, your mother will be fine, we will see to it, I promise," I vowed. "No more fear, Sam, it interferes with the transition. And believe me, you do not want to be stuck here for eternity."

Absently he nodded his head, and I could see him pondering something over, when his eye caught sight of something over my shoulder. "I can see it, my Lady." Sam blurted excitedly. "The light, it's getting brighter."

"Describe it to me, Sam, in detail."

"It is really beautiful, Miss, and I can hear music," he said, beaming brightly as his face lit up like a child opening a gift. "It's me Dad, he's came for me. Me Dad came for me…" Sam cried, stepping around me and walking toward a light that only he could see until he got closer, and then it was like a window opening. A bright light, too brilliant for me to stand. I was forced to shield my eyes and turn away, until I felt his presence had gone.

I stood still for a moment, basking in the glorious feeling of what I had just witnessed, when I was interrupted by the sound of crying as Brody, Quinton and Sam's mother, Mrs. Banning reached the top step. She ran to her son's prone body, laying lifelessly on the floor and fell to her knees sobbing uncontrollably. Pulling his head into her lap, she began to moan pitifully. My heart broke into pieces for her pain, but at the same time I was thankful that he had passed over, before witnessing his mother's pain.

The flood gates that I'd erected to perform my duties for Sam, now crumbled as I dropped to my knees next to her, and taking her into my arms, I held her as we cried together. Seconds stretched into minutes as the two of us cried for our own losses. "Shush now," I soothed, while rocking her back and forth, in my arms. "He loved you so very much, and he wanted me to make sure that you knew that," I rasped, choking back my own overwhelming feelings.

"Why?" she managed to whisper, before dissolving into a river of sorrow and tears again.

Brody placed a hand on my shoulder, trying to lend comfort. "Sam didn't say why, Mrs. Banning. I don't even believe he knew why. He was a little foggy on details, but he is at peace, now. He is not imprisoned here, forced to wander about earthbound. His father was waiting for him, to show him the way home," I declared, brushing hair and tears from her face. "Your son and husband are together and they are with God now. Nothing can change that." I glanced up at Brody, who was standing over my shoulder. "Could you ask Quinton, to find my mother and sister and let them now that I need them."

Taking Mrs. Banning's hand in mine, I drew her gaze away from Sam's lifeless body. "I need you to do something for me, Mrs. Banning, please look at me. Can you look at me?" I saw confusion mar her features, before she wordlessly answered by nodding her head, staring at me, without truly seeing me. "I need you to let go of Sam's body now, and let us prepare him for burial. It isn't him anymore, Sam is gone. He is in a better place and isn't suffering," I said softly, holding her hands in mine. "Mr. Beaumont is going to take you downstairs to your room so that you can rest. My mother and sister will see to everything. I promise to take good care of him and dress him in his finest."

Mrs. Banning silently stood up, then allowed Brody to lead her down the steps, handing her off to the head housekeeper, as Quinton returned with my mother and Coco.

Taking Mother and Coco by the hand, I turned to Brody and Quinton who were standing over Sam. "Would you give us a moment with Sam?" I asked, "I will let you know when we have finished and Sam is ready to be moved."

Simultaneously opening their mouths to speak, then thinking better of it, they silently turned and walked back down the steps. A few moments passed before I heard the door close.

"What's going on, Olivia?" Mother asked, taking me by the shoulders, forcing me to face her.

"I've already told you about Lilly in my letter, but I didn't tell you everything. I think she was murdered. Lilly was unable to remember anything about her death. At first I thought that Quinton or Brody could have been involved, then I came here. Coco ruled Brody out, but never had the chance to rule out Quinton. Now Sam is dead and he can't remember a thing past last night when he fell asleep. It's far too coincidental."

Coco pulled on the shoulder of my dress, "Tell Mother about their mother, Annabelle Beaumont," she insisted, "don't leave that part out."

"Who the devil is, Annabelle Beaumont?"

"She was the mother of Brody and Quinton.

"Was!?" Mother gasped.

"She died. The story is, she was taking a bath after the annual party celebration eight years ago, hit her head on the side of the tub, and drowning in her bath. She has been haunting the household ever since. But I'm not so sure that is the entire story," I added skeptically. "I feel like there has to be something more to it."

"How can we help?" Mother asked, suddenly pulling Coco and me as close as she could while looking down at Sam's body with pity.

"Well, mostly I need you both for moral support. But since you're asking how you can help, I need your advice of what to do after Coco touches Sam and tell me what she sees." I stated, as if it was obvious.

"Wait just a darn minute, Olivia Sophia Allen," Coco strongly protested, turning to face me. "I didn't sign up for this. I've never touched a dead person before. Who knows what will happen?" she added with an involuntary shutter.

Trying to sooth Coco's jumpy nerves and ultimately get her to do what I wanted, I turned her around to face Sam's body, and whispered into her ear. "It's perfectly normal to be frightened by something new, Coco, but if you think about it too long you will lose your nerve." Then I drove the nail home. "Of course, if it is too difficult for you, I will completely understand," I said, playing on her vanity. "After all, not everyone is as strong and brave as our mother or grandmother."

"Now that's just not fair, Olivia," Coco whined, poking out her bottom lip.

"You are the only one who can do this, Coco," I pleaded. "I would do it if I could, but I can't."

"Coco's right, Olivia, you shouldn't ask so much of her," Mother admonished. "She's too young to be pulling her into this mess," she said, with a wink.

"Fine, fine, fine, I'll do it! But mark my word, I'm doing this under duress," Coco said in disgust, yanking her gloves off one finger at a time.

I smiled to myself in triumph. "How can I help?" I asked, taking the gloves Coco shoved at me.

"You've already done quite enough, thank you very much."

Mother moved around to stand at Sam's feet and I stood at his head, watching as Coco kneeled down next to the body. Hesitated at first, she stretching her hands out, holding them over the body a moment. "Please, forgive my intrusion, dear Sam, but this is in the name of science," she said sarcastically, while giving me a sour look.

"Maybe this was a bad idea," I cautioned, looking around as a foul odor permeate the stale attic air.

"The ox is in the mire, Olivia," Coco said resolute, as she took Sam's hands in hers.

I knew Annabelle was lurking in the shadows by the odor assailing my nostrils, but I couldn't see her and it made me nervous. Turning and picking up a nearby lantern, I held it above my head. Slowly Annabelle floated from the corner toward me, with a sinister glint in her eyes. I tried not to wince and hold my ground, but I could feel my insides twisting. Something in her eyes scared me to my very core. I looked at Coco then back to Annabelle, and realized that she wasn't looking at me, but at my sister. I moved towards Coco, but my feet wouldn't cooperate, feeling as if they were made of lead. Then grabbing her arm, I yanked her to her feet, breaking the connection and dragging her to the stairs. "Hurry Mother," I screamed, while pushing Coco down the stairs ahead of me. Mother looked startled, but rushed to follow us down the stairs and the three of us burst through the door, startling Brody and Quinton as I slammed the door shut behind us.

"What the bloody hell just happened?" My mother demanded.

"Yes, Olivia, why the devil did you do that?" Coco cried with indignation.

Still leaning against the door, I must have looked like a crazy person, "Couldn't you smell her?

"Her who, Olivia?" Brody asked, sounding surprised.

"It was her, your mother, Annabelle Beaumont," I stated, shaking my head. "The way she was looking at Coco, I was certain she was going to do something bad."

"Olivia, she is a spirit. She can't hurt anyone," Coco said with confidence, as if she were an authority on all things dead and buried.

"She's different, Coco. There is something so sinister about her presence. I can't explain it, but she terrifies me."

"Are you speaking of our dead mother?" Quinton spat out, with disbelief. "You are a bail short of a full load, Olivia Townsend," he added, taking a menacing step toward me, clenching and unclenching his fists.

Brody grabbed his arm, forcing Quinton to stop. "That is enough!" Brody growled. "We've known there was something wrong here for years, and if Olivia says our mother's spirit is sinister, you can believe it. Now settle down," Brody ordered, the two of them standing toe to toe. Quinton looked as if he would throw the first punch. Seconds felt like minutes, then Quinton exhaled, taking a step back.

"Coco, did you see anything when you touched Sam?" I asked, stepping away from the door, still eyeing Quinton cautiously.

"It was strange, really, I couldn't see anything, but I could feel darkness and fear. It was as if Sam had been taken over by something," Coco said, wrapping her arms around herself.

I looked at her and goosebumps ran up her arms before she began to shake uncontrollably. "Coco, are you alright?" I asked, unable to hide my sudden concern.

"I'm just cold, Olivia. A hot bath and a big pot of tea, and I will be good as new," she smiled. "Good as new," Coco repeated, trying to keep her teeth from chattering.

Mother and I looked at one another, a silent message passing between us. "Mother?" was all I had to say.

"Hot tea and a bath, coming right up," Mother echoed, ushering Coco down the hallway.

Wrapping my arms around myself, I watched them all the way down the hall. "The two of you see to Sam's body since you are so confident that nothing bad will happen to you if you go up those steps. I am in desperate need of fresh air," I called over my shoulder as I ran down the hall, praying that I would make it outside before I heaved my guts up.

I was confident Quinton and Brody could move Sam's body to the parlor so it could be prepared for burial. The authorities would be called, probably arriving in the evening to take statements from everyone involved. Of course, my statement wouldn't include every detail. That would make me sound like a raving lunatic, and I had no need to tempt fate.

People back home in Ireland had become accustomed to my family's eccentricities without much fuss or concern. But it had taken them years to accept us. I couldn't expect people in this part of the world to be so understanding of my gifts. I would keep my mouth shut about the demonic spirit that lurked.

14

Something Sinister Lurks Among Us.

BURSTING THROUGH THE FRONT DOOR and slamming it shut behind me, I ran to my left and heaved everything into the bushes.

I felt my heart racing as I gradually stood up and turned around to find Brody standing three feet away with a ladle of water and a white handkerchief in hand.

"I thought you might need these," he said, holding the items out to me with a sly smile.

I looked up at the water and starched hanky before begrudgingly taking them from him. "Thank you," I added, rinsing my mouth, then turning to spit it out in the bushes as gracefully as possible, before dabbing my mouth and handing him the ladle back. Without a word, I turned and headed to the back of the house, in search of parsley or mint leaves.

Brody followed silently behind me as I pawed through the herb garden. Within seconds I found what I had been searching for — mint leaves. Grabbing a handful, I chewed on them. "Oh that is so much better," I breathed a sigh of relief, before handing a few leaves to Brody as I walked past him.

Clearly perplexed, Brody chased after me. "What do you expect me to do with these?" he asked, taking a hold of my arm.

"I meant to inform you earlier, you taste like a brewery," I quipped, glaring at his offending hand still clamped to my arm. He didn't immediately understand the stare, until my eyes slowly traveled back up to his. Realizing why I was glaring at his hand, Brody released me, and

I continued walking down the path leading into the trees. Still standing where I left him, he breathed into his hand, inhaling the foul odor of his own breath. "You're right, that is a bit rank," he announced, chewing on the mint leaves, rushing to catch up to me. "What happened in the attic?" Brody asked, walking alongside me as we went down the path.

Breathing deeply of the pine scent, I brushed stray hairs out of my face. I just needed a moment to think. *Do I tell him everything? And if I do, would he think me mad or even a bit off, like others before him?* My insides already feeling like a queasy mess, I needed to talk to someone before I imploded.

Gently taking ahold of my arm, forcing me to stop, his eyes looked pleadingly into mine. "Olivia, please, tell me what you saw. You were scared, I could see it in your eyes when you came out of the attic. Don't try to deny it!" He continued to prod. "What happened in the attic?"

"Let it go, Brody, please. You could never understand what I live with every single day," I said, trying to pull my arm free.

"Try me," he challenged.

"I'm not crazy."

"I never said you were," Brody scoffed defensively, spotting a fallen tree behind me, then pulled me in that direction. "I just want to understand how it works, that's all. I want to know about you," he said gently.

Still skeptical of his motives, I took a seat on the log and glanced up as Brody sat down next to me. "Lilly swore by you, and I didn't think she was crazy," Brody added, taking my hand in his. "Just tell me what you see when you communicate with the dead."

Uncertainty furrowed my brow as I gazed into his eyes and the sincerity I saw was so raw and open that I broke my own rule and decided to confide in him. Exhaling, I hoped I wasn't making a mistake. "Spirits find me, I don't know how or why, but they do. Sometimes they seek me out in the middle of the night, or walk past me on the street and realize that I can see them. And when I see them, it's as if they are flesh and blood, much like I see you, but slightly different at the same time."

Taking another deep breath, uncertainty began to gnaw at me. "I don't exactly know how else to explain it to you. They are the same, yet different, shinier." I glanced up feeling self-conscious. I was starting have feelings for Brody Beaumont and feared seeing him look at me the way others did when they discovered the truth about me. It always began with a look of pity, other times a look of horror, followed by absolute superiority. Then finally they looked around as if the wished to be anywhere but where they were, standing next to me.

Placing a hand on my chin, Brody turned me to face him. "I believe you. I am not trying to judge you. I just want to understand, that is all. Please go on."

"Your mother is the first evil spirit I've come across. She frightens me and I don't know how to deal with it. This has never happened to me before. I can actually smell her evil stench before I see her," I said sincerely, looking into his face to gage his reaction. "The worst thing is, I think she knows I am afraid of her."

"Tell me how I can help. What can I do?"

"There isn't anything you can do. Can't you see that? You are powerless to help," I admonished, pulling away and standing up, needing to place distance between us. "You can't fight her, and I don't know if I can either. How am I going to get her to go towards the light if I don't know if there is a light that will appear for her to go towards… I don't even know if there is a way to talk sense into her," I stammered, pacing back and forth. "There are too many unknowns." I stopped to look at him. "This is very disconcerting if you hadn't already guessed."

Standing now, Brody took a step towards me and pulled me close, until I was pressed tightly against him, forced to look up. "Stop looking at me like that," I said, tersely, halfheartedly, pushing against his chest.

With an innocent look, he questioned, "Like what?"

"You know exactly like what. As if I were a forest of dry timber and you were a passing thunderstorm," I countered, attempting to step back without any luck.

With a vice-like grip, Brody tightened his arm around my middle, tipping my head up by placing a finger beneath my chin. "I believe you are very descriptive when you speak," he smiled. "I like that," Brody said, his lips inching closer to mine as he spoke. "No pretense or game playing, just good honest, straight forwardness," he added, only a hair's breath away from my lips.

The sweet dulcet tones of his voice sent a thrill through me, and I opened my mouth to speak, when his lips slanted ever so slightly, touching mine. Very gently at first, the sweet taste of mint assaulted my senses, as his breath mingled with mine. I felt his tongue slip through my lips, sending a new sensation throughout my body. Slight tremors began to gather in the center of my belly. I sighed when his fingers tangled through my hair at the nape of my neck, and I shuttered as he deepened our kiss. Clinging to him for support, I felt a dizzying rush of blood flow to my head, resulting in a slight sway. I felt bathed in warmth, despite the chilly February afternoon and I sighed and leaned in closer.

Brody pulled back slowly and my eyelids fluttered open, to find him studying me with an intense look. "Why do you look at me like that?" I asked, suddenly feeling self conscious.

"You are so beautiful that I can't bear to tear my eyes from you." His words thrilled me making my head spin. I'd never known someone who knew my secrets and still looked at me with such wonton desire.

"You have lost your mind," I said defensively, pushing Brody away from me. I figured it could only be a matter of time before he felt differently about me.

"No, really, I am completely consumed by you," Brody confessed, taking hold of my arm as I turned to leave. "Maybe I am too forward, but I have never met anyone as bold and, well, honest before, and I find it captivating."

"You give me too much credit. I knew who you were in New York, and I tricked you into inviting my sister and me to your home," I admitted, casting my eyes downward, embarrassed I had stooped to such tactics. "How is that for straight forward and honest?"

"I know." Brody lifted my chin up as he grinned at me. "I knew what you were doing the entire time. I just wanted to see how far you would take it." He laughed. "Besides, sooner or later I would have convinced you to come here, one way or another."

"Why you duplicitous...."

"Ah, ah, ah!" Brody added, wagging his finger at me. "My father always says 'you catch more flies with honey.' And losing your temper won't get you anywhere in life."

Grabbing the offending finger, I bent it back until he cried out in pain. "And there are two things we are charged with in this life: living with our mistakes and endeavoring to learn from them," I snarled, before turning loose to walk back down the path.

Running to catch up with me, Brody spun me around. Undaunted by my bad temper, he smiled and dodged a kick to the shin. Looking down at me wearily, while holding me at arm's length, Brody clicked his tongue at me, as if scolding a naughty child. "A life lived without joy, is merely existence. The heart is like a flower, eternally brave, but easily crushed," he teased, "and turning loose of our fears allows one to speak directly to their heart, free from the burdens and trepidations of life's apprehensions."

"So, tell me, oh wise one, do you follow the teachings of Voltaire or Rousseau? Or perhaps you see yourself more of a Dalai Lama?" I asked with a sarcastic tone, unable to explain or even control my quickly changing moods.

Taking hold of both shoulders, Brody gave me a quick shake. "What is wrong with you, Olivia?"

"I don't know," I suddenly cried, wiggling loose of his grip. "I'm not usually so irritable and moody, but I feel agitated and maybe just a little angry." I gasped, taking a deep breath to calm the emotions that were stirred up inside of me. "Something is wrong." Instinctively looking toward the house, unable to explain why, I knew we needed to hurry back.

"You think that there is something wrong at home?" Brody's gaze drifted in the same direction.

"Yes," I cried, turning my gaze back to his. "And I think we need to hurry." Lifting my skirts up to run, Brody took hold of my arm to help quicken my step as we raced for the house.

Meeting us on the front porch, Father looked surprised. "I was just coming to find you"

"What's wrong?" I ask with a sinking feeling in my stomach.

"It's Coco, something has happened and your mother sent me to find you." I could hear the concern in his voice.

Turning loose of Brody, I screamed, "No!" then ran through the house, crying, "No, no, no, no, no," all the way up the stairs, taking them two at a time, nearly knocking over one of the housekeepers in the process. Darting down the hallway, I threw open the door to Coco's room with a loud bang. "What's happened?" I demanded, the second my eyes landed on Coco's still form. "What happened?" I demanded again, climbing into bed with her and pulling her close.

"I don't know, Olivia. She was eating hot soup and began to shake uncontrollably, telling me she was very tired and then fainted. I haven't been able to wake her." She was cold to the touch so I pulled the covers back to get a better look at her, just as Brody, Quinton and my father came through the door.

"Well, is she alright?" Quinton questioned.

"I knew she was up to no good," I said accusingly. "There was something in the way she looked at me. I should have listened to my instincts." I murmured angrily to myself, clutching Coco closer as I rocked Coco in my arms, trying to stifle the hysterical sob. "What have I done, Coco? Please forgive me for dragging you into this."

"Father has sent for the physician," Quinton said, sounding positive. "Olivia, Coco will be alright."

"No, no she won't." I sobbed, burying my face in her hair. "And I don't know how to fix her. There has to be someone." I demanded, eyeing Brody and then Quinton. "Think! You must have heard stories of such things when you were younger. Maybe you overheard the servants whispering in the hallway," I said desperately, licking my lips that had suddenly gone dry. "Think!" I shouted, observing a knowing look pass between Quinton and Brody as they hesitated. "Spit it out. I can tell you know something."

"There is someone the servants talked about years ago. I don't even know if I heard correctly. For all I know we were imagining," Brody added.

"But if he is real, Brody, it was years ago. What if he's dead by now? I haven't heard them speak his name in years." Quinton said.

"Who?!" Mother demanded.

"They said his name is Father something or other and that he lives deep in the woods… I don't know if the stories are true. It may have been something the servants made up, just to scare us straight." Brody admitted, "We were pretty bad to the servants when we were younger."

"Well, who wasn't?" I quipped, knowing too well how the staff made easy targets for privileged children. "But we need to do something. Standing here doing nothing is not an option. Brody, you go to the servants and ask them directly. Explain that it is a matter of life or death." I ordered. He nodded his head and quickly left the room. "Quinton, you see that transportation is arranged and waiting, in case we need to leave quickly. Quinton was walking out the door before I finished speaking. "Father, we need to get Coco by the fire and warm her up. She feels like an icicle."

Mother and I wrapped two quilts around Coco, then Father carried her over to the crackling fire where he sat as close as he could. I watched as beads of perspiration formed on his forehead, but he never complained. I saw worry and fear in my parents' faces, while the feeling of desperation gnawed at my heart, along with condemnation and guilt for allowing Coco to come along with me on this trip. I was pacing the room, deep in thought and self-incrimination, when Brody walked through the door.

"Well?" I asked, the moment his foot crossed the threshold.

"How is she?" Brody questioned, looking at Father sitting by the fire, with my mother next to him, consoling each other.

"Not good and I'm scared, Brody. I don't know how much time we have." I whispered so that my parents didn't hear me.

"I have confirmed with two of the servants that the man is real and that he still lives. They say he's an ex-priest and has performed countless miracles. But the real question remains whether or not he can help us. I will take Quinton to find this man and bring him back here," Brody said, turning to leave.

"We don't have that kind of time, Brody," I said, grabbing his arm, to stop him. "We will make a bed for Coco in the carriage and take her with us."

"There will only be room for three more passengers."

I looked up and noticed the concern on his face as something electric passed between us. "I will ride strapped to the luggage rack if I have to, Brody Beaumont, but I'm going with you."

"We are going as well," Mother announced.

Brody and I turned, guilt written all over my face as I realized she'd heard our conversation.

"Then I'd better tell Quinton to prepare the other carriage," Brody concluded, turning to leave.

"My wife and I will ride horses, if you don't mind," Father insisted, lifting Coco in his arms and following Brody out the door. "Two carriages will take far too long to prepare and it will only slow us down."

Brody stopped at the door. "But, sir, it is a very long ride," he cautioned, looking with concern at mother.

"We have ridden under worse circumstances, dear boy. My wife and I will make do," Father countered, leading the way out the room and down the hall. "Now run ahead and get the horses saddled. That's a good lad, and be quick about it. Daylight is burning!"

"Father!" I loudly protested, shocked by his disrespectful tone.

"You will hold your sister's head in your lap. Your mother and I will be alongside the carriage should you have a problem," Father instructed, while carrying Coco down the stairs and out the door. Mother ran alongside him, fretting the entire way before opening the door to the carriage.

"I cannot believe your rudeness, Father," I scolded, climbing into the carriage, waiting for him lay her next to me. Cradling her in my lap, Coco suddenly seemed so small and frail. I closed my eyes to stifle the tears that threatened as Father kissed my forehead, before stepping down from the carriage.

"Please tell them to hurry," I said, bringing Coco's head up to mine and inhaling deeply. She smelled so sweet and fresh, like a bouquet of flowers. Every morning Coco dabbed a little rose oil behind her ears. It was her favorite scent.

Lilly appeared in the seat across from me, with a concerned expression. "What happened to Coco, Olivia? Why isn't she moving?"

"I don't exactly know what happened to her, Lilly. What I do know is Annabelle Beaumont had something to do with it." I breathed deeply, trying to calm my frayed nerves. "Where have you been? I've been looking for you," I admonished, glaring at her accusingly. "How could you pit one Beaumont brother against the other? I never knew you to be so duplicitous." I lashed out, worried and frustrated over Coco's condition.

"What are you talking about, Olivia?"

"You promised yourself to Quinton and then kissed Brody on purpose," I scolded.

"Oh, that. It wasn't like that, exactly," Lilly said sheepishly, looking around uncomfortably.

"Oh, then how was it, *exactly*?" I asked, pinning her to the carriage wall with an angry stare.

"I guess I couldn't decide which one I liked better. I was certain when I left Ireland," she said with a childish pout, "but then half way across the ocean, I discovered that maybe I liked the other one."

"Oh Lilly, you are such a child. Honestly!" I retorted, turning my head to the side, heaving a heavy sigh of disappointment, as I looked out the window.

"Did you say something, Olivia?" Quinton inquired, as he climbed in the carriage, followed by Brody.

Nearly jumping out of my skin, I turned, and replied. "No. I was simply clearing the air. We need to hurry, please."

"Certainly," Quinton replied, wrapping on the outside of the carriage with his hand.

"Who were you talking to? I thought I heard you scolding someone," Brody leaned over and inquired, while fidgeting with Coco's blanket.

"No one of importance," I answered, forcing a smile before turning to look out the window.

"No one of import, you say!" Lilly bristled, before leaning over next to my ear, "I know when I am not wanted. I will be sitting up top, getting fresh air. It is a little stale in here," she added, before disappearing with an angry harrumph.

"Is anyone else bothered by the sound of buzzing insects?" I asked, swiping at my ear.

"I heard that," Lilly scoffed.

I was the only person to hear her complaint and I smiled to myself. I was reminded of times Lilly and I had disagreed or quarreled. I would get annoyed and ignore her and she would go away in a huff. We, of course, always made up, but it never got old to either one of us. I loved her so much. Averting my eyes as they suddenly moistened, I wiped at them with the back of my hand, while hugging Coco closer. I was determined not to lose my sister as well. "Can't your driver go any faster?" I complained.

Brody slid a small compartment door open. "Noah, we are in a hurry," he said, closing the door and turning back to me. "I would advise you to hang on to your seat, and perhaps your sister as well. The road can be very bumpy between here and our destination." He'd no more than spoken the words when our carriage lurched forward, bouncing about unexpectedly. I gave a little yelp, clinging to Coco with all my might. Brody changed sides, gathering my sister's legs up as he slid beneath her. "You look as if you could use some help," he smiled reassuringly at me.

Hesitantly I smiled back and then nodded. My nerves felt as taut as a piano wire ready to spring loose at the slightest provocation. And the nerve-racking ride didn't help. It seemed to take forever to reach our destination, but in reality, it was just over two and a half hours.

The landscape visibly changed, growing darker the deeper we went into the woods, and the road twisted and turned as an eerie fog settled in, close to the ground. I shivered inwardly as we came up to a quick moving river with a rickety, old bridge spanning cross it.

I glanced out the window and worried that the bridge wouldn't hold the weight of the carriage and horses together. It was then that I began to pray, in earnest, that we would make it across without incident as the driver pulled the carriage to a stop. Hopping down from his lofty perch to study the condition of the dilapidated old bridge in front of us, it was several minutes before he deemed the bridge safe enough to cross.

Looking down at Coco, I noticed her lips had taken on a bluish tinge and I worried even more that we wouldn't be in time to save her. Quinton, noticing my distress, bellowed out the window to our driver, "Don't spare the horses, Noah."

Our carriage sprang forward, with a jerk, and again I clung to Coco and the seat for dear life. A few more minutes passed before our carriage slowed and I looked out the window at a shocking sight. To call the rundown structure a cabin was being too kind. I could actually see daylight through the weathered boards. Then I saw him. A tall, thin man standing in the doorway, waiting as if we had been expected.

Mother and Father dismounted, then Father flung the carriage door open before we had come to a complete stop. Quinton and Brody gently handed Coco into his waiting arms, and I watched as they all seemed to move, in unison, towards the mysterious man standing in the doorway of the dilapidated shack.

A feeling of uncertainty flowed through me like a wave on a turbulent ocean, and I leaped from the carriage and ran to catch up. Placing myself between the man and my sister, I blocked his hand from touching her. "What is your name?" I questioned harshly. "What makes you qualified to help my sister?"

"Olivia!" Mother scolded, grabbing my arm to pull me out of the way. "Please, forgive my daughter's rudeness."

"I am not offended, my dear," he said, with a quiet, but kind tone. "All of God's children are welcomed in my humble home, even the skeptical ones." He chuckled.

I scrutinized everything about him, starting with his attire. The material of his coat and pants were worn and tattered at the cuffs. They were not dirty or torn, but weathered from years of washing. The fabric had been lovingly mended in places, which did nothing to detract from the man himself, who appeared to have been mended in several places, as well. His tall, thin frame was crooked and bent as he leaned heavily upon his cane, which he held in his left hand. His hands were ravaged by age and arthritis, with mangled, malformed fingers that gripped tightly to his silver-handled cane. Finishing my assessment, I looked upon his wrinkled and leathery face. He appeared weathered by elements and time. A feeling of peace washed over me when I peered into his eyes. I must have audibly gasped because his smile widened even more as he peered down at me reassuringly, unaffected by my discovery.

"I'm sorry. Please forgive me. I did not realize that you were… were…" I said, as he fumbled for my hand.

"Blind, my child. There are those who never see what is before them, even with the benefit of sight. I am at peace with my afflictions. They have never deterred me from doing the things my maker sent me to do." He replied graciously, touching my arm and running his hand down to grasp my hand. "I am Father Timothy, and it is my pleasure to serve you and your family, Olivia. I have been expecting your arrival."

"But, how could you have known we were coming?" I cried with disbelief, before a dagger of guilt speared my heart. After all, I was the last person to doubt another's abilities. How many times had I been wounded by the hurtful barbs of another's words calling my abilities into question?

"There are things of this world and the next which defy explanation, child. One simply must learn to exist on faith," Father Timothy said. The rich timber of his voice and words reverberated in my mind long after he finished speaking.

Gesturing for us to enter, Father Timothy stood to the side, ushering my family into his humble dwelling while I stood still a moment longer. Just as I stepped forward, he placed a hand on my arm leaving me shocked by the strength he still possessed in his twisted fingers.

Looking to be sure he truly was blind, I stared into his milky-colored eyes. "I wish to restore your faith in human kind, dear child, but I worry that I am too late to do so," he said gently, looking past me.

"I often worry about the very same thing, Father Timothy, but there is nothing to be done about that now. You need to help my sister because I can't," I insisted, placing his hand over my arm to lead him inside.

He smiled widely. "You are most kind to help an old man." Leaning on me for support, though somehow I doubted he truly needed my help, he continued. "Don't forget to invite your friend in, she is very pretty and welcomed in my home, any time," he added with a chuckle when he felt me hesitate. Rendered speechless, I turned to look over my shoulder. I hadn't seen Lilly since we left Rosewood, but there she stood in the open doorway, waiting for an invitation to enter. I motioning with my hand for her. "Come on, Lilly," I whispered.

I maneuvered Father Timothy toward the middle of the darkened cabin, where my father, who was still cradling Coco in his arms, stood. The sparsely furnished room had two well-worn chairs, a frayed love seat and a large wooden table, accompanied by two wobbly benches on either side. Father Timothy tapped his cane on the wooden table, and my father gently laid Coco down.

Stretching his crippled hand out to gently touch Coco's throat, his look turned to concern, before he smiled, finding the faint pulse he searched for. "The proof of life," he said, almost to himself. "Fetch me a bowl and mortar from the cabinet over there," Father Timothy instructed, touching my hand and pointing in the general direction he wished me to search. "Someone find my black leather satchel. It is well worn, and may be covered in dust," he said, again pointing in a general direction the item could be found. "I've not had much call to use it of late." Reaching above the table for dried herbs that hung there, he fingered then sniffed each one in turn, before breaking off a piece. "Mary, burn the sage and seal the room." He called to an elderly woman I hadn't noticed until now, who sat quietly in a dark corner of the room.

Mary was short and thin, almost childlike in stature, with thin brown hair pulled back and tucked beneath her untied cap. She wore a brown dress and apron tied at the waist, that I assumed had been white at some point, but now was tinged gray. She gathered a handful of herbs tied together with twine in her right hand, and lit the bundle on fire, which she quickly blew out. Plumes of gray smoke gently floated through the room as she walked from the opened doorway, working her way slowly around the tiny shack. The words she spoke as she walked were barely audible, but they sounded like a prayer, repeated over again.

Touching Father Timothy's hand, I held out the bowl and mortar to him. "Here, Father, I found what you asked for. Is there anything else I can do to help?"

"Yes. Hold the mortar in one hand and give me the bowl," he requested, placing herbs into the white marble bowl and setting it on the table in front of him.

From another corner of the room, Quinton shouted out, victorious, "I found the bag," he called, dusting the satchel off with his hand before giving it a blow, causing him to sneeze three times. Wiping his nose with his handkerchief before placing the bag down in front of Father Timothy, Quinton sneezed one more time.

"Very good, my son," Father Timothy said, touching Quinton's arm, so he could follow it down to the bag. "Now, let me just find the elements I need and we will be ready." Staring up, he rummaged about in the satchel. "Here it is," he cried triumphantly, pulling his hand out of the bag, while grasping a glass bottle filled with oil. Giving the bottle a sharp shake close to his ear. "This should have sufficient for our needs." His lips turned up with a satisfied grin, trying to hide his excitement. Removing the cork, Father Timothy began muttering strange words in Latin that I had never heard before, despite extensively studying the language. "Kneel down before me, child. I wish to give you a blessing."

"But Father, I'm not the one who needs healing," I protested.

"I assure you, that I have been doing this a long time. Now, please, stop arguing and kneel down," he ordered, reaching for my hand to pull me close and whisper in my ear. "Just do as I ask."

Marking my forehead with sanctified oil, he made the sign of the cross and placed his hands upon my head, muttering five words over again before moving on to Quinton, Brody and my parents. He turned in Lilly's general direction, and began to make the same gestures, before I turned him three inches to the left. "Thank you," he muttered before he continued the prayer.

"Why did you do that? Lilly is already a spirit. She can't die again."

"My child, there are worse things in this world than being dead; yet, even the dead need protection from certain unsavory elements," he concluded, over his shoulder. With this task completed, Father Timothy poured several drops of oil into the bowl of herbs, placed the cork back in the bottle and dropped it into the bag. Then reaching in with both hands, he dug around searching for something. Pulling out two more bottles, one square and the other short and round, he opened them and carefully placed a few drops to the mix. "I am ready for the mortar." He smiled, crushing the herbs and oil together while mumbling sacred words.

Suddenly the door and shutters flew open, making a terrible clapping noise as they hit the wall and loose boards, causing everyone to jump and scream at the same time. But Father Timothy never flinched, as if he had anticipated this happening.

My heart pounding in my throat, I began to shake all over, positive my legs would give out as a thick fog rolled in through the opened doorway. I thought it strange that the fog only came through the doorway, when the windows stood open as well.

Father Timothy rocked back and forth quickly, and his voice became louder. I realized the wind had begun to blow through the small shack, making a deafening noise. Leaves blew around just outside of the door, but never crossed the threshold, and I couldn't pull my eyes away from them. As they swirled around, I was mesmerized. It was as if there was an invisible barrier blocking the leaves from entering.

Slowly, a figure stepped from out of the fog, stopping at the threshold, unable to enter. Annabelle Beaumont stood glaring, disdain and hate coming from those cold dead eyes of hers. A disquieting chill traveled through me, and I began to shiver uncontrollably, unable to decide if I was going to be sick, lose consciousness, or both. I felt someone touch my arm and slowly I brought my eyes around to see who it was. My eyes traveled up his arm to Brody's concerned face. I could read the question in his eyes, but I was unable to open my mouth to speak. I turned once more to stare at the doorway and thought my eyes were playing a trick on me. Instead of seeing Annabelle standing there, it was my sister at the doorway, begging to be let in.

I looked down at Coco lying on the table and my mind questioned the truth of what I was seeing. I shook my head and closed my eyes and must have made a sound, because Brody forcefully turned me around to face him. I opened my eyes and I saw his mouth moving, but the only thing I heard was the deafening noise of the wind. I tried looking back at the door, but he refused to let me. Cupping his hands upon my face, Brody forced me to look at him. He looked scared, even shocked, and I tried to clear my mind and focus on him so that I could understand what was happening; but my mind felt like the thick fog had invaded it.

Brody suddenly looked away and my eyes followed his. That's when I saw Coco sitting straight up on the table, grasping her chest and gasped for air. The noise of the wind died down, then ceased, and I could hear everyone talking at once. My eyes wondered back to the doorway, and Annabelle was no longer standing there.

Mary, Father Timothy's housekeeper, ran to the close the door, placing a wooden bar across it, before closing and latching the shutters. I watched as she straightened her spine, adjusted her skirts and glanced about to ensure everything was back in its proper place.

Brody still tightly held my shoulders, concern knitted his brows. "Why didn't you answer me, Olivia? What did you see?" he asked.

I stared blankly at him, not sure what to say. How does one tell another that their mother is a demonic creature? Without a word, I turned to Coco, burying my face in her hair and clasping her tightly to me. "I was so scared, Coco I had lost you. Don't you ever do that to me again!" I scolded through my tears.

"Don't worry. I never wish to repeat such an experience again!" she assured me, wrapping her arms around my neck.

15

I Will be Right Behind You

MARY BREWED US SOME TEA and portioned out the spice cake she had baked earlier that morning, and we all humbly accepted the generous offer. An hour later, we prepared to depart.

"Mother, please take my spot in the carriage, I could use a bit of fresh air," I said, knowing that she didn't wish to be far from Coco's side.

"Don't be ridiculous, Olivia, it's getting dark and there's a terrible chill in the air. Why, you don't even have a coat to wear," Mother pointed out.

"I will wear yours. There are plenty of blankets in the carriage, so you and Coco will be very warm together," I insisted.

"If you really don't mind," Mother hesitated, looking toward the carriage, then back at me. "I would prefer to ride in the carriage," she smiled, placing her coat across my arm before she and Coco walked out together.

"I will be happy to ride the other horse, if it is all the same to you, Lord Townsend," Brody offered, stopping my father before he followed mother out the door.

"That would be most magnanimous of you, old boy," Father teased, smiling broadly at Brody before shooting me a sly wink as he removed his coat. "But you truly should trade me coats. Yours looks a little flimsy for the ride back. The temperature has dropped, and I won't have you catching your death's cold," Father insisted, handing Brody his heavy leather coat in exchange for his thinner one. "I would feel quite guilty, since I will be warm and toasty in the carriage," he continued, giving me a kiss on the forehead before turning to walk out the door. "Don't be long now, it is a long ride back and it is already getting dark."

"I will be right behind you, Father."

"I will see that nothing happens to your daughter, sir," Brody added solemnly.

"Aye!" Father omitted a noise, deep in his chest, that sounded like skepticism. "See that you don't, or there will be hell to pay," he tersely mumbled, shaking a finger at him over his shoulder as he continued to walk toward the carriage.

Rolling my eyes and exhaling loudly, I felt dismayed by Father's over protective nature. "Please, forgive my father's over-bearing nature," I said, forcing a smile. "Would you mind seeing to the horses? I need a quick word with Father Timothy before we leave," I added, with a nod.

Brody hesitated a moment before leaving. "Don't be long, your father was right. It is a long ride back."

"I promise," I said from the doorway.

Taking mother's coat from me, Father Timothy fussed with it a moment before holding it up to me. I smiled to myself, slipping into the garment. "You are a very brave girl, Olivia Townsend."

"I'm truly not, Father. I feel ill-prepared for what may come next," I said in a small voice, sounding anything but brave.

Taking a hold of my shoulder, I could feel the strength of his conviction. "How can you, or any of us, ever truly be prepared for the unknown, child?"

Placing my right hand on his chest, I took a step in closer and whispered, "What if I become paralyzed by fear the next time I come face to face with her? What do you suggest I do then, Father Timothy?"

Taking a hold of my hands, he grasped them both to his chest so tightly I could feel his heart beating. "You move forward, pushing past your fear, child. What else is there?" he asked, staring into my face as he placed a warm hand upon my cheek. "Otherwise you become stuck in one place, unable to move forward, yet unwilling to go back. Open your heart, my child and don't be afraid to live or make a mistake. There is no room in one's life for fear."

"Are we still speaking about my fight against this demonic spirit, or are you now speaking about other matters? Perhaps matters of the heart?" I asked, giving a small scoff. "Because it really sounds like you are telling me to follow my heart, right now."

"Perhaps the two subjects are not mutually exclusive," he said, giving me wide grin before he sighed. "Take the advice of an old man, or don't. This is really about your path. It is entirely up to you," Father Timothy added, cryptically. "Comme ci, comme ca. It is Italian, for…"

"I know what it means, Father Timothy. My grandmother has said the same thing to me many times. It is neither good nor bad — it is what it is."

"You are very wise for one so young," he commented, patting my hand. "Just don't out-smart yourself out of the life that you are meant to have."

"What do you mean by that?"

"Olivia, we have to leave now, before the fog gets any thicker," Father called out from the carriage door, sounding very urgent before shutting it with a loud bang.

Touching my shoulders, Father Timothy pulled my hood up to cover my head. "You will figure it out, dear child. You are a clever girl. You should go before the fog worsens and you can't find your path back," he said with a cordial wave in the direction of my father's voice. "Be safe, my dear," he added, giving me a gentle push, and a wave, as Mary stepped forward, taking ahold of his arm to lead him inside. The sound of the closing door brought me back to reality. I looked around me and noticed the fog. I shivered inwardly. It would certainly be a long, cold ride back.

Pulling up the collar of Mother's coat, and fastening the top button, I placed my foot into the stirrup to hoist myself up onto my mount.

I was beginning to regret my impulsive offer to ride back on horseback, because I was wearing a flimsy dress and forced to ride side saddle, which always made my back ache.

Brody steadied the horse for me while I situated my skirts, then he ran to the carriage, retrieving a blanket. "I thought you might need this," he offered, unfolding it and slipping it over my lap, resting his hand upon my leg longer than necessary.

I smiled as my eyes met his and our hands touched, causing me to jump as a spark passed between us. "How very gallant of you, Mr. Beaumont, and now I am in your debt," I teased, securing the corners around my waist and tucking the corner under me, so the blanket wouldn't slip off as I rode. The carriage began to pull away as we continued to stare into one another's eyes for a full second longer. Climbing into the saddle, Brody brought Zeus alongside of me. "Are you ready?" he asked, before kicking his horse forward.

The croaking frogs and chirping crickets sounded so loud, echoing off the dense fog in the darkening forest. We rode in silence for some time, each lost in our own thoughts, following the infused lights of the carriage lanterns.

Suddenly I involuntarily screamed, throwing the hood of the jacket off and waving my hands wildly about swatting at a bug that flew into the hood and then my hair. I must have looked like a crazy person, shaking my head and flailing my arms around. "Is it gone?" I screamed, throwing hair pins and spilling curls down my back.

Coming to my aid, Brody chuckled as he grabbed the reins from my hand to keep the horse from galloping away with me helplessly clinging to his back. "I think you got it. Oh wait —" he teased, sending me into another wild fit of screams and shudders. "No, it's gone."

I shuddered "augh," a noise I always made when I was creeped out by a bug, before swatting the last place the bug had been. "I hate bugs!" I emphatically stated, yanking my hood back up, taking the reins from him, irritated that he was still laughing. "If a snake falls out of those trees and lands on me..." I warned, pointing at the limbs above my head, followed by another involuntary shudder as I pulled the blanket off my lap, draping it over head.

"Snakes hate the cold, Olivia. They hibernate this time of year. You have nothing to worry about," Brody said with another chuckle, then a hearty laugh.

"I retract permission giving you leave to use my given name. You may address me as Lady Townsend from now on, you, you... Oh stop laughing at me, you baboon. It isn't funny," I finally managed, slapping at his leg. "I really hate bugs and snakes and slimy things. They make my skin crawl."

"Don't worry your pretty little head over all those slimy things, Lady Townsend, I'll protect you," Brody boasted, sitting a little taller in his saddle.

"You are so gallant," I added, with just a hint of sarcasm at the same time my horse tripped over something in the road and started limping. "What else could go wrong?" I muttered, pulling my horse to a stop.

Jumping down from his mount, Brody ran around the horse, to help me down. "Let me have a look." He ran a hand down the horse's leg. "He's thrown a shoe. I guess that means we double up," Brody smiled just a little too enthusiastically.

"If we can catch up to the carriage," I began, looking down the road for signs of the carriage lights, "I could climb in ..." my words trailing off. "Or... I could just ride with you. You realize that it is completely dark now and we don't know where we are going."

"Maybe you don't know where we are going, but I know these woods like the back of my hand," Brody stated confidently, deftly grasping my sides and helping me up on Zeus's back. "Here, take these," he insisted, placing both sets of reins in my hand. "We wouldn't want to lose a horse out here in the middle of nowhere."

Climbing up behind me, Brody draped the blanket over my shoulders. "Thank you. I was getting cold." I said, between chattering teeth.

"Well then, we best catch up to that carriage, so we can get you warm again." He tightened his grip around my waist before kicking his horse forward.

Pulling the blanket tightly around me, I didn't worry about falling off. "My hero," I murmured, so quietly I was sure he didn't hear me, until I felt his chest rumble with laughter. Relaxing my back into his strong, hard chest, I no longer felt cold and shivered now for a different reason.

"Now that I have you all to myself, there's something I've been wondering about," Brody asserted, his voice sounded like velvet to my ears, just before his hand rested on the dagger in my pocket. "What's this?" he questioned, probing the object protruding through the material of Mother's coat.

"That's the burning question that's been plaguing your mind? What's in my Mother's jacket pocket?" I asked with astonishment.

"No, that isn't what I wanted to ask you, but my hand kept bumping against it and I became curious."

Pulling Mother's jeweled dagger from the pocket, I brandished it in front of him. "This would be Mother's lovely jeweled dagger. She always carries it with her. In fact, Coco and I have our own pretty little daggers. I wouldn't dream of leaving the house without it." I bragged, feeling about in my dress pocket, before realizing I didn't have it. "Well, let me preface that statement, by saying that I normally wouldn't leave the house without my dagger, but today was a very unusual day." I said, turning to look at him.

"Let me get this straight. You normally carry a knife at all times?"

With a smile and a bashful laugh, I turned back around and placed mother's dagger back into the pocket. "Usually. Ever since my grandmother, Angelina was set upon by a band of pirates, it has been the practice of the women in my family to carry a dagger in their pocket at all times."

Brody expelled the air through his teeth, making a high-pitched whistle. "Your grandmother was taken by pirates?"

"Turns out that all pirates are not evil. Perhaps you will get the opportunity to ask my grandmother about her story one day. Although it is true, she was taken by ship full of pirates, she also won her freedom and liberated the family ship by playing a game of chance."

"Good to know," he muttered under his breath.

"So, what did you really want to ask me?"

"What causes a soul to be trapped on Earth, instead of ascending to the afterlife?" Brody softly asked, tightening his grip on my waist.

"Are we speaking in general terms and why, or are we speaking specifics?" I asked, snuggling deeper into the blanket and Brody's chest, looking for even more warmth.

"You do catch on quick," he exclaimed with a chuckle.

"And you thought that I was simply another pretty face?" I teased, elbowing him in the stomach. "I'm insulted." I laughed. "Well, I guess it really depends on the unique situation. You realize there are many different reasons why someone might be Earth bound?"

"No, I did not realize. That's why I am asking you."

"Some people get confused because their death is sudden, or unexpected, while others simply wish to watch over their loved ones," I explained.

"Do you think that is why my mother has stayed?" Brody inquired, nuzzling his nose in my hair.

I made an unladylike sound deep in my throat before I scoffed. "May I ask exactly what you might be doing to my hair?" I inquired, glancing over my shoulder.

Unfazed by my tone, Brody simply smiled casually and gave me a wink, "My nose was cold," he answered with a wicked smile.

"And you felt it appropriate to bury your nose in my hair?"

Giving me a measured look, Brody's voice turned gravely as he spoke, his eyes never leaving mine. "Your hair makes an excellent nose warmer and it smells nice."

I was suddenly shocked by the ease with which Brody maneuvered from gallant hero to seducer. "Oh you are a slippery sort," I teased again, turning around to face him, knowing that I was on a slippery slope when it came to Brody Beaumont.

Feigning coolness was my best defense against him. His natural, heady musk drifted into my nose, teasing and arousing my senses, causing me to feel lightheaded. Dropping his gaze to my lips, I felt a tingling anticipation, spreading like a wildfire.

"Whatever could you mean by that preposterous statement, my Lady?" Brody pleaded ignorance, as his tone turned even more seductive as his voice deepened.

"I think you know exactly what I mean by that statement," I admonished, still playing it cool. "You are very used to getting your way with women, and I, for one, do not intend to be a conquest."

"You could never be a conquest to me, Olivia." Brody assured me with such conviction that I was taken aback. His eyes seemed to darken, drawing me in even deeper to a place I never knew I wanted to go. Intently studying him a moment longer, before my eyes shifting downward to his lips, I knew he meant to kiss me and I wanted him to. In the heat of the moment, it felt right, there was no denying there was something about this man that drew me in, like a moth to a flame. I couldn't help myself, and it had been this way from the moment I laid eyes on him.

His warm, pliant lips covered mine as I answered his wanton kisses with my own. Heat filled me as a fluttering sensation teased at parts of me, both sinful and thrilling at the same time. The very acknowledgment of this fact made my pulse beat faster.

I felt Zeus slow and come to a stop beneath us. There we sat, on the darkening forest road, with the frogs and crickets to serenade us and the fog swirling around Zeus's legs.

Brody Beaumont filled my mind. The taste, the feel, the very smell of him had invaded my senses – my very being. This was complete madness.

The feel of his hardened muscles beneath my fingers propelled me onward, beyond the boundaries of propriety and into the realm of desire. His lips trailed their way to my ear and down my neck, sending ripples of goose bumps up and down my spine. I could feel my toes curling inside my shoes and I audibly sighed, then shivered when his lips once again landed upon mine.

Time momentarily stood still as we became lost in each other's kiss. The fierce pull of attraction caused everyone and everything to melt away, until nothing else mattered. His fingers brushed against the swell of my breast, and I felt them harden and ache as they strained against the gauzy texture of my slip. The sensation rippled over my skin and raced down my limbs, causing delicious feelings to cascade through me. The heat from Brody's body warmed me to the point, the blanket I held onto became stifling and no longer needed. I felt scorched where he touched me, and the heat from his hands alone could have started a fire.

He made a sound low in his throat that sounded like regret, as he pulled back slightly. Brody smiled slowly and the affect was devastating to my heart.

"You fit in my arms as if you were made for them from the beginning," he murmured close to my ear.

I could feel the hairs on the back of my neck stand on end and the air between us felt charged with electricity, like a thunder storm passing through. "Do you think a few pretty words whispered in my ear, are enough to cause me to lose myself to you?" I uttered softly, once I was able to speak again. "Why, you certainly take much for granted, Mr. Beaumont."

"There you would be wrong, Lady Townsend. I take nothing for granted when it comes to you." he rasped, curling a finger beneath my chin, so that I was forced to look into his eyes. Then he griped me fiercely against his unyielding chest until not even breath could pass between us. "Tell me the words you wish to hear, that would convince you of my sincerest devotion."

Tingles of desire, almost too exquisite to bear, filled my body as something inside of me melted. "Brody…" I gasped, before I knew what was happening.

Then I was caught off guard by the screeching of an owl flapping its wings over my head. Ferociously grasping a clump of hair in its talons, the creature began clawing at my head. Ducking my head forward, I was trying to make sense of the sudden attack from a normally shy creature. Brody began swatting at the beast with one hand, while holding tightly to me with the other, preventing me from falling. Zeus began to prance around nervously, frightened by my screams and the owl's unholy screeches.

Suddenly survival instincts kicked in and I retrieved the dagger from Mother's coat pocket, plunging it into the demonic creature, all the way to the hilt. Its wings instantly stopped flailing and the unearthly cries ceased. The owl fell to the ground, with my hair still in its claws.

"Olivia, look at me!" Brody cried, desperately trying to get me to face him. "Are you hurt?" I could feel his hands quickly assessing my head and neck. "Olivia, answer me, please."

I felt the blood trickling down the back of my neck and forehead, while my right ear felt like it was on fire. I knew enough to know I was in a state of shock, as I tried to do my own mental assessment.

Brody reached for my arm, forcefully turning me around to face him. "Olivia, say something to me!" he insisted, sounding frightened and far away to me. I could feel his hands on my face, and I know I was looking at him without really seeing him. "Olivia!" He shouted again, giving me a stiff shake. I managed to whisper a response between clenched teeth as my body began to shake uncontrollably.

"I'm fine."

He took the dagger from my hand and reached into my pocket for the sheath, placing it on the end of the blade, before slipping it into his pocket. Then wrapping the blanket tightly around my shoulders, Brody kicked Zeus in the side and headed down the road as fast as he could, pulling the lame horse behind him. I was now shaking almost convulsively, but it wasn't from the cold night air. My mind couldn't process what was happening, and I'm sure I slipped in and out of consciousness a few times.

By the time we made it back to the plantation, my parents were in a state of panic. They had started to worry because they thought we were directly behind them. Thirty minutes had passed, while they discussed the matter over with Harrison Beaumont, who had only just returned himself from a hunting trip with Prince William. Between the four of them, they decided to saddle fresh horses and search for us.

They ran into us on the road about a mile from the plantation. "What's happened?" Mother cried, and I could hear the relief in her voice, before she realized anything was wrong. "We expected you both half an hour ago."

"We ran into a problem and Olivia's been hurt," Brody called over his shoulder, not bothering to slow down or explain further as he squeezed me tightly to his chest. Realization began to break through my foggy mind as Brody continued to ride quickly toward the main house. He never broke stride as he dismounted, pulling me from the back of Zeus in one move. Cradling me gently, he carried me towards the front door.

Harrison ran ahead to open the door while my parents ran to keep up.

"Take her to the sunroom," Harrison ordered, "we can take a look at her there." Then bellowing out orders like a general, Harrison commanded attention. "Fetch me some hot water in a basin, bandages and salve and bring them to the sunroom, immediately."

"How did this happen?" Father demanded, close on Brody's heels. "I told you to keep her safe," he questioned angrily.

"I would prefer to go to my room, if you don't mind. I need a hot bath." I quietly spoke, as the effects of shock began to wear off.

"Change of plans," Brody called over his shoulder, turning mid-step and reaching the stairs in three long strides. "We are going up stairs, Father, see that someone prepares Lady Olivia's bath right away."

Touching the back of my head with one hand, I began to squirm in Brody's arms. "You needn't fuss over me. It is merely a few scratches. I will be fine," I insisted with renewed determination, as I stared at the blood on my hand. I would find out what had happened in this house eight years ago, to cause someone's spirit to turn so evil. I had no doubt that the answer to that question would lead me the answers I truly sought. What happened to my best friend, Lilly? "I am famished. Did I miss supper?" I asked, perking up as I looked at Coco.

"You concern yourself with food at a time like this? Olivia, you could have been killed," Mother pointed out, looking at my father for support, before continuing. "We need to leave this place with haste," she demanded, grabbing ahold of Brody's arm to halt his progress. "This is serious, Olivia Sophia Allen Townsend."

"Do you think because you used my full name, that I will change my mind?" I argued. "Put me down. I am perfectly capable," I ordered tersely.

I was rewarded with an immediate response when Brody dropped my legs to the ground while his arm remained around my waist, lending support, until he was sure I wouldn't faint away.

"Perhaps you should consider what your mother has to say, Olivia. The spirit of my mother may be too dangerous for any of us. I couldn't bear it if something happened to you or your family." Brody quietly weighed in on the matter, offering his opinion, as he studied my reaction.

"I'm not a quitter," I protested, while bringing my other hand up to my throbbing ear. I felt out of sorts and my head felt woozy. "I could really use something in my stomach," I said, continuing to walk to my room.

"It isn't a matter of you being a quitter. This entire situation has turned dangerous. I fear for you and your sister's safety," Mother reasoned, following me through the bedroom door. "It is my job to worry."

"I came here with a purpose and I will not be leaving here until it is done," I stated with quiet finality.

"Aiden, talk some sense into your daughter, I'm getting nowhere." Mother admonished, frustration evident in her tone as she blew air between her clenched teeth.

"And how do you propose I change her mind?" Father asked skeptically. "I have never had any measure of success when it comes to changing *your* mind. Once you have decided on something, the matter is settled," he added, with a cynical laugh. "She is by default a very stubborn and determined child. She has been that way from the beginning. I guess that apple didn't fall far from the family tree." He crossed his arms over his chest and gave mother a bland look.

"Agh! I give up." Mother blurted, throwing her hands in the air and marched down the hallway, slamming the door to her and Father's room.

I gave Father a grateful look. "Thank you for taking my side."

"It isn't a matter of taking sides, Olivia. It is a matter of knowing my limitations." Father insisted, giving me a stern, but measured look, before glancing down the hallway where mother had just stormed off. "Now, if you will excuse me, I think I need to smooth things over with my wife before I am exiled. Is that dog house outside large enough to accommodate a large man?" Father joked, halfheartedly as he walked away. As I watched his retreating form, I felt Brody touch my shoulder. "Maybe your mother is right, Olivia."

"Pish-posh! I am not going home without answers," I replied stubbornly, gazing up into his large, hazel eyes. The way he was looking at me nearly melted away every ounce of resolve I had left.

"Look at you, Olivia, you're covered in blood and that creature could have blinded you or caused irreparable damage."

"But it didn't, Brody, and I'm fine. At least I think I'm fine," I said glibly. "I will know better after I have a hot bath and get some food in me." I dismissed all his concerns with a wave of my hand.

Taking a hold of my arm, to stop me from going, Brody pulled me back around to face him. "I cannot continue to allow you or your family to be placed in harm's way. I won't do it," he admonished. Hazel eyes stared back at me with emotion.

"Then it is a good thing that you have no say in what I choose to do." I replied obstinately.

"My father was right about redheads."

"Oh, and how is that?" I asked, curious what his father knew of redheads.

"He claims they are nothing but trouble and quite pig-headed and stubborn," he answered, expelling air through his teeth, while raking his fingers through his hair. "He warned me to stay away from them, but I wouldn't listen."

Narrowing my eyes, I detached his hand from my arm and walked him to the door. I could feel Brody's eyes on me the entire time, as I closed the door behind him. Maybe he was right and I should pack up my things and leave, but that would be the coward's way out. And I, for one, was no coward!

I certainly didn't wish to place my family in harm's way, but I also refused to let Annabelle Beaumont have the last word in this matter. I would get to the bottom of this mystery, if it was the last thing I did.

Then a haunting thought struck me. What if this was the last thing I ever did?

16

THURSDAY, FEBRUARY 12, 1804
2 O'CLOCK IN THE MORNING

Sibling Rivalry

I AWOKE WITH A START, DISORIENTED at first as I lay perfectly still for several minutes listened for anything out of the ordinary. I heard nothing. The house was silent and unusually still, and this bothered me.

Slowly opening the door between mine and Coco's room, I listened to her even, slow breathing for a moment. Satisfied that she was well, I silently closed the door and donned my robe and slippers. Securing the sash about my waist, I walked to the hall door with a lit candle.

Anxious and unable to sleep, I thought a hot cup of tea and one of cook's delicious raisin scones, if there were any left, should do the trick. The hallway clock chimed two times, just as I opened the door. It was two in the morning, and would be a long time before sun rise.

Slipping down the back staircase, I wound my way around to the kitchen and was fortunate enough to find a few good embers still burning in the hearth. Stirring the ashes, I added two small pieces of wood to get the fire burning again. Checking for water in the kettle, I swung it over the fire to heat.

Then I found the pantry door and fumbled about looking for the tea tin I had observed sitting out the day before. Finding several tins in the pantry filled with interesting looking tea leaves, I smelled each one, before deciding on a soothing chamomile and rose hips blend. I placed the leaves in a delicate porcelain pot, added hot water and left it to steep, while I searched for scones. Returning to the pantry I lifted my candle high into the air to get a better view. Setting the candle down on a shelf to my left, I needed both hands free to rummage about.

Startled by footsteps behind me, I whirled around quickly. I drew my dagger at the same time and was caught off guard by Brody's quick reflexes, as he grabbed my dagger wielding arm, before I could do him any harm.

"Now hold on there, little missy, you could hurt someone with that," he said, a perplexed look marring his handsome face. It was as if he wasn't expecting me to be wielding the dagger, even though I had told him that I always had it on me.

"You shaved your beard completely off?" I said offhandedly, turning to resume my search, even though he still had ahold of my arm. Something felt slightly off and then suddenly whirling back around, I gasped. "I'm so sorry, Quinton, I thought you were Brody."

"It happens more often than you think." Quinton admitted, still staring at me intently.

"I am going to need my arm back," I awkwardly teased, feeling somewhat uncomfortable with his close proximity. Quinton didn't immediately take the hint. "I made some tea and discovered where cook hid the scones," I added, spying the basket when I turned around. Plucking it from the shelf, "would you like to join me?" I asked, still trying to dislodge my arm from his grasp.

"Yes, I do believe I'd rather enjoy a spot of tea, as you Brit's like to say," Quinton quipped, giving me his best effort of an English accent.

I laughed stiffly and pulled away, squeezing past him, as I made my escape from the small confines of the pantry, with candle in hand. "You realize that I am Irish, not English. Although I do suppose I have English blood in my, on Mother's side."

"It all sounds the same to me," Quinton laughed, following me out of the pantry.

"Do you take your tea with cream and sugar or do you prefer it straight and strong?" I inquired, trying to sound casual, while keeping him in my peripheral vision. "Though, I'm not quite sure how strong one can make chamomile tea."

"Just fix mine as if you were drinking it," Quinton answered, coming up behind me on the pretense of observing what I was doing.

"Please, sit," I insisted, gesturing with my hand for him to take a seat at the servants table. Then bringing the tray over, I poured out the tea and added two sugar cubes and handed it to him. On a separate plate, I served Quinton a scone with a generous helping of apricot jam that I had liberated from the pantry and a dollop of whipped butter.

"So, what keeps you up at night?" Quinton asked, peering at me over the rim of his tea cup, scrutinized my every move.

"It has been a strange couple of days, to be sure," I replied, sipping from my own cup.

"Are you any closer to finding what you came here for?" Quinton inquired, still studying me closely.

I thought it strange, the way he worded his question and I stopped mid-sip, then set my cup down. "I can't say that I am," I stated with a stiff smile, placing butter and apricot jam on my scone. "In fact, I have more unanswered questions than before," I added, with another measured smile, before taking a bite of my scone, then dabbing my lips with the napkin from my lap.

An uneasy feeling had begun to crawl up the back of my neck at this point, causing tiny hairs to stand on end. I started making mental notes of the distance to each doorway and how hard it would be to get my hands on a cast iron skillet, just in case I needed to slow Mr. Quinton Beaumont down. "So, what brings you down to the kitchen, at this unholy hour?" I inquired, pouring more hot tea into my cup and looking up, gesturing with the pot, to inquire if he required more.

Shaking his head, not before leaning forward in his chair, Quinton closed the gap between us. "Would you believe me if I said I could sense that you were down here, all alone?" he replied, giving me a seductive half smile, to seal the deal.

I scoffed, before answering. "No, I can't say that I would," I replied blandly, while bringing the hot cup to my lips. I leaned back in my chair as I set the cup back on the saucer and eyed him suspiciously.

"Well, it's true," Quinton insisted, picking up my left hand that had been resting on the table. He began to gently massage my fingers with his strong, lean hand as if he and I had been friends forever.

Alarm bells began to ring in my head as my body instinctively went taut, ready to jump into action. I tried pulling away, but he only held on tighter. I was beginning to feel trapped like a cornered animal.

"As soothing as your touch is to some, Mr. Beaumont, I find it most unnerving and would appreciate you un-handing me," I demanded in a low, calm tone, which would have been warning enough to anyone that knew me well. Yet, Quinton Beaumont was a man used to getting what he wanted and not terribly adept at picking up on subtle, social cues, because he continued to rub my hand. Still looking at me with a casual smile on his lips, the complete disregard of my wishes was grating. "I don't know what game you are playing at, but I can assure you, I am no push over. I have already asked you once to un-hand me. There won't be a second time, only consequences, Mr. Beaumont." I growled in a low, but deadly tone.

Quinton immediately withdrew his hands as if he had just been scalded. "Message received, Lady Olivia. My most sincerest apologies," he added, picking up his tea cup and taking a long sip, draining the cup of its contents. Then as an afterthought, Quinton turned to his scone and pretended to be interested in it.

"Brody warned me to keep my hands off you," Quinton said, half sulking. "Said that you were special, and I wasn't to try anything, or I would be sorry," he scoffed cynically. "I just never thought it would be you who delivered the hurtful blow."

"Well, clearly, you like to ignore warnings," I speculated. "One would have to ask themselves, why?" I added, somewhat confused by his ruse. Then it hit me, like a glass of water to the face. "Oh, you duplicitous lout. Now I see what you are about, and I can assure you that I am not as dense as all that," I declared, anger lacing my words. "Lilly kissed Brody, which he informed you about, explaining the misunderstanding, I might add. Never the less, you were still hurt by the act of betrayal and felt you needed to strike back. Even though it wasn't his fault!" I stated accusingly. "How very deceitful of you," I added with a chuckle. "And to think that I nearly threw a hot cup of scalding tea in your face, and pinned your hand to the table with my pretty little blade," which I produced from my pocket, just to drive the mental picture home. Quinton chuckled nervously, looking at the blade out of the corner of his eye.

"Well then, it is fortunate indeed that I chose to heed your warning and let go when I did."

"Yes, most fortuitous, for you," I assured, laughing again. "Perhaps your problem derives from your inability to pick up on polite hints."

"That has never been a problem before," Quinton bantered, as he took a large bite of scone and jam.

"I can assure you, that you would not make it in royal courts of Europe with your skill set," I teased, good naturedly.

"Perhaps not," he scoffed, choking on the dry scone as he looked past me.

I poured him more tea, then gave him a hefty clap on the back. Still coughing, Quinton put his hand up to warn me off as another round of coughing spasms irrupted. His face turning red as he took the offered cup from my hand, taking a deep sip of tea, quickly spatting it out, when it scalded his tongue. I ran to fetch some cold water, when Quinton jumped up, hopping about with his tongue hanging out.

"What the Devil is all of this?" Brody admonished, startling me in the process. I gasped, grabbing at my chest, then turned to witness him leaning against the doorjamb, with his arms folded across his chest, eyeing his brother suspiciously.

"Your brother was choking on a scone, and then burned his tongue on some hot tea." I retorted, bringing the glass of water to Quinton, who gratefully took it, downing the contents. "What are you doing lurking about in darkened corners?" I scrutinized, wondering how long he had been standing there and just how much he had witnessed.

"Something woke me and I couldn't go back to sleep," Brody answered, pushing off the doorjamb to join us, still staring his twin down.

"I have more tea and another scone," I said nervously, jumping up to retrieve another set of dishes. "How do you take your tea?"

"I will gladly take it any way you choose to give it to me," Brody answered, glowering at Quinton one last time, before possessively taking the seat next to me, as if warning him again that I was spoken for.

His double entendre was not lost on me. "Well, isn't this cozy," I stated, with sarcasm, while Quinton and Brody sized one another up. "Now all we need is for someone else to join us and we can have ourselves a proper party or perhaps a game of cards."

Brody and Quinton both mumbled something incoherent under their breath before taking a sip of tea. Brody leaned back in his chair first, giving me an innocent smile, waiting for me to look the other way, before throwing a piece of scone at Quinton's head. Quinton retaliated in kind by throwing a piece back, which missed and landed in my lap.

Eyeing the offending pastry in my lap before looking up, I casually flicked it from my lap. "In my day, I would have been sent to my room, straight away, if I dared to throw food at my sibling. Maybe you should try sticking your tongues out at one another, to make this childish display more complete." I scolded, taking another sip of tea. "You both realize someone will have to clean this mess up," I added, as they both postured in a threatening manner. "Honestly, the two of you are acting like spoiled children," I said, hoping to shame them before leaning back in my chair.

Just then the clock chimed three times and I saw Brody motioning with his head for Quinton to disappear. I glanced at Quinton, who was stubbornly staying put with his arms folded over his chest, as if to say, *I'm not budging*. The look of consternation on Quinton's face caused me to laugh out loud as I stood up, placed the tea pot, plates and silverware back upon the tray, finished or not. I didn't care, I was done. I carried the entire tray over to the counter and placed it down with a loud clatter. "Well, gentlemen, and I use that term loosely, I believe I will turn in. Please, excuse me," I said, blowing out the two candles on the table, then picking up the one I brought down with me, I began to walk from the room.

"Hold up, I'll come with you," Brody quickly said, jumping to his feet to follow me.

"I'm coming too," Quinton echoed, sounding nervous. "The last place I want to be is sitting here alone in the dark."

"Three's a crowd, Quinton, get your own girl," Brody grumbled, elbowing Quinton in the stomach as he caught up to us.

Smiling to myself, I was somehow entertained by their sibling rivalry. It was a little endearing. "You're not afraid of the dark, are you Quinton?" I teased.

"No!" Quinton answered too quickly, as he jumped at a shadow and clutched his chest. "I just don't like it much," he added, taking the steps two at a time, making sure that he was in the circle of light cast by the single candle in my hand. "I'm not afraid!" he insisted, reaching behind me to punch Brody in the arm when he chuckled, then outright laughed.

"Brody, don't be unkind. It's very unbecoming," I chided, jabbing my elbow into his side when he opened his mouth to tease Quinton further.

"What? It's funny," Brody added innocently.

"It's rude," I scolded, turning my attention back to Quinton. "Here, you carry the candle, so I can hold the hem of my robe up. There's nothing worse than tripping on steps, and it would be a shame if I started the back staircase on fire, before the big party. By the way, how many people are you expecting for this birthday celebration of yours?"

Gratefully taking the candle from me, Quinton sweetly slipped a hand under my elbow, to guide me up the steps. At this point, Brody's eyes bulged out and I thought he was going to bust a vein in his head. He then took a hold of my other arm, while I lifted the front of my night gown and robe up off the step.

"I feel like a delicate rose between two rather prickly thorns," I teased.

Both Brody and Quinton pointed at the other simultaneously saying, "he's the thorn."

"I believe I said two thorns," I stated flatly.

"The last two years we have had about a hundred and fifty people, give or take a few. Wouldn't you agree, Quinton?"

"We were up to a hundred and sixty-eight guests last year, dear brother," Quinton corrected playfully.

"I stand corrected."

"Wow!" I gasped. "Why do you invite so many people?"

"Our birthday parties have become legendary," Brody grinned. "Every year, some crazy, unexplainable phenomenon happens," he said with a shrug, "and well, word has spread. People just show up, with presents in hand, for the opportunity to witness what will happen next."

"After all, it would be rude to turn people away when they come bearing gifts," Quinton added, with a sly grin.

"What sort of unexplainable phenomena are we talking about?" I questioned with horror, stopping mid-step.

Quinton looked up as he thought on the matter. "Oh, remember when the fireplace shot out flames that one year, and nearly caught Father and Jackson on fire?" he chuckled nervously.

"You mean the year Father's coat tails were singed and he smelled like a smoke house the rest of the night," Brody confirmed, bringing his balled-up hand to his mouth, to stifle a chuckle. "Oh, oh, how about the time Mrs. Elliot claimed she was merely looking for the washroom, but made a wrong turn and ended up in Mother's library instead."

"I still remember her shrill screams as she ran all the way down the hallway, babbling incoherently, about the books trying to kill her," Quinton laughed, grabbing his side, trying to speak through the fits of laughter. "Remember when the two… chandel… chandeliers spontaneously burst into flames, melting wax all over the third course, six years ago?

"I believe that it was the second course, and it was five years ago."

"I stand corrected," Quinton conceded.

"Remember how the wax dripped onto Mr. Edgar's new wool wig and then into his soup? What a mess," Brody added, with another burst of laughter, before looking up at me and seeing the horror on my face. Straightening up and clearing his throat, Brody tried to stop laughing, taking ahold of my arm again. His only mistake was looking over at Quinton, which resulted in the two of them dissolving into another round of riotous laughter, forcing them to both sit down on the nearest step.

I stood over them, perplexed by their childish antics. "How can either one of you laugh at such things?" I asked bewildered.

"You had to be there," they said simultaneously.

Shaking my head in disgust, a foul odor drifted in the air and I put my nose up and sniffed the air. "Do you smell that?"

"I don't smell anything," Quinton answered, reaching down to pull Brody to his feet.

"That sulfur smell. You really don't smell it?" I questioned, turning to the top of the stairs while pushing Quinton's arm up. "Would you mind lifting that candle a bit higher," I nervously squinted into dark, before gasping out loud.

Dark, angry eyes stared back at me, shooting daggers in my direction as *she* made her intentions very clear.

Brody grabbed my arm, turning me towards him. "What is it, Olivia? What do you see?" he asked, giving me a slight shake when I didn't immediately answer him. "Do you see something at the top of the stairs?"

Suddenly, an intense rush of air blew past us, putting out the candle in Quinton's hand. I heard the candlestick hit the steps and roll all the way to the bottom of the staircase.

"Quinton!" I cried, trying to break free of Brody's vise-like grasp as he pulled me protectively against his chest. "Brody, where is Quinton? What happened to him?"

"Quinton, answer me. Quinton!" Brody called out, in the dark.

"Brody, make your way back down to the kitchen and get another candle," I insisted.

With his lips near my ear, Brody quietly whispered, "What the Devil just happened, Olivia? What was that?"

"That was a warning shot fired directly across our bow," I answered with an involuntary shiver before stepping down one step. "Go, Brody. Hurry! We need to find Quinton. I will feel my way to the wall, while you make your way down the stairs." His hesitation was palpable, and squeezed his hand tightly. "Please, Brody, you need to hurry. If you had seen her face…"

"Who, Olivia, who's face?" Brody's voice shook with emotion, as he spoke quietly to me in the dark.

"Your mother's. She was very angry about something," I added solemnly, fear caused my voice to shake.

"I'll be right back, don't move a muscle, Olivia. I mean it, don't you move."

"Don't worry about me, you just be careful." I cautioned, sitting down on the step and bringing my knees up, hugging them to my chest to try to stop from shaking.

A loud clattering noise from the kitchen made me jump. "Brody, what was that noise? Are you hurt?" I called, "Brody? Brody! Answer me!"

A soft glow of light came around the corner and was headed up the stairs towards me. "Do I hear concern in your voice?"

"What was all that noise?" I questioned between clenched teeth, trying to stop my them from chattering.

"I found myself wrestling with a chair. But not to worry, I won," Brody teased, coming up the stairs, casting a soft glow. As he came closer with the light, I frantically looked for Quinton. He was against the wall, three steps above me, in a fetal position, neither speaking nor moving.

Crawling up the steps, I closed the distance between us in seconds. "Quinton! Quinton, are you hurt?" I cried, gently touching his arm and then his face. "Please, Quinton, answer me."

"Quinton!" Brody called, shoving the candle into my hand. "Here, hold this," he ordered, pulling Quinton to his feet, placing an arm around him and leading him up the steps. I scurried around to the other side of Quinton, placing my free arm around him, locking arms with Brody. We slowly made our way up the remainder of steps and down the hallway to Quinton's room.

Reaching the room, I ran ahead, placed the candle on the night stand and pulled back the covers so Brody could lower Quinton into bed. Then scooping his feet up and removing his slippers in one motion, Brody lovingly tucked Quinton in.

"He will be fine in the morning," Brody assured me, not bothering to retrieve the candle, but instead guiding me toward the door. "He just needs sleep."

"So, this has happened before?" I questioned, stopping abruptly.

"Well, ah, yes ... a few times." Brody stammered, sounding unsure of how he should answer.

"And you knew that he was deathly afraid of the dark, and you still teased him," I said accusingly, narrowing my eyes.

"Well, yes, but I would never betray Quinton by revealing his secrets to a stranger outright."

"But you would tease and taunt him in front of me?" I said slowly, with a disapproving tone.

"We are brothers," he justified, "that is what we do. Surely you of all people understand the complicated relationship between siblings. You and your sister are very close. Right?" Brody reasoned. "Do you not tease one another, from time to time?"

"Well, yes, but we would never say or do anything to hurt the other. Especially if it had something to do with the other's greatest fear," I stated flatly. "Look at him, Brody, Quinton is laying there nearly catatonic. Why aren't you more concerned?"

"I am concerned, Olivia. I'm not a monster. It's just that there's nothing that can be done for him right now. He needs to sleep it off. Quinton will come out of this when he is ready," Brody reasoned, as he looked back at his brother. Then placing a reassuring hand on my shoulder, Brody continued. "I promise you, Olivia, Quinton will be just fine. He has been afraid of the dark ever since Mother died. There is no explanation for it and I don't know what happened that night because he won't talk about it." He continued, "Quinton's closed up tighter than a clam shell. So I don't know what caused this sudden fear to occur because he won't tell me," Brody explained, diverting his gaze behind me.

"I'm sorry, Brody, I never meant to imply that you were a monster," I said gently, placing a hand on his chest. Our eyes locked and I could see the love he had for Quinton. It was reflected in his eyes, even in the dark. "It was just…"

"What, Olivia?" Brody interrupted harshly. "You were curious because we look so much alike."

"What are you talking about?"

"Maybe you intended to sample us both and decide which one of us you liked better?" Brody said, emotion causing his voice to crack with a subtle disapproving tone.

"What are you talking about?" I repeated, confused by the sudden change in direction of our conversation.

"In the kitchen, earlier," Brody answered defensively, "when you and my brother were holding hands."

"I assure you, that it was not what you think," I countered. "Is that what you thought was going on between your brother and me?" I questioned, feeling anger bubbling up inside, staining my cheeks crimson. "Because I can assure you, sir, that nothing like that has ever crossed my mind." Turning my back on Brody, I took the last few steps to the door and yanked it open, only to have the handle knocked from my hand.

"I don't believe we are through talking."

"I beg to differ," I answered, angrily whirling around and placing my back against the door as I shot him a withering glare. "Perhaps I need to remind you that I am a woman, adequately able to protect my own self interests." I added, purposely placing my hand into my robes pocket, to finger the cold smooth steel of my dagger. "I've trained in hand to hand combat since I was twelve years old. My father insisted upon it. So, if you would like to give it a go, I'm game if you are," I stated menacingly.

Giving me a measured look, Brody nervously laughed. Then stepping closer, he placed a cautious hand upon mine, stopping me from drawing my blade. "No," he smiled, "I don't believe that I need reminding," he said, looking properly chastised. "Though I admit the thought that you and Quinton planned a secret rendezvous had crossed my mind, I see how ridiculous it was. I was jealous when I witnessed you and Quinton in the kitchen together …"

Giving him a haughty glare, "Why, that is simply the most asinine, pompous, arrogant …" I began sputter angrily at him, when Brody lowered his head and kissed me into silence. Bringing his free hand slowly up, he placed it behind my neck to pull me closer and deepen the kiss.

At first I was annoyed at him and wanted nothing to do with his obvious ploy to silence the stream of angry words. Seconds passed and I found myself placing my pot of boiling scorn on the back burner as I melted into his solid form. The heat from his body penetrated through the thin material of my night clothes and spread through me like a wildfire. My body had a mind of its own as my fingers became hopelessly entangled in his thick tresses. Our bodies molded together as if we were one, and I become lost in the moment as time stood still. The trauma of the past few minutes disappeared, like a puff of smoke. The only thing that was real to me in that moment was the man standing before me, wrapping his arms around me.

Pulling back slowly, Brody brought his hand to his chest and rested it over his heart, looking repentant. "I am a simple a man, flawed and full of weaknesses. I sincerely beg for your forgiveness. I had no right to accuse you of such duplicity."

Taking a moment to catch my breath before answering, I smoothed back the strands that had fallen into my face. "I will forgive you this once," I said pointedly, lifting an eyebrow at him, "but if you ever accuse me of duplicity again —"

"I won't!" Brody swore, crossing his heart and then left his hand resting over it.

"And by the way, I am still angry with you," I added, lifting my chin slightly.

"I know," he said, giving a good-natured chuckle. "I would be surprised if you weren't," Brody added, opening the door behind me. "Shall I walk you to your room?" he questioned, reaching for my elbow and gesturing toward the open door with his hand as he followed me through.

"No, thank you, I will walk myself back to my room," I said coolly. "Perhaps I am less afraid of all the many things that go bump in the dark than I am of you," I admonished.

"How can you say that?" Brody nearly whined, his voice shooting up an octave.

"Easy. I know how to handle things that go bump in the night, but you …" I let out a heavy sigh, "you are complicated," I answered, stopping to retie my sash. Then with another sigh I continued. "And then there is the other matter to consider." Brody patiently waited for me to finish adjusting my robe and look up at him.

"Oh, and what matter would that be?" He queried, with good-natured curiosity.

"I haven't decided yet whether I entirely like you."

Brody thought I was merely joking and laughed it off, until he saw the look in my eyes. "Oh, now you are just being cruel," he concluded dramatically, clutching his heart.

"Go ahead, play the court jester. But you need to take me seriously right now," I pointed out, walking down the hallway by myself in the dark. "Perhaps we should both sleep on it?" I called over my shoulder. He was flabbergasted, making a ridiculous sound as I walked away. I had to smile because Mr. Brody Beaumont had just received a proper comeuppance.

I continued down the hallway and turned a corner when Brody caught up to me as I reached my door. Stepping through the doorway, he placed a hand gently on my arm and I stopped, giving him a slow, but deliberate look. A long silent moment passed and neither one of us spoke. It was at that moment I saw uncertainly in his eyes.

"I'm tired, Brody," I said gently, placing a hand against his chest, to force distance between us. Ignoring my deliberate blockade, he pulled me closer and I knew I was susceptible to his charms. My emotions were all over the place. One moment I wanted him with every fiber of my being, and the next, he infuriated me to no end. I suddenly felt drained, unable to sort through what was between us. "I'm certainly too tired to spar with you again tonight."

He slowly nodded his agreement, then ever so tenderly, he cupped my chin and stared longingly into my eyes. Another long silence passed before he leaned down, placing a kiss upon one eye lid and then the other. I felt his warm breath against my cheek just before his lips touched my lips. I experienced the melting of my emotional iceberg, as the heat of that one simple kiss was felt all the way to the soles of my feet. I also felt the depth of his unspoken words as they touched my heart, nearly causing me to forgot my resolve.

A sound that was somewhere between a sigh and a gasp escaped my lips as Brody slowly ended our very intimate kiss. And without another word, he disappeared into the darkness of the halls like a shadow in the night.

17

WEDNESDAY, FEBRUARY 11, 1804

A Good Romance Will Either Grow and Bloom,
Or Wither and Die on The Vine

I TOSSED AND TURNED THE REST of that morning, unable to find a comfortable spot. The bed was either too lumpy or my pillow would go flat in one spot, but whatever the reason, I could not sleep.

Margot bustled through the door with a tray of tea and raisin scones still warm from the oven. "It's a beautiful morning, Miss, time to rise and shine," she gleefully announced, placing the tray down upon the table. The fire glowed warmly in the hearth as Margot opened the drapes with a sweeping motion, securing them back with a sash.

"What makes this day so beautiful, compared to any other?" I complained, sitting up in bed, shoving stray hairs from my face.

"It does appear someone has had a restless night's sleep and awaken on the wrong side of the bed," Margot cheerfully said, picking my robe up from off the floor, patiently waiting for me to drag myself out of bed. Coco picked that moment to walk through the adjoining room door.

"Good morning, dear sister. How did you sleep?" Coco asked, before being diverted by the smell of warm pastries. "Oh, scones, my favorite!" she blurted out randomly.

"Why is everyone so cheery today?" I grumbled sourly as I walked over to the fire to warm myself. "It truly is disgusting. I hope you made extra strong tea this morning, Margot."

"Rough night?" Coco questioned, with her usual, *I know your hiding something from me* tone. Taking a large bite of her scone, she paused a moment to look up at me. "Good heavens, Olivia, you look like *hell*."

"Very funny, ha, ha," I said, without any real humor.

"Here you go, Olivia, nice and strong," Margot assured, handing me a cup and saucer.

"Do you wish to talk about it?" Coco absently asked, diverting her eyes downward, trying not to sound too eager.

Looking at her over the rim of my tea cup, I took a moment to ponder exactly how much truth I would divulge. "I couldn't sleep, so I went down stairs in search of a scone and a cup of tea when I ran into Quinton, who, by the way, I innocently mistook for Brody. But only for a moment!" I emphasized. "But then Brody showed up and was jealous because he thought Quinton and I had planned a secret rendezvous." I continued in a blur of words, spilling my guts out before I could think twice about it. "And as we were all going up stairs together, Annabelle decided to make an appearance and scare Quinton nearly to death. So, Brody and I were putting him to bed, when we got into it —" Interrupting me at that point, Coco sat on the edge of her seat with a cup of tea in one hand and a half eaten scone in the other.

"So, when you say you and *Brody* got into it, do you mean that the two of you argued, or kissed?" se asked breathlessly, a look of anticipation on her face.

I looked at her then paused a moment. "Well, we argued, then we kissed, but I wish to point out, he kissed me to keep me from yelling any further at him."

Coco laughed. "He's smarter than I gave him credit for."

"It was at that point I told him I wasn't sure if I truly liked him or not."

"Oh, no you did not!" Coco scolded, placing her scone on her plate, and pinching the bridge of her nose. "Olivia Sophia Allen Townsend, you are the most infuriating person —" she said, emphasizing the word *infuriating*. "What in Heaven's name am I going to do with you?"

"Are you going to keep interrupting me, or do you want to know what happened next?" I snapped.

"Yes, yes, please go on," she waved her hand in the air, a gesture I'd seen our mother do a hundred times, and was struck by how similar the two of them had become. Shaking my head, to banish the image from my thoughts, I turned, placing my tea cup down on the mantle, before continuing.

"Where was I?"

"You had just said that you were not sure whether you liked Mr. Beaumont, or not," Margot interjected, looking up at me while she continued to make the bed.

"Oh, yes, yes, of course," I muttered. "He thought I was joking!"

"Then what happened?" Coco prodded.

"Well, then he laughed, until he realized that I was serious and we had a few more words and then —" I paused, not sure if I should tell her the rest.

"And then?" Coco prompted again when I didn't immediately continue.

I was looking into the burning fire when I happened to glance up and see Coco and Margot staring at me with a look of anticipation. Like a stage performer who has forgotten their lines, I considered my options and decided to leave my audience hanging on my last words. "And then the witch said to the little children …"

"Honestly, Olivia, that is so unfair of you," Coco pouted, putting down her tea and scone and Margot shrugged her shoulders and continued making the bed.

Coco stood up suddenly and covered the distance between us in three strides and just for a split second I feared she would strike me. I cringed when she grabbed me by the shoulders and shook me. "You started the story, darn you, tell me what happened."

I was about to say something snide, when someone knocked on the door. I was grateful for the distraction and excuse not to finish my tale. "Margot, would you mind getting that?" I suggested, while peeling Coco's finger off me. Picking up my tea cup, I sipped the luke-warm liquid, barely able to refrain from spitting it back into the cup.

Stomping her foot, Coco growled in disgust. "Honestly, Olivia, you can be so infuriating!" I smiled behind my cup and turned to see who had come to call on us so early in the morning. It was two of the upstairs maids.

"Our sincerest apologies for disturbing you, my lady. I am Jane, and this is Mildred," she began, casting her eyes downward. "We were directed to bring these dresses up to you immediately. They are for the costume party Saturday night. Mr. Beaumont thought they may need some alterations, and wished for you to have time to have them properly fitted."

"Put them both in the dressing room, we will look at them later," I instructed, waving my hand.

"Oh no, Miss, Mr. Beaumont was very specific about the dresses. If it is all the same to you, Mildred will place your sister's dress in the other room and I will hang this one up for you in your dressing room," Jane said politely, correcting me before dropping into a quick curtsy while lowering her eyes to the ground again. Then they both shuffled off, only to return a moment later.

Mildred stepped forward, bobbing her head and curtsied, a show of respect. "If there is nothing else you require, Jane and I will return at two for your first fitting. If that is acceptable, of course," she added, diverting her eyes and folding her hands into her apron.

"Thank you, Mildred, Jane, my sister and I will make ourselves available and we are most grateful for your assistance," I smiled, placing myself between the ladies and the door. "I wonder if I might delay you both a moment longer."

"What can we do for you, my lady?" Jane said, eyeing me cautiously.

"Would either one of you care for a scone? They are still warm," I offered with a gracious smile, sweeping my hand as I gestured for them sit.

"Regrettably, we must decline, Miss," Jane answered with an equally gracious smile, refusing to take the offered seat which forced me to remain standing.

"Then I will get straight to the point," I began, stepping closer to the two ladies. "I was wondering if either one of you were employed with the Beaumonts eight years ago and if you may have witnessed what transpired the night Mrs. Beaumont," I paused, hoping I wasn't being too indelicate, "died?"

The ladies merely glanced at each other before Mildred cleared her throat and Jane looked away nervously. Some secret message passed between them, but was quickly masked by propriety.

"Is that a yes or no, ladies?" Coco asked, bluntly.

"Begging your pardon, my lady, I am uncomfortable speaking on the matter, after what happened to Dusty," Mildred quickly spoke up when she saw Jane open her mouth to say something.

"You mean Sam. His name was Sam, not Dusty," I corrected, hoping that knowing the boy's real name would buy me some credibility with them. "Please ladies, I truly need to know what happened eight years ago. It could be a matter of life or death. I promise not to divulge anything you might tell me," I pleaded, hoping that I didn't sound too desperate. "I just need to know what happened to her."

Jane stepped forward, even after Mildred gave her a warning glare. "We both worked here eight years ago. I was new and had only been working for the Beaumonts for seven months when it all happened. Mildred here, started two years before me and was Mrs. Beaumont's personal maid. She could tell you better than me what really happened that night," Jane announced. I looked at Mildred, but the expression on her face, told me that I wasn't getting anything out of her. "But I doubt she will say anything to you. Her lips have been sealed tighter than a wine bottle ever since that night."

Taking Mildred by the hand, I led her over to the settee and forced her to sit down next to me. "Margot, hot tea please," I asked, holding out my hand when Margot brought the cup over, all the while maintaining eye contact with Mildred.

Mildred opened her mouth to protest, but then thought better of it, and closed her mouth with a slight scowl on her lips. I handed her the saucer with a fresh cup of hot tea on it.

"Now, where were we? Oh yes, you were about to tell me what transpired the night of the party eight years ago," I asserted, as if it were only a matter of time before she spilled her life's story to me.

At first Mildred sat there, with the steaming cup of tea in her hand, opening and closing her mouth, like a fish out of water. "Mildred, please. I wouldn't ask such a betrayal of you if this wasn't important," I implored. It wasn't long after that Mildred began to talk, as if she had been waiting for the right person to come along, so she could unburden herself of the secret from that night. And apparently, I had the right key. I noticed Mildred's hand was shaking, as she set the saucer and cup down on the table between us, without taking a sip.

Clearing her throat, Mildred began to speak. "I may have been Mrs. Beaumont's maid, but there were things that she kept even from me. All I know with certainty is that Mrs. Beaumont was very nervous the night of the party."

"Why do you say that?" I asked, perplexed by that statement.

"Because when I was putting her hair up that evening, she wouldn't stop fidgeting. It was as if she couldn't keep still," Mildred said, lifting her eyes gazing directly into mine. "I think it had something to do with her disagreement with her son that day. Just before I entered her room I overheard, Mrs. Beaumont and her son having a heated argument, which they abruptly cut off, when I came in the room."

"Which son?" I questioned.

Mildred swallowed hard and looked up and to the right, as if she was trying to remember. "I couldn't tell you for sure because I never looked up. Mrs. Beaumont didn't like us looking directly at her."

Licking my lips, I continued, "Well, did you hear what they were arguing about?"

Mildred nervously rubbed her hands together and began to squirm in her seat. Shaking her head, she answered. "No, not really. I always try to be respectful of my employer's privacy. I'm not an eavesdropper."

"I would never think such a thing of you, Mildred. I was just hoping to have some sort of idea of what happened before the terrible event," I gently prodded, touching her hand. "Is there anything else you can remember from that night?"

"Just that Mr. Beaumont, her husband, found the body. That is all I remember," Mildred concluded.

I saw Mildred's eyes begin to glisten and could tell that our conversation was upsetting her. Squeezing her arm, I said, "I would like to thank you for speaking with me. You've been very helpful."

"We really must return to our duties now, my lady. If there is nothing more, Mildred and I will return at two for your fittings," Jane said, interrupting us as she pulled her friend up off the couch. Placing a comforting hand around Mildred's waist, she led her to the door. I waited for the door to close completely, before I spoke.

"Well, that was somewhat enlightening," I stated ambiguously.

"You're kidding, right? She didn't tell you anything," Coco complained, as she walked over to stand in front of me, with her arms folded across her chest.

Smiling up at her, I stood and headed for my dressing room. "Oh Coco, you are so wrong. We learned that the night of the incident Annabelle was acting out of character. She was nervous and fidgety. We also know that one of the twins fought with his mother. Apparently it was very heated, yet we do not know what they discussed," I said, holding up the beautiful dress Jane had left for me. Silently I studied it a moment. The material was made of silky, red Chiffon and was very exquisite. Not your run of the mill red, but a deep, rich, burgundy red, so vibrant it took my breath away.

Looking at my reflection in the mirror, holding the dress up in front of me, I began to speak again. "We know that Annabelle's husband found her body the night of the incident, but the thing we still don't know, is how she drowned or…" I added, turning to find Coco and Margot standing two feet away, hanging on every word.

"Or, what Olivia?" Coco asked, with anticipation.

"Or who may have drowned Annabelle that night," I concluded, then waited for their reaction.

"You aren't serious?" Coco gasped.

"We can't rule out the fact that Annabelle may have been murdered," I admonished, hanging the dress back up. "It makes sense. Anabelle is angry. I know I, for one, would be angry if someone had drowned me and got away with it. If we can figure out what happened to Annabelle Beaumont maybe, just maybe, we can figure out what happened to Lilly."

"Olivia, we could resolve the entire matter so much faster if you would allow me go around touching people."

"Yes, but you know how it drains you when you do. Besides, after what happened the last time you touched someone, I'm not so sure that it would be prudent to tempt fate again. Annabelle is still lurking about," I added, touching her, expressing concern. "I do not wish to duplicate the experience. Do you?" I asked.

"No!" she answered emphatically. "I do not!"

"Then we will do this my way, and you will keep your gloves on."

18

The Green-Eyed Monster of Jealousy Comes to Call

TAKING CARE TO DRESS IN layers for warmth, I donned a green, long-sleeve, wool gown and sweater. The weather had taken a turn for the worse, and the skies were overcast, threatening rain at any time. With one last look in the mirror, I headed toward the door. "Margot, tell Coco I was tired of waiting for her and have gone downstairs," I called over my shoulder from the doorway. "Oh, and Margot, don't forget we are meeting back here at two for the fittings."

"I have not forgotten," Margot called back, stepping out of the dressing area with her arms laden down with clothes that needed to be washed or mended.

I smiled and closed the door. Walking to the stairs, I looked over the railing to see who was about, but only saw a maid quickly walking through the lobby toward the kitchen. Descending the stairs and through a hallway, I entered the sunroom and found my mother, father, Harrison and Prince William enjoying a leisurely cup of tea and pastries. Father and Harrison were discussing cotton business while Mother and the prince were having a lively conversation regarding matters of trade and commerce. I looked around the room but didn't see Brody or Quinton. I leaned over to whisper in Mother's ear.

"Do you happen to know where I might find Brody or Quinton?" blessing William with a brilliant smile as I stood up again.

"They left us an hour ago," she replied, looking over at William. "Your highness, do you know where my daughter might find Quinton or Brody?" she sweetly smiled.

"I believe I overheard them discussing horses and I would suggest checking in the barn, my dear," he answered, looking at me over the rim of his cup as he signaled for more tea.

"Thank you both," I called out while grabbing a scone off the tray, giving Father a quick peck on the cheek and an impish smile. Narrowing his eyes at me, the way he usually did when he thought I was up to no good, he opened his mouth to say as much when I cut him off. "Tell Coco that I will be in the barn. That is if she ever comes down," I added before sauntering out of the room.

I wandered down the hallway and turned the corner that lead to the kitchen because it was the quickest way to the barn. "Cook, I am in love with these raisin scones," I gushed, waving what was left of the scone in my hand. "I don't know what you put in them, but they are simply heavenly pastries," I called out as I passed by, snatching up a handful of apples pieces and placing them in my pocket, in hopes of making friends with the horses.

"Thank you, my lady. Coming from you, that is high praise indeed," she said with a smile, pretending not to notice that I pilfered her cut apples.

Smiling to myself, I opened the door, then scratched Brody's dog on the head as I passed by her sitting at the back door waiting for scraps.

Everything was so normal and wonderful at the moment I could almost forget about all that had happened. And if someone didn't know any better, they would have thought that this was a wonderful place to live. I felt relaxed, and yet there was an underlying tension that hung in the air. The sun was peeking out from behind a cloud and just as quickly it was gone again. A chilly breeze whipped up, making me shiver. Walking through the garden, I smiled and grabbed a few mint leaves to freshen my breath.

I was humming a tune, when Lilly startled me. "Were you looking for me?" she asked, with a smile.

"I was actually looking for Brody and Quinton, but you will due," I said, as relief washed over me, grateful it was Lilly and not Annabelle. "Where have you been?" Then looking at her closer, I noticed that her coloring was off. "Is something wrong, Lilly? You look strange."

Lilly shivered and looked up at the sky. "It looks like rain," she said, with a sad smile playing across her lips. I began to feel very concerned at this point. It wasn't like her to not hear my question.

"I really don't know what is the matter with me, Olivia. I feel so cold all the time. But enough about me, how is Coco doing?" Lilly asked, trying to sound cheery.

"She has bounced back and doesn't appear to have any lingering effects," I responded, feeling slightly concerned as our conversation took on a tone of normalcy, except for the whole part about her being dead. "I did, however, have a run in with you-know-who earlier this morning. Well, let me clarify — Brody, Quinton and I had a run in with you-know-who."

"Oh, that sounds awful. So, tell me what happened."

"Turns out Quinton has an un-natural fear of the darkness and things that go bump in the night ever since his mother died eight years ago, and I'm not sure what to make of it yet."

"And the puzzle gets more curious with every piece you find and put into place," Lilly mused. I began to walk toward the barn again, while Lilly followed,

"That is what I was thinking. Have you been able to remember anything more from the night you —?" I began to say, before thinking better of it.

Lilly gave me a sad smile. "It's hard to say, Olivia. Sometimes I think I've remembered something, and that is important, then it all becomes a blur again, fading away from my thoughts like a puff of smoke," Lilly concluded, with a shrug of her slender shoulders. "Do you know what I'm trying to say?"

"It's alright, Lilly. I don't want you to worry about it. I will figure this out," I assured her. "I'm on my way to the barn, so you be safe. I have this uneasy feeling that we are sitting on a powder keg and someone has already lit the fuse," I uttered as I turned to leave.

"Olivia," Lilly called out in a small voice.

"Yes?" Turning back, I looked at her.

"I know I never said it enough when we were alive, but I want you to know how much I loved being your friend, Olivia Townsend," Lilly said, her eyes glistening with unshed tears as she pulled her shawl tighter around her shoulders. "You were always so good at listening without passing judgement on me. I really loved that about you."

"You were always a good friend to me too, Lilly," I replied, emotion causing the words to stick in my throat. "I hope you know that I would do anything for you. You are like a sister to me."

I watched as a tear fell down her cheeks as I choked back my own raw emotion and tears. Then her willowy form faded away. Wiping away the moisture clinging to my lashes with my fingers, I turned back toward the barn and began to walk. By the time I reached the barn, I had my emotions in check and had pasted a smile back upon my lips, before sliding the door open and stepping inside. I heard boisterous voices and laughter at the far side of the building, and headed in that direction. Brody and Quinton had the two horses Prince William had given them as a birthday gift, in one large stall.

I leaned against the wooden door and poked my head inside to see what they were doing. The large stallion nickered and snorted near my face, before smelling the apples I held out to him, which he eagerly ate.

"Good morning, gentlemen, and what might you be up to, on this fine but chilly day?" I asked, keeping a wary eye on the horse directly in front of me. "Oh, hello there, big fellow, want to be friends?" I asked, cautiously reaching out my one hand with apple in it, then scratching his head with the other.

"I thought you would never get up," Brody blurted out from the far corner of the stall.

I smiled and leaned in further to see exactly what he and Quinton were doing. "Girls will be girls. We need our beauty sleep. I'm glad to see that you are up and about, Quinton," I casually mentioned, noting the warning look in Brody's eyes as he shook his head. I took this as Brody's way of cautioning me away from commenting further on events that occurred earlier.

"Thank you for your concern, Olivia, but there is really no need for it," Quinton said gruffly, without really looking up from his work. His mood seemed to be on the sour side, so I continued in a cheerful tone, but not overly cheery. "Have you decided on names for your newly acquired stallion and brood mare?" I asked, ignoring Quinton's foul mood.

"Yes, I believe we have," Brody answered, then cleared his throat as he stood up and straightened his back as if he had been stooped over for a while. "Samson and Delilah," he continued, walking towards me with a wry smile. "And just for safety sake, I would stay away from Quinton today," he warned under his breath so that only I could hear him. "He has been like that since he got up this morning." Then adding loud enough for Quinton to hear, "I think he grew fangs in the middle of the night. To tell the truth, he kind of reminds me of a grizzly bear with a thorn stuck in his paw."

Quinton was not so amused, grousing under his breath, something about a thorn up someone's posterior region before overly exaggerating his laugh, while he scraped at Delilah's hoof.

Brody ignored Quinton's slight, choosing to lean on the door by me and slyly touch my hand. "So, to answer your original question, Quinton and I are putting the two love birds together, to see if they are amenable to the idea of... well, you know, procreating." Brody said, giving me a sly look, then a wink.

I turned three shades of red, before recovering my composure as I pulled my hand back suddenly. "Oh, OH!" I gasped, taking a step back from the stall door, which caused Brody to throw his head back and laugh out loud.

A carriage pulled up outside, followed by loud, boisterous shouts of greetings. It was then that Quinton perked up, shoved a couple of tools into his back pocket. At the same time he pulled out a handkerchief to wipe his hands off.

"Who the devil could that be?" Brody questioned, scrubbing his hand across his stubbly face.

"I will give you three guesses and the first two don't count," Quinton grinned widely, followed by nasty chuckle. "The Olson's have arrived."

Brody groaned and a look passed between them before he unlatched the door and stepped out of the stall, followed by Quinton, who slapped his brother roughly on the back as he passed.

"Who are the Olson's and why do the two of you look like that?"

"Nothing but pure trouble in skirts." Brody said, taking my arm as he guided me through the barn. Quinton ran ahead and was already outside with the others. "I suppose you will have to meet them sooner or later, and now is as good a time as any," he said, pulling me along as if we were going to a funeral. "The Olson sisters have only missed two of our gatherings since we were ten."

As we stepped through the door, I saw Quinton lifting a young woman off the ground and spinning her around in a circle as she squealed with delight. Then he lifted the next young woman down from the carriage in the same manner. She had been waiting eagerly for her turn.

"Oh, Quinton Beaumont, you are a sight for sore eyes. Why, just look at you, so big and strong." The second girl was gushing just as Brody and I walked up.

"Why, Thomas Olson, you old dog, I thought you would never get here," Harrison boisterously yelled, slapping the man on the back as everyone stood around. "And this couldn't possibly be little Emily, or Patricia Olson, now could it? No, it couldn't be," he teased. "You are too grown up and beautiful to be those scrawny little girls."

Emily, the youngest sister, threw herself into Harrison's arms with another shrill scream. "Uncle Harrison, you just say the nicest things!" she cried with a thick southern drawl.

"Give us a big squeeze, Uncle Harrison," Patricia insisted, shoving her sister aside when their hug lasted too long for her.

Emily immediately turned toward Brody, breaking out in to a large grin. "Why Brody Beaumont, I can't believe you haven't given me some sugar yet," Emily whined, eyeing me as if I were nothing more than the lowly help, before throwing herself into Brody's arms. "Tell me how much you've missed me, cousin," she pouted, poking her bottom lip forward, "because I thought I would die if I had to go another year without seeing you two."

With a stiff smile, Brody quickly hugged Emily, then tried to peel her off of him. "Ladies, allow me to introduce you to Lady Olivia Townsend. Olivia, this is Emily and Patricia Olson, our second cousins, from Carolina."

I smiled pleasantly, giving Emily my best aristocratic once over. She was a pretty girl, on the lanky side of tall, with golden curls neatly styled and pinned upon her head. Her big blue eyes registered shock as I began to speak. "Miss Olson, it is a pleasure to meet you," I said, holding myself as regally as I could, nodding my head in her direction before turning toward her sister, Patricia, to my right. With a stiff smile and bored stare, I gave her my once over as well before speaking. "Please, allow me to introduce you both to my family," I gestured with my hand. "This is my younger sister, Lady Catherine Elizabeth, my mother, the Countess of Buckinghamshire, Lady Isabella Townsend and my Father, the second Earl of Buckinghamshire, The Right Honorable Lord Lieutenant of Ireland," I concluded with a satisfied smile, when Emily Olson's perfectly manicured, blond eyebrows shot up as recognition and horror bleached the color from her cheeks. Lifting the front of her gown and dropping into an immediate, deep curtsy, she then stood, placing her hand across her chest. My self-gratification was shallow, I know, but to see Miss Emily Olson receive her comeuppance, was worth it. I couldn't help smiling inwardly as she stood upright again, trying to make eye contact with me before diverting her gaze.

"Please forgive my sister," Patricia said, not really sounding apologetically at all, as she stepped forward, dropping into a proper curtsy in front of my parents. Her eyes slowly wandered up to mine with a knowing look, before landing on Brody. "Well, I am waiting for a proper greeting, cousin," she admonished, showing a row of perfectly white teeth as she did so. Opening her arms wide to him, she took a step forward as her light blue eyes looked into mine with a cool calculating glance. Patricia Olson had sized me up and dismissed me as no great threat to her claim on Mr. Brody Beaumont. And did I miss the smug, satisfied smile that played across her lips as she looked at me once again, before she laid her southern charm on good and thick? No. "Why, Brody Beaumont, I do declare, you get more handsome every time I look at you," she gushed. "I just don't think I can stand it."

I was having difficulty reading his reaction as he gave her an even wider smile. "Why, Patricia Ann Olson, you big flatterer, you. As I live and breathe, you and your sister just get more and more southern with each passing year," he belted out, over-enthusiastically, causing Patricia and Emily to grin even more.

"Now, who is the big flatterer?" Patricia questioned, giving Brody a halfhearted slap to his arm.

Thomas Olson slapped Brody on the back, then Harrison Beaumont began to laugh and slap Thomas on the back. This, of course, turned into a big, loud hug fest between the men as they slapped one another on the back, as Quinton stood back and took it all in a big grin on his lips.

Putting an arm around Patricia and Emily, Quinton said, "You girls get settled in and I will send word to Jackson that you have arrived. Then it will truly be a proper reunion. Just like old times," he said, leading them to the house. "I was beginning to think you two weren't going to make it this year."

Patricia laughed and gazed knowingly at Brody over her shoulder. I could tell by that look in her eyes she was playing at some game, one in which she felt she had already won. "Why, that is simply ridiculous, Quinton," Patricia whined, oozing insincerity from every pour. "I truly couldn't wait to be here. Why, I was just telling Daddy how excited I was this year. Picking out a party dress was surely a fun, but not nothing could compare to being here with you and cousin Brody."

The sugary sweetness pouring from her lips was enough to make me gag. I caught myself rolling my eyes heaven-ward as Brody took my arm, pulling me along behind the procession.

19

Let the Games Begin

THE MOMENT WE ENTERED THE house, Patricia made her move. Refusing to make further eye contact with me, she placed herself between Brody and me. The second she saw Brody preparing to sit down next to me on the couch, she plopped herself between us and motioned for one of the servants to bring her a cup of tea. Then she began droning on and on about all the fun times she and Emily had here when they came for visits. Patricia not only monopolized the entire conversation, she sucked up all the air in the room.

"Oh, do you remember how much trouble we got into, a few years back, when we snuck off to the pond and went swimming?" Patricia laughed, giving Brody jab in the ribs with her elbow and a knowing look as she recounted the story to Jackson, Quinton and Emily. "I remember your mother was fit to be tied."

"That's because we didn't have any swimming attire and we all stripped down to our under clothes," Quinton added, between bouts of laughter. "And do you remember your mother's reaction, Patricia? I thought she was going to succumb to a fit of the vapors and faint dead away in the dirt."

"Quinton Beaumont, you know better than that," Emily chided, "Mother would never succumb in the dirt, that would be too common. She always waited until there was a comfortable chair nearby."

"Let's not forget my father taking me off to the shed for a personal discussion." Jackson added, holding his sides as he laughed. "At least that's what *he* called it."

"Whatever happened when you and your father took a walk to the shed?" Brody questioned. "As I recall, there weren't any tears streaking your cheeks when you returned. Though I do remember your face was very red."

Jackson looked sideways at the girls and then began to laugh some more. "My pops told me about the birds and the bees that day." Then with a wry smile, he asked, pointing at Brody, "Did you really think I got a switching that day?"

"Well, to be fair, we were only nine and eleven at the time," Emily pointed out, with a sidelong look at Quinton.

"Yes, and you were all old enough to know better," Harrison admonished with a tone of humor. "At least most of you, that is," he glanced over at his sons.

"Harrison, leave them alone. Those were some good times, my friend," Thomas confessed, sounding nostalgic. "My Mary always looked forward to our annual visits with your family. She certainly loved it here."

"She is sorely missed, bless her soul," Harrison said, raising his cup in the air.

Suddenly, a vase crashed to the floor in the corner of the room and we all jumped, turning to see what had happened. No one could see her, but I could. Annabelle stood next to the serving credenza, her face contorted in anger.

Harrison growled under his breath. "What the devil?"

The head footman turned to one of the other footmen and instructed him to fetch a broom and dust pan. "We will clean that up immediately, sir, my apologies. I'm sure that one of the maids left the vase too close to the corner earlier."

Harrison wore a scowl as he stared into the corner, and I wondered if he was imagining his dead wife standing there. "I don't care about all that. Just get it cleaned up and bring us a pot of fresh tea. Mine has gone cold," he ordered, looking suspiciously at the corner again.

"Yes, sir, straight away." And with a snap of his fingers, the head footman dispatched someone to fetch a fresh pot of tea and a new tray of pastries.

I glanced over at Brody, who had been staring at me. Taking a deep breath, I felt penned in by the number of people and spirits in one room. "If you will excuse me, I think I need some fresh air," I announced, standing up trying to present a pleasant smile to everyone present. Placing my cup and saucer down on the table in front of me, I took a step toward the doorway.

"If you don't mind the company, I think I would like some fresh air as well," Brody called out, jumping to his feet and following me.

"But Brody, it is simply too cold outside. Why, I think it is going to start raining any minute now, and you could catch your death," I heard Patricia call after him. Her grating whiny twang annoyed me, and I clenched my hands as I looked back to see if Brody was coming.

Giving Patricia and anyone who cared to look up from their pastry a wink and sheepish grin, he barely broke stride as he answered his cousin's protest, "All the better, dear cousin. I don't recall inviting you to join me."

I heard a slight feminine growl of anger, followed by a delicate stomp of her booted foot because she didn't get her way. I smiled to myself as I left the room and quickly headed for the front door. Taking the offered cape from the butler on my way out, I didn't slow down until I was well away from the house.

"Olivia, wait, slow down. Have you lost the ability to hear me?" Brody called out as he ran to catch up to me and reached out to put a hand on my shoulder and slow me down a little. "Was that my mother, who broke the vase?" he questioned.

Facing him now, I struggled to get my breathing under control. "Yes, and the look on her face was pure venom. I sensed that she was jealous over the fact that your uncle spoke so highly of his dearly departed Mary, and your father never mentioned her."

"You're shaking, Olivia. What aren't you telling me?" Brody asked, as I looked up. There was honest concern in his eyes when he took me by the arm. "Let's walk, shall we?" he suggested.

I simply nodded, then turned toward the forest as he put a steadying arm under mine. We walked in complete silence for a while before I began to relax again. "I hope your family doesn't judge me too harshly, but I had to leave. I felt like I couldn't breathe and needed to escape that room," I explained.

"My cousins can have that effect on people. They're both a couple of whirling-dervishes of chaos, especially Patricia," Brody said, laughing to himself.

Looking up at him, I pulled us to a stop, then turned to face him. "Tell me about your cousin, Patricia unless, of course, it is none of my business."

"There's nothing to really tell," he said, brushing a stray hair from my face before cupping my chin.

Pulling back slightly, I wasn't buying his story, and was unwilling to let it go. "You honestly don't expect me to believe that load of manure you're pushing down the road, do you? She has been here less than an hour and already I've seen the furtive glances that pass between you two. And please don't tell me that it is all a figment of my active imagination!" I said, stepping back, pushing his hand away.

"Alright, you deserve to know," he began, taking a step closer. "I was infatuated by her, once upon a time. We were very young and it truly was a long time ago. I no longer have any real feelings towards her."

Eyeing him suspiciously, I continued to press the point. "Then you wouldn't mind telling me how serious your non-relationship was with your second cousin Patricia." I said, pressing the point.

"The thing is, well, it's complicated," he started, attempting to dismiss the entire matter altogether as he took me by the hand and leading me down a path to the right. "Come on, I want to show you a pretty brook and one of my favorite meadows. Maybe we can see some deer."

After three steps, I pulled away, forcing him to stop again and look at me. "I don't believe your situation is so complicated maybe you could use small words so I can understand. I'm normally not a jealous woman," I admitted, taking a couple of deep breaths to regain control of my emotions. "But the truth is, I have never had a reason to be," I calmly concluded. I was searching his face, trying to get answers to the question my heart was asking, when I thought better of it. "You know what? Just forget it. I think I would like to be alone, if you don't mind," I said, turning to leave, when Brody grabbed my arm.

"Now wait just a dog-gone-minute. I never said I wouldn't tell you. I simply said it was complicated and maybe, if truth were told, a little embarrassing," Brody admitted, combing his fingers through his hair as he desperately looked around for someplace to sit down. Spotting a clearing twenty yards away, he pulled me along behind him to an old stump. "Sit," he ordered, pointing at the stump.

Crossed my arms over my chest, I narrowed my eyes at him, fully prepared to launch into a long winded, expletive-filled rant about not being his dog, when he realized how his words had come out. "I sincerely beg your pardon, my lady. Please, won't you have a seat?" He playfully gestured with a gallant sweep of his hand.

Exhaling my anger away, I obediently sat down on the stump and waited.

"Patricia, Emily, Quinton and I have always been friends. Some would say too close. But heck, we all grew up together. And I mean that literally and figuratively," Brody began cautiously. "When Quinton and I turned seven, we initiated Jackson into our little gang, mostly out of necessity, because he was always at our place," he said, with a forced smile, as he stopped and massaged the back of his neck, as if he was uncomfortable continuing. "Our parents left us kids alone, a lot! We played and explored as we saw fit and I have to say, it may not have been the best strategic move on our parents' part, but they were busy," he added as his voice and eyebrows both shot up, slightly.

"Oh, and why is that?" I asked, already sure that I knew the answer and would not like the it.

"Because we found ways of entertaining ourselves as we got older, that were not always appropriate," he answered sheepishly, as his voice went up another octave. "Patricia may or may not have been the one who taught me how to kiss and well —" he implied, pausing to let that bit of information fully sink in. I took this as an admission of guilt and wasted no time continuing my interrogation.

"So, what are you trying to tell me, Brody Beaumont? That you and your cousin Patricia were intimate?" I asked pointedly, as I stood and walked out into the meadow. "Are you in love with her?"

"No... no, No!" Brody repeated, following after me. "We were young and curious, and I was, well, a little naive. You must believe me, that isn't who I am, now. She isn't who I thought she was, and I definitely know that she isn't who I want to spend the rest of my life with," Brody stammered as he continued to trail behind me. "I made a mistake. I was young and stupid. I need you to say that you believe me. Olivia!" Taking ahold of my arm again, Brody gently turned me around to face him and I begrudgingly looked up. For several long, silent moments we stood there, face to face.

"Well, that depends," I began, attempting to sound stern, all the while staring at his lips. His mouth looked so soft and pliant, I couldn't stop imagining them pressed against mine. I tried to focus on his face. I even tried being angry at him again, but I couldn't muster the emotion.

"Really," his voice sounded hopeful, "and what does your decision depend upon?" he asked. Dragging my eyes up to meet his gaze, I chewed on my bottom lip, before answering. "Convince me that you are truly over your cousin Patricia and that you have put her behind you. Swear to me that her lips will never again touch yours and maybe I will believe you," I assured with a slight pout, pulling roughly on the lapels of his coat. The image of his lips touching someone other than mine disturbed me, no matter how much I told myself it was ridiculous.

Brody broke out into a large grin. "I swear to you today, that no other lips shall ever touch mine ever again, except yours. You know what this means, right?" He chuckled, when I looked confused. "We must seal the deal."

"But I'm still mad at you."

"I know of no better way to get beyond you anger than to kiss it away," Brody stated, pulling me closer, as he tipped my chin up and lowered his lips to mine possessively. Slowly parting my lips when I felt his tongue tentatively touch them, a moan of pleasure escaped my throat. I felt exhilarated and light-headed at the same time. My heart raced and he pulled me even closer. I sighed when Brody pulled his lips away and touched them to my cheek as he whispered in my ear. "My lips shall never desire another, I swear." Trailing passionate kisses down my throat to the sensitive hallows of my collar bone, again I moaned as my fingers tangled themselves through his thick mane. I reveled in the sensations he caused, tiny goose bumps traveled the length of my spine, while tiny little hairs on my arms and at neck stood on end. "I never want this feeling to end." I breathlessly whispered. "Don't stop, I beg you."

This was all the encouragement necessary to send him into a frenzy, as he began to nibble his way back up my throat to my earlobes. I could hear his breathing becoming harsh and labored as his lips returned to mine. Large, strong fingers cupped my face, before capturing my hand to kiss and nibbled at my sensitive fingertips and inner wrist. I marveled at the ease and grace in which he moved, giving me so much pleasure. An involuntary shudder shook my body and I could feel my toes curling up inside my shoes.

Threading fingers through his hair again, I pulled his lips to mine, but this time I heard Brody moan deep in his throat and felt him shudder when I reached my hand beneath his coat. In that moment, our emotions were so pure and honest. I never wanted it to end. I clung to his solid form, drawing strength and warmth from him. I found myself drawing in harsh, ragged breaths as my fingers dug into the solid flesh of his back, before grasping at the material of his shirt to pull it free. I desperately wanted to feel his bare flesh against my hands, at the same time I was cognizant of his hands pushing aside the cape I wore, to cup my suddenly swollen breast through the thin material of my gown.

My fingers explored the different texture of his smooth, unblemished skin and washboard stomach as I ran my hand up the thin thatch of hair near his navel. The sensation only fueled the fire and I was instantly rewarded when I felt him shudder again, followed by little goose bumps forming beneath my fingers.

I cried out, when his tooth nicked my lip, but all was forgotten, that is until Brody expelled a breath and then groaned deep in his throat. Slowly pulled away, he captured my hands in his. Taking several deep breaths, he whistled through his teeth. "I do declare, Miss Olivia, you could charm a bear out of his coat in the middle of winter." Brody confessed, combing his fingers through his hair before looking down at his shirt and state of undress. "But there is a point at which no man can turn back from, and I do believe, we have slid our toes over that line."

My face flushed and my lips felt swollen as I tried to breathe normally again. I know that I should have been ashamed, maybe even embarrassed, but I wasn't. Instead, I smiled up at him boldly. "Perhaps you are right, Mr. Beaumont, some of us don't need to practice with our second cousins, before we get it right." I quipped, dabbing at my swollen lips.

Brody's eyebrows shot up, and his draw became thicker. "Oh, now look who is full of themselves," he teased, tucking his shirt into his pants.

"If you're not careful, I just may have to wipe that wicked smile from your lips, Miss Sass," he announced, reaching out to tickle me, before stopping suddenly, looking concerned. "Hold on here, did I do that?" He inquired, pulling out a handkerchief, and dabbing the blood from my lip.

"Perhaps you're not as experienced as you give yourself credit for," I teased.

"Would that be sass coming again from those sweet lips of yours?" Brody playfully tested, before I snatched the handkerchief from him and ran, laughing as I fled.

Squealing loudly as he caught up to me, pulling us both to the ground, we tussled in the thick grass a few minutes and in between tickles and passionate kisses I begged and pleaded for mercy, giving him my best southern drawl with a full pout, just the way I'd seen Patricia do earlier. "Oh my, Brody Beaumont, I do declare, if you aren't just the biggest, strongest thing to come along since, well, I just don't know when. Why, I could just eat you up." I taunted with a straight face, before dissolving into hysterical laughter as Brody began to tickling me again. "Stop, stop… please, I'm begging you. Please!" I squealed, gasping for air.

"Why, Miss Olivia Townsend, I do believe you have an evil streak," Brody proclaimed. "I think we need to examine that aspect of your personality a bit more." Ceasing with the relentless tickling, he didn't allow me to catch my breath before leaning down and delivering another passionate kiss.

We were both so lost in the moment, that we never heard Quinton approach. Clearing his throat twice, very loudly, Quinton stood over us. "It's funny really that you and I grew up in the very same household, and yet, this is your definition of taking a walk to get some air. And to think I've been doing it wrong all these years," Quinton admonished coolly, giving us a few seconds to digest his subtle reprimand, before clearing his throat and looking over his shoulder again. Then he leaned down a little closer and smiled. "We were sent to find you two. Your presence has been missed and is requested back at the house. The others are not far behind me. I sent them to search *the other clearing* but that won't delay them long once Patricia realizes I sent them on a wild goose hunt."

Narrowing his eyes at Quinton, "Damn it, Quinton, why would you lead them here, of all places?" Brody complained, jumping to his feet, and reaching down to help me up.

"I had no choice. Father sent us out to find you," Quinton said somberly. "You have some grass in your hair." He tried to be subtle, pointing at my hair, patiently watching as I shook my head, before simply reaching up and plucking several blades of grass and a twig out. "What happened to your lip?"

Brushing grass from his pants and coat before turning to me, Brody turned me around and brushed the back of my gown. "Your lip isn't that noticeable, really," he assured me, before taking a hold of my hand and leading the way back to the trail.

Jackson and Patricia came through the tree line just as we got everything adjusted properly. If looks could kill, I would have died three times over right where I stood. Patricia's eyes were seething with loathing hatred as she glared in our direction.

"Why is Patricia looking at me that way?" I inquired, leaning near Brody's ear.

"Like what?" Brody asked innocently, as if he didn't notice anything wrong.

"As if you left the two of us alone in a room together, she would rip my beating heart from my chest?" I replied in a whisper.

Quinton didn't miss a beat. Leaning in between us, he said, "Patricia Olson has coveted the Beaumont name ever since she was old enough to walk. And you, a mere interloper, comes along to ruin that for her, without even trying."

"Oh," I answered flatly, looking dumbfoundedly at him. "Thank you for clearing that up for me."

"Happy to oblige," Quinton quipped, smiling broadly. Wrapping his arms around our shoulders and stepping between us, he propelled Brody and me forward. Patricia's look told me that she had seen us holding hands and probably guessed why we were here, and what we had been doing.

Quinton called out in a jovial tone as we walked past the others. "Found them! I bet we beat you all back to the house," he called out, hurrying us past Patricia and Jackson. Physically turning my head forward when I stared a moment too long at Patricia, Quinton whispered, "I would like to avoid an all-out brawl between the two of you. Come along, children, nothing to see here," Quinton said, over his shoulder.

Patricia's sudden sour mood was not lost on any of us. Quinton continued to forge ahead paying absolutely no attention to the sulking woman behind us. I, on the other hand, couldn't ignore her and the daggers of death she was throwing at my back. Every so often I heard her snort something rude and derisive before Jackson could shush her, as he attempted to keep the peace. It felt like an eternity before we reached the main house. Just as we reached the door step, Quinton shoved me through the front door, then immediately blocked Patricia from entering. Oh, she tried to push her way past him, but Brody stepped in front of her, as well. Quinton used the excuse that he wanted to show her the new puppies. Patricia became instantly incensed, demanding that Quinton and Brody get out of her way. She even tried to convince them that she was merely exhausted and needed to lay down, but they knew her tricks all too well. They each took an arm and physically picked her up, escorting her to the other side of the house, where they kept her for another thirty minutes.

I heard the entire exchange as I slowly walked up the stairs. It wasn't that I was afraid of Miss Olson; on the contrary, I relished the opportunity to show Patricia how it was done. The real issue was who would protect her from me. Besides, my good breeding taught me that it was in very poor taste as an invited guest to eviscerate a member of the family.

Shutting my door, with a resounding slam, I startled Margot, causing her to drop the poker in her hand that she just used to stoke the fire.

"Honestly Olivia, you gave me a start. What has gotten into you?"

"Patricia Olson, that's who," I replied, contemptuously adding a growl of frustration. "I have never met anyone with so few redeeming qualities, "I said, continuing my rant, before noticing Margot shaking her head and pointing at Coco's door, "Margot, what in the world has gotten into you?"

The door opened between the two rooms and out stepped, Emily Olson with my sister Coco following behind her, hanging her head and looking dejected.

"I will be sure to inform my sister of your utter disdain for her, Lady Olivia," Emily sniffed, lifting her chin a touch higher as she made her way to the hallway door. "Thank you, Coco, for the very enjoyable afternoon," she continued, without looking at me again.

"Wait," I cried, but it was too late. Emily shut the door, with a slam. "I'm sorry —" I called out, halfheartedly, attempt to stop her.

"What is wrong with you, Olivia? Emily was nice. Now she probably won't speak to me again," Coco complained, stomping her delicate foot. "You are the worst, and I hope you get a pin stuck in your side," she concluded with the slamming of her door.

Slumping in a nearby chair, I placed my head in my hands, feeling utterly defeated. I didn't even look up when there came a knock at the door. Margot showed Mildred and Jane in. "It would serve me right," I murmured, under my breath, forcing a smile to my lips as I stood and followed the ladies in to the dressing room for my fitting. "How is your afternoon going, ladies? I truly hope that it is much better than mine."

"Yes, my Lady," Mildred's reply as Jane scurried ahead of us like a frightened mouse.

"Margot, do you think that I could have tea in my room this afternoon? I don't seem to be terribly popular with the general population," I said to Mildred, rolling my eyes heavenward. "Apparently, I haven't learned to play well with others."

Margot, who had followed us into the dressing room, began to laugh out loud, before she coughed, clearing her throat. "Terribly sorry, my Lady, I must have gotten a little dust up my nose."

All the three of us watched as Margot excused herself, "Most peculiar," Mildred commented before turning back to begin my fitting.

20

The Spirit That Passed Before Me

I HID IN MY ROOM THE remainder of the day and would have feigned a headache if it hadn't been for Mother shaming me into coming down for dinner.

I wore a green, chiffon, gown with long white gloves that came just above my elbow and my hair was fashioned simply with a thin, white satin ribbon running through the curls. Emerald earrings dangled, catching the light as I moved. Taking one last look in the mirror, along with a deep breath, "Well, here goes nothing," I murmured, to myself, slipping on satin slippers. "What do you think, Margot?" I asked, spinning in a circle to get her final approval.

"You look lovely. Now hurry along before you are truly late instead of fashionably late," Margot chided, shooing me along.

Checking the small clock on the mantle, I gasped and ran to the door. "Great, if one more thing goes wrong before dinner, I might as well crawl into bed and pull the covers over my head," I muttered, as the door closed behind me.

I looked up, then down the hallway, assuring that no one was about to witness my unladylike act as I lifted my skirts and ran all the way to the stairs. I slowed just as I reached the landing, to catch my breath a moment while smoothing my gown, along with a stray curl that had come loose. Then I gracefully gliding down the staircase and proceeded to the music room where everyone had gathered before dinner.

Stepping through the opened doorway, I was surprised to see Patricia sitting at an English spinet, while her sister, Emily, stood next to her playing a violin. "Of course, she plays the spinet, but can she carry a tune?"

I murmured sarcastically, under my breath, before silently making my way around several chairs, taking a seat next to my father, in the back row.

Father leaned over and whisper in my ear, "I was beginning to wonder if you were going to join us."

I flashed him an irritated smile before looking around the room, hoping this little impromptu concert wouldn't take long because I was famished. Patricia began to sing, which caused me to inwardly groan. I would have stood up and excused myself if it wouldn't have caused a scene. But I was in the very back row and had only just sat down. To keep my mind off of the gurgles and rumblings of my stomach, I began to recite poetry in my head. This served two purposes. One, it occupied my mind, and two, it distracted me from the fact that my stomach was eating itself.

The poem I decided upon was apply entitled, <u>A Spirit Passed Before Me</u>, by Lord Byron.

> *A spirit passed before me. I beheld the face of*
> *immortality unveiled—*
> *Deep sleep came down on every eye save mine—*
> *And there it stood, all formless, but divine:*
> *Along my bones the creeping flesh did quake;*
> *And as my damp hair stiffened, thus it spake:*
> *Is man more just than God?*
> *Is man more pure than He who deems even*
> *Seraphs insecure? Creatures of clay,*
> *vain dwellers in the dust! The moth survives you,*
> *and are ye more just? Things of a day!*
> *You wither ere the night, heedless and blind to*
> *Wisdom's wasted light!*

Upon concluding the last line of the poem, my eyes fell upon an empty chair at the other side of the room. Only the chair was not empty at all but was occupied by Annabelle Beaumont. Her eyes were closed and her head nodded along to the music. She looked so peaceful and serene that it was difficult for me to reconcile this Annabelle with the one I had been dealing with since my arrival. Slowly her eyes opened and the graceful smile upon her lips faded as she gazed into my eyes, as if she knew I was watching her. Swallowing hard, I clutched at the sudden knot in my belly. A wicked smile manifested itself as her lips turned up, and she narrowed her eyes as she fully realized my distress.

Standing, Annabelle walked over to Emily, then looked at me to gauge my reaction. She smiled even wider at this point and moved to Patricia, placing her hand upon her throat. I tried staying calm and not reacting, but it didn't seem to make a difference. It was as if she could hear the beating of my frantic heart and knew my every thought. In my head, the word *NO!* repeated, over and over again as I felt my eyes growing larger. I wanted to remove that grotesque smile from Annabelle's face, but of course I couldn't. The demonic sound of her laughter echoed in my ears as she threw her head back, letting out a shrill cackle. Then looking directly at me again, Annabelle shook her head, as her expression grew even more sinister. She walked towards Brody with intent. Placing her hands upon his shoulders, she leaned over, trying to communicate something to him in his ear. Not getting a satisfactory response, Annabelle placed her fingers around his throat, closed her eyes and tipped her head back as if she were enjoying the music again. Seconds later, Brody started to cough, and I could see that he was in distress as a strange look clouded his eyes. He stood up, quickly making his way to the door, as his face turned bright red.

I tried to be discreet, ducking out of the room through the side door, and quickly walking through the hall to the other entrance. Patricia's reaction to this noisy interruption was to sing even louder, drowning out any sound of Brody's coughing.

I found Brody down on the ground, hunched over, steadying himself against a wall, trying to catch his breath. The head butler was bent over him, attempting to help. The look on Annabelle's face was pure satisfaction, as she continued to squeeze his throat with her fingers.

Assessing the situation, I wasted no time, dropping to my knees and placing my arms around Brody's middle, then delivering several sharp blows to his belly with my fist, just as my grandmother had done once to a choking child. Annabelle evaporated immediately.

"What are you doing?" the butler protested.

"Saving his life, I hope —" I asserted, punching Brody in the stomach again. "Can't you see that he is choking?" I let go of him, as a hard piece of candy shot from his mouth, landing on the floor. Brody gasped for air.

One young maid and a footman stood gawking at the floor where the offending candy lay. "Well, don't just stand there, fetch Mr. Beaumont a glass of water," the butler barked. "Mr. Beaumont, are you hurt? Should I get your father?"

"No," Brody rasped, resting a hand around his throat. "I will be fine, just give me a minute." Then turning to me, he rested a hand upon my shoulder, as I helped him to his feet. Pushing his one hand away from his throat, I began to loosen his collar.

"Would you mind checking on that glass of water yourself, Mr. Frederics?" I politely requested, over my shoulder, never taking my eyes off of Brody's face.

"Of course," Frederics replied, looking as if I had just struck him, before hurrying off to do as I'd asked.

"Where did you learn to do that?" Brody questioned in a hoarse voice.

"It was something I witnessed my grandmother do before," I replied.

Brody pushed my hands aside when I boldly removed his cravat and unfastened the first two buttons of his shirt. "I don't feel it necessary to undress me here. I merely choked on a hard candy. But if you are still interested later, I will see what I can do about accommodating your desires," he teased.

"You didn't merely choke on a hard piece of candy, Brody," I announced, irritably, slapping his hands away to get a better look at his neck while pushing him into the nearest chair.

"What are you talking about? Of course I did. You can see the evidence clearly on the floor in front of you." Brody pointed at the candy, still lying there.

Cupping his face in between my hands, I brought his eyes around to mine. "Stop arguing with me. There are forces at work here that you cannot see."

"That is just nonsense," Brody stated, a look of uncertainty crossed his features as my words sank in.

"You need to sit still and let me look at you," I demanded, with a solemn tone, pulling back the collar of his shirt to check for marks. "Brody, did you grab your throat when you were choking? Because there are marks here, that look like somebody was choking you."

"Where?" Brody asked, jumping to his feet to look in the mirror for himself. "Well paint me crazy. There are marks on my throat," he proclaimed, as he stared at his throat.

Nervously I looked down the hallway for Frederics, "I think that we should fasten your collar, before someone sees those marks." Brody obediently sat back down in the chair with a look of disbelief on his face. He didn't move to fasten his collar, so I took the liberty of buttoning his shirt, when he suddenly pushed my hand aside to finish it himself.

Mr. Frederics came around the corner that moment with two glasses upon a silver tray. One contained water and the other contained Brandy. Brody automatically reached for the brandy and swallowed it down in one gulp, squeezing his eyes shut as the amber liquid burned its way down his already sore throat. Placing the glass back upon the tray, Brody stood up with a decisive move, "Thank you, Frederics, that will be all."

"Very good, Sir," Frederics replied, with a nod, handing the tray off to the maid, then pointed at the piece of candy still lying on the floor. "Do remove that offending confection before someone else is injured." Without a word, she smiled, bent over to retrieve the candy, and left.

Frederics excused himself, leaving to handle last minute preparations before dinner.

Leaning in close to Brody's ear, "I have a plan, do you wish to hear it?" I whispered.

"Yes, but I am sure it will fail," Brody announced, turning around to return to the music room, forcing me to follow him.

"Can't you be more positive?" I asked, irritated that he would dismiss me before hearing what I had to say.

Stopping abruptly, Brody turned to face me, and with a forced smile, said, "I'm sorry. Let me try again. I'm positive that it won't work."

"Don't you at least want to hear my idea before you dismiss it as rubbish?"

"Let's just say that I am suffering from shock and having a difficult time finding my footing. After all, you just informed that my mother, who has been dead for eight years, just tried to kill me," he whispered loudly, sounding slightly unhinged, looking up, then down the hallway as he pulled me to the side, pinning me against the wall. "Right now, all I really need is for someone to tell me that everything is going to be alright. That is all I need to hear! Can you do that for me?"

"Of course, Brody, I have no doubt that everything is going to work out just fine," I stated flatly.

Brody shook his head, "It doesn't work when I know you're lying."

"I wouldn't be so glib if I were you, Brody Beaumont. After all, it wasn't my mother who just tried to kill me from beyond the grave," I admonished in a loud whisper.

"Now that's just hurtful when you say it that way," Brody said glibly.

"Yes, yes, the truth hurts. Now, do you care to hear what I have to say, or would you prefer to be surprised?" I added, with a glib tone of my own.

Brody pulled me close, then leaned near my face so that we merely looked like a couple who chose that moment to be intimate. "Alright, but you might want to whisper it in my ear because these walls have ears," he agreed, with a seductive smile.

"And the staff have wagging tongues," I replied, trying to push him away.

"I'm serious, Olivia, if you say the plan out loud, I feel we won't get three steps before we are done in. So whisper the plan to me, and we just might survive the night and the staff can be damned."

Brody had a desperate look in his eyes, and I took a breath to calm my racing heart. "Very well, but you will need to follow the plan to the letter. There can be no deviating."

"I understand."

As Brody and I finished making plans, people began to pour out of the music room. Harrison, Prince William and my father were first. "If you two are quite finished, perhaps you would like to join us for dinner," Harrisons nonchalantly stated, as they walked past us. Quickly stepping apart, my face stained scarlet, then I saw the disapproving look on Father's face. Mother and Quinton were next to leave the music room, closely followed by Coco, Emily and Patricia.

Patricia had a look of anticipation on her face as if she were looking for someone, but then bristled the moment he eyes fell upon Brody and me. "I might have known the two of you would be skulking about in the hallway, like a couple of common…well I can't say it. My momma raised me better," she chastised, walking past us with her nose in the air.

"Well, I guess I just ruined all hope any kind of lasting friendship with Miss Patricia," I blandly stated, taking Brody's arm and followed the others into the dining room. Then I adding under my breath, "I truly hope I am not paired up with Saint Patricia for dinner or I might have to slit my wrists."

Brody put his head back and laughed heartily out loud. I should have been mortified, but it only caused me to laugh as well. Patricia, Emily and my mother all turned their heads to stare at us, as if we had suddenly lost our minds.

Sobering quickly, I elbowed Brody in the ribs. He looked at the others in front of us, then cleared his throat. "Lady Townsend, honestly, I wish you would learn to control yourself," Brody admonished, louder than necessary while smiling at those who had turned to stare at us.

I felt the color travel up my neck and color my cheeks. "I will pay you back, Brody Beaumont, mark my words," I growled under my breath while disentangling my arm from his.

"And here I thought you could take a joke?" Brody teased, retrieving my arm and placing it over his. "You really should learn to be less sensitive and enjoy life more," he remarked, leading to the table. "Shall we find your seat?"

"I believe I can find my own seat, thank you, Sir."

"I insist. It would be ungentlemanly of me to leave you stranded in the middle of the room," he chuckled, holding fast to my arm, preventing my escape as he looked at each name card. "Maybe I will get lucky and you are seated next to me."

"Oh, wouldn't *that* be a treat," I bemoaned.

Finding my name card, Brody pursed his lips together then pouted. I was seated between William and Quinton. Begrudgingly, he pulled out my chair and relinquished me to my dinner companions, before slowly making his way to his own seat. His mood went from unhappy to sour when he found himself seated next to Patricia.

I laughed out loud, then quickly covered it up by loudly clearing my throat and taking a drink of water when he glared at me.

Coco sat on Brody's other side conversing with her new friend Emily across the table from her, while Patricia rebuffed Brody by completely ignoring him and carrying on a lively conversation with Harrison Beaumont. I almost felt sorry for him, but then remembered how he had embarrassed me for his own amusement and decided that he got what he deserved.

The first course was presented and I noticed Coco had a strange look on her face as the footman ladled out her soup. I was curious about her look, until the footman came around to me. Inwardly I groaned to myself as the soup was ladled into my bowl. Split pea soup, the very bane of my existence. Coco and I looked at each other simultaneously, picked up our spoons with heavy hearts, dipping them into our bowls to retrieve a small amount.

Quinton leaned over and quietly said, "Not a fan of pea soup?"

"Not when I was forced to eat it nearly every day for three weeks straight, coming over here. Although, I will admit your cook is a much better cook than our ship's cook," I chuckled. "Perhaps, I may be permitted to borrow her for my return trip."

"You can try, but Cook hates ocean voyages. She claims that she nearly didn't make it the first time out."

"Pity. I guess that this means that Coco and I will be forced to pull up our boot straps and bear the return trip," I joked, "just as long as you send us with plenty of raisin scones."

"I will see what I can do," Quinton replied solemnly. "We can't have you starve to death."

"When do you return home?" Prince William asked, as he leaned over to join in on our conversation.

Turning to him, I replied, "I'm not exactly sure," I smiled. "Perhaps it will be soon. When do you return home, Prince William?"

"I always leave a couple of days after the party. It gives me time to recover from the festivities without wearing out my welcome," he replied, giving Quinton a wry smile.

William and Quinton began conversing about something of mutual interest while I sipped my wine and waited for the second course to be served. I glanced across the table and noticed Brody staring at me. Tipping my head, I smiled and took another sip of soup, followed with some crisp toast spread with melted garlic butter.

Harrison signaled the footman and the bowls were collected, followed closely behind by another footman serving game hens, while another served baked potatoes. A younger footman followed the other two and offered butter or white gravy to go over the hen and potatoes.

Prince William regaled us with tales of his trip to India and the time a monkey stole his shoes while he was praying, wearing them on his hands and pulling a funny face every time he put the shoes to his nose. By the time he was finished telling us about the monkeys antics, we were all laughing, and some guests were even snorting with tears rolling down their cheeks.

Everything tasted delicious and I was beginning to relax as the wine flowed and my stomach filled. What more could anyone ask for?

Frederics came in and whispered into Harrison's ear, then left again. "Please, join me in the drawing room. I have arranged entertainment for us all," Harrison announced, scooting his chair back as he stood up. He grinned widely. "So, everyone, take yourself a partner and no dawdling. Dessert will be served afterward, and I was told that cook has prepared something very special this evening."

Patricia turned to Brody with an expectant smile, but she hadn't been fast enough. He was already out of his seat before she turned around. Emily and Coco had linked arms and were walking out of the dining room door, as Brody began pulling on my chair.

"You're too late, brother, Olivia has agreed to accompany me to the drawing room," Quinton explained with a wry grin, waiting for the smile to melt from Brody's face. Then, as Brody looked completely defeated, Quinton stood and elbowed him in the ribs. "I'm just joshing you, she's all yours. How about I help you both out by occupying Patricia for the night?"

"I would be eternally grateful," Brody beamed, slapping Quinton on the back. "I'm sure you will make me pay for this later."

"That's a given," Quinton quipped, before turning with a bow, then kissing the back of my hand. "It's been a pleasure, Lady Olivia. Let me know if he gets out of line," he said, with a grin and a wink.

"Most gallant of you," I jested, giving Quinton a proper curtsy. "I'm afraid that won't be necessary since I am armed to the teeth and quite capable," I teased, winking back. "But the offer is most appreciated, none the less."

"The offer stands," Quinton assured me, looking Brody up and then down. "Just between you and me, I'm the better-looking twin."

"How can you say that?" Brody asked, feigning hurt. "We are identical twins."

"Simple, because it is true," Quinton laughed as he walked away.

"Your head was always bigger than mine, you conceited …" Brody called out to Quinton's retreating back.

"I've never experienced sibling rivalry between twins." I laughed. "Did I tell you that my mother is a twin?"

"No, I don't recall you mentioning that fact," he said, turning his attention to me. "Is Lady Isabella's twin as lovely as she is?"

"Well, that would depend on your point of view," I mused with a laugh. "While I consider Uncle Charlie a very handsome man, I don't think he would take kindly to being called pretty."

"No, I don't suppose he would," Brody admitted, lifting an eyebrow as he placed my arm over his, leading the way to the drawing room.

Taking a seat in the second row, Brody and I sat behind Emily and Coco. Quinton thankfully decided it best that he and Patricia sit in the back row, as far away from us as possible. I saw Brody make eye contact with his twin. They seemed to be having a secret conversation that only twins understood. My heart melted, because I was reminded of mother and Uncle Charlie and the way they could communicate with each other without using words.

Harrison had created a stage of sorts. The furniture was moved out of the room and the chairs were arranged in a half circle. A piano sat near the stage and lanterns, with reflective metal attachments straight from the local playhouse arranged on the floor with a back drop behind it.

When everyone was seated, Harrison stood up and stepped on to the makeshift stage. "Ladies and gentlemen, it is my great honor to present to you, the traveling troop of players from our very own *John Ellis Playhouse*. They have generously agreed to perform for us here tonight, and they are introducing their newest play entitled *A Simple Truth*, written by Mr. Joseph Jeffries III," Harrison announced, as a male actor stepped out from behind the backdrop and boldly walked onto the stage, giving a bow. "And here to help him perform this dark comedy is the incomparable Miss Fanny Sinclair," he stated with a flourish, as Miss Sinclair gracefully floated onto the stage, dropping into a deep, yet dramatic curtsy. "I will now turn the stage over to Mr. Jeffries, and his merry band of players for the remainder of this evening's performance," Harrison finished, leaving the stage and taking a seat in the front row.

Mr. Jeffries reached out, taking Fanny by the hand, and they both took a step forward giving another bow and curtsy, before Fanny floated from the stage, as Joseph made a show of looking after her longingly. "I feel privileged to bring to you my latest creation, *A Simple Truth*. As Mr. Beaumont has already explained, this is a dark comedy about a man and a woman," he began, leaning forward and wagging his eyebrows up and down, causing us all to laugh, before he continued. "A series of unfortunate events occur, and the results are, well, you know, laughable. So, I suggest you all sit back, relax and leave the singing and entertaining to us," he concluded. Then as an aside, he placed his hand to the side of his face as if he was letting us all in on a secret. "Your only responsibility is to laugh and clap in all of the right places and enjoy the show."

We all laughed again and began to clap. The air vibrated with excitement, and I found myself holding my breath with anticipation.

Coco turned around to smile at me, and I could read her every thought as her eyes glimmered with expectation.

The music began and the stage swarmed with activity as three stage hands, dressed all in black, brought out chairs and props, setting them down as the actors flowed through the doors, in front and behind us, beginning their performance.

Fanny Sinclair was a jewel to behold — fair skinned with rich chestnut hair and hazel green eyes that shined with mischief. She was willowy and thin, with tapered fingers and long slender arms. Joseph Jeffries III had dark skin, almost olive in tone, and his hair was such a rich dark brown it appeared black. His face had some stubble that only added to his masculine good looks and his thin stature complimented Fanny. They made a striking pair as they played their parts so convincingly that it was difficult to tell were the acting began and the individuals took up.

The play, from beginning to end, flowed well and was full of action and rousing songs that pulled us all into the plot, keeping us intrigued. I was captivated and entertained the entire time. Then, at the end, we were encouraged to join in the singing.

Prince William remarked, "Harrison, you're a sly old dog, you've really out done yourself this time." We all stood, loudly cheering and waited for the actors to join us for refreshments.

Mr. Joseph Jeffries III and Miss Fanny Sinclair exchanged furtive glances all evening long, and it was no stretch of the imagination to believe they were intimately involved.

I was fascinated watching the actors mingle with the gentry, as if they could fit in anywhere with their worldly lives. I smiled as Coco and Emily thoroughly questioned a young male actor who appeared to be about their age. He was telling them a story about the time he played Romeo on stage in Europe, and had to sneak away after the show. Apparently, the stage manager had absconded the playhouse's evening receipts, leaving the actors to defend for themselves. The two girls openly gawked when he told them about ducking behind a pile of rubbish to avoid being apprehended by the stage hands who would have beaten him, like they had a few other unfortunate actors.

I marveled at how easily everyone was drawn in by the thespians and their unique lifestyle. Even my parents were captivated by the young man's harrowing tales of life on the road and narrow escapes. As for me, I was perfectly content sitting back near the far corner of the room watching the chaos unfold, spooning my rice custard with golden currents and sweet cream on top into my mouth.

Everyone seemed to be talking at once, yet it wasn't difficult to listen to the individual conversations. Brody sauntered over to me and stood, looking down at me.

"Why are you hiding out in the corner instead of mingling with everyone else?" he asked, dragging a chair over and sitting down next to me.

"Who says I'm hiding out? Maybe I have the best seat in the house for the after show," I rebutted, flashing him a lopsided grin and spooning another bite of custard into my mouth. Looking as if he had just been struck by a bolt of lightning, Brody stood, walked over to the tray of desserts, and retrieved a bowl of rice custard; he then returned to sit down next to me. "Let's just see if this show is as good or better than the last one," Brody mused, spooning rice custard into his mouth, as he looked at them all with anticipation.

"The key is not to attract any attention to yourself. Try being a bit more nonchalant, and wipe that silly grin off your face," I chided. "Like this," I said, with a placid expression on my face, slowly took a scoop from my bowl, as if I were completely bored by the entire evening.

Watching me, Brody tried to get into character, mirroring my every move and facial expression. "Oh, you mean like this," he mimicked, causing me to laugh out loud because his expression made him look constipated instead of merely bored.

"No, no, no," I shook my head. "You're doing it all wrong," I said, reaching over to smooth out the wrinkle between his brows, and relax the stress lines on his face. "More like that. Now you've got it. You were trying too hard." I chuckled, placing my empty bowl on the table next to me.

Stifling a yawn, I covered my mouth, looked away, and that's when my eyes landed on Annabelle, lurking in a darkened corner of the room. I saw the dark and piercing glimmering of her eyes as she stared at me. Reaching over to squeeze Brody's arm, I wanted to get his attention while maintaining eye contact with her.

"Olivia, what's wrong?" he questioned, as understanding slowly dawned on him when I remained silent. "It's her, isn't it? Olivia, answer me," Brody demanded, giving me a slight shake. "What is she doing?" I stood up slowly, trying not to make any sudden moves as she began to drift from the corner towards the piano. The palpable chill in the room caused me to shiver, as I swallowed the lump that had formed in my throat.

"I believe she is deciding her next move."

"Why do you say that?" Brody quietly asked, leaning down near my ear as he followed me.

"Because she is smiling."

"Well, that is a good thing, isn't it?" he asked, perplexed by my concern. Taking ahold of my hand to turn me around and face him, he continued. "Maybe she is simply enjoyed the performance and is intrigued by the evening's festivities." Shaking my head to the negative, I tried to remove his hand from my wrist.

"Not bloody well likely. For some reason I can sense her intent, and it isn't good," I added, with another involuntary shudder as my voice cracked. "She is surveying everyone in this room, as if she is picking out her next victim. Do you understand my concern now?" Brody's Adams apple bobbed up and down as he swallowed hard.

"Oh, no you don't, you witch!" I exclaimed under my breath, swiftly my weight and moving towards Fanny Sinclair, grabbing a pitcher of water from the tray as I went.

"Olivia, what's the matter?" Brody sounded panicked following close behind me while trying to be discreet.

Quickly grabbing Fanny by the arm, I spun her around, dumping the pitcher of water down the back of her gown. Shock, then alarm registered on her pretty face. "What do you think you are doing?" she screamed, yanking her arm free.

"I'm terribly sorry, Miss Sinclair, please except my deepest apologies, but you were on fire and I didn't have time to say anything, before dousing your lovely gown," I explained, passing the empty pitcher off to Brody, who passed it off to a servant. "I saw you take a step backwards, and noticed that you were too close to that lantern, and well, I just reacted," I explained.

"Oh no, it is I who should be apologizing to you. You saved my life," Fanny gushed, while examining the damage to her evening gown.

Then turning to Harrison, who had come over to see what all the commotion was about, I pointed at the still lit lanterns. "Perhaps it would be prudent to extinguish the rest of the stage lamps and remove them, before anyone else catches fire."

Harrison's face turned completely white, mortified by what had just nearly happened to one of his esteemed guest. "I am so terribly sorry for the damage done to your gown, Miss Sinclair. Please, allow me to replace it," he cried, turning to one of his footman. He snapped his fingers. "See to these lamps before we set someone else on fire."

"Right away, Sir," the man answered, moving quickly with two other servants to clean up the mess.

"Perhaps we should move to the music room and conclude our evening there," Harrison announced, forcing a smile that didn't quite reach his eyes. "Frederics, would you lead our guests to the other room."

Grabbing Coco by the hand, I pulled her over to the piano where mother and Prince William stood, and waited until the prince excused himself. "If I were you, I would consider calling it a night," I said quietly, nervously looking over my shoulder, to make sure I wasn't overheard.

"We have a mischievous, if not spiteful, spirit who finds delight in disrupting the evening's activities with her dangerous pranks. I, for one, intend to give her one less target to aim for. The two of you would be wise to do the same," I added.

Then, turning to see where Annabelle had scurried off to when I ruined her fun, I caught sight of her lurking in the far corner again. "Oh, and don't forget to warn Father. I would hate for him to get caught off guard."

"Your father and I will make our excuses, then retire as soon as possible," Mother announced, looking around for Father, who was still talking to one of the actors.

"I will tell Emily that I am tired, and that I wish to turn in, or perhaps I could invite her back to my room for a game of cards. That way there will be even less targets for our demon spirit," Coco said, squeezing my hand.

"That is clever. The two of you need to be careful, and keep this between us," I said, looking around for Brody. I spotted him standing off to the side with his brother, Quinton and Patricia, quietly talking. I gave Mother and Coco a reassuring smile, and they left without another word. I stood a moment longer, observing the three of them interacting. Patricia had a fan close to her and Brody's face, obscuring my view slightly, but I could tell that she was leaning heavily against Brody, whispering something in his ear. He looked up with a guilty expression, as his eyes landed upon me.

As I approached, Patricia left and Brody and Quinton put their heads together and spoke quietly. Gracefully stepping around Quinton to place my back against the wall, I waited for them to finish talking. "Your deceased mother is having a bit of fun at the expense of us mere mortals. I think my family and I will be turning in for the evening."

Quinton looked concerned and put his hand on my arm to keep me from leaving, when I pushed away from the wall. "How will we know when she is going to strike again if you go up to bed?"

"With less people to attack, I believe she will get bored and go away. She really comes alive in large crowds if you hadn't noticed. If we refuse to play, she has no choice," I said with a shrug of my shoulders. "Then the problem goes away as well." I added, with a forced smile, "In theory."

"It makes sense," Quinton agreed, looking somewhat convinced.

Taking a hold of my arm, Brody saw Patricia coming back towards us. "I will see you safely upstairs. Just to make sure that you get there in one piece." Brody insisted, nodding his head in Patricia direction, acknowledging her presence. Patricia stuck out her lower lip in a pout as we walked past her, leaving Quinton to deal with her.

Leaning down by my ear, Brody spoke under his breath, "I guess she's mad at me."

"That isn't how it looked earlier," I admonished.

"What are you talking about?" he questioned, innocently. "We have been family for a long time. She gets mad, we make up," he said, looking over his shoulder. "She can be a little surly when she is angry, and right now she is madder than a little wet hen at me."

"And who could blame her? You really are a terrible host. Your cousin traveled a great distance just to see you and you constantly put her off," I stated with a straight face.

Brody chuckled quietly and began to say something back, but I silenced him with a look. "Do you remember the discussion we had earlier this evening?" I asked, squeezing his arm while staring at Annabelle, who had stepped out from her corner and was making her way towards us.

"Yes, of course. The one where we —" he began to say when I cut him off again.

"If you were about to reference the discussion, that we swore would never be spoken of out loud? Then yes, that is the one." I interrupted, flashing him a smile, and pulling him to a stop to keep him from intersecting with Annabelle who cut us off, walking through the doorway just in front of us.

We stepped out into the hallway, as I watched Annabelle walk through the wall, giving me one last bone chilling glare, before she disappeared into the music room.

Looking up at Brody, I couldn't hide my concern. "She has gone into the music room, so we are safe for the moment. I still wouldn't say anything out loud that we don't want her to know, just in case," I cautioned.

"Olivia, your hands are like ice," Brody said, stopping to rub them between his.

"I will be fine. Hopefully someone has thought to light the fire in my room's hearth," I scoffed, trying to brush it off as nothing.

"I have just the thing to warm you up," Brody cried, suddenly excited, as he turned, leaving me at the top of the stairs, "I'll be right back," he called over his shoulder as he ran down the steps. Giving me one last look, Brody grinned before disappearing around the corner.

Shaking my head, I continued to my room. A fire had been lit and my room felt warm and cozy. Bending down to stir the coals, I threw another log on the fire and watched as the flames began to jump back to life.

"Margot, are you here?" I called out and waited for a response, but none came. I figured that she didn't expect the evening to be over so early for me and was downstairs having dinner. I went around the room lighting lanterns with a stick that I touched to the newly blazing fire. When I was done, I stood by the fire to warm myself when there was a knock on my door. "Come in," I called out, expecting Brody to walk through the doorway. But instead of Brody, it was Patricia.

Shock registered on my face. "Well, isn't this cozy?" Patricia began, with a deceivingly warm tone.

"I guess I should have asked who it was before offering a blanketed invitation to enter." I said.

"And spoil that surprised look on your face?" Patricia continued, clicking her tongue and shaking her head at me. "That would never do," she crooned, taking the liberty of shutting the door behind her.

"If you don't mind, I would prefer that you leave the door open."

Turning around, Patricia gave me a sardonic smile, followed by a scornful chuckle. "Oh, but I do mind. You see, I wish to have a few words with you, Olivia, in private. If you don't mind? It could be a tad embarrassing and would prefer that we are not overheard." She continued walking closer while pretending to admire the room. "I have always loved this room." Bringing her eyes back around to look at me boldly, she looked oddly emboldened. "Brody can be so protective of his new, well, dare I say, plaything?"

"Why are you here, Miss Olsen?" I asked, placing my hand into my pocket and patting the warm steel of my dagger's handle.

"I told you, Olivia. Weren't you listening to me?"

"Yes, as a matter of fact, I was listening, Patricia, but I still don't see what you and I would have to talk about," I stated, moving away from the open hearth, cautious not to turn my back on her.

The room suddenly seemed small and confined as Patricia followed me, a half-smile forced to her lips, which didn't quite translate to anything pleasant. She continued to look around the room. "Is your hand maiden out at the moment?" she asked, leaning forward and looking into the dressing room.

"Margot just ran downstairs to fetch me some tea. She shouldn't be long," I stated confidently, even though my insides suddenly soured like milk that had gone bad. "So perhaps we can speak at another time," I suggested, walking towards the door, intending to show her out.

Cutting me off, Patricia quickly stepped in front of me. "Or, maybe you don't wish to be alone with me, for some reason. Perhaps, you are even scared of me?" she suggested, grabbing my right arm, prevent me from stepping around her.

"Or maybe I just don't like you very much and wish for you to leave. Now turn loose of me this instant, and get out of my room," I ordered, glaring at her defiantly.

For several long, tense moments, Patricia continued to squeeze my wrist as tightly as she could, weighing her options. Finally, she let go of me, and I jammed my right hand into my pocket and unsheathed my dagger. In a cold, calculating voice I continued. "Turning me loose was a very wise decision, indeed. Now, if you will be so kind as to remove yourself from my sight, our business here is concluded!" I stated, with finality, eyeing her coolly.

"Not quite."

"Oh, and what matter do we still have to discuss?" I asked suspiciously, walking back to the fire to chase away the sudden chill that settled over me.

"Brody's mine and you need to know that he will always be mine," Patricia stated with finality, as if everyone knew this simple fact. "We pledged our love to each other years ago."

"I noticed that you don't wear a promise ring," I said pointedly, turning to face her now. "Why is that?"

Glancing at her hand, then placing it behind her back, Patricia answered without blinking, "We swore to keep our love a secret from our parents, until we were old enough to consent and wed without their permission." Taking a few steps closer, Patricia stood next to me now, and I felt I had no other choice but to look at her. Her voice suddenly took on a new quieter tone as she continued, no longer sounded proud or brazen, but sad and pleading. "We sealed our promise to one another in the very same clearing..." she hesitated, "Brody took you to today. He was my first and my only..." She concluded by clearing her throat as her face turned red. "Well, I think you get the point."

"Again, why come to me? Why not confront Brody with your concerns?" I asked, unsure I believed her story.

With a single tear running down Patricia's face, she managed to look up at me with a quivering lip. "Because Brody has had these little dalliances before, and he always comes back to me in the end."

How could I be such a fool? Turning away, I stared into the fire. Could she be telling me the truth? Had I been led astray by a man who was promised to another in the most intimate of ways? My emotions were a jumbled mess. I didn't know whether to laugh in her face or congratulate her while expressing my deepest condolences for pledging herself to such a philanderer.

"I would never wish to stand in the way of another's happiness, Miss Olson. Brody is yours, I will step aside," I conceded, still staring into the burning fire. I felt my heart breaking as it rested in my throat.

"Somehow, I knew you were a woman of integrity and honor, Olivia," she proclaimed, wasting no time as she made her way toward the door. "Thank you again," she gushed as if the two of us were the best of friends."

"Oh, and by the way, Miss Olsen," I admonished, without looking up from the fire, "I do not recall giving you leave to address me by my given name." Turning slowly, my eyes found hers, as she hesitated a moment, with her hand resting on the doorknob.

"Please accept my sincerest apologies for the impropriety, Lady Townsend. It won't happen again," she said tentatively, flashing me a shy smile as our eyes locked.

"See that it doesn't," I demanded, as Patricia quietly closed the door.

Something didn't sit quite right with me, but I didn't have time to ponder the feeling further. I had no more than turned to stare into the glowing fire, searching for solace when I heard a loud knocking at the door. Irritated by the noise breaking into my thoughts, I brought my hand up and to message the area that was throbbing in my temples. "Who is it?" I barked, turning towards the door as it opened.

Poking his head cautiously around the door, Brody knitted his eyebrows together. "Is something wrong, Olivia? You sound angry." Stepping into the room, Brody carried a covered silver tray with a white towel draped over his forearm, just like the footmen at dinner. "I've brought you something that will make all your worries disappear," he announced cheerfully, closing the door with his foot. Then he walked across the room to present the tray to me.

Tears suddenly sprang to my eyes and I turned away, pretending to stare into the fire again, while bracing my hands on the mantle. Taking a deep breath, I held it to the count of ten, then slowly let it out before turning to face him. "I'm fine, Brody. Why wouldn't I be?" I said, forcing an awkwardly smile to my lips. I needed time to think. Patricia's words kept running through my head, *Brody has had these little dalliances before, and he always comes back to me, in the end.* "I guess I didn't realize how tired I truly was," I claimed, trying to sound convincing.

Placing his hand on the tray cover, Brody removed the lid, exposing the surprise. "Well then, this should help you sleep soundly," he said triumphantly, delighted with himself. "I brought you a glass of our special mulled cider."

Eyeing the contents of the two glasses suspiciously, I asked, "What exactly makes this cider so special?"

"It's a family secret," Brody explained with a wink, handing me a glass of cider, before taking one for himself and placing the empty tray on the table. "Cheers, bottoms up."

I sniffed the contents and pulled a face, causing Brody to chuckle. Then I tentatively brought the glass to my lips and sipped. The cider was fermented with extra sugar, making it sweet and tart at the same time.

"It is quite delicious," I gasped slightly as the warmed cider burned the back of my throat. "Wow, that is strong."

"Do you like it?"

I couldn't look him directly in the eye, he seemed so happy and carefree. *I guess he has all but forgotten his declaration to Patricia Olson in the meadow clearing, years ago,* I thought to myself, silently seething at him. I was angry that he made me hope for something that he knew could never be.

"It is very good. Thank you for sharing this with me," I said, with a stiff smile. "But I'm afraid I didn't realize how tired I really was. Everything has been happening so fast," I stammered, trying to come up with a plausible excuse to make him leave. I walked over to the call rope and gave it a good stiff pull, alerting Margot downstairs that I needed her assistance. "I'm terribly sorry, but I truly do have a frightful headache, and need to lie down," I shyly smiled, bringing my hand back up to my head, emphasizing my ploy. Reaching the door, I opened it, as a polite invitation for Brody to leave.

"But I thought I would keep you company," he objected, sounding confused by the sudden change in my demeanor. "I could rub your pain away."

"I truly am sorry," I said, looking downward and shuffling my feet. "Perhaps it isn't too late for you to join the others downstairs if you aren't yet ready to retire for the night," I suggested, downing the remaining cider in my glass, before placing it back upon his tray as he stepped through the doorway. "I'm sure we will see each other for breakfast in the morning," I added, looking up, knowing full well that I intended to avoid him for the remainder of my stay.

"But, but…" Brody stammered, as the door closed in his face.

I stood for the longest time, listening, waiting for him to walk away. I could feel my heart breaking in my chest and I closed my eyes to keep the tears from coming. But they came anyway as I thought of Patricia's lips pressed against Brody's mouth. I shook my head to clear the thought away.

I heard his heavy footsteps slowly walk toward the back staircase, leading down to the kitchen and had to stop myself from throwing the door open and running after him. Instead, I stood still letting the tears stream down my cheeks until I was certain he was gone. Then I ran to the bed, threw myself face first into the thick down coverlet, and cried bitter tears until I was spent and my tears dried up. I let loose with one last angry scream into my pillow before laying very still.

I heard Margot quietly enter the room and felt her touch my leg, softly calling out to me. Instead of answering her, I pretended to be asleep and waited for her to leave. Placing a blanket over me, she extinguished every lamp and candle in the room, but one. Margot left the lantern on the nightstand table lit, placing a handkerchief and glass of water next to it. Between the slits in my swollen eyes, I saw her hesitate a moment, before reaching out her hand to gently stroked my cheek. "Sleep well, my little princess. I'm here if you need me," she quietly murmured before turning in for the night.

It was only after she blew her light out in the next room, that I sat up to blow my nose and drink some water. Turning over in bed, I pulled the covers up, snuggling deep into the blanket. I tried to sleep.

21

FRIDAY, FEBRUARY 13, 1804

Father Timothy Comes to Chase Away the Evil

MY SLEEP WAS FITFUL AT best, as I tossed and turned the entire night. Every time I drifted off to sleep, visions of Patricia and Brody locked in an intimate embrace swam through my head, their mocking laughter tormenting my mind. I must have cried in my sleep, because my pillow was damp in the morning.

Margot didn't come in to open the curtains or roust me from my slumber. Instead, she took pity upon me and allowed me my privacy, so I could work out my inner demons.

When I awoke, I felt disoriented and groggy from lack of sleep. Crawling from under the covers, I trudged over to the window and opened the drapes wide, allowing the bright sunlight to permeate every corner of the room.

I turned, then noticed Margot had laid out a dark blue, wool gown for me to wear, with thick stockings to ward off the chill.

Turning toward the window again, I looked more closely at the trees and grass and noticed that everything glistened with white. Frost had incrusted the land overnight, leaving a magical glimmer upon everything it touched. In my mind's eye, I could imagine stepping out onto the frosty grass and hearing it crunch beneath my boots and feeling the nip of cold on my face and hands. Although the sun was out, the air would be sharp and cold, and the wind would no doubt cut straight through an individual with the precision of a surgeon's blade, leaving one flayed open and exposed to their very core. Which was perfect, I thought to myself, because it was just what I needed at the moment, and suddenly, I couldn't wait to get out of this house. Anything was preferable to this dull, gnawing pain that had taken a hold of my heart.

I was a fool. I had fallen hard, there was no doubt about that fact, and I wanted, nay, needed to escape from the confines of this stuffy house, even if it were for an hour.

Quickly dressing, I found my cape in the dressing closet and fastened the clasp as I hurried to the door. Listening for movement from the other side, I heard nothing, so I silently opened the door. Slipping down the back staircase, past the busy kitchen staff, I procured two raisin scones as I made my way to the back door. Looking over my shoulder, Cook gave me a wink, as I closed the door. I had made my escape.

Winding my way through the garden, then finding a narrow path that I had never been on before, I slipped into the woods. The path meandered through trees, past a stream, then came out upon a beautiful lake. The water was crystal clear with a thin sheet of ice along the bank and shallow areas. I found a fallen tree near the water's edge and decided to sit down for a while. Pulling the hood of the cape closer, trying to ward off the biting cold, I took a deep breath of cold, crisp air and sighed. The sight before me was so breathtakingly beautiful it nearly hurt. I pulled the second scone from my pocket and began nibbling on it while I marveled at the beauty that surrounded me.

"Isn't it magnificent here," Lilly sighed, behind me, and I jumped out of my skin, choking on the scone I'd been eating. Sputtering and coughing, I hit my chest with the heel of my hand, dislodging the piece of pastry lodged in my windpipe. "Bloody hell," I admonished between fits of coughing. "You scared ten years from my life. Don't you ever do that to me again, Lilly Ann Collins. You hear me?"

"Alright, alright, I'm sorry. I forget you can't see me all the time," Lilly conceded, stepping around the log to stand near me. "I thought you knew that I was there when you left the house."

"You were next to me the whole time?" I cried.

"Not next to you, behind you. I followed you out here," Lilly replied, turning to look at the lake. "This is one of my favorite spots. It's so beautiful that it makes me homesick."

I looked at Lilly and suddenly felt bad for being angry with her. "I'm sorry, Lilly, I didn't mean to yell at you," I groaned, taking a deep breath. "I just needed to find a quiet spot and, well, I thought this one would do."

"What's the matter, Olivia? You seem sad. Talk to me," she pleaded, sounding like the old Lilly I remembered. "Besides, who am I going to tell? You're the only person I can talk to."

It was her tone that made me feel like everything was going to be alright, and to be honest, I really missed our talks and knowing that she was just down the road from me. It had always brought me comfort, but that was never to be again. My best friend was trapped between this world and the next and that knowledge only added to my burdened heart. I had originally come here to solve the mystery of her death, but I hadn't yet. In fact, I hadn't thought of her in days.

"Oh Lilly, I miss you. I miss this," I said, waving my hand between us, feeling the sting of tears welling up in my eyes, so I turned my head to hide them.

"Olivia, you don't have to hide your feelings. I know what is in your heart, without having to see your face," she confessed, scooting closer to me. "You can't hide from me. I felt your pain last night. I guess it is one of the benefits of being dead if there can truly be a benefit. So, you might as well tell me what happened, Olivia Townsend. What has made you so sad?"

"Oh Lilly, I am such a fool."

"Why would you say such a thing?" Lilly scolded. "You are one of the smartest, level-headed people I know."

"I allowed myself to be duped by a philanderer," I cried, then buried my face in my hands as bitter tears came. "I'm so ashamed. Brody has made a fool of me, Lilly. I'm like a moth to the flame, and he's the flame!"

"What do you mean he's made a fool of you?"

"Patricia came to my room last night and told me how the two of them made a pledged to each other, years ago," I announced with a frustrated growl, angry at myself for crying as I roughly wiped away tears.

"Now, there… there… Olivia," Lilly comforted, looking as if she would put her arm around me, then deciding against it. "I've seen how he looks at you. I tell you, I just don't believe it, Olivia!" Lilly vehemently said. "If you ask me, it's that shady looking strumpet that is the questionable character here," she added, jumping to her feet. "Now that is enough of that, Olivia Sophia Allen Townsend. There will be no more of this crying business." Lilly ordered, wagging her finger at me. "If I could slap a little sense back into you right now, I would. But since I can't, you will have to snap out of it."

"You're right, of course," I sniffed, reaching into my pocket for a handkerchief to blow my nose. "And besides, I didn't come all this way to fall in love. I came here to find out what happened to you and make somebody pay!" I announced, with renewed purpose, getting to my feet so that I could look Lilly in the eyes, "and come hell or high water, that is exactly what I intend to do."

"That's the spirit," she cheered. "Shall we take a walk before you go back?"

"Yes, I think I would like that." I replied, giving her a half-smile.

Lilly and I walked for an hour, talking about everything, just like old times, and by the time we reached the house again, I was restored to my old self.

I noticed a Rosewood Plantation carriage in the courtyard as we came out of the woods. "Lilly, you stay here and keep out of site. I'll be back to find you when I can," I advised, giving her a reassuring smile. "Everything is going to be fine." Lilly smiled at me, turned to leave and disappeared into the forest.

Opening the front door, I walked toward the drawing room, which was the logical place to entertain newly-arrived guest. Removing my cape and gloves, I handed them over to a maid and watched as she took them upstairs.

I heard the happy exchange of greetings and walked down the hallway, bracing myself before entering the room.

The day before Brody and I had put our heads together and devised a plan. Brody and Quinton were to ride out today and fetch Father Timothy, and his housekeeper, Mary, spiff them up a bit and introduce them to their father, Harrison, as an old acquaintance.

"Olivia, allow me to introduce you to, Father Timothy," Quinton said jovially, just in case someone was passing by the room and looked in.

"How wonderful to meet you, Father Timothy," I cried, sounding cheerier than I was.

Instead of the raggedy, disheveled priest from the other day, Father Timothy was well groomed with brand new attire. His hair and beard had been trimmed and his nails manicured. He looked like a proper gentleman. Mary, his housekeeper and long time companion, was also wearing some new clothes. Her hair was simply fashioned upon her head and her half-gloves, made of a fine lace, showed off her recently groomed nails.

"My dear child, the pleasure is all mine," he smiled, putting down his tea down so that he could stand, with the help of Mary.

Coming up behind me, Brody seemed to appear from out of nowhere. "Quinton and I went to fetch him last night, because I knew how important it was to you," he said, just a hairs breath from my ear.

I turned with a start, because I hadn't seen him when I entered. "Thank you." I replied, while avoiding eye contact.

"We plan to distract the others, so that you, Mary and Father Timothy can do what needs to be done," he added, placing a warm hand upon my shoulder. "Olivia, what is the matter with you?" he asked, sounding put off because I hadn't looked at him when he spoke.

"I'm fine, Brody, there's just a lot to get done before tomorrow," I answered, again managing to avoid direct eye contact.

"Let me get you some hot tea, and you'll feel better," Brody suggested, gently touching my cheek with the back of his hand. "Olivia, you are like ice!"

Chancing a quick glance up at him, I thought I saw real concern. Then just as quickly, the pain of remembering how he had played me for a fool flooded my thoughts. I tried to smile, but feared that I was less than convincing when I pulled away.

Brody was right of course. I was frozen to the bone, but that was only because I wanted to forget the pain that had settled in my heart. I sat down next to Father Timothy on the couch and waited for my cup of hot cup of tea, so I could thaw my fingers.

Nodding to Mother and Father who were sitting in the corner enjoying a game of cards while sipping tea, I turned back to Father Timothy as Brody approached.

"Here you go, just the way you like it," Brody announced, handing me the saucer and cup. Glancing up, I grudgingly blessed him with a real smile, just as Patricia happened to walk in. Strolling over to us, she placed a possessive hand through Brody's arm.

"Where have you been all morning?" Patricia asked me, trying hard to sound concerned about my welfare. "Why, Brody has been positively beside himself with worry." Her smooth, southern drawl left the listener believing that she was truly concerned.

Looking up with a bland, disinterested gaze, I feigned a politely smile. "I needed some air, so I went for a walk. I'm afraid that from time to time I find the confines of any household stifling, and simply need to commune with nature."

With a surprised look, Patricia said, bringing her free hand up to her chest, "Olivia, my dear, it is unsuitable outside for man or beast, let alone a delicate little thing, such as yourself. Why I do declare, you are the strangest creature I have ever met. Don't you agree, Brody?"

Looking uncomfortable, he stared transfixed a moment at me, before turning to Patricia. With a cynical smile, he looked down at his cousin. "Actually, Patricia, I find Lady Olivia rather intriguing. Dare I even say, captivating. I have an idea, why don't we all go for a ride this morning," Brody announced to everyone in earshot, presenting Patricia with a huge smile, showing his teeth and clearly issuing a challenge.

I coughed, choking on the tea I had just swallowed as all the color drained from Patricia's face.

"Are you alright, my dear?" Father Timothy asked, reaching for my arm, trying to lift it above my head. "This always keeps me from choking." Eyeing Brody cautiously, I couldn't help but feel better, when I saw that wry smile upon his lips.

"Yes, Father Timothy, I am quite fine," I assured, taking back my arm. "Thank you for your kind assistance. I believe I am fully recovered now."

"Did I hear someone say that we are going for a ride?" Jackson questioned, entering the room.

"Yes you did, my good friend, and Patricia will be accompanying us, won't you Patricia?" Brody cajoled, giving Patricia a sly smile and a squeeze, as she began to stammer, searching for an appropriate excuse not to go.

"Oh, don't look at me that way. I know how much you love the fresh air filling your lungs on a day like this. There's nothing like it," Brody continued, making a real show of it, as we were joined by Prince William, Harrison, Emily and Coco. Looking around the room, Brody was soliciting support for his cause. "It's a beautiful brisk day for a ride. With a show of hands, who's with me?" he added, taking a head count as he looked around the room. "Come on, William, don't be timid, you know you want to go as well."

Looking as if he was being goaded into it, Prince William smiled, then raised his hand.

"Great," Brody exclaimed, with a triumphant laugh, "then I will tell them to saddle ten horses," he announced, turning to give me a wink.

"Of course, we will excuse, Lady Olivia, since she has already had her full measure of fresh air this morning."

"Thank you, good sir. You are most kind with your favors," I stated, with a bow my head, knowing that this was the excuse Brody had come up with to get people out of the house.

"That just leaves you, Father Timothy. Do you wish to join us for a ride?" Brody inquired.

"Oh no, my boy, I have had quite enough adventure this morning. But I thank you for the offer."

"I don't know, Brody, I think I would rather stay here with the Father," Patricia spoke up, voicing her protest. "I do believe that I feel a case of the sniffles coming on."

"But it will be fun, Patricia. Just like when we were kids," Brody assured her. Placing an arm around her waist, he walked her toward the door. "Now, you hurry on up those stairs and put on something warm, while Jackson and I see to the horses. It will be like old times, and we are going to have so much fun," he insisted. "And don't make me come up there to fetch you now, you hear?" Brody called after Patricia's retreating form, giving me a wink over his shoulder. "The rest of you, don't be long."

Brody's antics made me smile, but I still couldn't forget Patricia's words from the night before. *We sealed our promise to one another, in the very same clearing Brody took you to. He was my first and my only.*

One by one everyone left to retrieve warmer clothing for the ride, including Coco and my parents. But before my sister left she gave me a knowing smile.

Father Timothy, Mary and I were the only ones to remain, sipping our tea in peace, each of us lost in our own thoughts. We had a house to make secure from a certain unwanted spirit and I was anxious to get started.

"May I suggest we start in the attic and work our way down," Father Timothy said.

"Whatever you think best. You are the expert in these matters. You may consider me your lowly apprentice," I exclaimed, getting to my feet.

Father Timothy reached out to take my hand and keep me from leaving. His sightless eyes, appeared to look straight through me. "I just need to do one thing first," he added, reaching out his other hand to Mary. Obediently, she placed a silver medallion in his outstretched hand. Cautiously sitting back down, I looked at him, curious what he had in mind. "Now I am sure you are wondering what this is," he said, holding the medallion out for me to examine. Taking the medallion from him, I rolled it over in my hand, testing the weight. It was solid and must have weighed several ounces. Round in shape, the main body was made of bronze, encircled with a silver border that had been hand pounded and appeared to be very old. The metal looked as if it had been recently polished, but it still maintained its ancient, greenish patina. I held the pendent closer, trying to determine its origin. The image carved into the bronze portion of the metal was of a man with very large wings and a sword, which he wielded above his head.

"I wish you to have this medallion of Michael, the Archangel of protection, also known as The Angel of The Last Judgment," the priest said reverently, sensing my curiosity. He took the medallion from my hand, and slipped it over my head to lay quietly around my neck.

"Why are you giving me this?" I asked, feeling confused.

"Because, my dear, for those of us who have chosen to help the unseen spirits, it is important to have an extra barrier of protection," he answered, looking at me with eyes that had long since lost the ability to see what others took for granted. And yet, he could see things which the world would not wish to witness.

Staring at the medallion around my neck, I looked up to find Mary scrutinizing me. Looking back at Father Timothy, I could not contain my curiosity. "You make it sound as if there is a choice in the matter. But for me, it was never a choice."

Giving a derisive chuckle, he took my hand in his. "My dear child, there is always a choice. You just have to open your eyes to see it," he smiled. "Now, you are to wear this around your neck, always. It will protect you against the evils that lurk about. Never take it off!" he ordered, shaking a finger at me. "Promise me."

I felt goose bumps travel up my spine and the hairs on the back of my neck stood on end. "I promise, I will always wear it," I finally replied, lifting the medallion up to examine it one last time, before tucking it inside the top of my gown, hiding it from view. Some unknown feeling sunk deep into my heart and I found myself taking Father Timothy's warning seriously. "What do the words on the other side mean? I don't recognize the writing."

"The medallion comes with a promise, as well as a warning, to the person who wears it. You must be pure of heart, intending to do good with the powers given to you by the medallion, or you will suffer the consequences that surely will come," he replied, wagging his finger at me again. "So, make sure that your intensions are always good."

I felt a nervous knot working its way up from the pit of my stomach and swallowed hard to keep the bile down. I began to question my ability to fulfill such a tall order. I even questioned my motives. Were my intentions truly pure? Most importantly, were they pure enough?

"I can assume by your silence, that you are scared, but I wish to assure you that I know you are the one," Father Timothy admonished, patting my hands that nervously sat in my lap. "I had the very same thoughts run through my mind when I was given the responsibility of the medallion."

"How can you possibly know what it is that I am thinking?" I cried.

"Because, my child, I can," he gently answered, standing up, again with Mary's assistance, as she slipped his cane into his hand. "Now come along, we don't have much time before the others return," he advised. Obediently I stood and followed behind Father Timothy and Mary, lost in thought.

Beginning the purification process in the attic, Mary lit a bundle of herbs and passed it to Father Timothy, who began to chant ancient words, meant to banish any evil spirits from the house. He encouraged me to mimic his words as I held his arm and led him through each room, down the hallways and finally downstairs. Mary opened windows as we entered rooms and then came back around to close them when we were finished, allowing any trapped spirits and smoke from our burning herbs to escape. The servants averted their eyes and bowed their heads reverently as we came, finishing by passing through the kitchen.

Standing at the back door, after completing the process, I leaned in close to Father Timothy's ear. "Do you think it worked?" I asked.

"We shall see, my child. We shall see," he answered, with an exhausted smile that creased his face more than usual. "If you will excuse me now, I think I need to rest," he said, automatically putting his hand out to Mary, who took him upstairs.

A short thirty minutes later, the riding party returned, flooding the house with their ruckus laughter, as they pushed and jostled each other coming through the door. Jackson, Quinton and Brody playfully pushed and elbowed one another, while Mother, Emily and Coco followed behind, chattering away excitedly. Patricia followed closely behind, leaving no pretense of her displeasure, as she pushed her way past everyone to beat a hasty path up the stairs. Further evidence of her angry disposition manifested itself with the sound of heavy footsteps echoing off the walls, as she stomped her way up the stairs, down the hall, ending with a resounding slamming of her bedroom door.

Harrison, Father and Prince William brought up the rear, talking over one another, continuing their heated discussion over politics as they came through the door. It was very difficult to discern what the real point of their conversation was because of all the noise.

Harrison took a momentary break from the discussion to deliver his request to the butler. "Frederics, we need something hot to warm up our cold weary bones. Bring some tea for the ladies and something extra special for us gentlemen." Then as an afterthought. "Bring us some of that cider, right away," Harrison bellowed, before taking a deep breath and launching immediately back into his tirade about the European dollar and how it had destabilized the value of the American currency, while Father and Prince William heartily disagreed.

"Make that a special cider for me too," Mother called out, causing Harrison to stop mid-sentence with his mouth still open and stare at her. "Anyone else want some of Harrison's special cider," she asked, lifting her eyebrows defiantly, daring him to say something.

"I'll have some special cider too," I called out, stepping into the foyer to draw Harrison's attention away from Mother.

A look of shock crossed his features, before he let loose with a hearty belly laugh. "Frederics, to hell with the tea, just bring us some hot cider," he called, "it seems we have some real women among us this day."

Brody came over to stand next to me and slowly leaned in and ask, "Did you accomplish everything you needed to?"

With a small start, I turned, "So far, all is quiet. We shall see if it was enough," I answered, looping my arm with Mother's and accompanying her into the parlor. "What was the matter with Patricia? She moved through here like she was on fire."

"I'm afraid Patricia likes to be in control of everything and this morning I took that away from her," Brody ruefully laughed, walking alongside Mother and me. "We like to call her display of displeasure hopping mad," he concluded, sounding very unrepentant.

"I'm sorry to hear that," I murmured.

"Why? I'm not," he quipped, showing off a row of white teeth, before hurrying off ahead of us to join Quinton and Jackson.

"I am not exactly sure what is going on between you two," Mother commented, gesturing toward Brody with her head, "but I hope you resolve it before we return home."

"I'm sure I don't have the foggiest idea of what you are referring to, Mother," I replied, not daring to look her in the eye for fear she would see right through me.

"Deny my words if you must, Olivia Sophia, but I was young once too. Just know that you're not fooling anyone," she added, giving my arm a squeeze. "I've seen the way he looks at you. I've also seen the way you look at him when you think no one is watching."

"Don't be ridiculous, Mother," I scoffed, "I don't have time for such foolishness. Besides, falling in love isn't in my plans. I came here with one purpose in mind and that is to find out what happened to Lilly."

"If you say so, but I can't say that I fully believe you at the moment," she retorted, looking at me out of the corner of her eye. "Oh, honestly, Olivia when are you going to loosen up? You are far too reserved to be my daughter."

Groaning slightly, I exhaled and rolled my eyes skyward. The smartest move would have been to keep quiet and not give Mother any more kindling for her fire, but I couldn't help myself. "So, what is your point, Mother?" Pulling me to a stop, she forced me to face her.

"The truth is, I've been waiting for years for you to do something truly bold with your life. In my opinion, you are far too concerned with what others think of you that you have missed out on living, cloistering yourself away in your safe little room." Gently stroking my cheek, Mother cupped my cheeks, smoothing back a stray hair, tucking it behind my ear. "I realize you were concerned that your father and I would be angry with you for taking the ship, regardless of the reason," she asserted, giving me a reassuring smile. "But full disclosure, I was truly proud of you for taking such initiative and acting so boldly." She continued, as her eyes teared slightly. "But eventually your heart will make a choice, and you will no longer be in control."

Looking away skeptically, I scoffed, pulling Mother down the hallway with me. "I think you have gone soft in the head, Mother dearest. Besides, when I lose myself to such passions, you can be assured that I will take care not to lose my good senses, along with my head. You have nothing to fear, Mother, I have not lost my heart to anyone," I stated, with finality, knowing full well, that I had just lied to my mother. *I'm going straight to hell*, I thought to myself.

"That truly is a shame. Maybe you haven't fallen yet, but someday you will, and when that day comes, you must be willing to sacrifice. Mark my words," Mother asserted, wagging her finger at me.

My heart skipped a beat, as her words repeated over again in my head. "Sure, Mother, and then I will remember this conversation, implicitly," I skeptically scoffed, wishing to end our conversation before we entered the room.

Presented a cup of Harrison's special hot cider as we entered the parlor, a party atmosphere was present while we were regaled with stories of the morning's ride. I especially loved the retelling of Patricia's many excuses, as she attempted to get everyone to turn around and return to the sanctity and warmth of the main house. I found most of her justifications very creative. Brody and Quinton recounted the drama of the ride with some hilarious antics. They had me crying with laughter when they mimicked Patricia's southern twang, exaggerating her words as they reenacted each scene. Patricia's own father was chuckling out loud with the rest of us, until she unexpectedly stepped in to the room, causing Brody and Quinton to freeze mid-sentence.

I was unsure if she had overheard us and what we were discussing upon entered the room, but she acted as if nothing was out of the ordinary. In my opinion, Patricia Olson was an exceptional actress choosing to let the ridiculous parody of her flow like water off a duck's back, or she was choosing to take the proverbial high ground. Then there was the third choice: she really hadn't heard Quinton and Brody making fun of her ridiculous antics. Either way, no harm done, as my father would say, and I chose to believe that she was oblivious to the entire matter.

The remainder of the day progressed while maids, footmen and other household staff prepared the great hall, for the impending celebration.

Dinner that evening, was a simple affair of bean soup, crusty bread and ham, promptly served at seven. Throughout the entire evening's events I thwarted Brody's best efforts to speak alone with me, choosing instead to surround myself with people, then slipping away to the sanctuary of my bedroom the moment his back was turned.

Shortly after retreating to my room, at ten-thirty, I heard Brody tapping upon my door, quietly calling out my name, yet I chose to ignore his efforts to reach out and discuss what was bothering me. I warned Margot off with a shake of my head when she attempted to answer the door. Eventually, he gave up. I heard his halting footsteps retreating down the hallway, as he turned around several times, before leaving for good.

I could tell that Margot wanted to ask questions but thought better of it in the end. Helping me change into night clothes, she excused herself, then left to socialize with the other servants with whom she had formed friendships. Lying in bed, I was enjoying the warm glow from the fireplace and thinking about my next plan of attack when I heard another soft tap on the door. I thought Brody had returned, so I scooted down in bed and covered my head with the sheet. This was something Coco and I used to do, pretending to be asleep.

Realizing too late that I had neglected to blow out the candle on the night table, I heard the doorknob turn and someone step into the room. Closing my eyes tightly, I tried to slow my breathing down so that whoever it was would think that I was asleep. I nearly jumped when they placed their hand on the covers, to check the rise and fall of my chest. Then suddenly, the blankets and sheet were pulled back, and I opened my eyes to find Coco staring at me.

"Ah ha! I knew that you weren't really asleep," she loudly proclaimed, crawling into the bed with me, covering us both up again. "Who are we avoiding, Olivia Sophia?" Coco asked, cocking one eyebrow. "Is it me? Are you avoiding me?"

"Not very successfully, it would seem," I quipped.

When we were younger snuggling beneath the covers had been a favorite past time of ours. We would hide together while trying to evade detection from our parents or the nanny. We especially loved playing this game when it was past our bedtime. Now instead of a way to avoid bedtime, it had become a way for us to reconnect and share our deepest secrets.

Pulling me closer, Coco rested an arm over my waist. "Why did you turn in so early?" she questioned, with a knowing smile.

"I was tired and needed to be alone," I lied, knowing full well that she saw right through me, but figured I would attempt to sell the lie anyway.

Pursing her beautiful, rosebud lips together, Coco scoffed at the obvious lie. "You will have to do better than that, Olivia, if you intend to make me a believer," she said crossly, wagging of her slender finger at me. "Why are you avoiding Brody? He clearly likes you. And let's not forget, I've seen the future."

"Ugh," I groaned in frustration, closing my eyes and plugging my ears like a two-year-old. "I thought we agreed a long time ago that you wouldn't tell me the future, Coco. It would be wrong." I grumbled, pulling the sheet down, so that I could sit up.

"Come on, Olivia, spill it. What has changed so dramatically from yesterday?" Coco gently coaxed, forcing me to look at her while pulling my hands away from my ears. "You can tell me. I will even take the Sister's Oath, if you like."

After several silent moments, I relented, folding the sheet neatly over and smoothing it down, I began to speak. "Patricia has insisted that her and Brody promised themselves to each other, and that she gave herself to him years ago, making them betrothed." I quietly finished, too embarrassed to say anything more, as I stared down at my hands.

Making a sound in the back of her throat, suggesting complete disgust, Coco touched my face, forcing me to look at her. "Poppy cock! I have never laid hands upon that woman, but I can tell you for a fact that I don't trust Patricia Olson as far as I can throw her. I think she is a pathological liar," Coco gave a derisively scoff. "And I personally wouldn't believe a word that fell from her lips."

"Even though Brody has admitted to me that there was something between his cousin Patricia and him?" I challenged.

"Ah ha!" Coco interjected, waving a finger in the air. "But did he say that he was in love with her or that he intended to marry her?" she asked, narrowing her eyes.

"Well, no." I shook my head. "But that doesn't mean that the two of them haven't discussed it. What if this is just his pattern, and I am merely a dalliance before he settles down? Oh, oh, what if he intended to marry Patricia Olson all along, and decided that he wanted a last fling?"

"Olivia, you are such an idiot," Coco said candidly, shaking me by the shoulders.

"Yes, I know, because I allowed Mr. Brody Beaumont to get under my skin." I added, in a self-deprecating tone, "He was probably curious about the strange, mystical woman Lilly told him all about, and wished to know if I kissed differently than normal women," I said dejectedly, with an exhale of air, feeling completely defeated.

"No! I mean that you have lost your mind. I don't believe for one minute that any of those scenarios are true. Besides, you are a big, fat hypocrite," Coco pointed out, with another loud scoff.

"What are you talking about, Catherine Elizabeth?"

"Do you remember Jamie Bannon, and how the two of you swore your undying devotion to one another, forever and ever? You even told me that you would never love another, for as long as you lived."

"Well, I guess I should have seen that one coming," I interjected tersely. I felt as if she had just slapped me across the face. "I was ten years old, Coco, and we never sealed our promise with…well you know," I stammered, turning three shades of red. "There is that particular detail you left out."

"Oh, please," Coco let out yet another dismissive scoff. "I'll bet you that if I touched Patricia with my bare hands, we would discover that she has been with any number of young eligible men for the *supposed, first time*," she said, rolling her eyes skyward. Then, giving me a critical look, Coco took me by the shoulders and gave me another good shaking. "Grow up, Olivia. Brody is a man, so what if he has been with another woman?"

"So, what?" I gasped. "I've never lain with another man before! I've never came close."

"Need I mention Jamie Bannon again."

"You'd better not," I warned.

"Stop being such a prude, Olivia," Coco admonished. "What should matter to you is what happens here and now since he met you. Not some insignificant dalliance with his manipulative second cousin Patricia, that happened years ago. You need to realize that we live in modern times. Things have changed. They no longer stone men and women for their indiscretions."

"And when did you become so knowledgeable about matters between a man and a woman?"

Lifting her eyebrows at me, Coco sheepishly grinned. "I've touched a lot of people. Wow, what an education," she said, dramatically rolling her eyes toward the ceiling. "I've seen some things that can never be unseen," she added, shaking her head.

"What a burden," I said, with just a hint of sarcasm. "And I thought seeing dead people was tough."

"You scoff, but I am serious. There are images that are forever burned into my mind," Coco shuddered. "Mother, Father…" Her words trailed off. "Need I say more?"

"Alright, alright. You win and now that image is stuck in my head," I said, holding up my hands to stave off any more talk of our parent's personal life. "Perhaps you can teach yourself how to filter certain things out, so that you don't have to wear gloves for the rest of your life."

"I have been practicing. I've even made some progress," Coco smiled, patting my arm. "But enough about me, I came here to help you."

"You already have. Just by listening to me whine and complain, why, I feel better already. Now hurry up and get changed," I smiled, looking toward the other room. "I don't wish to be alone tonight. And if you hurry, I will even tell you a story."

"I will be right back. Don't you go to sleep without telling me that story," Coco called over her shoulder, hopping down from the end of the bed to hurry off and change out of her dress. "Margot, where are you?" she called out, on her way to the other room.

"You'll have to care for yourself, I'm afraid. Margot is downstairs." laying back against the pillow I laughed at Coco's youthful enthusiasm. As for Mr. Beaumont, I would have to analyze my feelings for him tomorrow, because all I wanted to do was retreat into my comfortable, safe place with my sister, Coco.

22

SATURDAY, FEBRUARY 14, 1804

Very Early in The Morning

COCO AND I WERE HUDDLED together, when something hit the window with a loud clatter, startling us awake. As our eyes popped open and we lay there staring at one another a moment, unsure of what had just happened, there was another loud clatter, causing us both to sit straight up in bed. Something hit the window again and we both jumped out of bed and ran to the window, throwing the curtains open wide to see what it was. Our eyes were drawn to several crows laying lifelessly upon the balcony landing. While we looked at each other, silently questioning what could have caused the birds to fly into the window, two more crows flew into the glass, startling us to the point that we screamed and jumped back.

The bedroom door flew open, causing us to scream again, even louder, and cling to one another for dear life, just as another bird flew into the window.

"What in the world?" Margot exclaimed, quickly joining us at the window to see for herself what was going on.

"The birds are just flinging themselves at the window," Coco declared while dragging me away from the window.

"What do you mean birds just keep flinging themselves against the window?" Margot questioned. "Look out!" she screamed, quickly closing the drapes, as another bird helplessly slammed to its death. "You two need to go in the other room. I will get some help." Margot insisted, shooing us out the door like a mother hen.

Out in the hallway, Coco turned to me and said, "That was most peculiar, don't you think?"

Quinton and Brody, who had been alerted to the commotion, came running down the hallway and saw us. "What's happened, and why is it peculiar?" Quinton questioned, peering at the startled expressions on our faces.

"Crows are flying into the window," I cried, "I've never seen anything like it."

Concern marred Brody's handsome face as his hand gently touched my arm. "Is anyone hurt?"

"We are fine," I said tentatively, looking up, "but the birds appear to be dead."

Quinton cleared his throat, drawing the attention of his brother. "We will see to the birds. We don't know why, but this happened before, one year ago today," he added, scratching his head. My eyes snapped up to Quinton's face.

"How many times has this happened before?" I questioned, as the flesh on my arm still tingled where Brody had touched me. From the corner of my eye, I noticed Brody scrutinizing me.

"Maybe seven years?" he answered, turning to his brother for confirmation.

Quinton nodded his head. "That sounds about right."

"Seven years, not eight?" I asked, just to clarify.

"No, seven years," Quinton confirmed. "Why?"

"Just gathering facts, that's all," I answered while opening the door to our room to call out to Margot. "Margot, perhaps you could gather some clothing for Coco and me, and meet us in Mother's room. We wouldn't want to be late for breakfast," I instructed, before closing the door again, just as another bird hit the window. "The room is all yours, gentlemen. I would advise you to enlist the help of Father Timothy," I added, taking a hold of Coco's arm to lead her down the hallway, without glancing back.

"That is an excellent suggestion," Brody called back to me, before dispatching a houseboy to fetch Father Timothy. I didn't need to look back to know that Brody was staring at me. I could feel his eyes. Turning the corner, I glanced back down the hallway and caught a glimpse of a slender figure, dressed in cream, quickly retreating in the opposite direction.

I had resigned myself to the fact that the entire day would be spent in preparations for the evenings celebrations, and yet the fact that Patricia was skulking about in the hallways spying on people made me curious. What was she up too?

"What is it, Olivia?" Coco asked when she felt me hesitate. Patting her arm, that was intertwined with mine, I smiled reassuringly.

"It's nothing, really. Let us go and roust Mother and Father to inform them of the wonderful news that we will be taking over their bedroom for a while."

Yanking on my arm, Coco stopped in the middle of the hallway, with a look of concern on her face. "We are planning to knock first, I hope."

"But of course, dear sister. I don't need any more surprises this morning," I added with a nervous laugh.

Coco laughed, covering her mouth. "Indeed."

The house was a buzz with excitement, as well as apprehension. And understandably so. It was like anticipating the guillotine blade dropping upon your neck, but not knowing how long the executioner intended to keep you waiting.

Coco and I returned to our rooms after breakfast, two hours later and found a fresh bath waiting for us, in front of the roaring fire.

I bathed first, because Coco wanted to visit beforehand with Emily. I, on the other hand, planned to hide in my room the rest of the day. I sunk down deep in the hot water, trying to sooth away a week's worth of pent up anxiety, as the lavender-scented water swirled just under my nose. "Ahh," I sighed deeply, after dunking my head under the water.

My mind was working overtime, untangling the mess that surrounded my best friend's murder. Then there was the new mystery of crows flying into windows every year for the past seven years. I wasn't quite sure what it all meant when a thought popped into my head. *If Annabelle Beaumont supposedly committed suicide eight years ago, why is she still here, causing turmoil for her family? If she wanted to die, wouldn't she have just passed over? Why stay and make everyone you loved suffer? It didn't make sense. What would prompt a prominent woman of society to commit suicide in the first place?*

Try as I might, I could not come up with a plausible reason. I needed to ask more questions to get at the truth. Then I started to wonder if Annabelle and Lilly's deaths were related at all? Could it be that one death set off a chain reaction that somehow caused the second death? I felt a dull ache in the pit of my stomach, like when you know you are about to be sick, but you try to deny it in hopes that it will just go away.

I reached behind me, pulling the medallion around to feel it. I had hung it over the side of the bathtub, while I still wore it, to keep it from getting wet. Somehow, just running my fingers over the weathered metal soothed and comforted me. I felt more centered and peaceful when I ran my fingertips across the surface of the ancient carvings, as I continued to ponder matters. Tapping my forehead a couple of times with the medallion I wondered what will happen if I never solve Lilly's death. Will I have to stay in this home indefinitely? No, that was definitely not an option. Eventually I would wear out my welcome, and my family and I would have to go back home at some point. I had an entire life to live, and I hadn't even begun it yet.

No, something was definitely coming to a head, I could feel it in every fiber of my marrow. But the when and where of it all was still a mystery to me. I sat in the tub pondering the matter further while staring into the fire, when a loud noise came from the window again. Startled from my musings, I turned my head toward the window to see what had caused the noise, and floating just outside of my window was

Annabelle Beaumont. And she looked angry. Well, angrier than usual. She must have just discovered that she was no longer welcomed to come and go from the house at will. Annabelle was locked out.

"Are you ready for me to rinse you off, Lady Olivia?" Margot teased, mimicking a very proper lady's maid.

I jumped with a yelp, while clutching at my chest, "I need to tie a bell around your neck, Margot. Honestly, you startled me."

"I can see that. What has you so jumpy, Olivia?" Margot gazed at the window, trying to determine what had me so transfixed. Margot had no idea that there was an angry spirit hovering at my window, shooting poison darts at me with her eyes. "What do you see out there?" she continued, walking over to the window and drawing the curtains shut.

"Thank you for that and as for what I was looking at, you really don't want to know," I advised, turning back around to face the fireplace. "It would only give you nightmares."

"Well, when you say it like that, of course I don't want to know. You can keep your demons to yourself."

"After seeing what awaits me outside, maybe I should stay where I am," I murmured, under my breath, just as Margot poured the water over my head.

I could hear the smile in her voice when she asked, "Did you say something?"

With a forced smile, I replied, "No, not really. Just help me dry off, so that my shriveled fingers and I can go enjoy this dance."

23

Gritting My Teeth And Preparing For Impact

CARRIAGES BEGAN TO ARRIVE AT six-thirty and I could hear the clatter of guests enjoying themselves every time the bedroom door was opened.

A light supper of vegetable soup, fruit, meats and cheeses was brought up to the room at five-thirty for Coco, Emily and me. Emily and Coco entertained themselves by gawking out the window, critiquing everyone's attire while I made sure to keep my back to the window. I did not dare take the chance that she would return and glare at me again. For all of my brave bravado of being able to take care of myself, Annabelle Beaumont and her steely-eyed glares frightened me to death. A chill had spread through me, like a cold front, and turned my blood to ice.

"Margot, would you mind stoking the fire and adding another log? It seems that I have developed a chill, and I can't shake it," I said, as an involuntary shiver shook my body.

"Right away, Lady Olivia," Margot answered, giving a curtsy, as she played the proper ladies' maid in front of Emily.

I watched Margot bend over and stoke the fire, then add another log. Normally, just the thought of Margot being all proper and such was enough to make me break out into hysterical giggles, but tonight it only made me smile.

"Olivia, is there something wrong?" Coco asked, looking concerned.

"No. I'm fine," I lied, staring at the glowing embers of the newly-stoked fire. "Just a little chilled. Nothing to worry about."

"But you would tell me if there was anything wrong, wouldn't you?" she questioned, placing a hand upon my shoulder.

Looking at Emily and then Coco, I forced myself to smile. "Of course I would. Now, stop worrying. Truly, I am fine," I assured her, patting Coco's arm where her robe covered her, being careful not to touch her skin, directly.

With that reassurance, Coco and Emily went back to discussing matters of importance — the handsome gentlemen they had seen entering the house, and which of them they intended to dance with first.

I smiled to myself and turned back to the fire, as the flames quickly kicked up. I could feel the warmth on my face, but my blood still felt sluggish and cold. Looking back upon that moment now, I can see where I had gone wrong. I believe I was blinded by inexperience.

I desired to be like everyone else who come to Rosewood that evening for the festivities. I wanted to drink, dance and flirt with eligible young men, and enjoy myself. But I wasn't just like everyone else. There was a reason I was present, at this moment in time. I had a purpose, a higher calling that wouldn't be denied or pushed aside. And yet, it was easier to close my eyes and shush the inner voices in my head telling me to prepare myself for battle. Somehow, I knew there was something bad coming my way because I could feel it in every fiber of my body. Instinctively I knew there was no way for me to stop what was about to happen, like two carriages that collide. You can see it coming from some ways off, but you are powerless to do anything to prevent it.

The only real decision left for me to make at that point was, should I grit my teeth and brace for impact, or do I turn and fight with everything I have left?

24

SATURDAY, FEBRUARY 14, 1804

Brace for Impact or Turn and Fight

IT WAS AROUND SEVEN-THIRTY WHEN Coco and Emily left my room to ready themselves for the party. They were so excited they could hardly sit still. I sat at the vanity, allowing Margot to fuss over my hair. She made curls, piling them all over my head and pinning them in place, with tiny pearl encrusted hair pins. The affect was stunning, as little white pearls danced in my hair.

Margot laced up my corset, cinching the ties so tightly that I could hardly breathe. "Explain to me again, the reason I have to wear a corset, Margot."

"This is a costume party, my dear, and the ladies of old wore corsets," Margot patiently explained, huffing and puffing as she pulled on the laces.

"Enough, Margot, or I shall expire before your eyes," I grumbled through clenched teeth while holding on to the bed post for support. "These things are barbaric."

"Ideally, your waist should be only eighteen to nineteen inches."

"Margot, my waist has never been very large, but I can assure you that I will never have a nineteen-inch waist. I enjoy food," I grumbled. Margot took pity on me, loosening the stays half an inch. "Oh, thank you, dear Margot. Now, I will be able to enjoy a sip of punch," I said, with a sarcastic tone.

"Count yourself fortunate that you have breath enough to still be cheeky. That alone should be of some consolation," she chided.

Stepping into the center of the gown, along with the layers and layers of underskirts that would give the dress flare, I waited as Margot pulled each layer up, tying them one by one. Finally, Margot reached down, pulling up the red brocade gown. She gently helped me slip my arms through the delicate sleeves.

The red dress was elegant in design, skimming low in the front and sitting just at the peak of my shoulders, with a delicate sheer-fitted sleeve. The material had both a satiny sheen and a tapestry pattern of delicate roses, in different stages of bloom. The material was truly exquisite, and the ladies had expertly altered the gown to fit me like a glove. The top of the dress tapered down, accentuating my tiny waist, with a full gathered skirt and large bow in the back. I truly felt like a princess.

Coco entered the room as Margot finished lacing me up, to let me know that she was ready to go downstairs. Her gown was equally lovely, white satin with a sheer gauzy layer skimming over the top of the skirt, tiny black rosebuds, embroidered along the bottom hem and again along the neckline. Coco had tied a black velvet ribbon around her throat, allowing the extra ribbon to flow down her back, with a single teardrop crystal resting in the hollow of her throat. One delicate crystal teardrop also hung from each ear, reflecting the lights when she turned her head. The design, while simple, was surprisingly stunning and she took my breath away.

"Oh Coco, I do believe you will be the most beautiful woman at the ball tonight," I remarked with a sigh, motioning for her to turn around and show me the back of her gown.

Spinning around the room, as if she were dancing with one of those handsome young men downstairs, Coco looked like she was floating an inch off the ground.

"Do you really think so?" she asked breathlessly. A knock at the door interrupted us.

"Margot, could you see who that is, please?" I asked, still staring at my sister's beautiful face.

"Of course," Margot replied, "should I send them away?"

"Find out who it is first," I answered, while reaching my hand out to feel the gown's material.

Opening the door a few inches, I heard, Margot talking to someone then swing the door open wide. "It's Miss Emily, my lady," Margot said, bobbing a polite curtsy, as she announced the guest.

"Oh, don't you both simply look glorious. I was wondering who would be picked to wear the red dress this year," Emily blurted out, with a wry smile. "And look at you. Why, I didn't even have to go downstairs to get my answer."

Coco and I were puzzled by Emily's statement, and simultaneously asked, "What are you talking about?"

"Well, this party has traditionally been a black and white ball, except for one woman who is chosen to wear the red gown," Emily said. "Of course, when Annabelle Beaumont was alive, she always chose the wearer. But since her death, a different woman has been chosen by the Beaumont men each year. Patricia was positive that it was her turn this year. Oh, won't she be shocked." Emily babbled on, as she ran her hand along the back of the settee, looking a little smug, as if she held all the great secrets of the world, and was deciding just how much to share with us.

"What are you saying, Emily?" I questioned, confused over the implication of wearing the red dress.

"Why, she is simply going to split a seem. Just wait until Patricia sees you coming down the staircase," Emily cooed, with delight as she laughed. "You must wait until I am downstairs, before you make your entrance," Emily insisted, with another squeal of delight. "Because I want to be standing next to her when you do. I want to witness her entire tirade," Emily confessed, with a mischievous gleam in her eyes.

"Perhaps I should change into something else," I remarked, looking down at the gown that had taken me forty minutes to get into, just a bit suspicious of her motives.

"Oh, don't you dare," Emily replied, turning to Coco for support. "Tell her to stay just as she is. Your sister has just as much right to be the woman in red as Patricia."

"Emily is right, Olivia. Don't you dare change out of that gown. You look absolutely bonny," Coco admonished, narrowing her eye and adding, "and if Brody wanted Patricia to be the woman in red, then she would be wearing that gown tonight, instead of you."

"Of course, you are right, but I still feel a bit uncomfortable," I admitted, turning to take another glance at my reflection in the tall, floor-length mirror. Grudgingly, I had to admit that they were right and decided that it was too late to change.

"You will be the belle of the ball," Emily giggled triumphantly, taking Coco's arm. "You take your time and finish getting ready, while we go downstairs to find the perfect spot so we may witness your grand entrance." Then stopping at the door, Emily turned to say, "Are you going to wear that chain around your neck?"

Drawing my attention to the medallion, Father Timothy had given me, I picked it up and looked at it. Father Timothy was a wise man, and he made me swear to keep wear the medal for a reason. I would not take a chance with my life, simply to be fashionable. "Well, yes, I was planning to."

"Well, I wouldn't, it's simply ghastly," Emily argued, taking Coco's arm and usher her from the room. Sitting in front of the mirror, I pondered what to do with the silver chain and medallion, I had promised never to take off.

"Don't fret, Olivia, Margot knows just what to do about that chain." Margot said, referring to herself in the third person. "When I am done, you won't even know that it is there," she added cheerfully, producing a thick, red satin ribbon. "We will just turn this thing around and drop the medal down your back and disguise the chain with a ribbon."

The high collar was genius and hid the chain completely from view once Margot tied the ribbon around my throat. The length of ribbon was tucked beneath my collar as well, hiding any sign of the ancient medal. Producing a pair of ruby earrings with delicately dangling pearls, Margot held out her hand and smiled. "I thought this pair would go well with that dress.

"They are perfect," I gushed, slipping them on, then sat back a moment to admire Margot's handiwork. Every hair was precisely in place and the faint blush of makeup only enhanced my features, instead of overpowering them.

"I believe I am ready to make my grand entrance," I stated with trepidation, feeling like the proverbial lamb being led to slaughter. Giving my shoulders a reassuring squeeze, Margot tied a dance card to my wrist with a matching satin ribbon and adjusted one last pin, before walking me to the door. Stepping into the hallway, I heard crystal glasses, clanking together and people visiting and laughing, enjoying themselves.

I took a deep breath at the top of the staircase, preparing myself for whatever might come at me. Quinton and Brody did say that their parties had become infamous for the strange happenings. I admit I was curious about what could happen with Annabelle banished from the house by a protective barrier.

I could see Harrison as I stood on the top step. He bellowed loudly, trying to get everyone's attention and quiet the crowd. "Ladies and gentlemen, may I have your attention, please." People continued to talk excitedly, despite Harrison's plea for quiet.

I took one last deep breath and began to descend the staircase. I had wished to exude an air of self-confidence and calm demeanor, despite my complete lack of it. Halfway down the steps, I heard Harrison bellow again. "Ladies and gentlemen, please, I wish to make a toast," he bellowed again, just as the crowd fell silent.

Harrison turned to look at me just as Brody dashed up the staircase, took my hand, and led me the rest of the way down the staircase, grinning from ear-to-ear.

"I was starting to wonder if you were ever going to grace us with your presence," Brody leaned down to whisper.

"If I had realized I would be the center of attention, I might have taken the back staircase down tonight," I quipped.

"And miss all the excitement? Father was just about to give the official toast that begins the evening's festivities," Brody commented, loud enough for his father to hear, as we passed by. Taking two glasses from a nearby tray, Brody handed one to me and turned to smile broadly at his father.

"As I was saying. I would like to welcome everyone to our annual winter ball and thank you for graciously joining us. It is my great honor to toast the start of another celebration, commemorating my sons Quinton and Brody. We would like you all to raise your glasses to another year of good health, good fortune and may everyone live well and prosper. Cheers!" he said, lifting his glass of Champaign into the air, just as the room broke out into loud cheers of "Happy Birthday."

"Cheers, my dear Olivia," Brody smiled, lifting his glass to me. "How does it feel to be the belle of the ball?" he asked, taking a sip of Champaign.

"If I had only been warned beforehand," I stated, lifting my glass in answer, before downing the contents. "By the way, Happy Birthday," I muttered, sipping from my glass as people shook his hand and wished him well.

"So, it is to be like that," he remarked between handshakes, before downing his glass of Champaign as he looked around, plucking the glass from my hand and placing them both down on a tray just as a server passed by.

Stepping onto the dance floor, Brody stood, waiting for me to join him. "The first dance is always a waltz," he remarked, lifting his arms into the proper stance, as if he already held someone.

"That is rather presumptuous of you," I said, standing in place and staring at him.

"What is?" he asked, stepping off the dance floor and taking a hold of my hand, paying little attention to the fact that I was not smiling back at him.

"To assume that I hadn't promised someone else the first dance."

"Don't be ridiculous, you've only just arrived downstairs," Brody pointed out, pulling me closer. "When would you have had the time?" he added, as the music began.

"That isn't the point. What if I wanted to dance with someone else?" I argued.

"Well, that would be ridiculous, because I am the best dancer in five counties. Six if you count Tucker," Brody teased, giving me a wink as he spun me in his arms and continued.

His good humor was quite infections and I nearly forgot why I was angry with him, until I noticed Patricia's scowling face from the edge of the floor, glaring at us both.

"Don't you just love a good ball? The rush and excitement, mingled with so much anticipation. The speculations of who will get lost in the hallways of this enormous home or take a wrong turn, with whom?" Brody speculated, as he prattled on, pretending not to notice the terse look on my face.

"A life of privilege, has left you blind in one eye," I stated rather flippantly, as we began another turn around the dance floor.

"Are you calling me blind?" Brody asked, good naturedly, seeming unperturbed.

"Would you say that a morally bankrupt individual makes for a very poor prospect?" I countered, coolly.

Looking slightly concerned now, but still not yet angry, Brody continued to smile pleasantly. "If you could be a little more forthcoming about the matter for which you speak, perhaps I could give you my honest opinion."

A furtive glance passed between us, and I was trying to decide if he was sincere or if he was truly ignorant about the reason I was angry. I gnawed at my bottom lip, uncertain whether or not I had made a mistake, judging Brody too harshly.

"Perhaps, if you would stop talking in riddles and speak your mind, the two of us could get to the heart of the matter," Brody chastised as his seductive voice sliced through me like a sharp knife.

"There you are wrong, Mr. Beaumont, I speak clearly enough for those with ears to hear."

I saw a change come over him, manifesting through his eyes. My last words had struck a nerve. "So, not only have you called me blind, but now you say that I am deaf, as well," he added, with a loud snort, then looked down at me. "This is not the way I saw the evening progressing at all." His eyes turned dark and stormy, crackling with electricity as they now met mine.

I was beginning to question the soundness of confronting him at his ball, but at this point, the ox was in the mire. "I was informed that you have promised yourself to another," I managed to say, just as the music ended.

Pondering me a moment longer than necessary, Brody abruptly stopped, curtly bowed to me as I dropped into a curtsy. "You have been misinformed," he said curtly, before walking away, leaving me standing alone on the dance floor with my mouth hanging open.

I didn't have time to process the unexpected information because I was approached by another young man who bowed, introduced himself to me as Mr. Emery Lafferty of Virginia, who immediately took ahold of my hand and began to dance me around the floor.

When that song ended, I didn't have time to escape the floor before I was handed off to Mr. Isaac Cumberton, of Roanoke. He was a pleasant man, in his late twenties, with tall, lanky features. His hands were far too soft and supple to have ever done any kind of manual labor.

He was followed by Mr. Dwight Dewitt, who enjoyed pontificating on the virtues of his modernized flour mill and extensive bug collection. And just as I was ready to throw my hands into the air and cry uncle, Quinton stepped in to rescue me. "I see that my brother has thrown you to the wolves," he laughed, sweeping me from the dance floor and over to the refreshment table, where he handed me a cold glass of punch. "Now, I wonder what would have made him do that?" Quinton mused out loud, giving me a sidelong glance, while picking out something to eat.

"I may have been given some bad information," I said sheepishly, mulling over the refreshment table and deciding that nothing truly looked good to me. "Of which I may have confronted him with said bad information whilst we were dancing," I added, trying to sound perfectly innocent, before quickly lifting the cup of punch to my lips and drinking the contents down.

With a lift of his eyebrows, Quinton smiled broadly as he popped a stuffed mushroom into his mouth and chewed. "That would do it," he mumbled with a full mouth while reaching for a piece of cheese. "Can I get you another drink?"

"Only if you lace it with something a little stronger than this," I suggested, lifting the empty cup up and looking around for a tray to deposit it on.

Taking my arm and tucking it under his, Quinton led me away from the table. "So, I am just going to take a wild stab at this and say that my cousin Patricia has been whispering nonsense into your ear."

Gasping out loud, I found it impossible to hide my surprise. "Are you psychic?"

Quinton threw his head back and laughed. "No, but I do know the intricate workings of my cousin's mind. She is conniving like that. She must have seen how Brody looked at you and worried that she could no longer manipulate him, like she used to."

"What do you mean, manipulate him like she used to?" I questioned, searching the room for any sign of Brody, hoping that I could apologize.

"She used to lead my brother around by the nose when we were younger," Quinton said with a chuckle. "It really was quite entertaining and pathetic at the same time, if you must know. Then Brody wised up and saw Patricia for the person she truly is."

"And who might that be?" Patricia demanded in a low growl, standing directly behind us.

Quinton answered, without turning around. "A catty, cruel, despiteful, self-indulgent, self-centered, narcissistic…" and then as if he just realized that she was standing behind him, Quinton turned and acted surprised. "Oh, have you been standing there long?"

"Don't play dumb with me, you ignorant…" Patricia fumed as her face turned red, her eyes darted from side to side, checking for who else might have heard their conversation.

"Ah, ah, ah." Quinton said, wagging his finger in Patricia's face. "You wouldn't wish to show your true colors to everyone present. However, I would wager any amount of money that half the male population in this room have already seen more than that."

Patricia hissed and attempted to strike Quinton across the face, but he was too fast for her, grabbing her wrist mid-swing. "Did you honestly think that I would just stand here and take it from you, Patricia?" Quinton hissed back, getting within an inch of her face. "You have the wrong Beaumont boy for that."

Looking as if she were about to break into tears, Patricia whined, "You're hurting my arm, Quinton Beaumont, you awful beast."

"You're very lucky that we are surrounded by a room full of polite society, or I would do worse to you and not think twice about it," he added, throwing Patricia's wrist back at her, as if the appendage offended him.

"You were always the mean one," Patricia pouted, looking around her to see if anyone felt sorry for her and would intervene on her behalf.

"What you really mean is, I was never stupid enough to fall for your lies." With a cruel smile, Quinton laughed, then took me by the hand, leading me away from her, and with those parting words Quinton and

I disappeared into the crowd. "You need to make things right," Quinton exclaimed, unceremoniously dragging me behind him, weaving his way through the crowd and coming out at the edge of the great hall.

Pulling back slightly, I was starting to feel indignant. "Quinton, I'm going to have to insist you slow down and stop dragging me about as if I were a prized mare."

With a chuckle, Quinton turned around. "Begging your pardon, my Lady, but did you just refer to yourself as a prized mare?"

"Yes, and I am not accustomed to being dragged about like this. It really is quite undignified," I bristled, looking down to straighten my skirts. "Have you ever been cinched up tightly in some antiquated corset to the point that you could barely breathe? Because I have."

Looking surprised, Quinton pursed his lips together as if he was thinking about it, and then replied, "No, I've never had an occasion to wear one."

"Well, thanks to your family's desire to play dress up, I am. And I can assure you, they are very restrictive. I can barely breath in this thing, let alone keep up with you whilst you drag me about, willy-nilly like this," I complained. "Now please, tell me why you feel this is necessary," eyeing him critically. "It is no small wonder that you haven't yet secured yourself a wife, to be sure. Who would marry such a brute?" I stated emphatically, glaring at him.

Instead of being insulted, Quinton threw his head back and laughed, wiping a tear from his eye, before replying. "Oh, how I do not envy my brother. You certainly are a hand full." Then grabbing my hand again, Quinton continued to pull me along behind him, through the doorway and down the hall.

"Quinton Beaumont, you turn loose of me, this instant! Do you hear me?" I berated, with my most stern tone. "I swear, you're as thick as manure and only half as useful, you dunder-head," which only made him laugh more. Between gritted teeth I hissed, "If I wasn't all trussed up like a Christmas goose, I would show you a thing or two."

"And I can assure you, my Lady, I look forward to that day with much anticipation," Quinton admonished over his shoulder. "But right this minute, you need to right a terrible wrong, and I intend to help you do just that," he taunted, with a smug smile.

Opening the door at the end of the hallway, he peaked inside, then turning back around and grinned. Giving me a wink he said, "Good luck and please, do try to sound sincere, Lady Olivia," just before shoving me into the darkened room, and quickly closing the doors behind me. I didn't really have a chance to react before I heard Quinton laughing on the other side of the door, as he turned the key, locking me inside.

Surprised by his rotten trick, I quickly turned around and pulled on the handle, to no avail. Then I pounded on the door, but Quinton only laughed from halfway down the hallway. Giving the door a good swift kick, I quickly realized the folly of my actions when my foot collided with the solid, wooden door and I began to hop about on my one good foot.

The fact that I was on my own quickly sunk in and I turned around to survey the room. I was in a man's study, a play room of sorts for grown men. I could make out a billiard table and saw that a fire was burning in the hearth on the far side of the room. Limping my way towards the light I stubbed my toe on a chair, cursing under my breath.

Drawing closer to the fire light, some one moved on the couch, catching my eye, causing me to jump. "Oh, you frightened me." I confessed, still clutching at my chest. Brody merely gazed up at me, before downing the contents of his crystal tumbler. "What on earth are you doing sitting here in the dark?"

Without answering, he held up his glass and waved it in the air. Then he stood and walked over to the liquor cabinet, to pour himself another glass full. "Would you like one?" he offered, looking over his shoulder at me. I could tell that he was still put out by our earlier conversation and waved him off. "Well, your loss," he added, before returning to the sofa and plopping down on the cushion. "Best *damn* whisky in all the states. That's because it came all the way from Ireland, not unlike yourself," Brody chuckled to himself. "Those Irish," he with a sarcastic tone.

Studying him a moment, I could tell that he was slightly inebriated. No doubt from indulging just a bit too much in his *damn fine* Irish whisky. That's when my guilty conscious began to gnaw at me, and I felt bad for ruining his party. Not to mention, being an idiot for listening to Patricia Olson. Desperately searching for something to say that would fill the awkward silence between us, I blurted out the first thing that came to my mind. "You know, you really threw me to the wolves, when you left the party abruptly."

"I'm so sorry, Your Highness, but I lost the stomach for making merry with everyone tonight," Brody answered with a cynical sneer, before taking another sip of his drink.

Turning to warm my hands, I took a deep breath and chanced a look over my shoulder. Quinton was right, I had made a tremendous blunder, and now it was up to me to fix it. There was no way around it. I owed Brody an apology. "I'm an idiot," I said, still facing the fire, too embarrassed by my behavior to face him. "And I realize that I'm completely to blame for that, Brody. I truly am sorry for doubting you. I was wrong to doubt you and wish you would except my sincerest apologies. Maybe you will let me make it up to you?" I concluded.

When he didn't answer me, I turned around to face him and found him staring into his glass of whiskey. For the longest moment, he didn't move or say a word. I found myself mesmerized by the way the firelight refracted off the liquid in his cut crystal tumbler. When I finally brought my eyes up to look into his, I saw the firelight dancing wildly in his darkened pupils. There was a storm brewing and the air in the room all but evaporated, like steam off a lake on a hot summer morning. My skin felt flush and my breath caught in my lungs. A devilish smile played across his sensuous lips and I knew in that moment, that I was in serious trouble.

Taking another deep breath, I walked over to where he sat and sat down next to him and, taking the half full glass from his hand, I downed the contents in one gulp. It burned like hell all the way down the back of my throat, and I began to sputter and cough.

Brody gave me one swift claps to the back, nearly knocking me onto the floor. "*Damn good* whisky," I managed to choke out while trying to catch my breath.

Brody threw his head back and laughed until tears streamed down his cheeks, so I stood up and walked over to the liquor cabinet, intending to refill his tumbler for him. But before I could pour out the liquid in the cup, I felt Brody's breath on the back of my neck as he covered my hand with his, stopping me.

I turned my head, curious why he had stopped me when I saw the look in his eyes and gasped out loud. My heart skipped a beat, and I'm certain that it must have stopped all together, for just a couple of seconds.

Placing his hands about my waist, Brody forced me to turn and face him. "I don't need more whisky, Olivia. Just the sight of you intoxicates me," he whispered, lowering his lips to within a hairs breath of mine. "I only need you."

I felt exhilarated as his lips covered mine. He was all I could concentrate on as I threw caution to the wind, along with my good common sense. But I didn't care. I needed him to forgive me for my harsh words and doubt. I felt cleansed from my sins.

His touch was warm as his hands gently clasped the back of my neck, wrapping his long, tapered fingers around my throat to draw me nearer, quickening my pulse and breathing as he deepened our kiss.

My own hands worked independent of me, splaying across his strong, muscular back and chest at the same time. I couldn't get close enough. Need and desire coursed through my veins, fanning the flames of passion. Heaving a sigh that bespoke so much more than words alone could express, I felt Brody's lips travel down the sensitive flesh of my throat, sending goose bumps through me, like ripples on a pond. An involuntary shudder rocked me and I softly moaned when his teeth grazed the sensitive skin of my collar bone, while his tongue playfully danced in the hollow.

I couldn't imagine anything more glorious as I clung to him, until the very moment I realized my feet were no longer touching the ground. Brody had lifted me into his arms and carrying me over to the couch.

Gently depositing me on the well-worn leather cushions of the study couch, Brody placed a pillow beneath my head. My eyes followed him as he stood back and took a deep breath as he gazed down at me.

Shirking out of his coat and vest, Brody threw the articles of clothing at the nearest chair, not caring that they slid almost immediately to the ground. Next his fingers quickly worked feverishly at the knot of his cravat, which he dropped on the ground, as he walked towards me. Our eyes never strayed from one another and the air was charged with electricity, leaving me breathless. I could physically feel the heat from his gaze as it travelled up and down my body and when the firelight caught his eyes again, I thought my heart would beat its way from my chest. *He is more handsome than any one man had the right to be*, I thought to myself as shivers of desire coursed through me.

I knew I was playing with fire, but the desire to feel his skin touching mine was so strong, almost desperate, and when he took me in his arms again, I smiled to myself because I knew he felt the same way.

I pulled back slightly and touched his face, the fires glow made his skin look like satin and I caught my breath. I wanted him with every fiber of my being as I watched his lips turn up into a confident smile. I wondered what he would think of me if he knew all of my deepest, darkest thoughts in that moment. Would he be shocked?

Our mouths came together, almost frantically, and I heard myself moan in pleasure as I melted into him. If I were truly a proper young woman, I would've gathered up my skirts, and run away as fast as

I could. Just that simple show of self control would have been a sign of good breeding. But who was I kidding?

Pushing the flimsy material from my shoulder, his lips again trailed passionate kisses down my throat and collar bone. I felt something inside of me melt and begin to ooze molten sensuality that was so liquid hot I feared it would consume me. It swept through me with such intensity that passionate flutters teased the lowest parts of my belly, sending sinfully wicked pleasure throughout. They were the most pleasurable feelings I had ever experienced. Suddenly I understood why poets wrote sonnets about it and women lost their virtue over it. I was hot, then cold and my head was spinning all at once. Resistance at this point would have been futile, as his teeth gently nibbled at the sensitive flesh of my shoulder, sending quaking shivers to my very core. He had a hold over me, and I refused to stop and ask myself why or how I could be free again. I only knew that it was an intoxicating emotion, and I never wanted it to end.

Slowly Brody pulled back and his eyes searched mine desperately, only my befuddled mind couldn't imagine why he would stop. "Olivia," he said, as if the effort of speaking were almost unbearable, "I want you to know that I wish to ask your father for your hand in marriage," he announced, still waiting for some sign of reaction from me.

I felt as if a bucket of icy cold water had been poured over my head, quickly sobering me. I stared at him for a few split seconds, before pushing against him to free myself from his embrace. Standing up on wobbly legs, I somehow managed to walk over to the fireplace.

"What is it, Olivia?" He sounded bewildered by my reaction. "I thought you would be pleased."

Turning around to face him, I felt my entire insides quaking for an entirely different reason. I was furious. "How can you possibly assume that you know what is in my heart when you have never bothered to ask me?" I replied calmly, despite the rage that bubbled up inside of me. "Not every woman is scheming to entangle themselves to a man and family. You couldn't possibly know me, could you, because you haven't bothered to inquire. So how can you stand before me now and profess to know what it is that I want?"

"But doesn't every woman want the security of marriage, before…" He stammered, grabbing his shirt from the floor when he stood up, sounding confused as he took a few steps toward me while slipping on his shirt. "Before you commit yourself to a man."

"You take much for granted, Mr. Townsend," I spat out between clenched teeth, before turning to find my way to the locked door at the other end of the darkened room. "And if you and your nefarious brother are quite through with your scheming, I would appreciate you unlocking this door."

Stopping to pick up his waist coat and jacket, Brody slipped them on before joining me at the door. Taking a hold of my elbow, he spun me around to face him. "What are you talking about, Olivia? I didn't know that you would come looking for me tonight. There was no scheming on my part," he asserted.

"Do you honestly expect me to believe that you didn't set this entire thing up, so you could bag yourself a rich heiress from Europe?" I spitefully hissed, trying to break his hold.

"Olivia, listen to yourself. You're not making any sense," he pleaded, sounding so sincere I almost believed him. "Why would I need a rich heiress from Europe when I have more than enough money to sustain a small army?"

Infuriated and incensed, I didn't wish to hear anything he had to say, let alone something that made sense. I struggled to free myself from his vise-like grip. He was trying to make me see reason, but I was beyond reason at this point and felt myself shut down. "Do you have a key to unlock this door or not?"

Trying one last time, Brody lowered his lips to mine and passionately kissed me, in hopes of recapturing the moment, but I was having nothing to do with it. When our lips separated again, I could see his eyes desperately searching my face in the dark. "Well, do you have the key or not?" I asked again, slightly less angry than before.

Silently, Brody let loose of me and reached into his trouser pocket, producing a key. Stepping closer to the door, Brody was about to place the key into the lock when the doors and windows began to rattle and shake violently. Jumping back from the door, we looked at one another as panicked screams came from the other side of the door.

"Brody, please, you must unlock this door, quickly," I pleaded, "something is terribly wrong."

Without a word, Brody jammed the key into the lock and turned it, pulling the door open with one move. We saw two servants quickly run past us toward the kitchen and away from the chaos of the main hall.

Brody grabbed my arm as I tried to run past him and our eyes locked for a split second. Then, if by reflex, he pushed me behind him, shielding me from any possible harm. "Stay behind me, Olivia, I mean it!" he ordered, before quickly running toward the great hall and the screaming voices.

I followed closely on Brody's heals, clinging to his shirt the entire time as he pushed his way past the chaotic people flooding out of the main hall.

Brody grabbed a man by the arm. "Hughes, where is my brother?" he yelled over the chaos.

"I saw him standing by the food table earlier, Sir. He was helping a young woman who had been knocked down," the man franticly replied.

"Mr. Hughes, have you seen my family?" I blurted out, grabbing his arm, preventing him from fleeing.

"I saw them earlier this evening, Miss, but I'm not sure where they are now," Hughes replied, before pulling his sleeve from my grasp and running away quickly.

"Don't worry, Olivia, we will find them. Just stay behind me and don't let go," Brody cautioned, before taking my hand to pull me along behind him.

"I see Father Timoth," I yelled.

"Where?"

"Over there," I pointed off to Brody's left.

Protectively, Brody shoved a man away as he blindly ran toward us, then clinging to my hand, we made our way toward Father Timothy standing against a far wall.

"Father Timothy!" Brody called out when we drew near.

"Father Timothy, thank the Heavens above you're safe. Where's Mary?" I asked, looking around for her.

"Don't fuss so, my child, I am sure she is safe. Mary went off to the kitchen just before all the chaos broke out," he replied, unperturbed by the commotion going on around him.

"Brody, find my family and yours. I will take Father Timothy out of here," I insisted, looking over the priest's head. As our eyes locked I could tell that Brody didn't want to leave my side, but understood the soundness of my thinking and relented in the end. Neither one of us wanted to drag a blind priest around the great hall while looking for our families.

"Fine, but you stay with Father Timothy, and don't leave his side for any reason," Brody hesitated. "I will find everyone and then come to find you both. Stay safe," Brody said, squeezing my hand before turning to leave. "Don't let go of her, Father," he called over his shoulder.

"I won't, my son. I'll keep her safe until you come for her," Father Timothy assured.

25

The Devil Comes to Call

CAREFULLY, I ESCORTED FATHER TIMOTHY from the great hall and ran into my parents just outside the doors. They were franticly searching for me and Coco.

"Olivia, have you seen your sister? We have searched the hallways and watched for her to come out of the great hall, but we haven't seen her," Father called to me, sounding desperate.

Pulling my parents close, I hugged them both tightly. "Don't worry, Brody is searching and will find her," I assured them, feeling relieved they were safe.

Holding me at arm's length, Father looked at Mother and then back at me. "Your mother and I will look as well. Don't move from this spot," he warned. "We will be right back."

"Please darling, don't go anywhere," Mother pleaded, as worry marred her delicate features. Then they both disappeared back into the hall.

Father Timothy grasped my hand suddenly, causing me to turn and look at him. "What is it?"

His eyes looked strange as he turned towards the front door, which hung open to the outside. Slowly lifting his and pointing with a bent, arthritic-riddled finger, Father Timothy whispered in a voice I barely recognized. "She's here for you, my child."

"Who, Father Timothy? Who's come for me?" I gasped, and held my breath. His words confused me as three more terrified guests ran past us. "What exactly happened, in that room?"

"The entire room felt like it was shaking. The windows and door rattled like the devil himself were trying to break in. And the noise was so deafening that I thought the walls would surely crash in on us all. Then someone panicked and started screaming, "The Devil has returned and we're all going to die." That's when people began to run around and scream, pushing and shoving one another other," Father Timothy exclaimed. "But the people were not the problem, Olivia. I felt an evil presence, the likes of which I have never encountered before, and I sense that she has come for you!"

"Me?" I cried, both shocked and horrified by his words. "Why would she be here for me?"

Just as I asked the question, the massive wooden front doors slammed shut, and everyone froze where they stood. There was a moment of complete silence. No one moved or even breathed. Then the doors flew open again, crashing and banging loudly against the walls on either side. People started running away from the front door and screaming all over again with renewed emphasis, as if the end of the world had come to drag them all down to hell. The gates of hell had been flung open, but the devil hadn't come for any of them. Father Timothy and I knew the truth. She had come for me.

My eyes flew to the open doors and the inky blackness beyond. The torches that lined the courtyard no longer illuminated the grounds because they were all extinguished. At first, the only thing visible through the doorway was darkness. Then, as if by magic, the dark sinister figure of Annabelle Beaumont appeared, hovering just beyond the threshold.

She had her back to me but turned her head around to peer at me over her shoulder. She wore an amused smile upon her lips, deliberately turning around slowly to reveal something wrapped in the folds of her cloak. A feeling of dread washed over me as Annabelle purposely pulled back the corners of her black cloak. At first, I tried to deny my own eyes, but the moment she removed her hand from over the mouth of her helpless victim, I could no longer dispute what I saw.

"Olivia, help me, please!" Lilly desperately screamed, trying to fight against her abductor. Sheer terror shook my body as everything and everyone fell away from my field of view. The only thing I saw was Lilly and that smug look on Annabelle's face. Then she turned and headed into the large yard, straight for the woods and beyond.

Father Timothy still held tightly to my arm when I disentangled myself from him. I could hear him speaking to me, but I couldn't understand the words coming out of his mouth as I moved towards the doors.

I was racked with fear, powerless to control the shaking in my legs as I put one foot in front of the other. Taking one deep breath at a time until I no longer noticed them, I kept moving towards the door. Every step I took forward, Annabelle took one step back, and I felt as if I was having a crazy dream, moving forward, just like she wanted me to, and yet I was no closer to freeing Lilly. Not really paying attention to where I stepped, my eyes locked with Annabelle's, I continued to move forward, lifting my skirts to gain some momentum as I pressed forward. A sudden surge of energy shot through me and I began to run, pursuing the two ethereal forms as they entered the woods. I felt branches tugging at my gown and hair but pressed forward regardless. It was at this point I merely followed the cackling laughter of the she-devil while she led me on a merry chase through the darkened woods.

My eyes adjusted to the darkness, and I was able to duck and dodged obstacles, climbing over fallen trees and around rock formations in my pursuit of them. I barely noticed the chilly night air as goose bumps formed on my arms and legs. The intense pounding of my heart beat between my ears, drowned out all other noise.

I had never been so scared in my life and began to question the rationale of my decision. Had I lost my mind? Why was I wondering around in this dark forest, chasing after a demon and my best friend who were already dead? Pushing those thoughts from my mind, Lilly's terrified face kept running through my head. She *was* my best friend, and I knew that I would do anything to save her.

Stopping for a moment to catch my breath, I rested my hand on a large tree trunk and listened for a moment. I had lost sight of them both, yet I knew instinctively that they were not far and had passed this way. I could feel it.

Suddenly a chill traveled up my spine, like bone cold fingers at the back of my neck. Then an owl hooted over my head and I jumped. It struck me that Annabelle had waited patiently for the full mantle of night to fall, before she called me out. *But why?*

I shifted my weight, taking a few steps back, blending into the shadow of a tree. I had been resting and listening to my surroundings when my breath suddenly crystalized into a mist in front of my face. I was merely a pawn in Annabelle's demented game, powerless to change the outcome, helpless to do anything but play my part. But I had come this far, I couldn't turn back now without playing to the end.

Something large and ominous rushed past me, then I heard her laugh, as if she were a child playing a merry little game of hide and seek. "Catch me if you can," she called out, laughing as she peered over her shoulder at me. The whites of her eyes stood out, like beacons in the darkness showing me the way.

Lifting my skirts, I ran to keep up with her, once again blindly pursing her through the woods. I found myself tamping down the bad feeling that gnawed at my insides as I chased her into a small clearing. My path was lit by the light of the full moon overhead as it played peek-a-boo with the clouds. An eerie-looking mist rose from the ground in ghostly clusters growing thicker as Annabelle disappeared into it.

A strange silence fell over this new landscape. I had never been to this part of the property. Trepidation poured over me like a bucket of cold water, so I stopped short of entering the thick fog and stood and listened again. I heard voices, people off in the distance calling out my name. Time had spiraled out of control, and I felt my mind growing fuzzy. Turning to scan the opened field I had just crossed and the tree line beyond, I knew I was being watched.

"Olivia! Help me. Help me, Olivia!" I heard Lilly call out. Then she screamed, and the sound traveled across the opened field, crisp and clear like a church bell being rung on Sunday morning.

Blood began to crash through my veins again, bringing my mind back into focus. Beads of sweat formed on my forehead despite the cold night air. I felt my breath coming in harsh ragged gulps as I ran through the clearing, yet despite my overwhelming fear, I forced myself to push forward. A portion of the moon disappeared behind a cloud, leaving me to deal with the semi-darkness and misty fog that continued to spread out before me. I gazed up into the night sky and momentarily wished for stars, sparkling so crisp and bright. The frost was settling on the leaves and blades of grass as I trudged through them, weighing the hem of my gown down with water. I suddenly felt like someone had just placed their cold, icy fingers upon my neck.

"Come and find me if you can, little sparrow," Annabelle taunted, sweeping into view and then out again. "Your friend is waiting for you." She called to me in a sing-song tone.

I began to move faster than prudent, but I counted myself beyond logical reasoning at that point. *Stay calm, focus*, I told myself, as I fought back the hysteria I felt inside. I stepped through the thick mist that seemed to choke the air from my lungs, leaving me gasping for breath. I'd entered the forest again, where branches tore at my hair and face, snagging the material of my gown.

"You are almost there, just a little further," Annabelle called out, in her lyrical voice, lulling me into a sense of complacency.

"If I wanted a game of cat and mouse, I certainly don't intend to be the mouse!" I screamed out of frustration. Her games and this bloody fog was enough to make anyone lose their mind, I thought as I followed the trail of light Annabelle left for me.

People sounded closer than before as they called to me now, but they were still too far away to help, so I pressed on, quickening my pace until I was running again through the darkness. The surrounding terrain changed from moonlit meadows back to shadows cast by the tall trees.

I was attempting to capture an elusive creature that truly could not be captured, all in the name of preserving my best friend's soul. The irony was not lost upon me. Yet, if I had stopped long enough to consider these facts, I might have simply quit the game and gone back to the house or called out to one of the many voices calling my name. But I didn't. I didn't consider the insanity of my actions or the danger I was in. Neither did I stop to consider that this cat and mouse game could get me killed.

The bush and undergrowth tripped my feet, catching my gown, tearing the skirt to shreds. Putting my hands up to protect my eyes and face from the low-hanging branches, I slowed my pace to a fast walk, instead of a full-on run.

"Come out, come out, wherever you are," I called out, through gritted teeth while maneuvering myself over a fallen tree.

Annabelle's menacing laughter echoed all around me, then suddenly she peered at me, stepping out from behind an old oak tree two feet away. The game was back on, as I picked up my tattered skirts and gave chase. She led me down a well-worn trail, making sure to stay just far enough ahead of me to give me hope that I could catch up to her. Every now and then, Annabelle would vanish, and I would have to follow the sound of her sinister laughter. All the while, my gut told me to stay alert because she was up to something.

I began to wonder what had happened to Lilly. I hadn't seen her for a little while. Where had she gone? When Annabelle had poked her head out from behind that tree, Lilly wasn't with her.

"Annabelle, where is Lilly?" I demanded, slowing down, then coming to a stop.

"We're almost there. Not much further," Annabelle replied with a sardonic grin. "Just follow me. I have a surprise for you."

Propping myself against an old tree stump, I decided I would rest a moment. Looking up, the clouds had parted, allowing moonlight to illuminate places on the ground between the trees.

"I do not think I wish to play your silly little game any longer, Annabelle," I called out in my own sing-song tone. That is when my ghostly companion reappeared, drawing menacingly near.

"There are ways I could make you do as I wish," Annabelle sneered. "But then that wouldn't be as much fun for me," she added with an evil smile. As soon as the words passed from her lips, a pack of wolves began to howl, calling out to the full moon.

I felt myself shiver as a strange metallic taste settled in my mouth — pure, unadulterated fear. The animalistic stench of anxiety clung to my skin. A strong musty odor assaulted my senses, causing me to feel ill. I desired nothing more than to wash the smell from my skin.

"Follow me or take your chances with what lurks in the dark," Annabelle warned, moving quickly down the trail again. Two more wolves off in the distance howled at the moon, but they were closer than the others, so I lifted the tattered remains of my skirt, and began to run.

"Wait, you're going too fast for me," I cried, peering behind me, expecting to see the fanged beasts right behind me. "I can't keep up with you. I'm going to get lost in the darkness, you deranged demon," I muttered through clenched teeth. I continued to run, headlong into the darkness. "And if I get lost, there will be no one left to play your silly little game." Sounds were coming from all around me, but I couldn't pinpoint their direction. I heard my name again and even stopped for a moment to listen.

"Nearly there, my little sparrow," Annabelle called to me, sounding excited and pleased with herself. "You'd better hurry. Those wolves are particularly hungry tonight."

Silently, I said a pray that someone would find to me before the wolves did, then I began to run in the direction I had last seen Annabelle. The sound of gunshot ricocheted through the crisp night air, and I froze in my tracks.

I broke out into another cold sweat when the wolves howled again. "Over here," I screamed, "I'm over here."

"What are you doing? Don't be stupid, you little twit. Don't you know that they can't hear you?" Annabelle hissed, next to my ear. "The wolves will get to you before they do. Run! Run like the wind! Run like your little friend Lilly did, and don't stop."

The nearby bushes began to rattle and shake violently, and I heard an animal growl. Screaming, I hastily ran down the darkened path, with little regard to where I was going. Annabelle's cackles echoed in my head, until I thought I would go mad. Blindly running through the darkness, I reached into the pocket of my gown and touched the cold, hard steel of my dagger. Dislodging the sheath, I pulled the dagger from my pocket and held it while I ran. Just holding the blade in my hand somehow comforted me.

"Olivia, stop! Stop!" Lilly screamed, appearing on the path in front of me. She had her hands up and was running straight at me. "You're going the wrong way. You have to stop!" She screamed again, passing completely through me. The sensation of her going through me was like hitting a wall, and I dropped to my knees, gasping for air. At first, I couldn't grasp what had happened, but then understanding seeped into my brain, like a ray of sunlight through the clouds, and I looked around for Lilly. She was kneeling beside me on the ground.

"I remember, Olivia, I remember everything now. It has all come back to me."

"I think I'm going to be sick," I said, as my stomach rebelled against the experience and I began to dry heave, staring at her dumbfounded.

"Did you hear what I just said to you, Olivia? I remember what happened to me. I know how I died," Lilly exclaimed, tears glistening in her eyes. "Annabelle took me and made me look at what was left of me while you two were playing cat and mouse."

I was still not comprehending Lilly's words, staring blankly at her. "You were headed off a cliff, Olivia, the very same cliff I fell from," Lilly said, pointing her finger in the direction I had been headed. "If you had kept going, you would have suffered the same fate I did."

Slowly, Lilly's words penetrated my foggy mind and I started to cry while crawling on my hands and knees toward the edge.

"Oh, don't cry, Olivia. Please, don't cry," Lilly begged, trying to comfort me as I continued to crawled along the ground, searching through the fog and dark. I crawled three more feet on my hands and knees when my hand felt empty air. Suddenly the clouds parted and the moonlight illuminated what stood before me. The cliff dropped off suddenly. On either side of me stood two large pine trees, with portions of their roots exposed and protruding from the grounds. There was a deep canyon with rocks below, and I had nearly gone over it.

The noise of my heart beating between my ears was so loud it drowned out any other sound for several minutes while I gasped for air. My entire body began to shake uncontrollably when I realized how close I had come to running headlong over the cliff. Then I realized Lilly's body was down there. "Oh, Lilly, I cried, "you're down there."

"Well, my body is down there, but I'm right here, right next to you, Olivia," she countered, sounding just like Lilly. "I need to tell you what I can remember." Taking a deep breath, I stilled myself and quashed the hysteria I was feeling. I needed to hear her story.

"Go on."

"I remember things had been flying off the shelves at me all afternoon, and I needed to get out of that place and get a breath of fresh air. I decided to take a ride and clear my head. It was late in the afternoon and Quinton, Brody and Harrison were gone. They had set out earlier that day for town, to conduct some business. I chose to stay home because I had a headache," she said, looking into my eyes. "The accident was my own fault, really. I was scared and got turned around when the bushes moved and startled my horse, which began running down a path I didn't recognize when I lost control of her. My horse ran off the cliff, Olivia."

Anguish washed over me, and my heart broke, as anxiety, anger and pain rushed in, all at once. I stared over the cliff into the canyon below and wondered how this could have happened. Then I began to rock back and forth, holding my sides. I'd held myself together for so long but now there was nothing left to distract me. It was inevitable that the pain of it would catch up to me. Letting loose with a long, anguished scream, that sounded more like a wounded animal than a human being, I found that I could no longer contain my sorrow.

I did not recognize the pitiful cries coming out of my mouth, but I felt the pain, clear down to my soul.

"Olivia, stop it. Stop making that god-awful noise," Lilly demanded, bending over me, trying to lend comfort, when there came a low growling noise behind us. "Olivia, you can't do this right now," she insisted, standing up and shielding me with her ethereal form.

I could clearly hear her concern, but I was too far gone with my own self-pity and grief to care. Gradually my cries subsided and, as I rocked back and forth wiping my eyes, I turned to see what had Lilly so worked up. That's when I jumped back, nearly slipping off the edge of the cliff. Quickly I brandished the blade that I still held in my hand, jumping to my feet, attempting to make myself look bigger.

"Oh, Olivia, you have to do something," Lilly fretted, wringing her hands, then stepping behind me as if she feared dying again.

"Come on, you devil's span, here I am!" I taunted one of the wolves to make a move while backing up and placing my back against the trunk of one of the trees behind me.

"Olivia, what are you doing? You're going the wrong way," Lilly pointed out, looking around nervously. "Stop it this instant! I'm serious, Olivia."

"It will be fine, Lilly," I assured her, never taking my eyes off either one of the snarling wolves which were advancing on me as I backed up. "I know what I'm doing."

"You're going to fall to your death, or get yourself shredded to pieces, Olivia. I don't call that knowing what you are doing."

"Shush, Lilly, you're making me nervous," I said curtly. "I'm scared too, and you're not helping."

"I'm making you nervous! Ha! Now, that's rich, to be sure," Lilly muttered to herself.

Bracing my back against the trees trunk, I couldn't go any further. Slowly leaning down, I picked up several good sized rocks, and slowly stood up, making sure I didn't make any sudden moves. A sulfur smell permeated the air and I knew Annabelle was nearby, watching her handy work.

"I know you're out there, Annabelle, you spawn of Satan. Show yourself!" I demanded, momentarily distracted by flashes of lantern lights coming toward us through the trees. The timber wolves crisscrossed one another in front of me, inching closer as Annabelle reappeared just behind them. Her smile was more of a sneer, and I could tell that she was pleased with my dangerous position. "Don't you wish now that you had listened to me and gone home, little sparrow?"

"Why do you keep calling me that?" I asked, nervously licking my dry lips.

"Because I can hear your heart beating wildly in your chest, just like a little injured bird," Annabelle laughed, clasping her hands together. "Isn't my little game just the most fun you've had in, well, forever?" She jeered, swooping in close to my ear. "I think you should watch that one." Annabelle pointed at the wolf to my right.

I was bracing for the worst, just as the wolf to my left leaped in the air unexpectedly. I screamed, instinctively wincing while holding my blade in front of me. At that same time, I heard the sound of a ricocheting bullet hitting something directly in front of me.

Holding my breath, at the same time, I braced for impact. I couldn't fathom why nothing was happening. Cautiously opening one eye and then the other, my mind refused to register what I was seeing. A large, gray wolf lay dead at my feet while the other one had vanished, probably frightened off by the gunshot noise.

Expelling my breath, I crumpled to the ground as my legs gave out, no longer able to support me.

"Over here," I heard someone shout.

Rolling over onto my back, looking up at the stars above me, I lay on the ground when shock, disbelief and gratitude washed over me. I was still alive and in one piece.

Lilly stood over me, with a big smile, "Olivia, you're still alive. You did it! She's gone," Lilly announced, before looking up at whoever was approaching. "You're safe, Olivia. You're safe," she cried, before disappearing into the mist.

I blinked, turning my head, when someone shined the lantern light in my eyes. I wanted to cover my face, but my limbs wouldn't budge.

Immediately recognizing my father's voice, I was again grateful and tears well up in my eyes. "Thank the heavens above, Olivia Sophia, I thought we had lost you for sure, this time." My Father cried, carrying on a one-sided conversation. "If Brody hadn't made that shot," he hesitated, bringing the lantern closer to assess whether I had been injured. Lifting one arm and then the other, I felt someone sit me up and check my back. "Well, I dare not say what could have happened to you if that wolf had reached you first," Father droned on, as Brody removed his coat and wrapped it around me. My eyes locked with his, just as Quinton came up behind them both.

"What's the matter with her? Why isn't she saying anything?" Quinton asked, sounding concerned as he squatted down, getting a better look. "Is she hurt? Are those scratches on her face from one of those mangy wolves?"

Father and Brody lifted me to my feet to see if I could stand, but I crumpled over like a rag doll. "I think she's in shock. Give her to me," Brody insisted, lifting me into his strong arms. "Quinton, grab that lantern. Lord Townsend, you watch our backs, in case we have any more fanged surprises." I could see more lanterns coming toward us, as my head helplessly bobbed around. People began calling out back and forth, but none of that mattered any longer to me. I was safe and Annabelle was gone, for now.

Holding on to me tightly, Brody quietly said, "I thought I had lost you. What happened, Olivia? I thought we agreed you would stay put and wait for me. I found your sister, by the way. She was hold up with Emily under the banquet table."

I could hear the anguish in his voice and I wanted to explain, but I didn't really have the strength to speak, except to say, "Lilly."

"What? Did you say something?"

"Is she alright?" Quinton questioned, dropping back to hold the lantern close to my face. I cringed, pulling away from the light, burying my face in Brody's neck as a moan escaped my lips.

"Yes, but I don't think she wishes to have the light directly in her eyes just now," Brody cautioned. "The light from Lord Townsend's lantern should be sufficient. Run ahead and tell the others that we've found her, then ready the horses."

Without another word, Quinton ran ahead.

I tried to communicate again, but exhaustion was quickly over taking me. "Lilly, needs help," I managed to whisper.

Looking from side to side, Brody pulled me closer. "Where is Lilly? Is she alright?" he whispered close to my ear.

"Safe now. Lilly's safe now…" I answered as my words trailed off.

I had earned a rest and felt my eyes closing even before I finished speaking. My head fell forward, lodging in Brody's neck as I slipped into a comfortable place where all the worries and cares of the world were absent. I was cognizant of people around me, but I was beyond caring.

"Is she still breathing?" I heard Prince William inquire, and I wanted to answer, *"of course I'm still alive,"* yet I made no effort to communicate further. Instead, I found myself enter a world filled with happy childhood memories of Coco and our dog Winnie. The three of us were always so happy together. The perfect playmates.

Oh, how I'd loved that dog.

26

SUNDAY, FEBRUARY 15, 1804
3 O'CLOCK IN THE AFTERNOON

Saying Good Bye to My Friends

I DIDN'T REMEMBER ANYTHING ABOUT THE ride back to the house or when I changed into night clothes. Yet, when I awoke with a start, I had a perfect recollection of all the horrors I had endured.

I jumped out of my skin a second time when I looked over to find Coco sitting in the middle of my bed, staring at me. "Would you not do that! It is very disconcerting to awaken and find you staring at me like that," I said sleepily, still feeling groggy and stiff.

"You realize how lucky you are to be alive, Olivia Sophia? What were you thinking?" Coco chastised, pulling me up by my one arm, then roughly shoved another pillow behind me so I could sit up. "Brody has stopped in, no less than three times, to check on you since carrying you in earlier this morning. He finally gave up and made himself a bed in the hallway, just to be near you.

"Is he still out there?" I queried.

"I told him that you would be fine, with rest. Then I forced him to go back to his room and get some sleep, but I don't think he did."

Mother jumped up from her seat by the fire, the moment she heard Coco talking. "Coco, stop torturing your sister like that. Hasn't she been through enough?"

Giving a derisive snort, Coco narrowed her eyes at our Mother. "There is no need to tell me what Olivia has been through, Mother.

I experienced the entire, horrifying ordeal, the moment I touched her," she grumbled. "How could you have been so reckless and foolish, Olivia!" she scolded, turning her anger back at me. Then with another derisive snort, Coco crossed her arms and deliberately bumped into me as she turned and leaned against the pillow next to me. Then giving me an extra shove and a nasty glare, Coco 'harrumphed,' to make sure I knew that she was displeased.

"I am terribly sorry that you couldn't have been with me in person for the rousing evening of parlor tricks and mind games, but I refuse to apologize for my actions. I was forced to make a spur of the moment decision. And while I will be the first to admit I may not have been working with all of my faculties at the time," I admitted, while being completely unrepentant, "if it is all the same to you, I believe it was my decision to make." I saw Coco roll her eyes up to Heaven, then heaved an angry sigh. I looked up at Mother as she gently touched my cheek.

"It was very brave of you, Olivia," Mother responded, sitting down on the bed next to me.

"You mean reckless and stupid, don't you?" Coco blurted out, giving us both an angry glare. I could tell that she was put-out because I hadn't sought her counsel before running off to chase after a demon spirit.

"Coco!" Mother said, raising her voice, "apologize to your sister, this instant."

"I will not. She is the one who should be apologizing to me," Coco argued, angry tears forming in her eyes.

"Mother, Coco's right. I was being reckless and stupid, and I almost got myself killed," I admitted, putting my hands up between the two of them to stop further argument. "I truly am sorry, Coco. I would never wish to leave you alone, without a sibling. Not for anything in the world. I promise never to do anything that stupid or idiotic again."

A single tear escaped, rolling down my sister's cheek. "Swear it, Olivia Sophia Allen! Swear it, on your life, or else!" she warned.

Putting my arms around her as tears formed in my own eyes, I whispered, "I swear it to you, Coco. I swear on my life," I said, kissing her tears as they freely fell from her eyes. "Now help me get dressed. I learned a thing or two about Lilly's untimely demise and need to confront several suspicious people about it."

A small sit-tub had been brought up to my room. Not the normal bath tub that allows one to stretch out and luxuriate, but a small tub, that only allows enough room for the occupant to fold themselves up, like an accordion, while water is poured over their head. Refreshing, but not very satisfying. I climbed in, curled up and sat quietly while Margot cleaned my body and soul. After that, she styled my hair and helped me dress in a dark green gown. It had a round neckline, long sleeves and a small train that dragged on the ground as I walked.

I was unable to maintain any feeling of warmth in my limbs since my midnight escapades through the foggy meadow so wrapping a thick shawl around my shoulders I sat staring absently into the fire glow with a hot cup of tea clasped between my ice-cold fingers. Perfect recollection of the many horrifying events assaulted my mind and had me breaking out into a cold sweat, once again. Remembering the way Annabelle had looked at me, and all the range of emotions that washed over me, I had truly feared being devoured by wild beasts. The strange metallic taste returned to me, as well as the sour feeling in the pit of my stomach. I remembered, with vivid clarity, the smell of fear as it clung to me. I was chastising myself for having such morbid thoughts, when I heard a noise behind me.

Lilly's voice was so quiet I almost didn't recognize it when she called out my name. "Olivia." Startled, I cursed under my breath as hot tea sloshed from the cup and onto the carpet as I jumped. I turned suddenly and cursed again when the hot tea spilled all over my hand, burning me. Lilly stood before me, wide eyed and concerned.

"Lilly, thank heavens!" I cried, as morbid thoughts quickly left me. I was shocked at seeing her in my room. "I have so many questions for you. The main one is how in heaven's name did you cross over the barrier Father Timothy and I put up?" I asked, setting the half empty cup of tea down and wiping my hands dry with my napkin.

"I don't know anything about a barrier. I just know that I didn't feel the presence of evil, so I came in to find you." Lilly's eyes searched my face as she walked towards me. "I needed to see you with my own eyes. I wanted to make sure that you were really unharmed before I left."

"I don't understand, Lilly, where are you going?" I questioned, baffled by her statement, as I took a seat.

Lilly's angelic smile said it all. I knew what was coming next, but I didn't truly want to hear it. She sat down next to me.

"I saw the light, Olivia and it is beautiful. I saw Mother and my little brother waiting for me on the other side. But I couldn't go before making sure that you were alright. I also wanted to tell you how much your friendship has meant to me."

A helpless feeling began to build up inside of me — that familiar pain of loss and remorse for all the times I had taken our friendship for granted. I think that solving the mystery of her death was a way for me to keep her alive in my heart, if even for a little while longer. But now, Lilly had come to say good bye, and I needed to find a way to let her go.

I felt tears already forming at the back of my eyes, and I knew that it was inevitable that they would fall. Quickly turning so she wouldn't see me cry, I had to find a way to say good bye to her, without her feeling responsible for my sadness.

"I have loved you for so very long, Lilly Collins. You have been my sounding board and my confidant for years. How will I ever make it through this lifetime without you? You realize that I am going to blame you if I muck the entire thing up." I teased, forced a laugh, then wiped at a tear that slipped down my cheek, before turning to face her.

I could hear the sympathy in Lilly's voice as she tried to console me. "I'm the one who mucked it all up, not you. I fell off a bloody cliff, for goodness sakes."

"Yes, but you didn't cover any of this up. Someone else did that all on their own. And you can be sure that I will get to the bottom of it," I assured her.

Lilly smiled again, then chuckled. "None of that really matters any longer. But there is something you can do for me, Olivia."

"You know I would do anything for you, Lilly."

"Will you tell Quinton that I'm sorry and that I really did love him. I was such a stupid girl. And I should know. I've had a lot of time to think about things," Lilly said, sounding self-deprecating as she tried to smile. "Do you think I would have made a good wife and mother?"

I smiled, holding back the tears that again threatened to fall. "You would have made the best wife and mother that any man or child could have hoped for. I'm sure of it!"

Lilly laughed and shook her head. "Oh, Olivia, you always were the better liar. Just tell him that I am sorry for being such a foolish girl and getting myself killed."

"I promise that I will tell him, Lilly," I added, choking back the tears.

"And also tell my father and sisters that I loved them very much, and that I am truly sorry for running off the way that I did. It was stupid of me."

Tears escaped my eyes and freely flowed down my cheeks as I forced a laugh to cover up the fact that my heart was breaking. "Oh, Lilly, you have nothing to be sorry for," I said, swiping at my tears. "But I will be sure to go and see your family the moment I get back home. I will tell them how much you loved them and explain what happened."

We sat there in complete silence for a moment. Neither one of us wanted to be the first to say the final good bye.

"I'm afraid there is no good way around the pain, Olivia. You must lean into it and embrace it," Lilly finally said, with a sad smile.

Forcing myself to smile back through my tears, I looked into her sweet face. "You're waiting for me to be alright with your leaving, aren't you?" Another forced laugh escaped as I wiped the tears from my eyes. "You realize that I will never be alright with this," I assured her, with a loud sniff. "You truly are my best friend, Lilly Ann Collins, and I am going to miss you with all of my heart."

"I know, Olivia. And don't you forget to live a very long and happy life, for me."

"I won't," I replied, seeing a bright light beside me.

Lilly's eyes were drawn to something in the light, it was in that moment that I knew it was time for her to go. "You better toddle off now. There might be a long queue to get in. You wouldn't want to be the last one to line up, just in case they close early or something."

"I can wait a little while longer, if you like."

"Love is supposed to be liberating, Lilly. You don't need my permission to go," I said, looking over my shoulder to see if I could glimpse the other side.

"I know I don't need your permission, Olivia Townsend, but I would still like to know that you are going to be alright without me."

Trying to keep up a brave appearance, I stood and walked over to the hearth and poked at the wood, pretending to stoke the fire. "Why, Lilly, I will be better than fine. I'll be great. Didn't you see the way I handled that formidable foe last night?" I exclaimed, then turning back around. "You really shouldn't worry about me. I can truly can handle myself."

Coming to her feet, Lilly stood folding her hands, looking down at the ground. "How very silly of me to worry. Of course, you will be fine, because you are a Townsend," Lilly replied. "You have always been the most capable woman that I've had the pleasure to call friend." With one last look around the room, Lilly turned and walked toward the light.

"Lilly?" I called out, before she reached the beam.

Turning around to look at me, I saw a magnificent light reflected in her eyes. She looked so peaceful that I regretted my momentary weakness. "I will never forget you," I confessed, swallowing hard to stifle the overwhelming desire to keep her with me a few moments longer. "Safe journey, dear friend." Lilly smiled and walked into the light.

I was truly happy for her, and yet, at the same time I mourned for the loss of what should have been our long and happy friendship. Images of the two of us sitting side by side, growing old together, flashed through my mind. We were talking and laughing together, discussing our grandchildren, and we each had a needlepoint hoop in our hand. The sun fell across Lilly's features in my family's sun room back home, and suddenly the pain of losing her pierced my heart. It really was a silly thought after all, I didn't really like to sew.

I felt myself crumple and sink to the floor, as if every bone in my body had melted and turned to liquid. I hit my knees hard. The pain I'd held in for so long came spilling out, like flood gates that could no longer contain the water, my gut wrenching anguish, bubbled up and overflowed. Curling up into a ball, I wrapped my arms around my knees and, with a rocking motion, cried all of my fear, pain and hurt into my skirts.

27

Please Take a Seat, The Confrontation is About to Begin

I ALLOWED MYSELF AN HOUR TO cry and mourn my loss, then gathered myself up, dried my tears, washed my face and went downstairs to begin the inquest. I was determined to get to the bottom of just who covered up Lilly's death, and why. Yet the bigger underlying mystery was the haunting of Rosewood Plantation, by the former Mrs. Beaumont. Once those questions had been answered, I would be free to return home to my seemingly normal life. And the sooner the better.

Pulling the shawl tightly around my shoulders, I couldn't shake the chill and thought it strange that I should still feel so cold. I further ignored the warning signs as I brushed away the strange feeling that was attempting to open my eyes to the impending upheaval that would soon follow me.

Making my way to the large sitting room, I peered in and saw Quinton, Emily, Patricia and my sister Coco sitting by the hearth, enjoying a cup of warmed egg nog before dinner. Father Timothy was asleep in a chair by the window while Harrison, Thomas, my father and Prince William were playing a rousing game of cards. Mother leaned over my father's shoulder, and Brody stood by the large window, looking out at the woods.

Coco broke the silence first. "Olivia, you finally came downstairs!" Brody turned from the window when he heard my name, quickly walking across the room to greet me.

"I was very worried about you."

"Yes, I heard," I teased, flashing him a big smile. "I'm terribly sorry to have given everyone such a dreadful fright," I interjected, looking up into his hazel eyes, "but as you can see, I am no worse for wear."

"Dinner won't be served for another hour. Come, warm yourself by the fire. I've saved you a seat next to mine," Brody said sweetly, as he gently guided me to a seat. The sincerity in his eyes, almost made me regret what had to be done. It would have been easier to simply sit down next to him and shut my mouth. But the recent pain of saying good bye to Lilly made that impossible for me to do.

"If it is all the same to you, I have a matter to broach, and I would prefer to do it while standing."

Confusion marred Brody's features, and I could tell that he was disappointed. I gave his arm a reassuring squeeze and Brody gallantly swept a hand out before him, giving me the floor.

Wasting no time, I cleared my throat to get everyone's attention. "Mr. Beaumont, I would like to start by saying my family and I are very grateful to you for your generous hospitality. Lilly's death took me by surprise and saying good-by to her again has left me, well, feeling out of sorts. So, I hope that you will forgive my bluntness, but I am feeling rather blunt at the moment."

"What is this all about, my girl?" Harrison impatiently blurted out.

"Well, as you may or may not know, I was born with certain gifts, and while I don't hold all of the answers to what happened to my friend, Lilly, I was hoping that someone in this room does."

Harrison, Thomas, Prince William, Patricia and Emily looked confused by my words. I took a deep breath, preparing myself for the fallout that would come from telling them why I was truly here. I also feared how they would look at me after learning the truth about me.

"I see by the looks on your faces, Quinton and Brody have been true to their word and kept my secret." I began, as nervous laugh escaped my lips. "I feel the need to unburden myself, so I have a little confession to make. I was blessed with the ability to see spirits. I can see by your faces that I need to clarify. I can see people after they have left their mortal vessels and before they cross over to the other side. Most spirits go towards the light naturally, while others get confused for one reason or another and are unable to cross over."

"What in tarnation are you rambling on about, girly? Brody, Quinton, do you know what she is talking about? Because I'm not at all certain I understand a word that has come out of her mouth," Harrison interrupted, with a dumbfounded look, glaring at his sons.

"Yes, Father, Olivia is trying to explain it to you if you would just be quiet and stop interrupting," Brody interjected.

Prince William, who was listening intently, decided to add his voice to the conversation. "Harrison, old friend, I wish to hear what the young lady has to say," turning to his longtime friend. "I once heard of a woman from India who was able to talk to the dead, and I, for one, find this all very interesting." Harrison blustered a moment and then fell silent so I could continue.

Looking up at Brody, I asked, "Where was I?"

"You were just saying something about spirits, before they pass —" Brody prompted.

Grateful that he stood by my side, I shyly smiled. "Oh, yes, thank you. After the spirits go toward the light, they are on the other side and I can no longer see them. I deal with people who died suddenly or tragically," I remarked, looking around the room. "Let me be clear, when someone dies suddenly, or traumatically, they often get confused and don't know to go into the light, and sometimes they refuse to cross over because of unfinished business. My friend, Lilly was confused. She didn't know what had happened, only that she was dead."

"Hold on a moment," Patricia interrupted, jumping to her feet, with contempt. "Is anyone else buying what she's selling? Because I'm not," she added, looking to see if anyone would stand with her. "Personally, I think this entire matter is pure horse manure."

Coco jumped to her feet, intent on defending me. "You should sit down and shut your mouth, Miss Patricia Olson, before I tell everyone here what you were doing last night, whilst everyone else was out beating the bushes searching for my sister," she hissed.

Patricia looked as if she had been physically slapped, and began to stammer. "What...what did you... just say to me?"

"You heard me. I didn't stut...tutt...ter when I spoke," Coco replied, narrowing her eyes at Patricia. Patricia's expressions went from angry to resolute, in a matter of seconds. She opened, then shut her mouth several times, before deciding it was in her best interest to sit down and not call Coco's bluff.

Taking a deep breath, I was irritated by the constant interruptions. I gave Patricia a passing glance as I brought my attention back to Harrison, Thomas and Prince William. "If there are no more interruptions, I would like to get to the point," I admonished, looking over my shoulder at the group sitting by the hearth. Quinton and Emily both shook their heads, so I took this as my cue to continue. "Lilly came to me a few weeks ago, confused and disoriented. She had not realized that she was dead at that point, but after I helped her see that she was no longer alive, I set out to discover the reason for her death. Lilly had no recollection of dying or even how it could have occurred. That is why I came here, looking for answers." I gave Harrison an apologetic look. "I would like to say how sorry I am for my ruse, but it couldn't be helped," I continued, with a slight incline of my head in Harrison's direction. "I do hope that I have not offended you."

Harrison smiled and leaned back in his chair. "No offense taken, my girl. But there is just one thing that I am curious about," he said, folding his arms over his chest. "What makes you think we have answers for you?"

I glanced over at Father Timothy, who had awakened from his nap and was sitting quietly in the corner, listening to everything being said.

"Honestly, Mr. Beaumont, just one thing I have said so far makes you curious?" I responded, with a skeptical tone.

"Point taken," he said.

"Well, Sir, let me see if I can clear things up for you," I began. "I believe that someone covered up the fact that Lilly was missing by leaving a letter behind stating that she had returned home. This was clearly a lie because she was already dead when the letter was discovered. She fell to her death while riding one of your horses. I might add she was being chased by ravenous wolves, just as I was last night." Then shaking my head, I began to pace back and forth with one hand on my chin and the other on my hip. Pondering different scenarios in my head, I continued. "No, Lilly did not write the letter that was found," I concluded, directing my next question to Quinton. "Quinton, who found the note Lilly supposedly left you?"

"One of the servants brought the letter to me. We had business in the next town over," he said, indicated his brother Brody and father. "When we returned, I had been home a couple of hours before Annie brought the letter to me." Quinton looked away as if remembering that day was painful. "Annie said she'd been looking for Lilly when she decided to search Lilly's room again. That was when she noticed the note had been left on the night stand.

"Did you keep the note?" I inquired.

Turning his eyes to, Brody and then back to me, Quinton answered, "No, I crumpled it up and threw it into the nearest fire. Truth be told, I felt betrayed, and I couldn't think straight," he admitted, looking down at his hands which were folded in his lap. "I was in love with her and thought she felt the same way."

"But that's just it, Quinton. Lilly was in love with you too. The thing with... well, you know," I broke off, before completing my sentence and revealing Lilly's betrayal. Taking a deep breath, I continued. "Before crossing over, Lilly made me promise to give you a message," I said, waiting for him to look at me. "Lilly loved you, Quinton, and she wanted more than anything to be your wife. She sincerely regretted hurting you, but more than anything else, Lilly wants you to move on, make a new life for yourself and be happy. That means that you must go on living, for both of you." I saw the tears well up in his eyes again as he looked down at his hands once more, nodding his head. He scornfully snorted, before tears dropped onto his shirt. A minute passed before he looked up, and smiled through his pain.

"Thank you, Olivia." He sounded grateful, as several more tears rolled down his cheek. "You've given me the closure I desperately needed. I will be eternally grateful to you for that."

With one last loud sniff, Quinton stood up, pulled out his handkerchief. Wiping his eyes, he blew his nose and walked over to the large picture window to stare out at the woods that were now cast in darkness.

"All right then," I said, turning back around to lock eyes with Brody, giving a reassurance nod before turning my focus back to the main table of people. "For the next portion of my little show and tell, I would like to call upon my sister."

"What the Devil is she babbling on about now, Brody?" Harrison bellowed, as his face turning a vivid red hue.

Mother intervened at this point. "What my daughter is trying to say, Mr. Beaumont, is that our family is quite unique. Both my daughters have special, but unique skills."

"Oh, Mother, you are too humble," I added.

"This isn't really the time, darling," Mother answered coolly, waving me off.

"Of, course."

Harrison looked as if he was going to bust a vein in his forehead. "You mean she talks to spirits too?"

Father threw his head back and laughed. "Not quite, Harrison," Father replied. Then he looked at Mother, still grinning widely. "I believe that was the exact look I had on my face when I learned that my girls were *special*."

"Stop it, Aiden, you're not helping," Mother scolded. "No, Mr. Beaumont, Coco has an entirely different gift." People started talking over one another and the room dissolved into chaos.

I loudly cleared my throat. "If I could have the floor back, please, I would like to continue." All eyes turned to me and the room fell silent.

"Thank you," I said, smoothing the front of my gown and adjusting my shawl, taking a moment to compose myself. "Maybe I am not explaining this very well," I conceded, chewing nervously on my lower lip.

Father Timothy made himself known, breaking his silence from where he sat in the corner. "You are doing fine, my child. It is the closed-minded people who refuse to open themselves up and expand their understanding so that they may comprehend the unexplainable."

"Thank you, Father Timothy, I couldn't have put it better myself," I replied pensively, taking another deep breath. I decided to take a new approach and hit the matter head on, instead of gracefully dancing around it. "If you please," I motioned for Quinton to take a seat. "I have had some time to observe what has been going on around here since arriving on your doorstep," I began to say. "For instance, did you realize that your deceased wife Annabelle has been haunting your home for eight years?" I asked, turning to Harrison. He began to sputter and cough as he choked on his whisky. "Of course, you did. You may not have been able to see her, but anyone living in this house had to know that something was amiss," I stated, looking Harrison in the eye. "So, let's cut through all the rubbish and get to the heart of the matter, shall we?" not waiting for Harrison to recover fully from his coughing fit. "Splendid. Something happened here eight years ago that caused the spirit of Annabelle Beaumont to be so traumatized that she would risk losing her eternal soul just to stick around and make your lives a living hell," I pointed out. Then I noticed Harrison avert his eyes, as did Thomas, Prince William and Quinton. With a smile that didn't quite reach my eyes, I paused a moment, for the dramatic effect and then continued. "Not ready to go there yet? Fine! Let's talk about the note found in Lilly's room. Since I don't believe your servant Annie to be the mastermind behind the note, let's assume that she didn't write it. So, who did?" I asked, looking around.

Again, everyone seemed to be looking elsewhere, instead of at me, so I decided that it was time to enlist the help of my sister. "Very well then, I am left with no other choice. Coco, if you wouldn't mind," I gestured with my hand for Coco to join me. "I will begin by asking for volunteers."

Prince William spoke up first. "Volunteer for what?"

"Coco can tell me if you are lying about something and what you are hiding, just by touching you. It really isn't all that invasive and I promise, it won't hurt a bit," I assured everyone with a cynical grin.

"Not invasive, you say," Harrison scornfully said, crossing his arms across his chest and leaning back in his chair.

I smiled. "Did I say that this was voluntary? I meant, if no one steps forward I will simply pick you."

Harrison began to sputter, making noises, as if he were about to protest. His face turning bright red again when Prince William leaned over and whispered in his ear.

Narrowing my eye, I looked Harrison in the eye. "That is of course, conditional upon the fact you have nothing to hide." Feeling my point had been made, I turned my attention back to everyone else and my eyes landed upon Emily and Patricia. "Would either one of you like to go first?" I enquired.

Raising his hand, then turning away from the window, Quinton walked towards me. "I will be happy to volunteer," he replied, but I could tell by the look on his face that he was neither eager nor thrilled by the prospect of his deepest, darkest secrets coming to light.

Pulling the nearest chair into the middle of the room, I gestured for him to take a seat. "Splendid. Before we get started, is there anything you would like to address or get off your chest?" I suggested half-jokingly.

Looking at me queerly, Quinton said, "I had nothing to do with Lilly's death. I loved her."

"I never had any doubt about that matter, Quinton." Giving me another strange look, he quickly looked away. I might as well say it, you're going to find out regardless.

"I was responsible for my mother's death," he blurted out. I could tell that his confession took every ounce of strength, he could muster, but I wasn't convinced that he was to blame. I was a good judge of character, and usually felt when someone was evil to the core. When I was near Quinton, I didn't feel that with him. What I had come to realize is, when I first met Quinton, he was suffering from a broken heart and a feeling of betrayal by the woman he loved.

Several loud gasps were heard, then loud whispers from a few people. I can only assume what they were speculating. Quinton chanced a glance towards his father. "I'm sorry father. Everything was my fault," he confessed, jumping to his feet to explain. "I argued with Mother that night, after the party," he added, with a guilty look. "I had just found out... something about... her that day and I was angry." Quinton gulped back emotion. My heart went out to him as he stammered, then turned to his brother, Brody. Quinton's emotions were so raw when he continued. "Mother's death was on me, and I'm sorry, Brody." Looking at Harrison directly, he didn't seem shocked or surprised by Quinton's confession, and I wondered why. Harrison stood and walked over to his son, placing his arms around him. Quinton melted into his father's arms and begged his forgiveness.

"Your mother's death isn't on you, son." Harrison comforted his grieving child, patting him on the back. "I am to blame. I should have seen it coming," Harrison said, pulling back a bit. I could see that they were both shaken. "These parlor tricks, while entertaining, my dear, have worn me out. Perhaps you will excuse me, but I think I would like to be alone," he announced, as he left the room without so much as a backward glance.

Thomas Olson was the next person to stand and announce he would not be participating in my little game of show and tell.

"I think I would like to dine in my room this evening," Thomas said arrogantly, while giving me a nasty glare. "Girls, you will join me, of course!" he insisted.

"It would be our pleasure, Daddy," Patricia answered, lifting her chin into the air as she passed by me so there would be no question that I had just been snubbed by her entire family.

Prince William smiled broadly as he turned to my father. "Closed-minded sods," he derisively mocked, "so little understanding. Perhaps your daughter Coco would care to give me a reading?" he mused, turning to look at her.

"I don't do readings, Prince William," Coco corrected him, with a mocking tone. Still, she was amused by his open-mindedness and eager nature, as she walked towards him, while removing her gloves. I watched as the prince squirmed nervously in his chair. Throwing her gloves down on the table, Coco could contain herself no longer, and began to laugh. "Alright, I'm willing to give you a go, granted you don't take offence if I reveal something embarrassing."

Prince William sighed with relief while rubbing his hands together like a pleased child, getting his way. "What do you need me to do? Wait, how embarrassing are we talking about here?" he questioned, still grinning from ear to ear. Coco was doubly amused by his eagerness now, and motioned for Father to move so that she could take his seat. Father promptly stood up, pushed his chair closer and waited for Coco to sit down.

She took a deep breath, then exhaled. "You don't have to do anything, your Highness. You merely sit and let me do what I do." I left them to their amusements and walked over to Father Timothy, who was trying to get out of his chair with the help of his cane.

"Would you like me to find Mary for you?" I asked, taking a hold of his arm to help him up.

"No, no, I will be fine. I am very proud of you for not backing down." he confessed, patting my hand. "That Mr. Beaumont is a slippery one."

"I agree. He's hiding something, I'm sure of it," I said, letting my eyes land on Brody who was off in a corner talking quietly with Quinton. "I truly wish that he could have been more forthcoming with information."

Father Timothy let out a long sigh, drawing my gaze back to him. "Mary and I will be going home in the morning."

His words made me feel suddenly anxious. "But... there... there is so much I... I still don't understand," I stammered, finding it difficult to keep the panic from my voice. "What if I have questions or... or something bad happens? What if I completely muck things up?"

Patting my hand again, he chuckled. "There, there, my child, you will be fine. I have the utmost confidence in you."

"But I am scared. What if I handle things completely wrong, or... or do something that disrupts the balance between Heaven and Earth?" I pointed out.

"You will be fine. I have written my experiences down with Mary's help, of course. I've asked her to give my book to your handmaid Margot, and she has assured me that she has done this. So, you see, there is nothing to worry about," he said confidently, patting the back of my hand again. "Come, walk me to the stairs I am suddenly very tired, and I would like to lay down," he grimaced slightly as we began to walk.

"Is everything alright, Father Timothy? You don't sound like yourself," I said, voicing my concern when I noticed he had gone pale.

Giving me a slow smile, he looked as if he was going to say more, then changed his mind.

"Things are as they should be, my child. Always remember that. They have a way of working out the way they were intended."

I had a strange sensation go through me, a premonition that something unpleasant was about to happen, but I pushed the feeling aside.

"Let me take you to your room, and then find Mary for you. It would be a shame if you took a wrong turn and got yourself lost," I suggested.

Placing his hand on the railing, Father Timothy forced me to stop. "I will be fine, child, stop your fussing. Go back to your family, and have a nice evening," he insisted. "But yes, if you happen to see Mary, would you send her up to me?" he added, calling over his shoulder as he climbed the steps. "But only if you see her. Don't forget what I told you."

"I won't, Father." The strange sensation continued to gnaw at me, while I watched him slowly climb the steps. I decided that I would find Mary regardless of his assurances.

I found her in the servant's dining hall, taking supper with Margot and the others. "Mary, Father Timothy has gone up upstairs for the evening. He insisted he was feeling fine, but I am worried about him. I thought him pale, and said as much, but he insisted on going upstairs alone, anyway. Perhaps you wouldn't mind looking in on him, soon," I cautioned, wondering if I was making a fuss over nothing."

Sweet Mary smiled with the patience of Job and set down her cup of tea. "Thank you, Miss Olivia. I'm sure he will be fine. Father Timothy is a very private man, and won't let no one but me help him. Please don't take offence," she advised.

"Oh, I wasn't offended, Mary, I was merely concerned," I replied, feeling silly now for making such a fuss and interrupting her supper. "Well, I will leave the matter in your capable hands."

Mary added as I turned to leave, "Thank you, Miss, I will look in on him in a moment. There has been so much going on the last few days, I'm sure that he's just tuckered out. That's all."

"I'm sure you're right," I answered, before turning to leave.

Returning to my family, I entered the room to find everyone gathered around the table. Prince William was laughing, amused by something Coco had just said to him.

"What have I missed?" I inquired.

"Your sister is most remarkable," Prince William said, still laughing. "Most remarkable, indeed."

"That she is, your Highness," I agreed. "Did anyone happen to see where Quinton or Brody disappeared to?"

"I'm sorry, darling, we didn't see them leave," Father replied, still chuckling over what had been said.

That was curious, I thought. "Where could they have gone and what were they up to?" I murmured to myself.

"Did you say something, Olivia?" Mother questioned.

Turning to look at her with a pleasant smile, I said, "No, Mother, everything is fine," turning to glance at the door, "just fine indeed."

28

You Can Not Always Choose Your Destiny

QUINTON AND BRODY RETURNED TO the drawing room a few minutes later, inviting us to adjourn for dinner.

While the main course was being served, I watched as the butler leaned down and whispered something in Brody's ear. He and I were seated next to one another and I was surprised by his reaction.

"What? I don't understand," Brody gasped, then trying to look inconspicuous, he motioned for Frederics to lean back down, and he whispered back.

Frederics stood up and quietly answered, "Very good, Sir," before walking down to the other end of the table.

The same feeling of dread I'd felt earlier washed over me once more, and I had just leaned over to ask what had happened when Brody placed his napkin to the side of his plate, and scooted his chair back in one fluid motion, leaving the room without saying a word to anyone. I watched Frederics lean down and whisper to Quinton, who turned white as a sheet. Then he too stood up and followed Frederics from the room. No one else seemed to notice anything out of the ordinary as they continued to eat and talk normally, which I found strange.

Feigning a headache, I excused myself and followed Brody, Quinton and Frederics up the stairs, taking care that I was not seen by them. At the top of the stairs, I peered around the corner to see where they were headed and watched as they turned another corner. Dashing down the hall to the next corner, I peeked around the corner again. They stood talking quietly outside Father Timothy's bedroom, but I couldn't hear from where I stood. Then Brody became very animated, waving his arms in the air, and that's when something strange occurred.

Father Timothy stepped between them, then walked towards me, and no one reacted. Brody, Quinton and Frederics continued talking as if they hadn't noticed the priest walk directly in front of them.

My curiosity was replaced with shock when he drew nearer, and I noticed he wasn't using his cane. His eyes looked directly at me, as if he could see me. But that would be ridiculous, because he was blind. It was in that moment I knew— Father Timothy was dead.

So many things flashed through my mind; I should have known something was wrong, I should have listened to my instincts, and maybe I could have saved him. I should have tried harder, I should have walked him to his room. What if Father Timothy had known it was his time, and that's what he wanted to tell me but couldn't find the right words.

I must have gasped out loud, because all three men stopped talking and turned to look down the hallway towards me as I dodged back around the corner, hiding myself from view. I was dumbfounded and looked about for someplace to sit down. I felt light headed and couldn't catch my breath, but mostly I felt ill prepared for what would come next. Spotting a chair on the other side of the hall, I made my way to it and sat down. Concentrating on slowing my breathing by taking deep breaths, I wagged my finger at Father Timothy as he advanced on me. "This can't be happening."

"Don't waste your time being sad for me, child, I am completely healed. Look at me, I can walk and see again. I don't feel any pain and I'm at peace," Father Timothy said, trying to assure me as he drew nearer. "I haven't felt this good in thirty years."

Taking a couple of deep breaths to stave off the tears and panic that assaulted me, I looked at the ground and then my hands, to avoid making eye contact. "I don't know... oh, what is the matter with me?"

I stammered. "You would think that I've never seen a dead person before," I joked, slowly bringing my eyes up to meet his.

"You are a very brave girl," he gently coaxed, giving me one of his slow grins that I'd come to cherish. "I know they don't quite know what to make of my sudden death," he continued, directing my attention down the hallway and the men standing at his door. "I suppose you will need to step in."

"Yes, of course," I agreed, turning my attention back to Father Timothy, and gasped, "Mary, she must be devastated!"

I could tell by his expression that something was bothering him. "Mary is saddened by my passing, but will recover. We have discussed my eventual demise, she knows what to do and will make my burial arrangements. Don't worry yourself over such matters," he said, with a grim look. "I need to tell you something, Olivia, and I need you to stay calm and hear me."

"Oh, how do you expect me to stay calm when you begin a sentence like that?" I pointed out in a loud whisper, glancing down the hall to see if anyone had come around the corner because they had heard me.

"Annabelle Beaumont is not yet finished seeking revenge," he warned, pensively studying my reaction.

Jumping to my feet, I gasped loudly. "What?" Father Timothy turned to walk back down the hallway and peer around the corner, checking again to see if the three men had heard me.

I following closely behind him, I too peered around the corner. Brody, Quinton and Frederics were no longer standing in the hallway. "What do you mean it's not finished yet!?" I questioned angrily.

"You need to stay calm," he advised me, turning back to look at me. Closing my eyes, taking several deeper breaths and walking back down the hall to where I had been, I mumbled to myself, before opening my eyes and look at him.

"I can do this, I can do this."

"I don't have much time, child, I already feel the other side beckoning to me."

Although I was angry, I knew that he was trying to say good-bye to me. But I couldn't help feeling bereft and helpless, knowing that I would be left all alone to deal with Annabelle Beaumont. "What if I fail?" I cried, feeling sorry for myself.

"You cannot fail, as long as you are true to yourself."

"But what will happen if I do?" I whined.

"Your fear holds you back. Believe in yourself and you will never fail."

"I will miss you very much. I hope that someday I am as wise as you."

"Learn to listen to your heart and follow your instincts," he said, with a sad chuckle. "Your destiny is preordained, therefore it is out of your hands. Accept it, and stop fighting so hard against it."

Nodding my head, I smiled. "Listen better, obey my instincts and there is no getting around destiny. I believe I've got it," I replied, wishing that he could stay longer.

Smiling, Father Timothy shook his head, because I had over-simplified his words. "It's important to ask yourself what matters most." Then shaking his head again, he waged his finger at me and continued. "A simple question really that doesn't always come with a simple answer."

I looked at him a moment, reflecting on his words, wishing more than anything that we could continue talking, but noticed him looking past me again. I knew his time was short. "Thank you for staying long enough to allow me to say good bye. I will never forget you, and don't worry about, Mary. I will see to her and make sure she knows you are at peace," I smiled, looking over my shoulder, still hoping to glimpse the other side. "God speed, Father Timothy. A part of me is envious of you, if truth be told," I admitted, seeing him hesitate. "Please don't stay for me. I'll truly will be fine, truly."

"I know that you will, child. I have no doubts about that," he assured me, with a lopsided grin. "It's just that you look so forlorn."

I tried to smile, forcing a laugh, which sounded hollow to my ears. The pain of loss was becoming overwhelming, and I worried that he could see right through me. "I feel like I have been saying good-bye a lot, today," I confessed.

"It will get better." He smiled and walked past me toward the light.

I watched him disappear, crossing over to the other side. Tears slid down my cheeks, which I wiped away with my hand. I could have stayed where I was and given into the temptation of my heart to mourn my loss, but there was work yet to be done.

I walked down the hallway, intent on intervening. Stepping into Father Timothy's room, I noticed Quinton had his arm around Mary's shoulders, trying to console her as she quietly wept by the fire. Then with a loud sniffed, she stiffened her back a bit more, making it even straighter than normal. From where I stood, I could tell that she was attempting to be resolute and not dissolve into a puddle of sorrow. Yet it was difficult not to mourn the loss of her longtime companion. Brody was standing near the bed, looking down at Father Timothy's body while speaking quietly to Frederics.

"I wish to assure you that there was no foul play involved with his death," I called out from just inside the doorway.

Four sets of eyes turned towards me.

"Did you say something, Olivia?" Quinton asked.

With a sad, but confident smile, I stepped even further into the room. "Yes. I said, there was no foul play. Father Timothy died of natural causes," I added, walking towards Mary, feeling the need to offer my condolences. "That is what the three of you were trying to determine, is it not?"

"Ah, well, yes, how'd you —?" Brody stammered, creasing his eyebrows together. "How did you know?" he began, before remembering who I was and that I spoke to the dead. "Yes, well, never mind."

Quinton gratefully relinquished his position next to Mary, so that I could take his place. "So, it is safe to assume that he came to you," Quinton asserted. Looking at Frederics, I smiled and stayed silent, until he took the hint, politely excusing himself.

"Very good, Sir. If there will be no further need of my services, I would like to inform the staff about Father Timothy's passing," he said, inclining his head to Brody, Quinton and finally me, before turning to leave."

I called out to Frederics, before he reached the door. "Mr. Frederics."

"Yes, Miss, how may I be of service?" Frederics inquired in his impeccable English monotone.

"Will you be sure to make arrangements for Mary and ..." pausing, I looked at Mary, patting her hands, before looking back at Mr. Frederics. I continued. "Father Timothy is to be transported back home in the morning. I've been assured Mary knows what to do after that."

Frederics looked towards, Quinton and then back at me once he received an affirmative nod. "Very good, Miss," he said, before quietly closing the door.

Brody joined Quinton behind the couch, as I turned all my attention to Mary.

"I am so very sorry for your loss, Mary, but I have a message from Father Timothy. He wanted me to make sure that you knew he was at peace," I said, looking into her tear-filled eyes as she tried to hold them back. "He is no longer in pain and the most amazing thing is he can see again," I added, then watched as a few tears trickled over the dam of Mary's resolve, gently sliding down her plump cheeks. "He wants you to be happy, Mary, and not mourn his passing."

Mary nodded and tightly clasped my hands. "Your gifts are sent from Heaven above, dear girl. Don't ever forget that," Mary said with a solemn sigh as she held back the rest of her tears. "You have brought such comfort to this old woman's heart and I am eternally grateful to you for delivering Father Timothy's message." Pulling a battered old rag from her pocket, Mary loudly blew her nose and wiped her eyes.

Impatiently, I motioned for Quinton to hand me the crisp, white handkerchief he always had stuffed in his front trouser pocket. Slow to respond, Brody removed his handkerchief and placed it in my hand, deliberately brushing my fingers. I gazed up into his eyes and saw admiration reflected back at me. Shyly I smiled before turning my attention to Mary.

"Why don't you let me have that old hanky and I will have someone launder it for you," I said, replacing it with Brody's clean one. Mary relinquished the dingy piece of cloth, fingering the soft fabric of the new handkerchief before tucking it with a grateful smile into the waistband of her well-worn skirt.

"You need to inform the others what has happened. I will stay with Mary," I said, looking over my shoulder at Brody and Quinton. "Toddle off now," I added, "and don't worry, we will be just fine."

They didn't need to be asked twice. Happy to be dismissed, they nearly stepped over one another getting to the door.

I sat with Mary on the couch until the wee hours of the morning as she recounted stories of Father Timothy and his bravery. It was around two in the morning when Mary finally ran out of steam, falling asleep on the couch.

Covering her with a blanket, I tip-toed down the hallway and back to my own room where I collapsed into bed, falling fast asleep.

29

MONDAY, FEBRUARY 16, 1804

The Other Shoe Will Eventually Drop, It Always Does

"WHAT WAS THAT?" I CRIED, awakening with a start and grasping simultaneously at my chest. My eyes darted about the room, searching franticly for what had startled me awake. Sitting up and pushing myself against the headboard, I pulled the covers up, clutching them tightly to my throat— as if that would somehow protect me from whatever had gone bump in the darkness.

Slowly my eyes started to adjust to the faint light peeking through the drawn curtains. Squinting as I swept the room, paying attention to the corners, I didn't see anything. I jumped from bed, and ran to the security of the daylight on the other side of the curtains. Throwing the fabric back, I murmured. "Where there is light, darkness cannot dwell."

Quickly turning back around, my eyes fell to the corner of the room where the light didn't quite touch. At the same time a feeling of menace percolated through my veins. Taking a step backward at the same time, I reached for the medallion that rested between my breasts, and held it out in front of me.

"What exactly do you intend to prevent with that silly little thing hanging about your neck?" Annabelle purred, stepping out from the darkened corner into the light, like a snake slithering from its hole to bask in the sun.

Cautiously, I stepped away from the window, clearing my throat. "Perhaps, it isn't the useless little trinket you would have me believe,"

I countered, fingering the medallion while keeping a wary eye on her. She slowly walked about the room, pretending to be interested in my things.

Sitting down at the dressing table, Annabelle looked down at my hairbrush and pins before her. Then with a steely glare, she looked into the mirror and smiled at me. "I will allow you this one small victory, for now," she conceded. "Revel in it, if you like, because it will be your last. Now leave my house before it is too late for you," Annabelle warned before disappearing, leaving behind her foul odor.

Breathing a sigh of relief the moment she disappeared, I ran to the bed to retrieve my robe and quickly slipped it on. I was attempting to tie the sash with my shaking hands, when Margot opened the door, causing my to crying out. "Oh, I hate it when you do that!"

"What on earth is the matter with you, Olivia? You act as if you just saw a ghost." Margot teased, carrying in a tray. "Do you see how that was funny, because you see ghosts all of the time," Margot giggled to herself while setting the tray down on the table.

Not really feeling the least bit amused by Margot's joke, I splashed water onto my face and grudgingly took the towel she handed me to dry my face. "I'm not really in the mood, Margot."

With a slight chuckle, Margot turned her back to me and poured out some tea, and handed me the cup. "Well, aren't we in a mood, this morning." Handing Margot the towel in exchange for the cup of tea, I stepped closer to the hearth, trying to chase away the sudden chill I felt.

"She's back," I said plainly.

Without really thinking about who I might be talking about, Margot absently asked while going about tidying the room, "Who's back, Olivia?" And then, before I could answer her, Margot stood straight up and whirled about to face me. "Oh no! You don't mean her!"

Taking another sip of hot tea, I nodded my head. "Yes, and she is up to her old tricks. She couldn't wait for me to awaken this morning, so she knocked that book off the shelf." I indicated by nodding my head in the direction of the fallen book still lying on the floor.

Looking about the room as if she expected to see Annabelle lurking, Margot stepped closer to me and began to whisper. "Is she here now?" Margot asked, talking out of the side of her mouth while her eyes darted wildly about the room. Pausing with my hand mid-way to my mouth, I let loose with a yawn.

"No Margot, she left just before you walked in. Why do you think I was so jumpy?" I questioned with a bland tone, taking another sip of tea.

Coco came bolting through the adjoining bedroom door, still tying the sash of her robe as she shut the door with a resounding Bang! "Bloody hell," she exclaimed, pointing a finger at the door, her voice shaking as she continued, "several books just flew off the desk at me."

Lifting the cup of tea in a salute to her, I smiled. "It's definitely more effective than a rooster crowing. Wouldn't you say?"

Coming to stand next to me, Coco narrowed her eyes. "I fail to see the humor in being startled awake, Olivia. I was genuinely scared," she added, taking the cup of tea from my hand and quickly drinking it down.

"Join the club," I blurted out. "Only I can see the evil in her eyes when she confronts me," I pointed out with an incredulous tone, plopping down on the cushion of the couch. "Take my word for it, the term *scared to death* takes on an entirely new dimension when she looks directly into your eyes."

Coco stared at me for a moment as if she were trying to envision it. "No thank you!" she stated emphatically with an involuntary shiver.

Shaking my head, I added with a derisive snort, "Welcome to my world. Believe me, I wish I had a choice in the matter."

"You can keep your gift. Suddenly it doesn't seem so wonderful anymore," Coco said, pouring another cup of tea and adding a cube of sugar to it.

Margot came out of the dressing room carrying a dark, navy blue gown. "I thought this dress would be appropriate for today. I will also begin packing once the two of you are dressed. Your father informed me that we will be returning home today."

I felt both relieved and hesitant at the same time. I nodded my head in approval and quickly dressed. Margot arranged my hair in a simple style, pinning my hair up, with two braids wrapping around the top knot. Then she helped Coco into a dark gray gown, tying a purple ribbon around her waist and throat.

I absently stared out the window at the courtyard below, enjoying the coolness of the glass against my temple. I watched as people went about their duties, seemingly oblivious to the goings on in the main house.

Coco sat at the dressing table mirror as Margot fashioned her hair in a new style one of the house maids had told her about.

"Margot, do you know if Mary has left yet?" I absently asked, still staring at the courtyard below.

Margot quietly answered, with hair pins in her mouth. "She left early this morning, shortly after the rooster crowed." Removing the pins and sticking them into Coco's hair, Margot looked up. "Why?"

Looking away from the window a moment, I shook my head. "No particular reason. I really wanted to say good-bye," I answered, turning back to the window, lost in my own thoughts.

"Do you want to know who also left this morning, just after the rooster crowed?" Coco asked, with an air of mystery.

Still lost in my own thoughts, I absently replied, "Sure, I'll bite. Who also left this fine residence to brave the cold before the sun was even up?"

"The Olsons, that's who! They scurried out of here and into their waiting carriages, with servants in tow. Why, I don't even think they were completely packed. I had my window open and I heard one of the maids complaining about not having enough time to pack anything,"

Coco exclaimed, sounding a lot like the women back home who we made fun of for spreading gossip. "Then I heard the other one say that it wouldn't be a problem, because she'd left instructions for anything left behind to be shipped to the Olson's residence, later."

When I didn't immediately answer back, Coco prodded. "Well, what do you make of that?"

"I wouldn't waste too much time on the matter, Coco. I'm sure that it's nothing," I assured, still looking out the window and half listening to her.

Coco, who didn't wish to let the matter be, began to sputter, "Nothing!? You tell me that it means nothing?" she scornfully sputtered. "Why, how can you say such a thing? It has to mean something!"

"I'm sure that it means something, Coco, don't get me wrong. But nothing that you or I need to be concerned about," I replied, glancing at her over my shoulder. "Honestly Coco, you have your fingers in more pies than you could every eat."

"What is that supposed to mean?" she questioned, sounding slightly offended.

With a smile, I turned back to the window, enjoying the solitude of the trees. "It just means that you worry about things that you don't need to. Let the Olsons sort out their own affairs. *You* should really worry about *you*. Believe me when I say you will live longer. There is a very old saying— 'One who has his fingers in too many pots at once is bound to burn them.'

"I think you just made that up. Why, I've never heard of anything so ridiculous in my life," Coco scolded.

I laughed, knowing that Coco knew me too well, and that I was completely teasing her. Turning from the window with a genuine smile, I whispered, "Just tell me that it made you pause and think, if even for a moment."

"Ha, ha, ha," Coco responded, without any real humor, "you got me. Happy now?"

"Immensely," I replied with another large smile.

"Honestly, Olivia, I never grow tired of your platitudes," Coco cried. But her biting words assured me of the opposite.

I turned around and continued to gaze out the window when three riders come into the courtyard and dismounted, one of them bringing a hand up to shade his eyes as he stared up at me.

Recognizing Brody, I rested a hand against the window and smiled. He handed his reins off to a stable boy and then said something to Quinton and Jackson who both looked up and waved before walking their horses into the barn.

I stepped away from the window and poured myself another cup of tea. Nibbling on a raisin scone, I admired Coco's hair. "That style looks very pretty on you."

"Do you really think so?" she asked earnestly, as she turned her head from side to side to get a better look.

"Of course, I wouldn't say it if I didn't mean it. It makes you look very grown up." I smiled. "I guess it is a good thing Father has decided that it's time for us to leave. We wouldn't want all of the handsome men in the region to flock to Rosewood seeking your hand. Besides, I'm sure we have worn out our welcome by now."

"After that little fiasco in the parlor yesterday afternoon, I think you might be right," Coco retorted, still looking at herself in the mirror.

"Never mind that, after this morning's unexpected visitor I don't intend to stay around and find out what she meant —" I stated, then immediately bit my tongue, because I'd said too much. "Margot, do you know where I might find Father?"

"I believe he went out with Mr. Beaumont and Prince William, early this morning," Margot said, standing back and admiring her handiwork.

Coco turned in her seat, then motioned for Margot to move out of the way so that she could see me. "Might we discuss what you meant, when you stated that you didn't care to find out what *she* meant this morning?" Coco questioned.

I gave an involuntary chuckle. "It really doesn't matter." I said, evading my sister's question, just as someone knocked at the door. "Oh look, someone is at the door. I'll get it."

Jumping up, Coco chased after me. "Don't do that," Coco scolded. "You come back here, you coward. Tell me what she said."

Opening the door, I found Brody with a smile on his face, just as Coco grabbed my arm. "Olivia, what did you mean?"

"Please, Coco, not now." I said awkwardly, shaking her off, and taking a step back from the opened door. Then with a stiff smile, I gently touched her face. "Please, may we discuss it later? Perhaps you could go find Father, and I will come downstairs later."

Giving me a disapproving glare, Coco stomped her foot. Then turning to Brody, she shot him a very brief smile before turning back to me. "This discussion is not over, Olivia. You will tell me what you meant," she hissed between her teeth before shooting Brody another forced smile. "You can lay money on it."

Feeling color shoot up to my face, I begged, "Later, please," before looking up to see, Brody studying me.

With a nod, Coco relented. "Don't be long, Olivia," she blurted out, over her shoulder as she sauntered down the hall, "we are leaving for home today."

I watched as the smile left Brody's lips and his eyebrows furrowed together. Gesturing with my hand for him to enter, he followed closely behind me as I led him into the room.

"When were you planning to tell me?" he inquired. I held my hand up to silence any further discussion in front of my loyal, but talkative, handmaid. "Margot, I know you wished to start packing right away, but would you mind beginning with Coco's room?" I requested stiffly while walking towards the sitting area.

"Of course, my Lady, whatever you need," Margot answered, sounding so proper I did a double take as she bobbed a curtsy, then left.

A self-conscious laugh escaped my lips and I looked over my shoulder at Brody. "Now, where were we?"

Crossing the room in three strides, Brody looked concerned. "We were discussing the fact that you are leaving today."

Looking up at him, I smile sweetly. "Were we? Is that truly the reason you came all the way upstairs? You wanted to discuss my leaving today? I asked.

He slowly reached out his hand and I avoided his touch by skirting around a chair and walking to the couch. "That hardly seems fitting for a last conversation. Tea?"

"No." he answered, waving me off as he took the seat next to me. "Why are you leaving?"

"Because my father feels that it is time to go," I answered before giving him a quick glance and pouring myself a cup of tea.

"Hog wash!" Brody stated emphatically, jumping up from the couch to walk over to the large window and look out.

"I must admit I am baffled by your anger. After all, you had to know that I would be returning home at some point," I said, coming to my feet to join him at the window. "My family and I have intruded upon your family's generosity long enough," I pointed out, looking at the beautiful trees beyond the barn, then taking another sip of my tea.

Brody turned to face him. "But you could stay, if you wanted to."

"Don't be ridiculous," I cried, avoiding eye contact as I placed my cup down on the nearest table. Glancing over at him, I was taken aback by the intensity I saw in his eyes.

"Why is it such a ridiculous idea?" he questioned, sounding hurt by my rejection.

"Because I have no ties keeping me here," I argued as he took a step and pulled me in his arms. Halfheartedly pushing against his chest to free myself from his embrace, I added, "And besides, I wouldn't wish to live here, with the current occupants," then suddenly realizing how my words could be misinterpreted. Immediately shaking my head, I leaned into him. "I didn't mean it like that, please forgive me for the way that sounded. What I meant to say, and should have, is your mother is back and she paid me a visit earlier this morning."

Grasping my shoulders in a vice like grip, Brody looked concerned. "She didn't hurt you again, did she?" he asked, sounding almost desperate.

Shaking my head again, I gently placed my hands against his chest and smiled up at him. "No, but she did warn me to leave," I admitted with a nervous laugh. "I don't have to be asked twice. I know when I have worn out my welcome," I joked, trying to lighten the mood.

Pulling me closer, Brody hugged me tightly to him. "Oh, thank heavens," he gasped, clasping my head to his chest. "You had me worried." He pushed me away, holding me at arms-length. "I don't know what I would have done if something had happened to you."

Lifting my eyebrows, I added. "You sound too serious for someone who just met me a week ago."

"A week and four days," he corrected. "I met you a week and four days ago."

Pushing off him, I took a step back. "Thank you for making my point. So much has happened to us, in such a short time, Brody. We haven't had the opportunity to truly learn anything about each other. Everything is happening far too quickly for me," I admonished.

"I know everything I need to know." Brody said, taking a step closer.

I took another step back and turned to seek refuge by the hearth. "Like what, for instance?"

"Like, I love you and want you to be my wife."

Turning on him, I felt flattered and angry at the same time. "What else? People don't build a lifetime together on such a flimsy foundation of, 'I love you and wish to marry you.' That is ridiculous. Can you hear yourself?" I protested. "I need something more."

"And if you weren't going home today, I could give you something more," Brody reasoned, taking my hand in his. "But you're leaving, so I've run out of options, opportunity and time."

"I cannot accept your proposal," I said flatly, pulling my hand from his. "I'm sorry."

Pulling me into his arms, Brody boldly kissed my lips, refusing to yield to my feeble attempts to push him away as I finally surrendered, pulling him closer. I heard him sigh with desire and couldn't help but answer back with my own sigh.

After a few minutes, I felt him slowly pull back, ending the kiss — to my great disappointment — as he looked down at me. A slow smile began to form, traveling all the way up to his eyes and I knew that he thought he had won. He was assuming I would naturally agree to marry him at this point, but he hadn't changed my mind. I saw the hope in his eyes. The very same hopes I was about to dash to pieces, like a ship tossed against the rocks. I opened my mouth to tell him the truth when we heard someone screaming,

"Margot!" I shouted, looking over my shoulder while Brody and I ran to the door. "Margot? Hurry! Something is wrong!" I shouted again, as Margot came running from the other room, with her brows creased.

"What is it? What has happened?" she cried.

"I'm not sure. But we are going to find out," I replied, throwing the door open and stepped into the hallway, witnessing total chaos as servants ran from room to room, knocking and yelling for everyone to get out.

A young man I'd seen a few times before ran towards us, shouting for us to get out of the house. Brody grabbed his arm, refusing to turn him loose. "What is the matter, Henry? What is happening?"

Frightened and desperate to be on his way, Henry seemed confused by the question. He attempted to pull his arm free before regaining his composure enough to answer. "The house is on fire, Sir! We need to get everyone out!"

"Where is the fire?" Brody shouted, trying to sound calm, but I could tell the news had thrown him.

Henry blinked twice and then took a breath before answering. "In the master bedroom, Sir. It started in the master bedroom."

Jumping into action, Brody held on to young Henry's arm for a moment longer. "Where is my father? Is he in the master bedroom?" he demanded.

"No, Sir," Henry said, glancing at me before saying anything more. "He left early this morning with the Prince and Lord Townsend. My brother Frankie has gone in search of them."

Giving Henry a reassuring smile, Brody held him by the shoulders, "Henry, I need you to listen to me," he said, giving him a slight shake. The boy continued to struggle, attempting to flee. "I want you to gather everyone you can, and tell them to form a water line. Get as many buckets as well." Brody said briskly, then gave Henry another sharp shake when the boy looked away. "Henry, this is important. Tell Mr. Frederics to collect the sand buckets and bring them to the master bedroom. We need to get sand on the fire, before it gets away from us," Brody instructed, looking Henry in the eye, insuring that the boy understood.

"Yes, sir. I will find Mr. Frederics, straight away," Henry yelled as he ran down the hallway, repeating random words, as he went. "Sand, water line, lots of water, Mr. Frederics —"

We watched him just long enough to see him turn a corner and then we ran in the opposite direction.

I picked up my skirts, making it easier to run after Brody. "I knew she was up to no good this morning when I saw her."

"Who, Olivia? Who was up to no good this morning?" Brody called back to me, over his shoulder.

"Your mother!"

Grabbing my arm, he pulled me to a stop, mid-step and Margot ran into me. I stared blankly at him, certain he must have known.

"I don't care who you two are speaking of, we need to leave this house immediately!" Margot cried, grabbing my arm.

"Margot, please don't fuss so, I will be fine. Brody will be with me. He wouldn't let anything happen to me," I said, turning to him. "Will you, Brody?"

"I will guard her with my life," Brody replied with one hand over his heart as he looked at Margot. "You should take the back staircase and go out through the kitchen. Olivia and I will find out what happened and then we will leave as well. I promise. I will drag her out of here myself if it becomes too dangerous."

"I can't leave you in this burning house, Olivia Townsend. Your mother would skin me alive," Margot loudly protested.

"Margot, I have to see if Annabelle is behind the fire and if I can help. I promise that I will be careful. Now go!" I insisted. I felt for Margot as she stood before me, wringing her hands together in her apron. She had been deathly afraid of fires since her father had been burned alive in a factory accident ten years earlier. The screams of her father and the other men trapped in that burning building still haunted her from time to time. I could only imagine how it was affecting her, faced with the reality of being in a burning house now.

"We will just go down the hallway, a little farther, and see if we can help, Margot. If it looks serious or too dangerous, we will turn back. I swear it," I called over my shoulder, as I gathered up my skirts and hurried after Brody, who'd grown tired of waiting as I argued with my maid. "At the first sign of trouble, I will get out."

I watched as Margot rung her hands again, trying to decide if she believed me or not. Then turning, Margot hurried for the back staircase.

Brody gathered up two buckets of sand as we quickly ran toward the master bedroom. Smoke billowed out through the opened doorway when we rounded the corner.

Quinton, Prince William and Harrison arrived, from the opposite direction as us, with two more buckets of sand each.

"What the devil is going on?" Harrison cried, rushing towards the smoke, then entering the room and throwing sand onto the burning bed. Brody and Quinton followed closely behind Harrison, throwing their buckets of sand onto the flames. At the same time, Prince William and Harrison began pulling down curtains that were burning, piling them in the middle of the floor, to stomp out the fire.

Without forethought, Brody and Quinton grabbed their father, dragging him from the smoldering room. Harrison had not stepped foot in that room for eight years, taking up residence in the room across the way and down the hall.

I stood just outside the doorway with Brody's handkerchief over my mouth and nose watching everything transpire. I could see Annabelle pacing back and forth inside the room, agitated that her sons had removed their father from her grasp.

Suddenly Annabelle lunged forward toward me, stopping shy of the doorway, which caused me to jump backwards, startled by her erratic behavior. I bumped into Prince William.

"What is it, my dear? What did you see in there that frightened you so?" William asked, lending support and preventing me from hitting the floor. "Why, you're shaking like a leaf!"

"Annabelle started the fire on purpose," I blurted out, grabbing Brody by the arm. "Why is your dead mother still so angry, Brody?" I questioned, looking between Harrison, Quinton and Brody and seeing a look of guilt and secrecy passed between them. "I've seen that look pass between you three before. That day my sister was in the library and the books flew off the shelf and hit her in the head," I said, pointing an accusing finger at all three. "This enormous secret the three of you share is the reason Lilly is dead!" I shouted. "Is it truly worth protecting if someone else dies today?"

Prince William stepped in between me and Harrison, his oldest, and dearest friend. "You don't know what you are talking about,

Lady Townsend. These three men are the epitome of propriety. There are no secrets to be had here today!"

Again, Annabelle flew at the door, causing me to jump back, disgruntled by the Prince's words.

"Then, Prince William, maybe you could tell me why Annabelle has taken exception to your statement?" I asked.

"This is all just cheap parlor tricks and dramatic showmanship," the prince protested, turning to look at the three men.

I added with a loud scornful scoff, "So, when it suits you, your mind is open to the possibilities of the unexplainable, but now, it is all hog wash and parlor tricks. What do you say gentlemen, is it time to end the web of lies that has shrouded this home in darkness for eight long years? Does the truth see the light of day, this day? Or do we continue as if nothing is amiss, protecting the lies, until the day you all die?" I countered. "Because from where I stand, it would appear Annabelle is prepared to burn your house down, just to make a point," I said, narrowing my eyes at them all.

Brody stepped forward first. "My mother was having an affair with Jackson's father, eight years ago, and I confronted her about it two days before the party. She denied the entire matter ever happened, but I knew the truth," Brody shouted, turning towards the open doorway.

"Well, that hit a nerve," I stated, when Annabelle stopped pacing the room and stood in the doorway, looking at her son.

There was so much pain mirrored on both of their faces, but I knew that this was not the lie that had kept her earthbound.

"That isn't the problem here, Brody. You knowing about your mother's affair isn't what killed her, nor do I believe it to be the reason for her distraught nature and angry disposition. Something else happened to cause her to remain earthbound," I mused out loud, looking into her eyes. "No, there's still more to this secret, and it lays somewhere between the three of you," I concluded, turning around to study Harrison, Brody and Quinton.

Quinton stepped forward next. "I found out about our mother's affair, as well, only I confronted her the night of the party," Quinton retorted, his voice shaking with emotion as he spoke, lowering his head as tears formed in his eyes. "Mother and I had a terrible fight. The entire household heard us arguing," he continued as words stuck in his throat. "The next morning, mother was dead, found by her maid, drowned in her bathwater. I'm the reason she killed herself." I looked over at the doorway, trying to gage Annabelle's reaction as the room began to smolder anew, ready to reignite into flames at the slightest provocation. Shaking my head, I looked back at him, squinting my eye. "No, Quinton, I don't believe that is what happened."

Quinton looked up at me, large tears remained. "How can you say that? You weren't there. You couldn't possibly know what truly happened," he screamed, narrowing his eyes at me, then pointing at his mother's room. "Ask her," he insisted, taking a step closer to the doorway. "Ask her why she did it if you really can speak to the dead," he admonished.

Shaking my head again. "There is something more to this than a simple argument between a mother and her son," I insisted, unperturbed by his skepticism. Pursing my lips together and looking at Annabelle again, I continued to ponder out loud. I found it curious that she was completely focused on one person, in particular. I couldn't really tell which one of them it was, as they were all huddled together. I first took Quinton by the arm, moving him away from everyone else. "Although the real culprit might not have minded you thinking that your mother's death was by her own hand or even your fault, I find it unlikely that a woman like Annabelle would have taken her own life." Next, I took a hold of Brody's hand and moved him three feet in the opposite direction.

"What are you doing, Olivia?" Brody questioned, moving to follow me back to the group. I put my hand up, motioning for him to stay put.

Another glance in Annabelle's direction proved that it wasn't Brody or Quinton that she had been focused on, so I continued. "Please humor me a moment. I promise that I will not waste your time with cheap parlor tricks," I explained, looking toward Annabelle again, noticing that she was still staring at the same spot where Prince William and Harrison now stood. "Prince William, if you would be so kind as to stand against that wall over there," I said, pointing my finger.

"This is most disconcerting," he protested, refusing to budge.

"Just do as she asks, William," Brody dryly stated.

Grudgingly, Prince William crossed his arms over his chest, then stepped to the far wall. "Is this the spot you wish for me to stand?" he asked, pointing at his feet, cynically.

I smiled, knowing how hard it must have been for a man of his standing to take orders from a mere woman such as myself. "Yes. That will do nicely," I answered sweetly, while turning around to look at Annabelle once again. It was as I had suspected. Annabelle's eyes had never moved from their original spot.

Still watching Annabelle's face, I began to speak. "So, we have heard from your two sons, Harrison. Yet, we have yet to hear your account of what happened that night your wife died," I inquired, turning my gaze on Harrison and scrutinizing his body language. "So, here is your opportunity to tell us what happened, to your best recollection."

"There really isn't much to tell, Lady Townsend. After the guests all left and my sons went up to bed. I stayed downstairs to go over paperwork in my study," Harrison replied, unable to look me in the eye. I found it strange that Harrison suddenly felt the need to address me in such a formal manner and was unable to look at me. It was at that moment Annabelle became enraged, and all four men jumped, startled by the sound of books hitting the walls, as flames in the room jumped back to life.

"Is that so?" I questioned, suspiciously. "You would have us believe that you did paperwork after entertaining guest all evening long. Hum,"

I uttered out loud once more. "There is one person who would disagree with that statement."

Both Harrison and Prince William lunged forward. "This is absurd. My house is about to burn down, and you want to stand about asking me stupid, idiotic questions."

Blocking the doorway and preventing them from entering, I laughed out loud before continuing my interrogation. "I am convinced that your dead wife will extinguish the flames once you are honest with us, Harrison. You see, her eyes have been locked on you ever since you came down that hallway, and that makes me ask myself, why?"

Looking uncomfortable, Harrison began to shift his weight from side to side. "This is ridiculous," he blustered, trying to push me to one side.

"Is it really, Harrison, or did I hit a nerve?" I countered, standing my ground.

Brody and Quinton both stepped forward. "If you have nothing to hide Father, then answer Olivia's question," Quinton demanded, eyeing his father suspiciously.

"Why is Mother so focused on you, Father?" Brody questioned, pushing his father back a few steps.

"What really happened that night?" Quinton asked, taking a step forward, coming shoulder to shoulder with Brody, causing Harrison to take two more steps back.

I noticed that Harrison's right hand had begun to shake as he brought it up to rake his fingers through his hair. I marveled at the similarities between father and sons. Brody also had a habit of pulling his fingers through his hair when he was stressed.

"Her spirit won't rest, nor will she leave your home, until the truth comes out and she is able to find peace," I stressed. "Perhaps this is your opportunity to bring your dead wife a little peace, Harrison."

Harrison looked up, and suddenly it was written all over his face. Guilt, shame, disgrace. The strain of concealing his lie for so long had taken its toll on him, and he seemed to age before our eyes. It was all there, in his eyes.

"It was an accident. I didn't mean to kill her!" Harrison cried, bringing his hand up to his mouth, to stifle his pain filled cry.

I noticed that both his hands shook now. I worried that he might have a heart attack, as blood drained from his face.

"I came upstairs after the party and overheard you arguing with your mother," Harrison said, turning to Quinton. "I had suspected her infidelity for months, but I'd had no real proof. I even confronted her about my suspicions, but she convinced me that I was crazy for thinking such a thing of her. I felt like such a fool." Harrison spat out the words as if they left a bad taste in his mouth. Staring into the room, Harrison looked directly at her, as if he could see Annabelle standing in the doorway. Tears of pain, sprung to his eyes as he continued to speak. "After Quinton left the room, I watched her undress and get into the bathtub. She had the maid pour her an extra large glass of whisky, which she sipped on, while soaking in the hot water. Then came the moment I had been waiting for, Annabelle sent her maid away for the night. I stood there for a few moments, in her dressing room, trying to decide what I would do next. With every passing minute, I became even more furious. She had made me look like the fool, and I felt so small. But that wasn't the worst of it." Harrison continued through gritted teeth.

"She had sullied my family's good name, without any regard to my boys and how it would ruin them. I decided to confront her, but she only laughed in my face, calling me an impotent, little man and ordered me to get out of her room and leave her alone!" Harrison scoffed, clenching his fists, as he stared into the room and the equally angry eyes of his deceased wife, as the flames grew higher. "Imagine that, she was ordering me to get out of her room. The very same room that I had generously provided her for all those years. The ungrateful witch." Harrison growled. "Why, I became so incensed, that I could no longer see straight. I don't remember what happened next. I must have held her under the water, because an hour later, when I looked at the clock, when it chimed again, I had this sick feeling in my stomach. I looked down at my wet clothes and, wondering why I was soaking wet, I looked at Annabelle as she floated in the bathtub, not moving. I panicked! I knew that I had done something unspeakable to her, but I just didn't remember doing it. The next thing I remember was changing into some dry clothes and slipping downstairs to my study. I fully expected that I would be taken away in handcuffs when the gruesome discovery was made. But I wasn't. Instead, the maid who found her swore that her mistress had been acting peculiar the night before, and she told everyone that Annabelle had killed herself. No one ever questioned the maid's word, and everything went back to normal."

"But it didn't go back to normal, did it, Harrison?" I argued, defiantly glaring at him. "Because Annabelle's spirit was violently torn from her body, and she has tormented every living soul of this house, along with the dead, ever since. And it is all because of you!" I cried, pointing an accusing finger at him.

"Olivia!" My father yelled, as he rounded the corner down the hallway, sounding shocked by my harsh, bold words. Grabbing ahold of my arm, Father shoved me towards Harrison. "You apologize to Mr. Beaumont, this instant, young lady!"

"I will not," I unflinchingly proclaimed, reaching down to peel his fingers from my arm, leaving my father speechless.

Then turning on Harrison again, I took a bold step forward. "Tell me honestly, Mr. Beaumont, does it require a lot of courage on your part to be so ordinary?" I asked, glaring at him. My words had the desired effect, as a look of pure shock mixed with disgrace crossed his features.

"Olivia! You have crossed the line!" Father scolded. "Come with me this instant!" he insisted, clamping an iron tight grip on my arm again, intent on dragging me down the hallway.

Angrily I yanked my arm free from him. "I am not yet finished with what I came here to do. So, respectfully Father, I will ask you not to touch me again," I growled, between clenched teeth. With his mouth still open, my father, The Right Honorable Lord Lieutenant of Ireland and Earl of Buckinghamshire, was struck speechless, as he took a tenuous step backwards. He stared dumbfounded at me, as if he had never seen me before.

"Olivia—" Brody began, only to cut his words short when I glared at him as well.

Facing Harrison Beaumont, I quickly advanced on him as the flames beyond Annabelle suddenly spiked once more. "You have managed to stay silent all these years, allowing your own son Quinton to bear the guilt and blame for his mother's death. Why, Harrison? Don't bother to make excuses for yourself," I drilled on, silencing him by my angry tone. "It was because you are basically a selfish man. You, you… cowardice monster!" I screamed, pounding on Harrison's chest, punctuating each word with my balled-up fist.

Wrapping his arms around me, Harrison pulled me tightly against him, as bitter tears rolled down my face. I breathed harsh, ragged breathes, striking him again and again until I calmed down. Lifting my head, I whispered in his ear, "Tell me how you have managed to live with yourself?"

Harrison recoiled, as if I had physically struck him across the face. Turning to look at his sons he stammered, "Well, I… I…" looking behind him into the burning room.

"There has to be so much anger and malice inside of someone to do all of this," I motioned, pointing at the flames that were suddenly raging out of control.

"Olivia!" Brody cried again, but this time he gently touched my arm, trying to defuse the tension as servants continued rushing down the hallway with buckets of water to throw on the fire. None of them paid any attention to us, emptying their buckets on the flames, then rushing past us again. The fire jumped higher than before, as if the servants had thrown fuel on the flames instead of water.

Harrison and I never broke eye contact, and I could tell that he was thinking over everything I had accused him of, along with every incident that had occurred in his home the last eight years. "I never meant for any of this to happen. Nor did I mean for anyone to get hurt." He meekly said, "I need you to believe me," he pleaded, looking into my eyes and then into those of his sons.

"But you did hurt people," I gently argued. "And because of your silence and selfish acts, my best friend Lilly has paid for your mistakes with her life. Your sons have suffered needlessly. Where does it all end, Harrison? When is it enough?"

Looking at Quinton and then Brody, Harrison's features crumbled and he began to cry. "I'm so sorry," he repeated, covered his face with his hands and openly weeping. "I would take it all back if I could."

Brody put a hand on his father's shoulder to lend his support, but Quinton just crossed his arms defiantly. I wanted to feel sorry for Harrison, but I was too caught up in my own anger, grief and loss to have much pity for him.

"Tell that to your deceased wife," I suggested, moving to one side and pointing into the room. "She is standing in the doorway. She hasn't moved since you arrived."

Wiping his eyes and then taking out a handkerchief, Harrison wiped his nose and looked me in the eye. "I am truly sorry for Lilly's unfortunate death and for my part in covering it up. I should have been honest when she went missing. It was wrong of me to cover up one terrible mistake with another," he admitted, blowing his nose into his handkerchief with a loud honking noise. "I knew that it was wrong at the time, and you are right about me. I have been a coward for far too long. It was just easier to close my eyes to everything that was happening and to the part I played in creating it. Once I covered up what I did, believe me when I say I was willing to do anything to keep my secret." Harrison continued, giving me a sad smile. "You are a very stubborn woman, but you have been right about everything. I wish to thank you for uncovering my lies and opening my eyes to the truth."

I shook my head, confused by his words. That's when Harrison gave me a reassuring smile. "It is all going to work out just fine, my dear. You will see. I intend to correct my wrongs," he said, taking my hand and placing it gently into Brody's. Then tenderly touching his son's cheek, Harrison hugged his son tightly. "I would keep my eye on this one. She will never let you get away with anything." He laughed sadly, then turned to Quinton. "I am sorry that I caused you to suffer so needlessly. It was never my intension, son." He gasped, hugging tightly to Quinton, clapping him on the back as he smothered his tears against Quinton's shoulder. "I would give anything to be able to give you back your Lilly," he said, pulling back to look at Quinton, "and for that I am truly sorry, son."

Two more servants rushed past us, dousing the flames with the water they carried. Two rushed the other way, with empty pails in tow.

Harrison turned to his oldest, dearest friend, Prince William, and embraced him, giving him several hearty slaps on his back. "I can never thank you enough for the years of friendship you have given me. You have been a sounding board to me for so long, and for that I am grateful. Perhaps, if I had confided in you from the start, things would have turned out differently."

"I am honored to be your friend, Harry, and look forward to the many years to come, old friend," William remarked, as a strange look crossed his face.

Harrison looked up and smiled. "I am no longer afraid to face the consequences," he confided, "in fact, I am relieved, like a burden has finally been lifted from my shoulders. Promise me you will look after my boys, William."

"You sound as if you are saying good-bye, Harry," William remarked, looking at his friend with concern.

Shaking his head, then stepping back a couple of steps, Harrison looked over his shoulder and then back at us. "It's not that I don't love your company," he replied nervously, taking another step towards the door, "it's just that I need to put an end to it all. I need to pay for my crime. No matter how justified I felt at the time, I was wrong." Harrison concluded, turning with purpose and taking two more long strides into the room.

Brody and Quinton tried to grab their father's arm, before the door slammed in their faces. Quinton grasped the doorknob, trying to turn it, but it wouldn't budge. The metal burned his hand, causing him to jump back and cry out in pain. The door was locked. Then Brody tried to break down the door by slamming his should into it, but the door wouldn't budge.

"Hurry, find Mrs. Bell, the housekeeper. She will have the keys on her," Quinton yelled to the servant boy, sloshing water all over the floor as he ran towards us. The boy froze in place for a moment, surprised by the new orders. Immediately setting the buckets down in the middle of the hallway he ran back down the hallway as fast as he could.

I stood frozen in place, watching in horror as Quinton, Brody, William and my father attempted to break down the door. We heard Harrison begin to scream out in pain as the flames consumed the room. Suddenly, the four men hit the door with renewed vigor, attempted to get inside.

Then an eerie silence fell over the household, as the sound of burning timber ceased. There was no longer any sound coming from the master bedroom, and Quinton and Brody both put their ears to the door. Desperately, they began hitting at the door with their shoulders, repeatedly screaming out their father's name.

Mrs. Bell came around the corner, keys jangling from her waist as she half ran towards us. "I can't do a thing until you two move out of my way," she scolded.

Quinton and Brody jumped back, but still hovered over Mrs. Bell's shoulder. Her hands shook as she tried several keys in the lock before finding the right one. Brody nearly tore the set of keys from the housekeeper's waist as he shoved the door open before she could remove the key from the lock and get out of the way.

I watched as they rushed into the room, only to come up short, a few feet inside of the door. Quinton brought his hand up to his mouth and nose, then turned, throwing up. Brody stood perfectly still, almost as if he couldn't believe what he was seeing.

The smell that exuded from the opened doorway was shocking. I stifled a cry of shock at the gruesome scene I was witnessing, never having smelled burned flesh before I too began to gag, covering my mouth and nose with my hand.

The fire was all but extinguished, except for the spot where Harrison lay. His body still smoldered. The remains of his flesh, clung to his bones like a Christmas turkey that had been over-cooked. Harrison was curled up in a fetal position, his body charred beyond recognition as if the fire had been particularly hot in that one spot. My father tried to pull me away from where I stood, but I refused to budge.

The two servants rushed into the room with buckets of water, stopped suddenly, then carefully setting their buckets of water down, they reverently left the room to inform the other staff of what had happened.

What no one else knew yet was that there would be no more mysterious fires threatening to burn Rosewood to the ground, or unexplainable occurrences threatening innocent lives. Because Annabelle Beaumont's tormented spirit no longer lingered in that house or on this earth, for that matter, she was gone. The price for her untimely death had been met and she was satisfied. Annabelle had taken the one soul she was after all along.

I stepped out into the hallway and immediately located the half empty bucket left behind earlier by the young boy. Leaning my head over it,

I proceeded to heave up everything in my stomach. Then I began to dry heave, unable to stop myself as the memory and smell of Harrison's burnt remains kept assaulting me. My father gently placed a hand upon my back and led me through the hallway, down the stairs and out the front door. The bright sunlight blinded me at first before the reality of it truly hit me. The entire house felt different. Annabelle Beaumont was truly gone.

My mother, sister, and Margot all anxiously clambered around me. I don't remember what they said to me or if I even answered back. I was in a daze, watching as servants rushed in and out of the door, making sure the household valuables were removed.

People shouted and ran back and forth, and I didn't even have the strength to tell them that their efforts were in vain. All I could do was sit by silently and watch.

30

THURSDAY, FEBRUARY 19, 1804

Everything Was a Blur

THE NEXT FEW DAYS BLURRED together as a pall of grief hung in the air, like the lingering smell of smoke from the fire.

Brody and his twin, Quinton, busied themselves with funeral arrangements while my family and I delayed our departure out of respect for Harrison.

I avoided both Brody and Quinton, ashamed over my behavior before Harrison's untimely death and the part I played in his demise. I needn't have concerned myself, for I saw Brody only a handful of times from the back, as he and Quinton rushed off to attend to the family business. I even caught a quick glimpse of them one morning from my bedroom window as they rode through the courtyard, on their way out.

Truth be told, I wouldn't have known what to say to either Brody or Quinton, had they bothered to seek me out. I was filled with guilt, and I didn't know what to do with it. Guilt over the way I had confronted Harrison. Guilt for the anger I harbored in my heart. Guilt for not being a better friend to Lilly when she needed me the most. But mainly, I felt so guilty for causing Brody and Quinton to lose their father in such a horrific manner. I couldn't get beyond it. I felt responsible for the tragedy.

Father and Prince William helped with the clean-up after the fire, attempting to make things feel as normal as possible for Quinton and Brody.

I kept myself busy, waiting for Harris's funeral to be over, by taking long walks with Coco. Mother was, of course, in her element, pitching in where needed, making household decision, so Quinton and Brody had a chance to grieve their loss.

I, on the other hand, was certain that no amount of goodwill by me could possibly erase my part in Harrison's death. So, I found myself on the outside nervously looking in.

A rider was sent out shortly after the tragedy to locate and bring back the Olsons. Patricia, Emily and Thomas Olson had stopped in the neighboring town, sixty miles away. They were informed of Harrison's death and returned quickly, Patricia was only too happy to lend her support to her grieving cousins.

I took my meals in my room, attempting to be as inconspicuous as possible, blending in with the wallpaper whenever possible. Yet there are times one can't help but stick out like a sore thumb. The day of Harrison's funeral I came downstairs for breakfast, around nine o'clock. I dressed in a simple, if not understated gown of midnight blue, with a modest, rounded neckline. It was fitted at the bustline and went straight down to the ground with a small train and capped sleeves. The simplicity of the cut and the color made the gown seem more elegant than it really was. I chose not to wear any jewelry, other than the ancient medallion Father Timothy had given me tucked inside of the bodice.

Coco was sitting next to Emily when I entered the room, the two of them quietly discussing something of importance at the far end of the long table.

Patricia looked up, scowling at me as I entered the room, letting me know that she was in a particularly foul mood. I would be speculating, mind you, but I figured things didn't go well upon her return.

I poured myself a cup of tea and dropped two cubes of sugar in when Brody walked through the door looking around, as if he were searching for somebody. My breath caught in my chest as he turned toward me and began to walk in my direction. He truly was a handsome man, who managed to take my breath away whenever he entered a room, and he didn't even know it. His hair was still damp and his face looked freshly shaven. Brody wore a simple black morning coat, trousers, white linen shirt and black cravat, and the scent of saddle soap and sandalwood teased my senses as he stood close to me with a nonchalant grin on his face.

Leaning down near my ear, Brody whispered, "Please forgive my recent neglect." Then he straightened back up and poured himself a cup of tea.

Surprised, I hesitated a moment, before smiling to myself. Preparing my plate, I said casually, "No apologies necessary," moving down the buffet line and picking out a piece of bacon, a poached egg and toast.

Brody followed close behind, even purposely bumping our plates together so that he could touch my hand. "It wasn't your fault," he said, looking towards the dining room door, as Quinton walked in.

"It is most kind of you to say so, but I still feel very responsible," I replied with a shy smile, before falling silent.

I glanced up, acknowledging Quinton with a bob of my head as he retrieved a plate, then stood close to Brody to fixing his breakfast.

Quinton looked down at me and smiled cordially. "Would you two just do something already and get it over with. The suspense is killing me," he whispered.

Brody immediately elbowed Quinton in the ribs, causing him to cringe, then laugh unapologetically.

"I apologize for my ill-mannered brother. You would understand if you knew how many times he was dropped on his head as an infant," Brody teased, before turning a shade darker.

"has he asked you yet?" Quinton leaned in to inquire, purposely ignoring Brody's insult to change the subject.

"Ask me what?"

The three of us turned to stare at Patricia, when she made a guttural sound of disgust, "Argh!" as she scooted her chair back, loudly scraping it against the wooden floor, before making a show of throwing her napkin down upon the table. Then she glared at each one of us and angrily left the room with her nose in the air.

"Let's hope that it doesn't rain too hard this afternoon, during the grave site portion of the ceremony, or I'm afraid Patricia just might drown herself," Quinton stated, off-handedly, before the three of us turned and began preparing our plates again, as if nothing had happened.

"Where were we?" I said, "oh, yes, we were just discussing whether or not Brody had asked me about something," I concluded, carrying my plate and tea over to the far end of the table and sitting down. Brody and Quinton quickly followed, jostling one another, before setting their plates down and sitting on either side of me. I was rather surprised that they both managed to make it to the table without spilled their plates onto the floor.

"I was thinking..." Brody began to say, correcting himself as soon as Quinton cleared his throat rather loudly. "*We* were thinking that it would be nice if you would consent to ride with us to the church and then walk between us at the funeral." Surprised by the request, I began choking on the mouthful of tea I had just inhaled.

Quinton leaped up and began telling me to put both my arms in the air as he proceeded to pull them up and hold them there for me. Then Brody jumped in, thumping me on the back several times. Thankfully my sister was watching us and yelled across the table at them.

"Turn loose of her this instant, you big ape's, before you kill her," Coco called out, advancing on the two of them with a look of hellfire and brimstone in her eyes. Brody and Quinton immediately let go and stepped back as if they were truly afraid of incurring her wrath.

Placing a glass of water in my hand, Coco ordered me to drink it down while glaring at Quinton and Brody. "Were the two of you raised by a pack of wolves?" she scolded. "You could have caused her real harm, gentlemen," Coco added, as she headed back to her seat, shaking her head, but satisfied that I was going to live. "Honestly,

I don't know what either one of you was thinking," she murmured under her breath.

They kept an eye on Coco as she walked back to the other end of the table, waiting for her to take her seat before they would sit down again.

"Your sister is truly a force to behold when she is protecting you," Quinton quietly whispered to me, slowly bringing his eyes back around to look at me. Then, chancing one last look down to the other end of the table, "I think I might be in love with her."

"Don't be ridiculous, Quinton. Coco is far too young for you," Brody whispered.

"I am a patient man. I can wait," Quinton said, dragging his eyes back down to the other end of the table."

"Since when?" Brody quipped.

"My sister is right, the two of you are ridiculous. Why in the world would you want me by your side today? That position is reserved for family. What about your uncle and two cousins? They are your family," I pointed out.

"Because we do," Brody proclaimed, taking my hand in his. "Besides, we discovered the true motive behind Uncle Thomas's visit this year —"

"He wanted to borrow money from our father. It seems, Uncle Thomas has made a couple of bad investment deals as of late and now finds himself between a hard spot and a really hard spot," Quinton announced boldly, finishing the sentence for Brody. "And then there is dear, sweet cousin Patricia, who is looking for a husband and figured her old, reliable, cousin Brody, would be an easy mark— I mean good fit. Only when she turned up, there was some genuine competition for her," Quinton continued, even though he knew that Brody was embarrassed by the whole matter.

"Would you please stop talking?" Brody admonished Quinton, glaring as if he were about to punch him square in the jaw. "Patricia does not figure into my future plans," he continued, looking at me from the corner of his eye, "and I would very much appreciate it if you would accompany us to our father's funeral."

"Of course. If it means that much to you, it would be my honor," I replied.

Later that day the coffin was carried from the parlor and placed on a hearse drawn by two matching, black horses. Reverently and silently, people climbed into carriages after Harrison's lovely polished coffin was loaded into the hearse.

I sat on the bench of the lead carriage with Brody by my side, and Quinton directly opposite me. The procession of mourners followed behind us, twenty carriages deep, and I gazed out the window at the cold, gloomy sky as we trailed slowly behind the hearse. It smelled like rain was coming.

We traveled about five miles to St Peter's Church, a small, white-washed building in the township of Clarksburg. It had been the Beaumont family church for three generations. I was told on the ride over that there were four rows of benches, all bearing the Beaumont family name, front row center.

Stepping down from the carriage, Quinton exited first. Helping me down, Brody followed. Dutifully, I walked between the two men as we made our way up the six steps. Just before stepping through the tall wooden doors, I felt a single drop of rain hit my nose. Inside the small church we were greeted by the parson. A tall, thin man in his late thirties, balding slightly at the top of his head, he wore a long white robe and a slightly tattered, purple sash that hung around his neck and down the front of his robe.

The floor boards creaked in spots as we made our way down to the front row, where we took our seats, then waited somberly for others to be seated. The entire time I felt Patricia's little poison daggers hitting the back of my head as she glared at me from the third row. Instinctively knowing she wanted nothing more than for me to turn around so she could express her displeasure, I purposely stared straight ahead.

There would be no viewing of the body today, for obvious reasons. Harrison Beaumont's body rested comfortably in a satin-lined, solid oak casket, polished to a high glossy finish. The casket stood at the front of the room, just under the pulpit, draped with a thin, white linen cloth, to keep it from being too stark and dreary.

Two vases of wild flowers sat on either side of the pulpit where the parson stood and cleared his throat. He began to speak in a sing-song voice, extolling Harrison's virtues as a husband and father. Several amusing antidotes were shared by close family friends, further expressing Harrison's virtues and kind nature, followed by a twenty-minute sermon, at which time the parson commended Harrison's soul to God.

I remember thinking how strange it was that the small building echoed as it did, sounding as if three people were talking at the same time, despite the room being mostly full. I looked up and noticed the pitch of the roof was high, so the sound bounced around in the rafters before coming back down.

The parson inclined his head and the bells began to ring, signaling the pall bearers to attend to the casket. They carried Harrison's body out through the side door. The congregation stood and followed silently behind.

The sky was much darker than before, and now threatened to burst open and pour down upon our heads as we stood around the gravesite. The parson looked concerned and began speaking even before everyone had gathered, sprinkling holy water around the gravesite and onto the coffin as it was lowered into the ground.

Brody stepped up and threw a shovel full of dirt upon his father's casket and then handed the shovel to me. I took my turn and passed the shovel to Quinton. Each person in line paid their respects by shoveling a small amount of dirt upon Harrison's casket before returning to their carriages and making the short, five-mile drive back to Rosewood.

Just as Brody, Quinton and I reached the carriage, rain began to fall in sheets. The water that ran down the closed windows of our carriage reminded me of tears, which was something no one in our somber little group had bothered to shed.

A light meal had been prepared and waited for us as we entered the house at Rosewood. The atmosphere was reserved as people spoke in hushed tones, ate their food and paid their respects to Brody and Quinton. Then afterwards, everyone mingled waiting for the rain to ease. After nearly two hours of rain, heavy at times, people began to leave, hurrying from the house while the weather held, trying to avoid a long, soggy, ride home. Even Patricia, Emily and Uncle Thomas made their polite excuses shortly after lunch and left for home. I slipped out the side door, taking a seat on the porch while Brody and Quinton said their good-byes.

The air was crisp and clean after the heavy rain and everything smelled of rich soil, pine trees and wet grass. I'd always loved that smell, because it smelled like hope. Hope of good crops to follow in the spring to feed hungry mouths. Hope of things being washed clean, for a fresh start. Hope of better things to come, just around the corner.

I was watching the puppies bounding around, tumbling and rolling over one another near their mother when Brody came around the corner and I smiled up at him. He pulled a chair up next to mine and sat down. "Are you cold?" he asked, gazing intently at me. "I could go inside and fetch your wrap."

"No, I am fine. But thank you for asking," I replied, glancing over at him. I noticed a strange intensity to his stare. "What is it? Did something happen?" I felt concerned.

"Yes, Olivia, something has happened," he answered, pausing before taking my hand into his, to place a kiss in the palm. "I wanted to broach a subject and I don't know of any other way than to come straight out with it."

"You sound quite serious."

"I truly have enjoyed our time together, and fear that I will be lost without you when you leave," he expressed tenderly.

Momentarily caught off guard, I froze. "Oh, don't be ridiculous, Brody," I cried, pulling my hand back suddenly. "I can't believe that you are broaching this again. I told you that I cannot marry someone I hardly know."

"Why the hell not?" Brody blurted out, sounding hurt by my rejection and suddenly looking away.

I could see the sheer disappointment in his face, but it couldn't be avoided. "Because so much has happened between us in such a short time. Our emotions are all tangled up and exaggerated. When everything settles down, you will see," I answered, placing my hands on either side of his face, forcing him to look at me. "You just lost your father. Your house has been haunted for years by your dead mother. There are a hundred reason why getting married to a complete stranger would be a mistake."

"But it doesn't feel like a mistake to me. I've fallen in love, but perhaps you don't feel the same way."

"You have fallen in love with the idea of me. You couldn't possibly be in love with me because you don't really know me. Not the way you should, to make such a commitment to me for the rest of your life," I pointed out, trying to get him to see reason. "Please, you must see that."

"The only thing I can see is you leaving tomorrow. You will walk away, climb on a ship and cross an ocean, and I will never see you again," he replied, with a quiet desperation to his tone. "Tell me honestly, do you even have feelings for me?"

"Yes, of course I do! But that doesn't change the fact that we would be making a mistake, Brody." Standing up, I took two steps forward, gripping the railing to support myself. "It just isn't enough."

Coming up behind me, Brody gently placed a hand on my arm, and I turned around to look up at him. "Why Olivia? Why isn't it enough?"

"Because I am afraid, Brody." I softly answered, feeling tears spring to my eyes. "Afraid that the emotions we have for each other aren't real. Afraid that you will wake up one morning, a week from now, or a month from now and discover that you have made a terrible mistake."

Pulling me closer, Brody kissed my lips, cheek then my forehead, hugging me so tightly I thought he would break my ribs. I felt his heart beating wildly against my cheek. "I have never felt anything in my life so pure or more honest than when I am with you, Olivia Townsend," he announced, holding me at arm's length now, forcing me to look up at him. "I will try to understand your apprehension, but I have never been more sure of anything in my entire life. I implore you to reconsider my proposal." Then leaning down, Brody covered my mouth with his and we melted into one another. It was an emotionally charged embrace that bespoke more than mere words alone.

It told me that he too had hopes. Hopes for a future together. But more than that, he desired me above anyone else.

31

Friday, February 20, 1804

It's Complicated

I WAS FEELING VERY TORN, EMOTIONALLY speaking, and I didn't know what to do.

Brody and I sat on the porch for hours, discussing our hopes and dreams for the future. We talked of his desire to open a textile factory nearby that would rival my family's establishment in London. I shared with him my desire to help others who had been burdened by earthbound spirits, like his own family. Then Brody asked me again, on bended knee, to marry him. I was drawn in by his conviction and charm, suddenly unsure of my earlier resolve to bid farewell to him for now. It was one thing to say that you needed more time to get to know a person, and an entirely different matter to willingly walk away from them, not knowing if you would ever see them again. Yet, I was still unable to freely give him the answer he sought.

We parted that evening with Brody's question hanging heavily between us, and I went to bed feeling troubled and weighed down by my erratic emotion and inability to make a decision.

Coco wandered into my room around one o'clock in the morning, slipping quietly beneath the covers when she thought I was asleep. I was grateful for the company and the fact that she was exhausted, for I was in no mood for long conversations with her tonight about questions I was not yet ready to answer. She quickly fell asleep, resting her hand across my waist, as she had done since we were children.

Around three-thirty, I found myself wide awake, staring out of the window, and drawing comfort from the solitude that spread out before my eyes. The wind was gently swaying the trees, and it reminded me of a ballet as the branches swayed one way and then back the other. The moon shone brightly, lighting the tops of the trees and the courtyard below, as it sent strange shadows dancing upon the ground.

I no longer sensed the presence of a tortured soul bound to the earth by hate or anger, as I had when I first arrived. A sense of peace and tranquility had fallen over the household of Rosewood. Everyone seemed to breathe a collective sigh of relief, no longer fearing for their lives or wondering who would be the next victim of the angry spirit that had resided there. The only person in the household now who seemed ill at ease was me. Time was short and I needed to make a decision. A life-changing decision.

I began to wonder if I turned left, instead of right, at this proverbial fork in the road, would it really change the outcome of my life? Would I still end up where I was intended to? Or could one bad decision put me down the wrong path, negatively impacting the course of my life? Did I stay, making a life with Brody, or did I take the chance that the moon and stars would align themselves again at some point and bring us back together?

The new day had dawned brighter than the day before. The rain and clouds had departed, leaving clear skies. The rooster began to crow, but he didn't awaken me, because I was already wide awake. I had been tossing and turning, unable to sleep, knowing that we would be leaving as soon as the luggage could be loaded into the carriages.

"What is the matter with you, Olivia? Did something happen?" Coco sounded concerned, climbing from bed to join me at the window.

I gave a reassuring smile, that wasn't completely convincing at all. "No, nothing has happened. I just couldn't sleep."

Coco touched my sleeve as I turned to look at her. "Tell me what is wrong, and please, don't say nothing. I can tell when you are lying to me."

I smiled again, to keep from tearing up. "You were always so intuitive. Can you let this one go? Just this once?" I begged, gently stroking her cheek. "I don't know if I can talk about it without getting emotional," I added, walking back to bed and climbing beneath the covers. The only thing I wanted to do was pull the covers over my head and make time stand still a little while longer. Because no matter how many scenarios I played out in my head, I couldn't shake the feeling that my destiny required me to leave for home with my family. It was as if the universe were telling me what I should do, and all I wanted to do was argue with it.

"Is this about you and Brody?" she questioned, peeling the covers back, denying me the peace I dearly sought.

"Coco, stop it. I told you to let it go," I replied crossly, pulling the covers back up to my chin and gripping them tightly, before turning away from her, grousing in a low tone under my breath. "Go back to sleep. It is far too early for this."

Refusing to be ignored, Coco climbed over me and snaked beneath the blankets before I could stop her. "Too late, I'm awake now." With a guttural sound deep in my throat, I growled and clenched my teeth, turning over in bed and taking a majority of blankets with me.

"Ah ha! So, it *is* about you and Brody! I *knew* it! Is that why you were tossing and turning all night," Coco pestered, trying to force me to turn loose of the covers. "You really should tell me what you are struggling with. Maybe I can help."

Growing more impatient with each passing second, a character flaw in my personality that I attributed to lack of sleep, rather than to the fact that my heart was breaking, I lashed out at her. "Coco, go back to your own room and leave me alone. You really are like an annoying boil upon my —"

"Olivia Sophia, I am warning you, don't you dare finish that sentence!" Coco sputtered, as she glared at me. Finally, Coco "harrumphed," deciding she was madder at me than she was curious and climbed from my bed, quickly leaving without another word.

At the time, my actions were childish, I will admit. But they were affective, and frankly, the only thing that I could think of. I needed her to leave me alone. How was I going to wallow in my own sense of misery if Coco continued to pester me with questions? I couldn't hear myself think, and I was quickly running out of time. I still didn't know what my answer would be or what I was going to do.

Trying to sleep was impossible, so I climbed out of bed, pulled on the servant's bell, and requested a strong pot of tea and a hot bath. Then I splashed water on my face, brushed my teeth and waited for the tub and hot water to arrive. Someone else had requested a hot bath that morning, to be brought up as soon as they awoke but, fortunately for me, I was up first.

I found comfort in the warmth of the water as Margot poured it over my head. Lathering my hair up with oils and botanicals of lavender and citrus she mixed for me, I washed the suds from my head but didn't immediately climb out of the bath, deciding instead to sit and ponder matters until the water had grown cold.

Wrapping myself in a sheet, then twisting my hair up in a smaller cloth, I slipped into a robe to keep warm. I wandered over to the window, with a fresh cup of hot herbal tea in hand, and watched the changing colors of the sky as the sun came up over the trees. The sky had begun to turn a dusky pink and vivid orange just behind the tree line, and it took my breath away. About that time, Margot came through the door.

"If you continue to do for yourself, little missy, there will no longer any need for me," Margot grumbled, while heading into the dressing room to retrieve a dress for me.

I laughed and turned back to the window. "You are irreplaceable, Margot," I teased, mockingly.

"That's not what you said two days ago," she quipped, as she came back from the dressing room with a dark green, wool gown in hand. Looking at the dress before Margot laid it out on the bed, I chuckled to myself as I remembered just exactly what I had said to her two days prior. It had been an unkind statement, but I hadn't meant a word of it. "You do realize that I wasn't serious, right?"

"Of course," she replied with a smile. "Now come over here and let's get you dressed before you catch a chill."

Something moved in the courtyard below, catching my eye as I looked down to see a single rider on horseback, coming out from one of the side trails. He lifted his eyes up to my window, and I knew by the turn of his head who it was. I wondered if he had been as restless as me and had gone out for an early morning ride to settle anxious nerves.

Slowly pulling my eyes away from the window when he turned and headed for the barn with his mount Zeus, I focused my attention on the task at hand. Getting dressed.

Turning back to Margot, I smiled, deciding that even though I didn't yet know what I would say to Brody, at least I would be properly dressed when I saw him again.

I desperately wanted to see into the future and determine what would happen between Brody and myself, but of course, I didn't have that ability. So, like everyone else, I would have to make a decision and then live with whatever came afterwards.

I let Margot blather on about the friends she had made, as she went into detail about their lives. Normally, I would have found all of her idle gossip fascinating, but instead, I was lost in my own thoughts as she dried and brushed the tangles from my hair, styling it in a new way something she had learned from her new friends at Rosewood. Then she busied herself, packing up the rest of my belongings, still carrying on about different people, as she did so. In those moments, my future suddenly became clear. I didn't feel the need to interrupt her, so I left the room without her even noticing.

I needed to find Brody, to tell him what I had decided, without second guessing myself, or changing my mind.

I walked past my parent's room and noticed several trunks being moved out, then realized that I had even less time than I'd imagined.

Moving down the stairs, I was desperate to find Brody. Passing by the sunroom, I found a housekeeper tending to her duties. "Excuse me, but have you seen Mr. Beaumont this morning?"

"I just saw Mr. Quinton Beaumont in the sun room having breakfast. I am sure Mr. Brody Beaumont went upstairs twenty minutes ago and has not come downstairs yet," the young woman answered with a pleasant smile.

"Thank you," I replied, turning around to head the other way. I smiled to myself, and wondered if the bath I had pilfered earlier had been intended for Brody after his ride.

I heard talking coming from the sunroom as I passed by. Father, Mother, Prince William and Quinton were discussing India and many of the delicacies they had eaten while there when I entered the room.

I walked along the outskirt of the room toward the buffet, and noticed that Mother stood up when she saw me. Wondering over to join me at the buffet as I buttered my scone, she poured herself a fresh cup of tea. My stomach was tied into knots, and I was having a difficult time deciding what to have since I didn't feel very hungry. Yet our journey would be long, and I knew that I needed something before embarking on the sea voyage.

"I was wondering if you were ever coming down. Have you seen your sister?" Mother asked casually.

Sheepishly I smiled and looked away. "Well, yes and no," I coyly replied, searching for the right words to explain to Mother what I had done. "Funny thing about that, you see, I may have angered her first thing this morning," I whispered

"You what!" Mother gasped while sounding disappointed in me. She whispered back, "What did you do, Olivia?"

"I may have told her that she was an annoying boil on my —"

"Olivia Sophia, you didn't!" Mother scolded, looking over her shoulder to see if anyone else at the table had overheard us. Suddenly I felt like a five-year-old being taken to task by her mother.

"I'm sorry Mother. I didn't really mean it. It's just, well, she wouldn't leave me alone."

"That is no excuse, young lady," Mother exclaimed. "You need to find Coco and apologize to her before we leave. Because I, for one, do not intend to sit in some cramped confines of a carriage and then a ship, while the two of you feud all the way home. Do you hear me!?" Guilt and anxiety suddenly hit me as I cast my eyes downward. "Yes Mother, loud and clear. Can I at least eat my scone before I hang myself upon a cross?"

"I will have Mrs. Bell wrap several up for you, and you can eat them in the carriage. Now go!" Mother ordered as she pointed her finger in the direction I had just come from. Obediently, I did as I was told, placing my plate down on the buffet as I turned, glancing over at my father and Quinton as they stared at me. All conversation at the table had ceased, and I realized that part of my discussion with Mother had been overheard. I felt my cheeks flush with embarrassment, and grabbed a scone from my plate, to spite Mother, then quickly left the room.

I returned to my room that I shared with my sister when the adjoining door opened and there stood Coco. She took one look at me and averted her eyes, walking past me as if I wasn't even there.

I groaned inwardly, and ran after her. "Coco, please, stop," I called, yet she continued to walk towards the door as if I hadn't said a thing. "Please, Coco," I pleaded, "I'm sorry. I didn't mean what I said to you earlier. I'm an idiot," I meekly added, stepping in front of her, and then I saw the pain I had caused her, evident by the look in her eyes. Taking a few steps, I threw my arms around her stiff frame. "I really am sorry for my words, Coco. You didn't deserve them."

"I'm still angry at you," Coco mumbled against my neck.

"As you should be. I was very cruel, and inconsiderate, and thoughtless, and I should be severely flogged for it."

"Yes, you should," Coco grumbled next to my ear. "But I will forgive you, just this once, because I am so saintly for putting up with you," she conceded.

I chuckled in her hair so she wouldn't think I was making fun of her as I gave her another tight squeeze. "Yes, yes you are."

"Oh, go on with you," Coco pushed against me. "You're suffocating me."

I smiled, then kissed her cheek. "I promise to never say such cruel things to you ever again."

"See that you don't," Coco said sternly, still pouting a bit. "I'm hungry. Shall we go down to breakfast?"

Shaking my head, "I have to take care of something."

"Are you finally going to talk to Brody about, well, you know?" Coco prodded, with a half smile.

Momentarily taken aback, I gasped. "How did you know?"

Holding up her hands, to show me that she was only wearing one glove, Coco smiled impishly. "I was putting my gloves on when you stopped me."

"Why you little…" I blurted, before narrowing my eyes and shaking my head.

"Don't forget your promise!" Coco squealed, and took a step back. "You were the one who stopped me, remember?" she justified.

I shook my head and took a deep breath. "Fine," I relented. "Yes, I am going to speak with Brody. Any final words for me? Wait, never mind. That would be cheating."

Looking conspiratorial, Coco lifted her eyebrows and smiled. "So, what are you going to tell him?" she asked, "as if I don't already know."

Conceding defeat, I threw my hands into the air. "I don't know. You tell me. You touched my arm, remember?"

"You have to believe me, I stopped when it got too intimate," Coco confessed. "What I really want to know is are you staying or going?"

With a solemn tone, I admitted, "I know what I need to do. But it isn't what I want to do. Does that make sense?"

Looking into my eyes as she pulled her glove on, Coco's smile faded. Then taking my hand in hers, she whispered, "It makes perfect sense, Olivia. And for what it is worth, I'm sorry." Hugging me, Coco gave me another measured smile as she pulled away. "This isn't the way I saw any of this going, you know. Are you sure about your decision, Olivia?"

My emotions were all over the place and I struggled to contain them. I kept telling myself, that I wasn't going to cry. "I wrestled with this matter all night. You know how Father always tells us to go with our first instincts?"

"Yes. So?"

"Well, I feel that it is excellent advice, and I have decided that I need to go home," I concluded stoically.

"Then I will be downstairs having breakfast while you find Brody and tell him of your decision," Coco said soberly, opening the door for me.

I walked down the hallway a few feet, before turning around. Coco had a pensive look on her face, and I didn't understand it at the time. "Am I making a mistake?"

"A decision made for all the right reasons is never a mistake, Olivia. Just make sure that you are making this decision for all the right reasons," Coco advised, before turning around and leaving me in the hallway to ponder her words.

32

Time Waits for No Man, or Woman for That Matter

I STOOD IN THE MIDDLE OF the hallway a few moments longer, pondering my sister's last words to me, until a young man stopped to ask if I needed assistance. I smiled, shook my head, then continued on my way. Standing outside Brody's door, I was working up enough courage to knock when the door suddenly opened.

Brody stood in front of me, smelling of sandalwood soap and freshly laundered linens. My heart skipped a beat and my cheeks flushed warmly. He looked surprise. "I was just coming to find you," he muttered, motioning for me to enter, while stepping into the hallway to look up and then down to ensure that no one would be witness our clandestine meeting.

Stepping into his bedroom, I suddenly had a feeling of trepidation wash over me. "I saw you coming back from your ride earlier. Couldn't sleep?" I called over my shoulder as I walked even further into his room.

Brody's bedchambers were very masculine in décor — from the leather couch and leather upholstered armchairs in the sitting area near the hearth, to the thick, dark wood of his enormous, four-poster bed near the middle of the room, with the sheets all tousled from the night before. Hesitating a moment, I sauntered over to the window, stepping around a pair of dirty socks, a bath sheet and his riding clothes piled up in the middle of the floor. His room was on the opposite side of the house as mine, with views of the row houses peeking out between the tree tops.

"It seems that I wasn't the only one," he exclaimed, walking up behind me while I gazed out at the vistas beyond the trees. "And judging by the look on your face when you came through my door, I'm not going to like your answer very much. Am I?"

Turning around in his arms, to face him, I tried to smile. "Well, that all depends on whether or not you are a pragmatist," I answered coyly.

Touching my face gently, Brody scoffed and tried to smile back, equally unsuccessfully. "I've never known someone to answer a marriage proposal by asking the other person if they were a pragmatist," he teased, pulling me closer and wrapping his arms around me, just a bit tighter. I could feel his heart franticly beating in his chest as I laid my head against his chest, and knew the moment his heart broke in two because mine was breaking, too.

I pulled back slightly to search his face for any signs of anger, but there was none. I only saw the love he had for me written all over his face as he tried to understand my decision. The look in his eyes nearly made me change my mind.

"I truly do feel deeply for you, Brody Beaumont, and I wish with all my heart, that I could give you a different answer. And if circumstances were different, and I were an ordinary woman…" My words trailed off, leaving the sentence unfinished as I cast my eyes downward.

"But you're not an ordinary woman and you never will be," Brody concluded, gently stroking my cheek with his thumb. "That is why I love you so very much, Olivia Townsend. You never mince your words."

Chancing a glance, I brought my eyes up to look at him. "In my position, I can't just decide to get married, then run down to the church the next day. There are bands to be taken out, and the proper waiting time has to be observed." I blathered on before rolling my eyes as I remembered the most important reason I could never simply marry as I pleased. "Not to mention needing to seek the king's permission first. Why, I would never be able to go home again, otherwise. It is just unheard of!"

Nodding his head as if he actually understood my dilemma, Brody placed an index finger to my lips. "Shush now. You're making my head hurt with so many details," he teased. Then with an understanding smile, Brody tried to laugh. "Perhaps getting married right now is not the best idea I have had."

Lowering my eyes when I realized how ridiculous I sounded, I took a deep breath. "Brody," I tentatively said, looking up at him.

"Yes?" came the simple reply as he patiently gazed down at me.

Fighting back tears, I took another deep breath and chewed on my lower lip. "If circumstances were different, and I were an ordinary woman —"

Placing a finger across my lips again, he said, "I know," fighting back his own emotions as he lowered his head to gently kiss my lips. The bitter sweet moment was almost more than I could bear, as I buried my head into his chest, hugging him tightly. My emotions were too raw to look him in the eye, so I turned around in his arms. Brody continued to hold me tightly against him while we stared out of the window, pretending to take in the beautiful views. I forced myself to breath in and out, giving myself time to gain control, before speaking again.

"Brody?" I said in a whisper, trying not to betray myself. I heard him swallow hard.

"Yes, Olivia?" he answered, after a long pause, bending down near my ear.

"Will you walk me out to my carriage? I don't think that I will be able to walk away on my own," I confessed, as a tear rolled down my cheek.

Brody didn't immediately answer me, and I felt him take a hesitant breath as his chest rested against my back. Brody swallowed hard, then took a deep breath before he answered me. "I'm not entirely sure that that will be in my best interest. After all, I don't want you to leave," he replied, trying to sound light.

I wiped the tear from my cheek before turning around in his arms. "But you have to!" I demanded, sounding half like a child who had just been denied their favorite treat after dinner.

He smiled, then nodded his head and I watched his atoms apple bob up and then down, as he wordless answered me. I knew that I was asking the world of him, at that moment, and I laid my head against his chest again. He brought his hand up to cradle the back of my head tightly to his chest, and I thought to myself how much I wished that this moment would never end. But then I heard the clock strike ten o'clock and knew that my father would come looking for me soon. I didn't wish to be found alone in Brody's bedchamber.

"If we are going to get you on your way, we had better go now," Brody suggested, as he turned loose of me to retrieve his coat from the back of the chair.

While slipping on his coat, I observed him nonchalantly swipe at his cheek with the back of his hand and loudly cleared his throat. "Now then, don't just stand there unless you expect me to carry you down the stairs like a sack of potatoes," he teased, stepping to the door and opening it a crack to check the hallway in both directions before motioning to me to join him.

Standing just behind him, I tried to lighten the mood by jokingly saying, "I believe one should always examine another's bedchamber before agreeing to marry them," I admonished, giving his room one last glance before stepping into the hallway. "Besides, I can't believe that I seriously considered saying yes to you, before I realized how messy you were."

"Hay!" Brody cried, trying to sound hurt, as he picked up my hand and placing it over his arm like a proper gentleman. "Preposterous, I say!" Brody finally replied, sticking his nose into the air like a highborn when they smelled something stinky. I found myself wanting to giggle at him, despite the circumstances, and instead took another deep breath to keep from crying.

We walked through the hallways, and down the staircase, arm in arm, making light conversation.

"What is the first thing you are dying to eat when you return home?" Brody asked, as he remained looking straight ahead. I could tell that walking me out to the carriage was excruciatingly hard for him, and I was grateful.

"Shepherd's pie. Mrs. McDougal, our cook, makes the best Shepherd's pie," I replied, trying to keep the conversation light.

Father suddenly appeared through the front door, looking frantic. "Oh, there you are. I've been looking everywhere for you. Well, come along, we don't have all day," he said impatiently, rushing back out the door.

Brody and I continued our little game of make-believe as he walked me over to the group of people gathered to say their good-byes. His brother, Quinton and Prince William were talking to Mother and Coco when we walked up.

I smiled up at Quinton and laughed when he brazenly winked, leaning down to give me a farewell hug and whisper in my ear. "You do realize that he's the runt of the litter," he indicated, by pointing at Brody and jerking his head to the side. "So, scrawny and sickly," Quinton teased.

I couldn't help but smile at Quinton. "Thank you for welcoming my family and me into your home," I said, trying to be gracious and ignore the brotherly banter.

"We wouldn't have a home if it weren't for you," Brody pointed out.

Looking up at him, I smiled. "If you ever find yourselves in the canyon and happen upon Lilly's bones, would the two of you mind giving her a proper burial?"

Simultaneously they answered, "Of course."

Stiffly smiling, I felt my eyes began to tear up. "There is so much dust in the air here, I will be glad to get home so my eyes can stop watering," I complained, dabbing at my eyes with my finger. Brody and Quinton both immediately pulled clean handkerchiefs from their pockets, shoving them at me. Taking the handkerchiefs, from their outstretched hands, I laughed. "Thank you, both," I added graciously. "It seems that you don't know how much you need one of these until you don't have one," I joked. "I will send you each a box for Christmas."

"We look forward to receiving them," Quinton said, after an awkward pause, as Brody became suddenly mute.

Turning to Prince William, who had finished saying his farewells to my father, I stretched out a hand and dropped into a deep curtsy. "It has been a pleasure meeting you, Your Highness."

Taking my hand, Prince William chuckled. "The pleasure has been all mine, Lady Olivia. I hope to see you and your family soon. Your father has extended an invitation to me and my expanding brood. I hope to be take him up on his generous offer before too long," he chuckled again. "After my wife delivers, of course."

"Of course," I concurred.

"Olivia, we need to be off," Father called through the carriage door, sounding impatient.

I smiled and waved, suddenly feeling very awkward myself as a nervous laugh escaped my lips. "Time waits for no man, so I've heard or, in this case, woman. Thank you again for your hospitality, gentlemen," I said pensively, turning to Quinton and then Brody.

"Safe journey home, Olivia. I hope the wind stays at your back," Quinton exclaimed, elbowing Brody in the side to shake him out of his stupor. "Come along, William, I want to show you something in the barn," he said, unexpectedly kicking at Brody and giving him a sly look when he looked up.

"Well, I guess this is good-bye, for now," I pensively said, still looking after the retreating backs of Quinton and William.

Taking my arm to lead me over to the carriage, Brody walked me the last hundred yards in silence. There really wasn't anything left to say. I knew in my heart that if Brody had asked me to stay one more time, I would have thrown caution to the wind and said yes. But he didn't ask again.

Helping me to step up into the carriage, Brody held on to my fingers, instead of letting go. I turned and gazed down at him and for a moment. I thought he was going to say something as I watched his lips move to form a word, but he didn't. I even opened my mouth to say something back, but propriety caused me to hold my tongue, as the moment passed and he turned, shutting the door.

I sat down next to the door, staring out the window as our carriage pulled away from Rosewood. Brody never moved a muscle, he simply stood there, like a statue, until we were out of sight.

Mother, Father and Coco talked while I sat perfectly still, silently staring out the window. No one let on that anything was amiss, even when I dabbed at my eyes and blew my nose with the handkerchief Quinton had given me. Then bringing Brody's handkerchief to my nose, I inhaled deeply. His scent filled my senses, as I carefully folded the material into a neat little square and placed it into my dress pocket.

I knew that I wanted to recall the way he smelled the last time I saw him. I wanted to preserve this memory, no matter how bitter sweet it was, for as long as I could. Preventing it from fading away, to be lost to that secret place all old memories eventually go.

An hour into our journey, Coco leaned over and whispered into my ear. "Do you know what happens when you burn a bridge?"

I looked at her, still feeling bereft, and sad, "No, but I'm guessing you are about to tell me."

Coco smiled understandingly. "You learn to swim."

I closed my eyes, leaning my head against the carriage wall and just breathed. At that moment, I felt my world turning darker and wondered how it would ever return to the way it had been before. Yet, somewhere deep inside of me I knew that life would continue to go on, my heart would still beat tomorrow, my lungs would take another breath of air, and I would place one foot in front of the other. I knew that my feelings of sorrow were intensified by the fact that I had been given a choice. My hand sat on the carriage seat between us, balled up into an angry fist. Coco reached out, touching my hand while carrying on her conversation, as if everything were normal.

I remember feeling grateful to her for that small act of kindness.

Our ship journey home was long and torturous, made even more so by the fact that I spent most of my time up on deck looking back towards the direction we came from, instead of forward in the direction we were going.

At the time, I truly felt that my heart had been left behind at Rosewood, like an amputee who feels phantom pains from a missing appendage. The painful experience taught me something, however, and that was that life will give you heartbreak to grow, for those are the things that cause real change in our lives and in our hearts. Having this knowledge at the time did not make the pain any less, for my heart continued to ache.

Mother and Father did their best to pull me out of my depressed state, but I didn't make it easy on them. We never discussed the reason for my heartache, although I'm sure they believed me to still be morning the loss of my friend, Lilly, so they made allowances for my behavior.

Yet, Coco knew the truth and she kept my secret, never pressing me for answers or voicing her opinions. She simply watched over me and, like a guardian angel, she was my saving grace. I was lost in a pit of despair, unsure of how to climb out. She'd wrap a cape around my shoulders when I stayed too long on deck or brought me a corn muffin, forcing me to eat it while talking incessantly about absolutely nothing. Sometimes she watched over me from a distance, and took care of me when I wouldn't take care of myself.

Just before we made landfall, I concluded that something must change. So, it was with this thought in mind, I decided I would move forward with my life. What was done was done, and I would learn to live with my decision.

I began keeping this journal to express the hidden things of my heart, so one day, when I looked back upon my life, it would all somehow make sense. But more importantly, I never wanted to forget the love I could have had.

Something else came from our journey home. I stood back and took an accounting of my life. A long, hard look, as some would call it, and I realized that I didn't like what I saw. I'd become short-sighted and filled with contradictions, and this disturbed me. I had all of these emotions rattling around inside of my heart and my head, and I truly didn't know what to do with them.

The petty jealousy towards Patricia had filled me with so much anxiety, I had lost sight of my purpose. I was not pleased with my short-comings and decided that a change was in order. I was a complicated mess of a human, and it was not what I had envisioned for my life becoming, at all. I needed to discover my true self and find a healthy balance between the old me and the new me.

I told myself that day that I would do whatever it took to change my situation and find myself again. No longer would I allow fear or longing to cloud my judgement.

33

FRIDAY, MARCH 5, 1805

True Love is Never Really Forgotten

WINTER THAT YEAR IN DUBLIN was harsh, and spring came suddenly today, chasing the memories of cold weather away from our mind. Occasionally a cool breeze would whip up, but the sunshine on my face felt particularly glorious. Even the flowers and trees had begun to awaken from their deep winter slumber.

Shortly after returning from the colonies, I went to see Lilly's younger sisters, Rose and Iris. They were inconsolable over the news of their sister's death. Lilly's father, Mr. Collins, required me to explain what had happened to his precious daughter, but still he couldn't wrap his mind around it all. He was unable to grasp the reason Lilly's body hadn't been retrieved. Most Irish believed that a soul could never find peace if their remains were not buried in the hallowed ground of the church cemetery. I did my best to comfort them as we grieved her loss together. Eventually, I was able to calm his fears, assuring him that I had witnessed Lilly crossing over with my own eyes, and that she was truly at peace now.

My reputation as a healer of lost souls began to grow, and instead of reviled, I was being contacted by people from neighboring counties to remove unwanted spirits from homes. Sometimes I was simply asked to explain what happened to their loved ones, once they passed away. My consuming work, like a balm to my own heart, brought much needed comfort. At times I was far too busy to dwell on what

I had left behind or what might have been, and yet, there were quiet moments that allowed my mind to dwell on my past. It was like an anchor around my neck, weighing me down in a pit of self-despair. In those quiet memories, I was reminded of what I had given up for the sake of propriety.

A mighty change had begun inside of me as I was forced to stretch beyond myself to help others. I found that I could take a deep breath again without the pressing pain in my chest reminding me with every beat of my heart just how much it hurt. I now felt liberated because I had a purpose.

I sent Brody and Quinton each a box of the finest Irish handkerchiefs money could buy. I'd even dared to hope that Brody would receive my package and understand the subtle message associated with it. I still cared for him and he would always linger in my thoughts.

I arose early, today, with the intent of visiting the village orphanage and render my services since I had no other pressing matters to attend.

I tried to visit the children once a week and help the nuns out where I could. I loved surprising the children with a basket full of freshly baked pastries that I shamed our cook into providing for me, with Father's blessings, of course.

I dressed simply, donning a gray dress with a green ribbon loosely tied, just beneath the bust. I wrapped a green wool shawl around my shoulders to ward off the early morning chill and collected my basket of pastries on my way out the door.

I felt an odd sense of hopefulness today that left me feeling anxious and lighter somehow. I felt optimistic that I would be pleasantly surprised by my day.

Father came upon me on the road in his lovely official rig and offered me a ride into town, which I graciously accepted. "I am on my way to meet with potential investors in our textile business. Your mother and I are looking to expand. I wanted be sure you will be home at a reasonable hour for supper this evening."

"I didn't realize that you were looking to take on investors. Are we financially sound, Father?"

"Yes, yes, of course. Your mother and I were simply considering an expansion, and well, we need someone we can trust. You can give us your opinion this evening. I will be bringing them home for supper since they have come such a great distance. Perhaps you and your sister wouldn't mind gracing us with your musical talents."

I smiled and conceded. "Of course, it would be my pleasure," I said and kissed him on the cheek before stepping out of the carriage and waving good-bye.

It was always a long day when I visited the orphanage because I would get lost in the children and forget the time. The children were just completing their assigned chores when I arrived with my goodies, and they mobbed at the door, trying to poke their little hands into the basket. The head nun, Sister Mary, sternly scolded the older children for pushing the younger ones out of the way to get to me. Smiling my apologies to Sister Mary, I felt terrible for the children assigned chores for their infraction. But they all quickly lined up to get their portion of porridge, then stood in line to choose a treat from my basket, starting with the youngest.

Later, I read stories and helped the younger children practice their letters while the older girls brushed the younger girls' hair. I'd brought satin ribbons from home saving the best colors for the older girls because they always ended up with the short stick in my opinion. I washed cheeks and hands, then snuggled as many little ones as I could, for it is my expert opinion that little children can never have too many hugs.

Then I said my good-byes at four o'clock in the afternoon and began my long walk home. I waved to people I knew on my way, picked a handful of wild flowers from the side of the road and stopped a couple of times to chat with people who had questions about loved ones who had recently died.

I was at the bottom of the hill, beginning my climb to our home on top when I saw Coco, frantically waving her arms in the air. Concerned, I began to climb the hill more quickly, pushing myself forward by shear will as I ran the last four hundred yards up the hill.

Coming to a stop in front of her, I found myself very winded and leaned over, bracing a hand upon my knee so I could catch my breath. "What is it? What has happened?" I asked anxiously, between breaths as I gasped for air.

"Nothing is the matter, Olivia. In fact, everything is very well, indeed," Coco replied jubilantly, as a young puppy, I hadn't noticed before stepped out from behind her skirts and licked me on the nose.

Jumping back in surprise, I cried out and grimaced while staring at the dog. "What the bloody hell is that?" There was something that felt very familiar about her. She was tall and lean, with long sleek lines and a light, chocolate-colored coat and, as I continued to study the dog's unique white patch on her mussel, it hit me like a brick to the head. That was Brody Beaumont's puppy, the one he had shown me, all grown up!

"It's our new dog. Well, yours, really," Coco gleefully announced with a small giggle. "Isn't she beautiful, Olivia?"

"What are you babbling on about?" I asked bewildered, still not understanding what was going on. Then pulling my eyes away from the dog, I gasped, just as Brody walked around a grouping of trees, a hundred feet away from us. "Bloody hell!"

"I thought you would be happy about the dog, Olivia," she cried, sounding confused by my reaction. "I haven't told you the best news yet."

"Brody Beaumont is here," I gasped under my breath, watching him as he walked towards me with a confident smile on his face.

A look of shock crossed Coco's face, before she turned around to see what I was staring at. "Ugh! I told him to stay put," she blurted out, sounding rather disgruntled for having her surprise blown. "Come on girl, let's see what kind of trouble we can get into, somewhere else."

I didn't hear anything else my sister said because my world seemed to narrow down to a small pin hole. And all the while, there was a loud noise between my ears, like the sound of waves crashing upon the rock.

My mind and heart were racing, and suddenly I didn't know what to do or say. I simply stood, frozen in place, like a startled deer while Brody approached me. As he drew nearer, the first thing I noticed was his facial hair. He had grown his beard back, and his hair had been recently trimmed. He looked absolutely polished in his tailored, dark gray, three-piece suit and black leather shoes. Then I touched my hair, and remembered that I was a mess. It was at that moment I prayed for the ground to open up and swallow me whole. This was not the way I had imagined us meeting again. In my daydreams, I had always been the one all neatly manicured and put together.

"You're looking well," Brody lied, in his rich, warm, masculine tones that reminded me of melting caramel.

Self-consciously, I touched my hair again, knowing that he was only being polite. "You are most kind, good sir," I replied with a nervous laugh as I dropped into a proper curtsy. "But I'm sure that you didn't travel all this way, just to bring me a dog and flattering words?"

"I did promise you a dog, and I always keep my word," he assured me, with a wry smile. "She's smart as a whip. I trained her myself," he continued, letting his gaze fall upon the dog he spoke of, across the field with Coco. Then his tone turned more serious as he looked at me. "I had some business to attend to in Dublin."

"That's rather cryptic, without being specific. Would you care to elaborate?" I asserted, trying to read his face.

Ignoring my question, Brody's serious look turned mischievous, as he flashed me another brilliant smile. Taking ahold of my arm, Brody tucked it into his and pulled me along, as he began to walk the grounds like he had already been here. "Your sister tells me that you volunteer your time at the town orphanage. I also understand that you have been very busy helping others benefit from your gift," he mentioned casually.

"Yes, I have been rather busy of late," I answered, looking over my shoulder, scrutinizing my sister a little ways off but close enough that she could keep an eye on us as she played with *my* dog. I began to wonder what else she had been discussing with Brody Beaumont...

"It would seem that my sister has been doing a lot of talking. What else have you two been discussing in regards to me?" I questioned, pulling him to a stop so I could scrutinize him.

He chuckled a little and kept walking, casually changing the subject. "I was told that it was a difficult winter and that you received a lot of rain this year."

"Yes, it was a very long winter," I said, pulling on his arm, forcing him to stop walking again and face me. "Brody?"

"Yes?"

"Why have you come here?" I asked bluntly.

"I told you why."

"Actually, you've told me nothing," I pointed out. Narrowing my eyes, then lifting one eyebrow, I turned my head slightly. "So, why don't you tell me the real reason you have come all this way just to visit me."

"Who said anything about me traveling here to visit you?" he questioned, taking a moment to study me. I could tell that he was weighing his options, whether or not to tell me the whole truth. "My grandfather always told me there was no true educational benefit from a second kick from a mule," Brody said, narrowing his eyes to mimic my suspicious glare. Then he gave me another brilliant smile, showing off his beautiful white teeth. "I thought I would test his theory."

"Brody Beaumont, are you comparing me to a kicking mule? Because if you are —" I paused for dramatic effect, making him squirm just a bit.

"No!" he cried, suddenly looking alarmed.

Then I began to laugh and Brody looked very confused, which only made me laugh harder. "Because you wouldn't be the first person to do so," I cried between fits of laughter. "You should have seen your face."

Suddenly, Brody's arm shot out, pulling me up against him, forcing me to stop laughing, as I laid my head against his chest. I could feel his heart beating wildly and for some reason that thrilled me.

"Oh, Olivia, I truly have missed you so much," Brody confessed.

My pent-up emotions from the past year hit me like a brick wall. The fact that I was a mess no longer mattered and everything else melted away. I wrapped my arms around him, gulping back my tears and reveling in the feeling of being in his arms again.

"I'm afraid that when you left me, I experienced a feeling that I had never felt before," Brody admitted, still holding tightly to me, as the timber of his voice reverberating through his chest wall.

I quietly murmured against his chest, "Oh, and what might that be?"

"I thought that once your carriage pulled away, my life would return to normal and that I would be fine again, that my heart would stop feeling like it was being torn in two. But I wasn't fine, and my heart continued to ache like it was about to burst into a million pieces. When your carriage was out of sight, that I realized I needed you. Suddenly, I couldn't imagine my life without you," he admitted, gently tilting my chin up to look at him.

I couldn't believe what I was hearing, as his lips slowly touched mine, and we kissed so passionately, I thought my heart would burst. He had stolen my heart, the very moment he first touched my hand in New York. The very man who sent tingling jolts of electricity racing through my veins, ricocheting off the walls of my chest and piercing my heart completely. His velvety tongue caressed mine and he tasted of mint. I knew that he had wandered through our garden before coming to me and it sent my heart soring, until I also realized that he had waited more than a year to come after me. Pulling back, I pushed against him slightly.

"Then why didn't you come after me sooner? I cried, punching him in the arm as I pushed completely out of his embrace. "Why would you wait so long to tell me how you felt?" shaking my head slightly as a tear ran down my cheek. Taking a few steps away and turning my back to him, I felt baffled by his delay. "If you truly loved me, why would you wait so long? I have been tortured all these months thinking that you didn't really care. And for what?" I cried, abruptly turning on him. Brody merely stood still as if he was confused while I unleashed my frustration on him.

"Ouch," he cried, bringing his hands up to clutch his heart, as if an arrow had just mortally wounded him.

"Why? Why would you do that to me?" I sniffed loudly, wiping bitter tears aside with my one hand and then the other. He swallowed hard, and I was unable to read his thoughts. He took two steps closer and paused, unsure if he should touch me or not. It felt like an eternity before he came to a decision. He reached out a hand to pull me up against him again, despite my feeble attempts to free myself.

Brody wrapped me in his embrace, refusing to turn me loose. Silently he stared down at me trying to get his own emotional daemons under control. "I was hurt when you didn't pick me. I even convinced myself that you had been playing me for a fool the entire time, and that you didn't really care for me," Brody said, taking a deep breath. I saw his eyes water and he looked up to the sky a moment, blinking his eyes. When he looked back down at me, he was once again in control. "I was devastated when your carriage pulled away. That was, until I received a letter."

Gently touching his face, I took a breath, trying to hold back more tears. "Oh Brody, I'm so sorry. Truly I am. I would never knowingly try to hurt you," I replied, pulling a handkerchief from my pocket and blowing my nose. "You must believe me."

Brody stopped me as he closely examined the white piece of cloth. "What is this?" I looked down at the material in question, all crumpled up in my hand. Suddenly I felt embarrassed that he was examining my soiled hanky.

"Where I come from, they call it a handkerchief. What do you call it?" I teased, trying to retrieve my hand and soiled hanky.

With a strange look on his face, Brody let my hand go. "No, I mean, that's my handkerchief. The one I gave you before you left."

Absently looking at the white cloth again, I gave a sigh of relief. "Yes," I replied, placing it back into my pocket. "I'm almost embarrassed to say that I have carried it with me all these months. It reminded me of you. It even smelled like you, until I continually blew my nose in it and had to wash it." I gave a little chuckle. Looking back up at him, I was curious about what Brody meant when he said that he was devastated before he received a letter. "You mentioned that you received a letter. Who was it from?"

Brody smiled and gently stroked my cheek with his thumb, drying a stray tear that remained. "Your sister, Coco."

Looking at him suspiciously, I questioned, "And what exactly did this letter say that turned the tide in my favor, so to speak?"

"The details are unimportant," he replied, quickly diverting my attention back to what he considered to be important. "What does matter is that Coco wrote to me and explained everything. Suddenly it all became quite clear, why you made the choices that you did." Then with a wink and a smile, he continued. "No harm, no foul."

I looked around Brody, searching for my mettlesome sister. "I guess that depends on your point of view," I muttered, under my breath.

Taking a hold of my shoulders, Brody spun us around, switching places with me. "Your mother and father have been gracious enough to invite my brother and me to stay," he informed me, pulling me along as he started to walk again.

My overwhelming desire to seek out my sister and her loose lips and interrogate her suddenly shifted. "Oh?"

Brody's attempts to sound like an upper crust Englishman, made me laugh. "Oh, did I neglect to inform you of the other letter I received? How droll of me. Terribly sorry, love." He chuckled, knowing full well he sounded ridiculous, as his southern drawl, mingled with his fake English accent. "When I wrote back to your sister and expressed my excitement—"

"You did what?" I blurted out, interrupting him, mid-sentence.

Stopping our forward progress, Brody mustering up patience, as if he were dealing with a child as he gazed down at me with a thoughtful look, "You realize that this would progress more quickly, if you would simply stop interrupting me every other word."

"Terribly sorry, love," I mimicked his terrible accent, with a forced smile, "do go on."

Indulgently, he patted my hand and continued as he pulled me along towards the Atrium then opening the door to allow me to proceed him. "Now, where was I?"

"You were telling me about the letter you received," I said, forcing a pleasant smile to my lips.

"Oh yes, thank you," he replied amiably, "I received a letter from your sister, about a month after she had written to me the first time. It seems that she had told your parents of our desire to open a textile mill. Did you tell her?"

"No, but I bet I know how she knew."

"Anyway, they invited Quinton and me to come for an extended stay. Most generous of them, don't you think?"

"They did what?" I blurted out, somewhat shocked, before recovering and clearing my throat. I forced my mouth closed. "Yes, very generous, indeed."

"Naturally, after telling you about my desire to open a textile business, I thought you had mentioned something to them and, of course I was thrilled," Brody continued. Taking ahold of his arm again, I fell silent as we walked around, looking at the potted plants and flowers.

"So, other than the letter from my sister and parents, is there any other reason you came half way across the world to visit?" I quietly asked.

Brody looked at me then leaned over to examine a lovely flower. "This is an unusual plant. Do you have any idea where it came from?" he asked.

"A tropical island my father stopped at a few years back. He said it reminded him of my mother and that he had to bring it back to her," I replied, a little impatiently. "Why won't you answer my question?"

"Which one? You seem to be filled with so many questions, I'm not exactly sure which questions you are referring to," he admonished, still examining the flower before turning back to me with a smile on his lips. Pulling me closer, Brody stroked my cheek with the back of his fingers. "We have wasted far too much time being apart. I am here now, and that is all that matters to me." Leaning down, just a hair's breath from my lips, Brody added, "I have loved you since the first moment I looked into your eyes and offered you my handkerchief. Do you remember?"

"Yes," I sighed, feeling my world suddenly shift beneath my feet.

"I am here, and I intend to stay as long as it takes," he whispered, gently kissing my lips. Pulling back a mere inch, he added, "even if it takes forever. Because I discovered two other truths that day your carriage pulled away from me," he said with a lopsided smile.

"And what truths would those be?" I whispered breathless, as my heart skipped a beat.

"There are two types of people in this world, well, three really, if you count the fence sitters," Brody grinned.

"Oh?"

"Yes. Those who run away at the first sign of trouble, and those brave souls, willing to stand and fight," he nibbled of my ear. Involuntarily, I shivered, as a thrilling felling caused my spirits to soar.

"And you believe that you are brave enough to stand and fight?" I challenged.

"No, my dear, Olivia. I know that I am," Brody assured, reaching down and picking up my hand, to place a loving kiss in the palm of it.

"What is the other truth you discovered?" I asked, breathlessly.

Exhaling, Brody gave a wry smile and kissed my fingers, then drew me in even closer as he wrapped an arm around my waist and said, "I could never stop loving you, even if I tried."

Unable to speak, I felt tears of joy spill down my cheeks. I had waited for what felt like an eternity to hear those words from him. Wrapping my arms around his neck, I kissed him with such passion, that he would never again doubt my devotion to him. I wanted to shout my love for him from every rooftop and church steeple in Ireland. I was finally in the arms of the man I loved with all my heart, and I didn't intend to turn loose of him, ever again.

Epilogue

SEPTEMBER 12, 1807

Rosewood Plantation

BRODY WAS TRUE TO HIS word, enduring months of protocol, precessions and wedding planning. He did not fully appreciate our exceptional luck, but I did. I counted us fortunate that King George III had always had a soft spot in his heart for me. The normal waiting period for those who did not hold favor with the king was two to three years. And even with that, there was never any guarantee that King George would even grant us permission to wed. But Brody was knighted and bestowed an honorary title of Lord Beaumont of Strathmore. Ten months later, we were wed, the 14 day in February, on his birthday, in the year, 1806, at the Christ Church Cathedral, in Dublin. The ceremony was well attended by our immediate families, and by Prince William, Prince Edward the Duke of York and of Albany, who was the younger brother of King George III.

Although our wedding was attended by several dignitaries, for the most part, our celebration was small and intimate — if you can call one hundred and seventy-six guests an intimate gathering.

Arianna Lilly Elizabeth Beaumont was born on February 17, 1807, almost exactly one year after we married. That day started out, much like any other day, except for the overwhelming feeling of excitement I felt.

Even before Arianna was born, I knew her. Because of my unique gift, I had an advantage over other women who could only dream of what their child would look like. I was afforded the rare opportunity of seeing and talking with my child before she was ever placed into my arms.

She had a beautiful cherub face that made me smile, and sparkling blue eyes that danced with pure mischief. I knew that I was going to be in trouble the moment I heard her laugh. The sound of it was infectious, and I wondered how her father and I would ever tell her no.

My entire family made the long ocean voyage, *across the pond*, as father was fond of saying, to anxiously await the impending birth.

I felt invigorated by my family's presence under one roof, and it was a wonderful time. There were healthy debates over politics and rousing games of cards. But my favorite memories of that time were the walks I took with my mother and sister. Although brisk at times, we enjoyed the comradery of our long talks.

It had taken Brody and Quinton nearly seven months to get the textile factory up and running, with the help of Father and Uncle Charlie. This was a special time in our lives, and I learned many principles that have stayed with me still to this day. And that is, that I am responsible for helping my fellow man, even if they cannot be seen by anyone, other than me. I live in a world that can be filled with so much fear, anger and darkness that it is important to remember that my light has to come from within and shine outward like a beacon for the world to see. I have often asked myself why the light shines from some and not others? But I have since discovered that this light is the light of goodness, love, charity and kindness. Something that evil cannot exist in.

I still find it distressing to think that there was ever a time in my life that I stopped believing in magic. But I did, and when I turned my back on the poor departed souls who could not help themselves because I was made to feel ashamed of my gift, I was lost.

So, when I rediscovered the world around me was filled with magic after all, I counted myself all the more fortunate because the real magic was in my ability to love and be loved. And when I gave myself over to the beauty of such a simple act of giving and receiving love, it opened my eyes, allowing me to truly live again. After all, if there were no limitations to overcome, life would lose all its joy and purpose.

It was during the time Brody was knighted that I discovered that he and Quinton had retrieved Lilly's body from the canyon, taking them six months to locate and recover her. My promise to Lilly had finally been fulfilled and upon landing in Ireland, Brody and Quinton went to see the Collin's family. Quinton made a plea, giving a heartfelt apology to them, and begging Mr. Collins forgiveness for stealing his oldest daughter away. He told Mr. Collins that he would spend the rest of his life trying to make amends for his selfish, cowardice act of betrayal.

We buried Lilly five days later, next to her mother and infant brother, on a gloriously, warm day. I suspected that Lilly had some pull with the man in charge, demanding that her special day be filled with warm sunshine for us all to enjoy.

Over the many months that followed, Mr. Collins was moved by Quinton's selfless acts of attrition, and even offered him his forgiveness, which went a long way in healing them both.

I visit Lilly's grave whenever I am home, and think of her every day. She will never be dead to me, because I carry her with me in my heart and thoughts, always.

Stewart

Charles Edward Stewart
25 Jan 1739 - 10 Mar 1744
Buckingham, England

Jonathan Edward Stewart
18 Nov 1716
Buckingham, England

Jonathan Edward Stewart
25 Jan 1739
Buckingham, England

23 Feb 1738

Clarisse Emerson Allen
04 May 1720
Buckingham, England

Angelina Margaurite Amelia Stewart
02 Mar 1744
Buckingham, England

25 July 1763

Jude Gerard Deveraux
'Duke of Bayonne'
02 Mar 1739
Bordeaux, France

Lineage

Charles Philippe Deveraux
29 Jan 1764
Bayonne, France

Honore Gerard Deveraux
02 Mar 1744
Bayonne, France

Olivia Sophia Allen Townsend
07 Nov 1783
Ireland Dublin, Leinster

Nicolette Clarisse Deveraux
9 Dec 1769
Bayonne, France

Catherine Elizabeth Townsend
07 Nov 1787
Ireland Dublin, Leinster

Isabella Monique Deveraux
29 Jan 1764
Bayonne, France

14 Feb 1806

29 Feb 1783

Lord Beaumont of Strathmore
14 Feb 1777
Rosewood Plantation, West Virginia
America

Aiden Larkin Townsend
'Viscount of Buckinghamshire'
25 Jan 1757
Ireland Dublin, Leinster

Arianna Lilly Elizabeth Beaumont
17 Feb 1807
Rosewood Plantation, West Virginia
America

Printed in the USA
CPSIA information can be obtained
at www.ICGtesting.com
LVHW040154180724
785858LV00016B/75

9 781946 146076